do you dare?

LYLAH JAMES

To Oliver–
My best friend and my partner in crime.
Thank you for believing in me.

What happens when a dare goes too far?
Maddox Coulter. Reckless bad boy. Infamous playboy. My nemesis.
And now my best friend.

I know he'll never leave me hanging. He knows I'll never refuse a
dare. Everywhere we go, we turn heads, but it's not like that.

Until it is.

For one of us, anyway.

I've always known he would be my downfall. But I trusted him to
catch me.

He proved me wrong.

Maddox has gone too far, and I don't know if I want to rein him in
or push us further into dangerous territory.

He tells me those three little words that I crave. Three little words I
want from no one else.
I dare you.

Except this time, it's no simple dare. This could burn us to the
ground.
"I dare you to fuck him.

PROLOGUE

Lila

His presence was a warm heat behind me as we walked into the bar. He was close, really fucking close. I could *feel* him. I could *smell* him. He was so close, yet so far out of reach. A dangerous temptation dangling right in front of me.

I wanted to turn around and wrap my arms around him, bask in his warmth. We've hugged and cuddled plenty of times before, but since the Charity Gala, everything has been different.

He has been different.

Somehow, there was a wall between us now. I couldn't break it or walk around it. It was exhausting and scary – watching the change in him, seeing him so...cold and withdrawn from me. Sometimes, it felt like he was battling something inside his head. I waited silently for him to come to me, to speak of his worries, so I could find a way to soothe him. Like always.

Except...it started to feel as if *I* was the problem. As if he was hiding from *me*.

A week in Paris. This was supposed to be fun and exciting. An adventure for us. Day one and it was already going to waste.

I chewed on my bottom lip as we walked further inside the dim room. It wasn't overly crowded, but everyone here looked fancy. After all, this was one of the famous hotels of Paris; wealthy and posh people came here often. "I didn't think the hotel would have its own bar. Fancy. I like it."

"It's nice," he replied. There was a roughness in his voice, except his tone was robotic. No emotions whatsoever.

What's wrong with you? What did I do?

I paused in my steps, expecting him to bump into me. He didn't. Instead, I felt his arm slide around my waist as he curled it around me. Our bodies collided together softly, and I sucked in a quiet breath. His rock-hard chest was to my back, pressing against me, and I could feel every intake of breath he took. His touch was a sweet, sweet torture.

Fuck you. Fuck you for making me feel this way. Fuck you for tempting me and leaving me hanging. Fuck you for making me fall in love with you...

"This way." His lips lingered near my ear as he whispered the words. He steered me toward the bar stools.

We sat side by side. From the corner of my eye, I watched him as he ordered our drinks. His voice was smooth, and it slid over my skin like silk. Soft and gentle.

Lost in my thoughts, I didn't notice the man standing next to me until his hand touched my shoulder. I swiveled to the left, my eyes catching the intruder. Yes, intruder. He was interrupting my time with *him*.

Maddox Coulter – the balm to my soul but also the stinging pain in my chest. He was sweet heaven and the bane of my existence.

8

"Remember me?" the man in the suit asked with a tiny grin.

Yup, I did. He was the owner of the hotel. We met him when we checked in yesterday.

"I saw you across the bar, and I knew instantly, you had to be the pretty girl I met last night." His English was perfect, but it was laced with a husky French accent. I had to admit, it was kind of sexy. Mr. Frenchman stood between our stools, separating Maddox and me. He blocked my view of Maddox and I. Did. Not. Like. That.

"Thank you for helping us yesterday," I replied sweetly, masking my irritation.

His emerald eyes glimmered, and his grin widened. Mr. Frenchman was your typical tall, dark, and handsome eye candy. And he wore an expensive suit that molded to his body quite nicely. "It was all my pleasure."

I nodded, a little lost at what else I could say. I wasn't shy or uncomfortable around men. But this one was a little too close for my liking, and since I had zero interest in him, even though he could definitely be my type, given the fact that *someone else* had all my attention, I didn't want to continue this conversation.

"Lucien Mikael." He presented me with his hand. I remembered he told us his name last night, but I didn't tell him mine.

I took his palm in mine, shaking it. "You can call me, Lila. It's nice to make your acquaintance."

Instead of shaking my hand, he turned it over and brought my hand to his lips. He kissed the back of it, his lips lingering there for a second too long. His eyes met mine over our entwined hands. "My pleasure, *ma belle.*"

Oh dear. Yup. Mr. Frenchman was flirting.

I glanced around Lucien and saw that Maddox was lounging

back in his stool, his long legs stretched out in front of him, a drink in his hand, and he was staring directly at me. His face was expressionless.

Lucien turned to the bartender and said something to him in French. I didn't understand the words, but I quickly figured out what he said when he turned back to me.

"It's on me. A treat for a lovely lady."

I was already shaking my head. "Oh. You didn't have to –"

His hand tightened around mine. "Please, allow me."

"Thank you."

Lucien opened his mouth to say something else, but he was interrupted by the ringing of his phone. "Excuse me, *chérie*."

As he moved away, I caught sight of Maddox again. Our eyes met, and I stopped breathing. His gaze was dark, and his jaw was clenched so tightly that I wondered if it'd crack under the pressure. I could see the ticks in his sharp jaw as he gritted his teeth. His face – I didn't know how to describe it. Anger made his eyes appear darker, almost deadly. A shadow loomed over his face, his expression almost threatening. There was a predatory feel in his glare as he watched me closely.

He constantly pushed me away, putting more and more distance between us. Why was he so angry now? I couldn't tell. I. Couldn't. Fucking. Think. Especially when he stared at me like *this*.

Maddox was maddening. He pulled and pushed; he loved and hated. I always thought I understood him better than anyone else. But right now, he confused the hell out of me.

"Lila." My eyes snapped away from Maddox, and I looked at Lucien. He was apparently done with his phone call, and his attention was back on me. Before I could pull away, he gripped my hand in his once more. "If you need anything while you are in Paris, please call me. I could take you sightseeing. I know many beautiful places."

He let go of my hand, and I turned my palm over to see his business card. Smooth trick, Mr. Frenchman. "Umm, thank you."

Lucien leaned down and quickly placed a chaste kiss on both my cheeks before pulling away. "Au revoir, *chérie.*"

I didn't watch him leave. All my attention was on the man sitting beside me. He took a large gulp of his drink.

"He likes you," he said, once Lucien was out of hearing range.

"Jealous?" I shot back immediately.

A smirk crawled onto his face, and he chuckled, his wide chest rumbling with it. "He wants to fuck you, Lila."

My stomach clenched, goosebumps breaking out over my skin. My breath left me in a whoosh. His words were spoken dangerously low, although the harshness in his voice could not be mistaken.

"How would you know?" I retorted, angry and confused. He played with my feelings, turning my emotions into a little game of his. Maddox had me in knots, twisting me around like a little plaything.

He grunted, shaking his head, and then he let out a laugh. As if he was sharing an inside joke with himself. "I'm a man, like him. I know what he was thinking about when he looked at you like that."

"Maybe he wasn't thinking about sex. Maybe he's a gentleman. Unlike you." I was playing with fire, I knew that. I was testing him, testing *us.*

"*I dare you,*" he whispered so softly, I almost missed it. Maddox looked down at his glass, his fingers clenched around it. Even in the dim lights, I could see the way his knuckles were starting to turn white.

He was giving me a dare *now*?

He didn't finish his sentence, and I wondered if he was contemplating his dare. Maddox's jaw flexed from obvious frustration. For a brief moment, I thought maybe he wasn't angry at *me*. Maybe, he was angry at *himself*. He was fighting *himself*. Could it be that the problem wasn't me?

He drank the rest of his drink in one gulp and then slammed his glass on the counter, before swiveling around in his stool to face me. Maddox stood up and walked a step closer to me, until my knees were touching his strong thighs. He leaned forward, caging me in between the counter and his body. Our gaze locked, and he licked his lips. He had me captivated for a moment until he mercilessly broke the spell.

"I dare you to sleep with him."

I reared back in shock. *Wh-at?* No, I must have misheard him. This couldn't be…

"What?" I whispered, my throat dry, and my tongue suddenly heavy in my mouth.

Maddox's eyes bore into mine, staring into my soul. When he spoke again, his deep accented voice danced over my skin dangerously. "I dare you to fuck him, Lila."

A trembling started in my core and then moved through my body like a storm. Not just a quiet storm. A tsunami of emotions hit me all at once, reckless in its assault. I submerged under the dark waves, suffocating, and then I was being split open, so viciously, it sent tiny cracks of my heart and fissures of my soul in all directions. I clamped my teeth together to stop myself from saying something –anything that would make it worse.

We had done too many dares to simply count on our fingers. Countless silly dares over the years, but we had never dared each other to sleep with other people. Granted, I had asked him to kiss a girl once; they made out, but it was years ago. But our dares had never crossed that line.

Sex... that was never on the table. We never explicitly talked about it, but it was almost an unspoken rule.

"What's with that look, Lila?"

My eyes closed. I refused to look at him, to look into his beautiful eyes and see nothing but pitch black darkness. He wasn't looking at me like he used to. The light in his eyes was gone.

It scared me.

It hurt me.

It was destroying the rest of what was left of me.

"Look. At. Me."

I didn't want to. I didn't want him to see the hurt in my eyes.

"Open your eyes, Lila," he said in his rich baritone voice.

I did as I was commanded. He crowded into my personal space, forcing me to inhale his scent and feel the warmth of his body. "Are you serious? Or are you already drunk?" I asked quietly. It was hard to breathe with him this close.

"I never take back a dare."

And I never lose. He knew that. We were both very competitive, and to this day, neither of us had backed down from a dare.

Maddox's hand came up, and he cupped my jaw. His fingers kissed my skin softly. He smiled, but it didn't match the look in his eyes. "What's wrong? You don't want to do it?"

"I don't play to lose." *Asshole.*

Maddox leaned closer, his face barely an inch away from mine. Our noses were almost touching. My heart fluttered when he tipped my head back. *Take back your dare. Take back your dare, Maddox. Don't make me do this.*

He curled his index finger around the lock of hair that had

fallen out from my bun. His minty breath, mixed with the smell of alcohol, feathered over my lips. I wanted to beg him with my eyes. Maddox tugged on my hair slightly before tucking it behind my ear. He moved, and my eyes fluttered close once again...*waiting*... a desperate breath locked in my throat, my chest caving, and my stomach clenching.

He pressed his cheek against mine, and his lips lingered over my ear. "Don't disappoint me, *chérie*."

My body shuddered, and I breathed out a shaky breath. He tore my heart open and left me bleeding. He pulled away and stared down at me.

Maddox was mocking me. Taunting me.

He never stopped being a jerk. He just hid it behind a sexy smile and a nonchalant expression.

I thought he had left his asshole ways behind. But no, I was wrong. So fucking wrong about him. About *us*.

Friends. We were friends.

I thought maybe... he wanted *more*. More of me. More of us, of what we were or could be. I was so goddamn wrong.

Maddox Coulter was still an asshole behind a pretty mask.

And I was the stupid girl who fell in love with her best friend.

CHAPTER ONE

Lila

"**M**otherfuck–" My mouth snapped shut before I hissed out another painful breath as my knees threatened to buckle under me.

The coffee table stared back at me innocently, and I glared in response. *Little shit.* I gave it a kick, with my uninjured leg, just for the heck of it.

My morning was a mess already, and I fought the urge to take out my anger on the coffee table. Granted, it just bruised my knees, but in reality, the fault was mine.

My alarm didn't go off, which obviously meant I woke up late. *Very late.* First period classes had already ended, and it was halfway through second period. Then, in my struggle to get dressed hurriedly, I ended up tearing a hole in my white and pristine school blouse. Great. What a lovely morning already.

Scrambling away from the little table, I ran out of my grandparents' house and quickly locked the door behind me. I had to catch the bus in two minutes, or else I was going to be mega-fucking-late. The next bus wouldn't be here for another thirty-five minutes.

As I ran to the nearest bus stop, I quickly went over my morning list in my head. Four very important things. Phone – yes. Earphones – yes. Keys – yes. My English assignment – yes.

Everything seemed to be in order. Now, I just had to make it on time for my third period class, so I could submit my English essay on time. Or else...

I shook my head, refusing to even think of the consequences. My heart started to race and beat erratically at the mere thought of getting a zero on this assignment.

No way. It would ruin my perfect record of straight As. My grandma liked to joke and say I was paranoid and a little *too* OCD about my marks. My grandpa, with a proud little laugh, would say I was a perfectionist. They weren't exactly wrong.

My perfect GPA, plus my thousand hours of community service and volunteer work, would get me into Harvard. And it was all that mattered. Harvard was my path. It was my destination, and it was where I belonged. Maybe my grandparents were right. Maybe I was obsessed with the idea of *"perfection."* But I didn't care. If perfection would get me everything I wanted, then *Miss Perfectionist* I'd be.

The bus came on time, and I successfully climbed in without any more bad luck. My favorite seat at the back of the bus was waiting for me. It gave me the perfect view of the whole bus, and it was a window seat. Once my earphones were in, "Hands to Myself" by Selena Gomez started to blast in my ears. I leaned my forehead against the cool window and watched the world move.

This was probably my favorite part of my morning routine. I'd always been an observer, and one could learn a lot in a ten-minute bus ride.

Not long after, the bus came to a stop, and I walked out; I stopped on the pavement for the briefest moment to stare at the large and old, yet hauntingly beautiful and fancy, building in front of me.

The Berkshire Academy of Weston.

The private school for the rich and the corrupted. Kids of infamous judges, senators, government associates, and some of the highest paid lawyers and doctors in the United States.

I wasn't one of them. My father *was* a high school teacher. My mother *was* a nurse. And I was the quiet and poor girl amongst all the famous, wealthy spawns of the devils themselves. I didn't belong here. But I *chose* to be here.

48.2% of Berkshire Academy of Weston graduates end up at an Ivy League College – Yale, Princeton, Dartmouth, or Harvard.

That little fact was the reason why I chose to enroll in this school during my junior year. Now, I was a senior at Berkshire. A few more months, and I'd be out of here.

I took in a deep breath and inhaled the fresh September air. It wasn't too cold yet. The fall season had just begun, and the leaves were just starting to turn red, orange, and yellow. It was a beautiful time of year – the time where the trees end up naked, silently awaiting their rebirth once again. The end of something beautiful, while waiting for a new beginning.

"Lila!"

My thoughts came to a halt, and I turned to see Riley coming my way. She waved animatedly, and I couldn't help but smile. Riley was a sweet, wild girl, and my only friend at Berkshire.

Her pretty blonde locks bounced as she hopped over to me. "Are you late, too?"

I nodded with a sigh. She perked up cheekily. "No way! Miss Smarty Pants is late? Jesus, I need to write this down. ASAP."

The urge to roll my eyes was strong, but I refrained from doing so. "You have Advanced Calculus next, right?" I asked, switching the subject.

I usually loved to join in on the teasing, but I wasn't in the mood today. Waking up late had made me a tad grumpier. My knee was sore and ached every time I took a step – a constant reminder of how *amazing* my morning had been so far. Grumpy Lila was no fun.

Riley looked thoughtful for a second. "Yeah. I do," she responded after a long second. "You?"

"English. We have twenty minutes before our classes start."

"I actually need to see my teacher before class. Did I mention I hate math? Yeah, I probably did a hundred times. We have a test next week, and I'm pretty sure I'm going to flunk it." Riley's normal cheerfulness disappeared, and her brows tensed with a frown. She looked deeply saddened for a moment, but just as quickly, her expression changed, and she was back to happy Riley once again. "I'll see you at lunch?"

I grabbed her hand before she could leave. "If you want, I can help you this weekend with Calculus."

She smiled brightly, her whole face shining like the moon. "Really? Thank you, babe. How about we talk more about it at lunch? We can pick a time and place."

"Sounds good to me." I let her hand go, and she waved before running through the gates.

I looked down at my phone. Fifteen minutes until my next class. It was enough time for me to grab an iced latte. *Perfect.* Maybe sugar would help my mood.

18

The coffee shop was only a few feet away, sitting right next to the campus. It was pretty much only visited by the students of Berkshire. It wasn't lunch yet, so when I walked in, the shop was fairly quiet. I ordered myself an iced latte with extra whip cream and went to stand next to the heater. "Sugar" by Maroon 5 continued to play in my ear, and I softy hummed along to the song.

When a blast of cool air hit the back of my legs, I turned around to see a group of loud boys walking into the coffee shop. I instantly recognized a few of them from my classes. The Bennett Twins were part of the group. The boys kept the door opened, standing right at the entrance. Half of the group were wearing the required Berkshire uniform – pants, shirt, tie and blazer. The other half were in their gym clothes or football uniforms.

Jocks. *Ugh.*

Rich. Loud. Foul-mouthed. Annoying. A bit *too* wild. Everything I stayed away from, and everything I despised.

Whatever.

Ignorance was bliss. I turned back around and focused on my playlist instead, my foot tapping impatiently on the floor. The barista was taking forever, and I desperately needed my sugar. I could feel the group of boys coming closer to me, and I half-listened to them order their own drinks. In my peripheral, I could see them pushing each other around, bumping shoulders, and shaking with laughter. Their teasing rung louder than the music blasting in my ears.

"Here you go!" I lifted my head up when the voice called out in a singsong tone. Finally! My mouth watered as the young lady handed me the iced latte, and I almost drooled at the sight of extra whip cream. *Heaven.*

"Thank you." I cleared my throat and sent her a grateful smile.

God bless your soul, woman.

I swiveled around while simultaneously putting the straw into my mouth. But I never got the chance to take the first sip of my heavenly goodness. Nope. My happiness only lasted for two seconds flat.

Before I knew what was happening, a rock-hard wall bumped into me. I heard someone swear under his breath. It happened fast, too quickly for me to catch on until it was too late. The world spun and tilted on its axis. My eyes closed as I expected the impact of me hitting the floor, but my face didn't kiss the ground. I stayed suspended in the air, my body bent backward.

Someone was holding onto my arm…really…*really* tightly. Two heartbeats later, I was back on my feet again. I finally opened my eyes, and a shaky breath expelled from my lungs.

The first thing I noticed was that his navy colored blazer was wet. My coffee… "Shit. Sorry. I am so sorry," I muttered, absolutely horrified.

Then, I inwardly groaned. First – why was I apologizing? *He* bumped into *me*. His fault. Not mine. Second – My iced latte was gone.

My heart was still beating too fast and too hard after the little scare, and it felt like it would thump right out of my chest. *Wait…*

I looked down at myself and saw that my white shirt was soaked, and my pink bra was now quite visible to everyone. Oh, that was where my iced latte went. *Amaaaazing.*

Mood level: Extra grumpy with just a touch of bitchiness.

I let my eyes travel the length of the *wall* that bumped into me. Okay, not a wall then. He was definitely human. But a rock nonetheless. I had felt those hard muscles when he knocked me over. It was like a truck hitting me, and I swore he must have given me a

20

concussion from that whiplash.

My gaze went up and up...and up. *Jesus Christ,* he was tall. I was basically a midget next to him at five foot two inches.

My eyes stayed longer on his stomach, and for a brief moment, I wondered if he had six-pack abs. His wide chest caught my attention next. He was tall and lean, but still muscular and a bit bigger for his age. I could instantly tell he played football – his strong arms and muscular shoulders told me so, and he had a gym/sports bag thrown over his right shoulder. His school blazer molded to his upper body perfectly. Deliciously.

Sweet Mother Mary... I was supposed to be angry, right?

When my gaze finally landed on his face, my eyes decided they'd been blessed. A classic gorgeous boy. Chiseled jawline that could give you a papercut if you touched it? Check. Piercing eyes? Check. Thick eyebrows? Check. Plump lips made for kissing? Check. Intense good looks? Double check. He was a fine specimen, and I wanted to put him under my microscope for a closer look.

His dirty blond hair was curly and the tight curls ended a good inch or two above his shoulders. It gave him a surfer look, a bit wild and outgoing.

Wait. Hold up.

I stumbled a step back and took a good look at his face. My lips parted, completely dumbstruck, and I choked on my saliva silently. *Are you kidding me?*

Out of everyone... out of 325 boys at Berkshire, I had to bump into HIM?

He eyed me up and down, his gaze scanning my body leisurely like I had done to him. My cheeks flamed, not because he was checking me out – no, because he had obviously caught *me* checking *him* out. Could this day get any worse?

21

He cocked his head to the side, his deep blue eyes flashing with mischief. His eyes caressed my bare legs and then he followed the path up. My beige school skirt came to mid-thigh, only a few inches above my knees. He seemed to take great pleasure in watching my bare skin.

Slowly, his gaze moved up. Mister-Who-Bumped-Into-Me blatantly stared at my boobs. For fuck's sake, he was so goddamn obvious. The corner of his lips tilted up, and he gave me the perfect swoon worthy smirk.

He chuckled, a deep laugh that came out roughly from within his chest. "Well, I guess that'll perk them up a little."

Huh?

His buddies snickered and chortled with laughter. Cole Bennett, one of the twins, even doubled over and wheezed like he had just heard the best joke of the century.

I followed his gaze to my chest and then I looked back at him. Wait...was he...did he...just...?

My body tensed, and I straightened my spine. "Excuse me?"

My brain had finally caught on, and I could feel the steam coming out of my ears. How dare he!

I crossed my arms over my chest, my cheeks burning hot, and I held back an irritated growl. Yes, my boobs were *petite*. The two mounds were almost non-existent compared to the other girls my age, and they basically stopped growing when I was fourteen.

But. He. Did. Not. Have. To. Rub. That. In. My. Face.

Oh wait, I forgot. He was an asshole. *The* asshole.

Maddox Coulter.

Berkshire Academy's Star Quarterback.

Reckless bad boy. Infamous playboy.

The Casanova of the senior class and its golden boy.

And yes, a Class-A jerk, with unparalleled levels of douchebaggery.

Maddox was well-known in Berkshire. His face was catalogued into everyone's brain and heart, and I wanted nothing to do with him. Except, out of 325 boys in our school, I had to bump into him today.

He was still smirking, and I let out an irritated sigh. "Are you going to apologize to me or not? You bumped into me," I seethed, shoving my empty cup between us.

His dark blue eyes narrowed on my boobs again. Apparently, Mr. Coulter had a short attention span because he chose to ignore my words and decided to focus on my tits instead. The same tits he just insulted.

I crossed my arms over my chest again and glowered at him and his buddies. His gaze finally met mine, and I hated that he had such beautiful eyes. He didn't deserve them.

Maddox shrugged, quite nonchalantly. "You were in my way. Whoops."

Is he serious?

He took a step forward, his bigger body closing in on my small frame. "I have an extra shirt in my locker. I'll give it to you, considering the one you're wearing is soaked."

His voice lowered into a raspy tone when he spoke his next words. "But one condition. If I give you my shirt, I get to keep your bra. It's *cute*. I love the little flowers on them, baby."

I stumbled back, aghast. I knew he was immature, rude, and vulgar, but this was a whole other level of douchebaggery. *Murder is a crime, Lila. You could go to prison for a very long time.*

My eyes narrowed on him. "You know what? I don't have time for this. Go take your shitty attitude and try to impress another girl with it."

Maddox blinked, his goofy smile disappearing for a nanosecond, before his eyes lit up, almost as if he loved me rebuffing him.

I swiveled around, dumped my empty coffee cup into the garbage, and decided to walk away from Maddox. Too bad he was standing in my way, refusing to budge. I inwardly rolled my eyes and pushed past him. He was standing so close that I was forced to touch him, our bodies slightly rubbing against each other as I went by. A cocky smirk was plastered on his stupidly handsome face.

Fine. He wanted to play... then I'd play.

After taking two steps forward, I did a little side twist, which allowed my bag to hit him. *Bullseye.* When I heard a hiss of pain, I knew that the corner of my bag had bumped into his crotch, and his dick probably felt the impact, too.

I turned my head and gave Maddox a look over my shoulder. He had doubled over and was cupping himself between the legs. "You were in my way. Whoops," I said lazily, repeating his earlier words.

My middle name is 'Petty Bitch.' I didn't have time for a reckless bad boy, but I also wouldn't let him play me like his other fangirls.

His ocean blue eyes locked on mine, and they darkened the slightest bit. Maddox straightened his spine and stood at his full height again. He was imposing, his presence almost owning the whole coffee shop. I sent him a sugary sweet smile before walking away.

If I didn't leave this coffee shop in one minute, I was going to be late for my English class.

The intensity of his gaze burned into my back. I could feel the heat of it, of *him.* My cheeks flamed, and my body grew warmer. I knew he was looking at my ass. I could *feel* it.

Maddox Coulter was officially on my shit list.

CHAPTER TWO

Lila

I was on time for my English class and successfully submitted my essay – all thanks to the spare shirt I had in my locker. The one I wore this morning was soaked from my spilled iced coffee by the boy who shall not be named.

As soon as the bell rang, indicating the start of class, Mrs. Levi started her lecture about Greek Mythology. She went back and forth from the textbook and writing notes on the chalkboard.

Science might be my passion, but English was my favorite subject. I loved reading, loved learning about the language - every little piece of it. My interest began with Shakespeare, although it was Edgar Allen Poe who made me fall in love with English.

"Deep into that darkness peering, long I stood there, wondering, fearing, doubting, dreaming dreams no mortal ever dared to dream before."

I may or may not have memorized most of his poems after reading them over and over again. There was just something eerily beautiful with the way he weaved his words together.

"Medusa has several myths about her life, the most common ones are of her death and her, rather, painful demise." Mrs. Levi's voice snapped me to the present as she introduced us to the history of Medusa. "This will be our focus for the next two weeks. Your next assignment will be based on this particular topic, so make sure you're doing your research at home and come to class with your questions. The essay will be fifteen percent of your final mark. We'll be discussing it in more depth the next couple of days."

She continued to talk about Medusa, and I wrote down all my notes, marking the important ones with my red pen. I liked to keep my things organized, even though to other people, it seemed a bit too OCD.

Halfway through Mrs. Levi's lecture, my hand paused, and my pen came to halt. It had been a few minutes now, and I couldn't ignore the *feeling* anymore. My skin prickled, and my back seemed to warm under someone's intense stare. I could feel the tiny hairs on my arms stand on end. It was a strange feeling, and I couldn't concentrate on Mrs. Levi anymore.

I always sat in the front row of all my classes, but usually, I was invisible to everyone.

Today though... someone was staring at me *hard*.

It was impossible not to *feel* it.

The stare burned into my back, scorching me... waiting for a reaction, until I was forced to peek over my shoulder.

Our eyes met first.

Mine – widening with surprise. *His* – with amusement.

My jaw went slack, and I stared back, hard. No fucking way.

He was sitting in the last row at the back of the class, in the corner, next to the wall. There was a large gap between us, but I still felt him.

Maddox Coulter had both his elbows on the desk, his fingers threaded with his chin resting on them. His blue eyes danced with mischief, and when I continued to stare back, his lips crooked up in a lazy grin.

Well... shit.

I faced the front of the class again and mentally berated myself. Could this day get any worse?

How could I have missed him?

It was only the third week of school, and I never paid attention to whoever was sitting at the back. My focus had always been on Mrs. Levi and whatever she was teaching.

Knowing Maddox, he had probably skipped more than half of the classes in the past three weeks. I knew of his reputation. He rarely came to class, and when he did... he came with drama and a whole lot of assholery.

I mentally face-palmed while chewing on my lower lip, nervously. In the heat of the moment, I acted without thinking; granted, he was the douchebag in this situation, but nobody ever crossed Maddox without dealing with the repercussions.

With my best nonchalant expression, I quickly peeked over my shoulder again. He was still staring... and he caught me looking, *again*. His eyes were the deepest blue, shimmering with intensity. He lazily rubbed his thumb back and forth across his squared jaw while he cocked his head to the side, raising one lonely eyebrow almost mockingly.

Maddox watched me like he was sizing up his *prey*.

I didn't like the look he was giving me, and I didn't have any interest of being on his radar.

He might be *the* player, but I wasn't about to be played. *Try again, Coulter.*

Giving him the most exaggerated eyeroll I could muster, I sent him a frigid smile and then turned back around to face Mrs. Levi.

During the rest of the class, I tried my hardest not to pay attention to Maddox. It was the longest fifty minutes of my life as I fought hard not to fidget in my chair. He continued to stare, and I could feel it – feel him smirking and silently taunting me.

My fingers clenched and unclenched around my pen, and when the bell finally rang for lunch, I let out the deepest sigh of relief.

"Maddox, I'm going to need you to stay back for two minutes," Mrs. Levi announced, with a hard look.

"Can't, Teach. Got stuff to do."

"You either stay or you have detention for two weeks. Decide, Mr. Coulter."

There was one very important fact about Mrs. Levi, and it was why she was my favorite teacher: she took no bullshit from *anyone.* She wasn't intimated by Maddox or *who* he was.

All the students looked back and forth between Mrs. Levi and Maddox, holding their breath and *waiting.*

"Class, you may leave for lunch."

There were groans and whispers as everyone got up and started piling out of the classroom. Everyone had been waiting for drama – with Maddox in the middle of it. *Ha!*

I stood up too, following the herd. Curiosity got the best of me, and I looked back over my shoulder, one final time. Maddox was still sitting back in his chair, his arms crossed over his broad chest. His gaze followed me as I walked out of the class, and by *me,* I meant my ass.

I noticed Colton Bennett, twin number one, standing beside Maddox's chair. They muttered something to each other, and

28

Colton's gaze found mine before he chuckled at something else Maddox said.

Maddox might be on my shit list, but… I had a feeling I was on his now, too.

Riley waved at me as I stepped into the loud cafeteria. She was already sitting at a table, and I smiled, walking to her. "Hey!" She spoke through a bite of her chicken sandwich. "I got you one, too."

"Thanks, babe." I settled opposite her and took the sandwich she offered. It was our thing. Sometimes, I would buy her lunch, and other days, she'd return the favor.

"So, what exactly do you need help with in Math?" I munched on my cold sandwich and watched Riley pout.

"Everything," she mumbled, pouting even harder. "It makes no sense to me! The only genius who can help me is you."

I raised an eyebrow at her. "Why do I have a feeling this friendship is only one-sided?"

"Bitch, yes, I'm using you for your abilities to teach me Math."

It was a lie; we both knew that. Riley and I stared at each other for a second before we chuckled.

We became friends during junior year, after Jasper – another football star of Berkshire Academy -- broke her heart. That was a tamed way of putting it. They dated for six months; he was the perfect gentleman at first. When she finally gave him her virginity, he broke up with her two days later. She later found out Jasper had been cheating on her all along, and he only dated her to win a fucking bet. He spent the rest of the year spreading stupid rumors about her. She lost her cheerleader friends and sweet Riley…? She

became another outcast. I was there and watched her crumble –
going from Miss Popular to a nobody.

What happens when outcast number one meets outcast number two?
Of course, they became best friends. I was the new student, and
Riley was my first friend. It was a done deal.

"So… I heard whispers in the hallway," she started, eyeing me
closely.

"Huh?"

"About a girl who dumped coffee on Maddox Coulter this
morning." Riley left the sentence hanging before taking another
bite of her sandwich.

My heart thudded in my chest, so hard and so fast. Choking back
a cough, I quickly sputtered, "Dumped coffee on him? Excuse me!
He *bumped* into *me* and spilled my coffee down the front of *me*."

Riley sat back in her chair, taking the last bite of her lunch. "I
didn't say it was you, but thanks for confirming that," she replied
around a mouthful. "Your name was mentioned once, but I didn't
want to believe anything until I heard it myself from you."

Sweet Lord! Rumors were already going around?

"So, he bumped into you?" Riley pushed, looking quite amused
at this sudden turn of events.

"*Yes*," I hissed under my breath. "He didn't even apologize! My
shirt got wet, but thank God, I had a spare in my locker."

"Why am I not surprised? Do you think Maddox is the type
of guy to apologize? Think again, babe. I've known him since
elementary school. Coulter doesn't apologize. *Ever*. Everyone bows
down to him."

I huffed in response, and Riley shrugged. "He's the golden boy."

To the people of Berkshire Academy, he was a god amongst
mortals.

To me? He was just another boy who had too much power in his hands and didn't know how to use it. Maddox was no hero to me.

If he expected me to worship the ground he walked on, like all of his fangirls, he was about to be thoroughly disappointed.

Riley leaned forward and tapped me on the nose with her index finger. "Stay out of his way, Lila. He'll fuck you up so bad and leave you broken. Boys like him can't be trusted."

Her voice was thick, and I could see the emotions playing on her face. Jasper really broke her. Her scars were not visible; she hid them with a pretty smile, but I knew she still hurt inside.

"Don't worry. I have no plans to play his game."

Riley squinted at me. "I don't believe you. You're competitive by nature, Lila. If he pushes, you're going to push back twice as hard."

I bit my lower lip and gave her a sheepish look. She was right...

"How about this? I promise not to fall for him."

"One less girl in Maddox's harem," she agreed.

I rolled my eyes. "Okay, today is Thursday. How about we meet up on Saturday? I'll go over whatever you need help on with you then."

Riley nodded before her cheeks flushed. "You'll have to start at the beginning. Don't kill me."

"This is going to be a loooong Saturday." She kicked me under the table, and I hissed out a laugh.

"Bitch." Riley threw her empty plastic bottle at my head, laughing.

The rest of my day was uneventful. I stayed out of Maddox's way. There were a few whispers in the halls about me, but I ignored them, too.

I felt pretty confident that, after today, everyone would forget about the coffee shop scene, and Maddox would most definitely forget about my existence. He had plenty of girls to distract him.

Except... I had never been more wrong in my life.

The next day, my nightmare began.

CHAPTER THREE

Lila

The next morning, I found Maddox outside our English class. He was leaning against the wall, his long legs crossed at the ankle with his hands stuffed in his pockets. His expensive leather shoes were shiny and wrinkled free. He was missing his navy blazer, but his pristine white shirt was rolled to his elbows, exposing his strong forearms. His tie hung loosely around his neck.

He was *pretty* to look at – I had to admit, but the sight of him annoyed me.

There was a curvy blonde girl attached to his side, practically plastered against him. She whispered something into his ear, but he wasn't paying attention. Maddox looked bored, and the poor girl was trying too hard. *Run away, don't fall for his charms.* I wanted to shake some sense into her.

The moment his gaze fell on me, he slowly grinned.

My blood simmered, and I pressed my lips firmly together, refusing to acknowledge him. I tilted my chin up and marched forward. If I ignored him, he'd go away – I told myself.

Too bad it was nothing but false hope.

When I tried to walk into the classroom, Maddox pulled himself away from the girl. She protested, but it died in her throat when she noticed it was useless.

He shifted sideways and placed his arm out, blocking the door and effectively stopping me from stepping inside. "Hey, Garcia."

Maddox threw me his signature smirk in an attempt to *melt* me. I rolled my eyes. "Coulter," I said in acknowledgment. "You're in my way."

I tried to push past him, but he didn't budge; granted, he was a whole foot taller than me, but Maddox was an immovable wall. "It's quite comical that you think you can move me."

There was just *something* about Maddox that irritated me. It was like he had hit a nerve I didn't know I had. He made me feel edgy. I didn't know why I felt like that, but I was defensive around him.

"A knee to your dick will move you alright. So, either you move with no injuries, or your baby making machine will be in danger." I cocked my head to the side while holding my bag over my shoulder and waiting for him to move.

My lips crooked up in my fakest and sweetest smile.

Maddox stared me down for a second before he eventually moved, bending slightly to his waist and putting his arm out to motion inside the classroom. "Ladies first. After you."

I rolled my eyes a-fucking-gain because he was so goddamn annoying. Pushing past his hard body, I walked into class with a huff and settled in my chair. He sauntered inside like he owned the room and walked past me to his desk at the back of the classroom.

Maddox purposely brushed against my shoulder as he did so. "Whoops, my bad," he muttered gruffly. I could hear the laughter in his voice.

My fingers clenched into a fist, but I held back.

My days continued like this.

I noticed him following me around. Sometimes, he would call out my name loudly in the hallways, bringing everyone's attention to me. Other times, he would purposely bump into me in class or the cafeteria. I often caught him doing nothing but following silently behind me. He knew it annoyed me, and he did it on purpose. To. Irritate. Me.

A week ago, I was completely invisible to Maddox Coulter.

Now, I was the center of his attention.

The deal breaker was when he broke into my locker and stole my spare shirt. He even left a note: *What's the color of your bra today?*

Actually no, that wasn't the worst part.

The worst part was when he decided to reenact a scene from Romeo and Juliet in the cafeteria...

He was Romeo, standing on the table, and loudly confessing his undying love to Juliet for the whole room to hear.

Who was Juliet?

Oh me...

He was being dramatic and overly exaggerated his performance for one reason only: to embarrass me.

Everyone stared... snickered... laughed, until Riley and I were forced to leave the cafeteria; we ended up having to eat lunch under a staircase. I hated hiding, I hated the attention, and Riley... she was about to blow up.

Maddox was waiting for a reaction, he was egging me on... pushing and pushing, waiting for me to *snap*, like I did in the coffee shop. But I vowed I wouldn't play his stupid games.

He would eventually stop, I convinced myself. He'd grow bored of me soon enough, I told myself. I was wrong again.

On Thursday, a week after handling his nonsense, Maddox still hadn't given up.

"Uh-oh. He's here. Maybe we should make a run for it now." Riley went to stand up, taking her lunch tray with her.

"Sit down," I hissed. "We're not running away. We're going to eat lunch, and we're going to ignore him."

"He's coming our way," she reported, shaking her head. "Oh fuck, here we go again."

My back straightened, and I prepared myself for what was coming. I nodded at Riley, letting her know it was okay. Her eyebrows pulled together with a frown before she leveled a hard glare at whoever was standing behind me.

I felt Maddox before I saw him. His presence surrounded me, and I locked my jaw, gritting my teeth together. He grabbed the chair beside me and turned it around before sitting down, straddling it. Maddox leaned forward, using the back of the chair as an armrest. His friends settled around our table, grabbing their own chairs and joining us. Riley released a long, exasperated sigh.

Without speaking to me, he reached for my tray and grabbed my apple. With great annoyance, I forced myself to look at his face. His long dirty blond hair was pulled back into a small, messy man-bun. The rest of him was immaculate. The small diamond stud in his ear glinted in the light, briefly catching my attention. Maddox locked eyes with me, before taking a bite of my red apple. "Hmm juicy."

"That's my apple."

"It was lonely. I'm giving it some attention," he said, taking another huge bite.

I dropped my fork with a loud clank. "Put. The. Apple. Down."

Maddox was unfazed. "Or what?"

"You'll regret it, Coulter."

He let out a deep chuckle, as if my threat meant *nothing* to him. "You're all bark and no bite, Sweet Cheeks."

Sweet Cheeks? Excuse me…?

"You know what you remind me of? A little chihuahua trying to fight a bigger and stronger dog when she knows she can't win. Careful or you'll end up with a nasty bite, Garcia."

I snatched my apple from his hand and leaned forward, bringing our faces closer. "Did you know that chihuahuas are known as an aggressive breed when they're moody, and when they *do* bite, they bite *hard*. Careful, or you'll end up with a nasty bite, Coulter."

I brought the apple to my mouth and took a bite before I realized what I was doing. Maddox's eyes flared before his lips quirked up. "I think we just shared our first indirect kiss."

Oh, for fuck's sake!

Colton snickered before stealing a brownie from Riley's tray. She hissed, and her eyes hardened with a glare. The girl before Jasper would have exploded. The new Riley? She stayed quiet.

"That was a lousy kiss. You can do better than that, man," Colton said, his six-foot-something frame shaking with mirth.

Maddox grabbed my chair and pulled me closer to him, the four legs making a loud screeching sound. The whole cafeteria was watching now. I could feel their stares burning into me.

"What do you say, Garcia? Shall we put on a show for these asswipes?" His voice lowered, holding a suggestive tone.

"Not interested. Your lips probably hold more disease than a pig's asshole." I handed him back the apple, giving him my best smile. "Consider this charity. Next time, I won't be so gracious."

The boys hollered at my response.

Maddox stared, his blue eyes pointedly holding mine. He was

still grinning. I didn't know why he kept doing that – smiling like he was having the best time of his life verbally sparring with me.

I found it neither entertaining nor funny.

Pushing away from the table, I stood up and grabbed my empty tray. Riley followed suit, and we left the cafeteria.

Maddox and his buddies didn't follow.

Mrs. Levi gave me a nod of approval, and I let out a relieved sigh. "That was a fabulous explanation, Lila."

"Thank you." I started to take my seat, feeling quite pleased with myself. I had spent two hours last night writing my essay, rereading all my notes and writing out this analysis.

"I disagree." A deep baritone voice interrupted my happy moment.

Heat crept up my neck, and I flushed under the sudden scrutinizing stares coming from the rest of the class. Including *his*.

"Excuse me?" I said through gritted teeth, turning around to face Maddox. He was sitting, laid-back, in his chair.

Maddox leaned forward in his chair, crossing his arms over the desk. When he spoke, his tone was flat and disinterested. "Sometimes we're thrown into a difficult situation where we need to make a difficult choice. Sometimes, it's not the best *or* the right choice. But maybe, it's the only option we have."

"Could you elaborate on that, Maddox?" Mrs. Levi demanded.

"Throughout Greek history and mythology, Medusa has always been viewed as a villain. You made a good point that Athena is an anti-hero, but you also went ahead and painted Medusa as a villain, yet again. Medusa was once a very beautiful woman - one who was an avowed priestess of Athena. She spent her days and nights in Athena's temple. Here's what we all know... she was punished for breaking her vow of celibacy. Athena cursed her, and Medusa became the woman with serpent heads. But... was it really her fault? History said she had an affair with Poseidon. Some say he seduced her, but the article that Mrs. Levi assigned us to read revealed that it was a lie to hide the fact that, in reality, Poseidon had raped her. She was never given the chance to plead her case or to speak for herself. Poseidon said Medusa seduced him, and in a fit of anger and jealousy, Athena cursed her. Once turned into a monster, she brought terror to the temple and anyone who stepped foot inside was instantly turned into stone. Now, it's easy to categorize Athena as the antagonist. After all, *she* was the one who gave the magical mirror to the warrior, which was used to turn Medusa into stone and eventually killed her. But could it be an act of mercy?" Maddox paused, cocking his head to the side, thoughtfully. "Maybe Athena regretted turning Medusa into a monster. Maybe Athena discovered the truth about Poseidon. Maybe... killing Medusa was the only way of granting her peace. Neither Medusa nor Athena is a villain. I would say they're both anti-heroes who were thrown into a very shitty situation."

"Wow... umm that's a very interesting way of looking at it, Maddox. A very in-depth analysis, I have to say." I could hear the shock in Mrs. Levi's voice. She probably wasn't expecting that.

Me? My whole body strummed with embarrassment.

"Your analysis would have been better if you took a moment to think outside the box. Consider this constructive criticism," Maddox said, his gaze on mine. "I hope you don't mind my little tip."

I bit on my lip, trying so hard to hold back from saying something stupid in front of the class. "*Thank you.*" The words tasted bitter on my tongue.

Pressing my lips firmly together, I retook my seat.

I was hyperaware of Maddox staring at me. He hadn't skipped one English class since he made it his goal to irritate me. Maddox made sure I could feel his presence at *all* times.

He didn't want me to forget – I was the prey; he was the hunter.

As soon as the bell rang, I was the first one out of class. It was hard to admit... but I was running away.

Riley was already waiting for me in the courtyard. "Uh oh. That expression tells me Maddox pulled another one of his asshole moves again."

I threw my hands in the air, holding back a frustrated scream. "He embarrassed me in front of the class."

"What did he do *this* time?"

Riley and I settled down, cross-legged, on the cold grass. I handed her the sandwich my grandma packed for us this morning, Riley's favorite. Turkey, lettuce, cheese and homemade smoked mustard. We bit into our sandwiches while I recounted what happened in class.

"Are you pissed that he was right and made a smarter analysis than you... or, are you pissed that he called you out in front of the class?"

"I –" My mouth snapped shut because Riley...was right. She knew me so well. I'd always been competitive by nature.

I made an aggravated sound at the back of my throat before admitting the truth. "Okay, fine. I'm pissed he had a better analysis, *and* I'm annoyed he called me out like that. And, he called it *constructive criticism*. Maddox can shove it up his ass. He was trying to embarrass me."

"We've established that. You're on his shit list, but you're letting him get to you, babe."

I chewed aggressively around my last bite. "I'm not."

Riley was right, though.

Maddox Coulter, with his pretty smirk, pretty eyes and surfer hair, was having the time of his life messing with me, and I was letting him.

I clenched my fists on my lap. *Not anymore.*

CHAPTER FOUR

Lila

First, I heard my mom scream.

Then, there was silence. It happened within a nanosecond. The world tilted suddenly, my vision blurring, before everything went black. I sunk into a very dark place. For the longest time, I stayed there... awake... fading... heart beating... numb... lost...

The silence slowly faded away, a buzzing noise replaced it, filling my ears. It felt like the only thing inside my head was static.

My throat was dry, scratched raw from the inside, and I couldn't make a sound.

Mommy? Daddy?

I couldn't see anything. Everything was so dark... so empty...

I remembered the sound of crushing glass, mixed with the distinct cracking of bones breaking. I remembered my mom screaming, and my dad... I remembered...

Pain came next.

My bones and fragile organs felt like they were being crumbled and smashed into a tiny, suffocating box. I couldn't breathe. It hurt so much. My torso burned like acid was being poured on it. There was a knife dug, painfully, into my chest... no, not a knife... I didn't know... but it hurt. It felt like a knife or a hammer being pounded into my chest.

I blinked... forcing myself to breathe. I couldn't. My lungs contracted with such force that I was afraid they would fold into themselves. When I coughed, agony strummed through my body, and my cracked lips parted with a silent scream.

Mom... Dad...

I couldn't speak. The buzzing noise wouldn't stop in my ears.

The taste of coppery blood pooled in my mouth; it tasted bitter, and I could feel it soaking my tongue and the inside of my mouth. Blood...?

No...

How...

What...

I remember...

The fight...snow outside... in the car... mom... dad... me...

I remember the screams...

My bones felt like they had been mangled together, and my chest, it was being carved open. I lifted my head up a bit and looked down at my chest to see... blood. Everywhere. So much blood.

I sucked in cramped air and tried to scream, tried to breathe, but my lungs refused to work.

No. No. No. Please. No. Oh God, no.

MOM, I wanted to scream. DADDY.

The pain never ended. The darkness never faded away.

I woke up with a gasp, my mouth open in a silent scream. Drenched in a cold sweat with my heart beating way too fast, I tried to suck in desperate breaths.

Ten. *Inhale.* Nine. *Exhale.* Eight. *Inhale*

I didn't die. I wasn't dead.

Seven. *Exhale.* Six. *Inhale.* Five. *Exhale.*

It was only a dream, I told myself.

Four. *Inhale.* Three. *Breathe.* Two. *Exhale.*

My chest hurt; the pain was almost crippling.

One. *Breathe, damn it.*

Hot tears stung my eyes as I held them back from spilling over my cheeks. I rubbed my chest, trying to alleviate the hammering ache. A whimper escaped past my chapped lips, and I choked back a sob.

Don't cry. Don't you dare cry.

I breathed through my nose, the fear slowly receding back, and I locked a cage around it. The pain and the taste of coppery blood faded away, and my senses came back to me.

Just a dream, I told myself.

Except...

My eyes closed, and I sniffed back my unshed tears. I did as my therapist had trained me to do--count backward from ten and breathe. So, I did, and while doing so, I locked the *memories* away.

Once my racing heart calmed to a soothing beat again, I got off the bed and started my morning routine.

While combing my hair, my eyes fell on the picture frame on my nightstand. A picture of me on my thirteenth birthday. I stood in the middle with my parents on either side of me. We were laughing; our faces smudged with cake icing.

My lips twitched at the memory, a phantom of a smile as I reminisced our time together.

I laid the hairbrush down beside the small frame. My fingers slid over the picture, caressing their faces. "I miss you," I whispered to them. "But I'm okay. I promise you. *I'm okay.*"

They kept smiling back at me.

"Lila!" My grandma's voice broke through the moment. "Breakfast is ready."

"Coming!"

I grabbed my bag and strode out of my room. Sven Wilson, ex-military man and now a retired veteran, my dearest grandpa sat at the breakfast table. With a newspaper in his hand and Grandma Molly making us pancakes, it was a typical morning.

"Good morning," I greeted them with a smile.

"Sit, sit. You're going to be late."

"She's fine. Lila is rarely late for her classes," Grandpa said. He winked before taking a sip of his tea.

I winked back because I knew he had my back. Always.

Grandma handed me a plate and patted me on the cheek. "How's school, sweetie? You've been holed up in your bedroom or the library. We haven't had time to talk."

"It's going good," I replied around a bite of my pancakes. "I like my teachers. Do you guys need help at the store? I can come over during the weekend."

Grandpa waved a hand, shaking his head. "No need. We can handle it."

I held back a smile. He refused to acknowledge that he was getting older, and they did, in fact, need help. Both of them were in their seventies, and they could no longer run the grocery store on their own. But Sven Wilson was stubborn.

"How about we put a hiring sign up? I'll do the interviews and even train them for a few days."

"Maybe that's a good idea," Grandma agreed, a tender smile on her lips.

"Got it. I'll put the sign up this weekend. I'm sure you'll get plenty of students who want to work part-time."

I quickly finished my pancakes and stood up. "Thank you for breakfast." After quickly pecking them both on the cheek, I waved goodbye and ran out of the house.

The cold breeze of October hit me, and I breathed in the morning scent. It poured last night. The smell of grass after the rain teased my nostrils, and it soothed me.

If it were any normal day, I'd say today was going to be good. But my days were no longer *normal*. Not since Maddox decided I was his plaything.

It'd been a week since the Medusa argument, and Maddox was still irritating as always, if not worse.

God give me patience.

I was standing in line in the cafeteria, waiting to get my food, when I saw him. Our eyes met, and Maddox stalked closer, as if he was on a mission. *Shit.*

I quickly put my earphones in and stared hard at my phone. Maddox came to stand behind me, the heat practically rolling off him. I could sense people staring at us, again... waiting for another dramatic scene. I'd quickly become everyone's favorite joke.

Berkshire Academy was a shark tank.

You see, in Berkshire, only the strong survive. The weaker are preyed on, chewed up, and spit out like garbage.

Maddox was on the top – the pack leader. He was *the* King, and he wore his crown with a cocky grin. He was untouchable to his rivals, and he was every girl's favorite dick to ride.

And I wanted nothing to do with him.

His body brushed against mine as he slid closer to me. Maddox nudged me with his elbow.

I ignored him. "Hey, Garcia."

I scrolled through my playlist, refusing to acknowledge him. "Damn, are you ignoring me?"

When I didn't reply, Maddox let out a mock gasp. "You wound me."

I rolled my eyes for the umpteenth time but continued to ignore him. I didn't expect him to be so bold, but when he reached forward to pull my earphones out, I released a low frustrated growl.

My body swiveled around, and I faced him. The first thing I noticed was that he was wearing his full Berkshire uniform today. The navy blazer molded to his chest and shoulders like it was tailored made, especially for him, and the beige slacks didn't hide how strong his thighs were. Instead of putting his hair into another messy man bun, he left it loose today. The tight, blond curls ended up a good inch above his shoulders.

"Do you know that when people have headphones in... it means they don't want anyone to speak to them? That's the universal sign for Stay-The-Fuck-Away-From-Me-And-Don't-Speak-To-Me," I snapped, loud enough for the people around us to hear. *Ugh.*

If looks could kill, he'd be seven feet under right now. Irritation bubbled inside of me at the fact that I had been checking him out.

Yeah, he was hot. So what? Maddox was a fine specimen to look at. Too bad, he had an aggravating personality.

Maddox leaned closer, a little smirk playing on his lips. His hot breath feathered over the skin of my exposed neck, and when he whispered in my ear, his voice was low and deep. "I'm not everyone though. I'm special."

He pulled back, his blue eyes glinting with mischief. "And I know you want me to talk to you. We didn't see each other yesterday, and I wasn't in class today. Miss me, Sweet Cheeks?"

Ha! I had two very peaceful days, and I wasn't complaining.

Crossing my arms over my chest, I let out a laugh with absolutely no trace of humor. "Cocky much?"

"I love the sound of that word coming from your lips." His gaze shifted to my lips for a second, watching them with rapt attention before he met my eyes again.

I felt the blood rush between my ears. and I attempted to hold back my growl.

"Say it again," he calmly demanded, which pissed me off even more. "Slowly this time."

I took a deep breath before letting it out. I was trying so hard not to punch this dude. "Listen, Coulter. You need to back off, or I'm going to do something really bad."

"Like what?" He was testing me, pushing and pushing – waiting for what I'd do, or what I was capable of.

"I don't know. Maybe punch your dick so hard it'll retreat back into your asshole. Have you ever heard of personal space?"

My body was tight as a bowstring. He was too close to me, so close I caught the scent of his cologne and aftershave. He smelled clean and…

I didn't like the way my body suddenly decided to appreciate the way he looked or what he smelled like. "Take a step back. Now," I growled.

Maddox took a step *forward*, crowding into me and forcing me against the wall. His blue eyes darkened and all signs of mischief were suddenly gone. "I don't listen well to demands. I think you know that already. I always do the opposite. Did you, by any chance, want me closer?"

I brought my hands up and pushed against his chest, but he wouldn't budge.

"You're so full of yourself."

"You could be full of *me*. Time, date and address. You choose, Sweet Cheeks," he rasped in my ear, his lips whispering over my skin.

What… the… fuck?

A voice interrupted us before I could explode. "Next."

The lady at the end of the food line called again. "Next!"

Maddox pulled away, and I could finally breathe again. I hadn't even realized I was holding my breath or that my heartbeats had been strangely irregular.

I shouldn't be feeling this way. I wasn't weak.

No, in a tank full of sharks – I would *not* be preyed on.

Straightening my spine, I pushed past him without a second glance.

Fuck you, Coulter.

And game on.

CHAPTER FIVE

"Do you want to go to the haunted house this year?"
I couldn't remember the last time I'd been to a
haunted house. I hated them as a kid, but my dad
would always hold my hand through them. With him, I was safe,
and nothing about the haunted houses scared me.

Every Halloween, Berkshire Academy builds its own haunted
house on the school grounds. It was a tradition that started a whole
decade ago, and to this day, we still honored it.

I took a bite of my pizza, chewing while I contemplated Riley's
question. "I guess we could check it out."

She clapped her hands, her face lighting up with excitement. "I
heard it's scarier than last year. They're going all out this time. It'd
be fun! How about some girl time? We go to the haunted house then
a sleepover at my place? Movie and pizza?"

Riley continued to chatter with enthusiasm while I tried to

ignore all the eyes on me. It was difficult when they made it so obvious. The cafeteria had become a nightmare now. I could have tucked my tail between my legs and made a run for it; I could have hidden – but I was never one to accept defeat.

Since Maddox had made me his prey, I'd been the center of attention. A year ago, when I enrolled at Berkshire, I got used to all the judgmental eyes.

Lila Garcia, the 'poor' girl. I didn't have Louis Vuitton shoes or Chanel bags or the latest iPhone. I didn't prance around with a kilo of makeup on my face nor was I a cheerleader who constantly rubbed herself against the jocks. I wasn't a *follower*.

I'd always been the outsider, but after a few months of critical eyes on me and their constant judgment, they had forgotten about me. I blended into the crowd and soon became invisible. It made life easier.

Until Maddox.

Now, the girls looked at me with contempt, like I was the dirt under their feet. They gawked at me with envy because I had Maddox's attention while the boys stared at me with obvious interest.

None have made a move though.

Riley said I was Maddox's trophy. Nobody would dare to approach me. The moment he laid eyes on me, I became untouchable to the rest of Berkshire Academy.

Ha, lucky me.

Riley snapped her fingers at my face, causing me to flinch. She smiled sweetly. "Ignore them, Lila."

I hummed in response before taking another bite of my cold pizza.

"So, haunted house and then sleepover?" Riley asked again.

"Okay, I like that idea. I'm not a big fan of haunted houses though."

"I'll hold your hand. It'll be romantic! Me and you, walking through the dark. I'll protect you from the bad guys." She cooed, like a romance hero – way too dramatic.

"Funny. Very funny. If I didn't know better, I'd say you were into pussies."

She paused, looking thoughtful for a moment. "I kissed a girl once. A few years ago. It was a dare, and I liked it. She had really soft lips, and she said I was a good kisser. Wanna find out?"

When she leaned across the table, puckering her lips up, I let out a small laugh. "Um no. Stay away from me, Riley."

"I'm disappointed," she said with a cute pout.

Riley's gaze landed behind my shoulder again, before she blushed and quickly looked away. "Okay, that's it. What's going on?"

"What?" She feigned innocence, batting her long lashes at me.

I half-looked over my shoulder before facing her again. "*Him.* You keep looking at him and blushing. What's up?"

"Nothing." She was too quick with the denial. I call bullshit.

"Riley, who is he?"

I saw the moment she gave in. Her eyes softened, and she chewed on her bottom lip. "That's Grayson."

"And?" I kicked her under the table, demanding more answers.

"I heard some whispers in the hallway. They weren't really nice. He was bullied a bit last week. Jasper and his friends were being assholes, but Grayson just ignored them and walked away. Apparently, he was living on the streets for a while before he was recently adopted by a famous lawyer and his wife. They can't have kids. We don't know much about him yet, but he's in two of my classes."

I looked over my shoulder again, finally taking a good look at Grayson who was sitting at the far end of the cafeteria in a corner by himself. "I didn't know you were into nerds."

Grayson wore a black pair of glasses perched on his nose, and he was reading a book. I could see the appeal and definitely understood why he caught Riley's eye.

"He's a nerd, but did you see him? He's hot with a capital H O T. But he's kinda moody. He doesn't really talk to anyone. Typical loner. But he's smart and we bumped into each other last week. Remember the bruises on my knees? Yeah, Grayson took me to the infirmary after I fell down, and he noticed my knees bleeding."

Aha... I remembered that incident. I had found Riley in the infirmary; she was alone, but now that I remembered – she had been blushing heavily and was a stuttering mess.

"Well, at least he's not an asshole."

Riley let out a dreamy sigh. "He's sweet. Except he barely spared me a glance. I said *hi* to him a few times, and he just... ignored me. Apparently, he doesn't like when people talk to him."

"I didn't think the nerdy ones were your type..."

The last boy Riley dated was a jock and an asshole. After Jasper, it made sense why she'd swear off all the guys like him.

"Fine, I'll confess my secret. I like nerds. There's just something attractive about them."

I couldn't deny that Grayson was indeed appealing to the eye.

"Hot and moody nerds, you mean."

Riley popped a piece of mint gum into her mouth. She looked over my shoulder again, where her new crush was sitting. "Exactly," she chirped.

I quirked up an eyebrow at her. "*Grayson*, specifically."

"Yeah. Too bad he won't even look at me." The pout was evident in her voice.

"Is that why you wore extra makeup today, curled your hair, and rolled your skirt higher?"

I already knew the answer, but I still wanted to hear it from her.

A nervous laugh bubbled out of her, and she twirled a lock of hair around her finger. "You noticed that?"

My sweet friend. Gripping her hand over the table, I gave her a small, comforting squeeze. "Just be yourself, Riley. If he likes you, you'll know."

She let out a sigh, her eyes moving to Grayson one last time before she focused on me. "So, what's up with you and Maddox?"

I crooked my finger at her, and Riley leaned closer, as if we were about to share a secret. It kind of was – *a secret.*

"He wants a fight? I'm going to give him a fight."

Riley's face lit up, and a huge smile spread across her lips. "We're going to be bad?"

Well, if she put it that way... then yeah, we were about to be very bad.

"Oh, we're going to play *his* games, but with *my* rules."

She slapped the table loud enough to rattle our trays and smirked. "I'm in!"

My lips twitched, and I held back my own smile. Maddox was about to be bested at his own little, shitty game.

"Can you see him?" I asked, leaning closer to Riley. It was two hours after school, and we were hiding in the hallway, which also overlooked the huge football field. Where, very conveniently, the boys were practicing. They had a very important game in a week, and I heard the coach was being extra hard on all their asses.

"I can't believe we're hiding with binoculars, Lila. But yeah, I can see him. He's playing just fine. Did you put a lot of the powder in his pants?"

"No, just a little, but enough to make him lose his mind."

An unladylike snort came from Riley. "You're so fucking petty."

I let out a mock gasp, but the urge to defend myself was strong. "He started it."

"Aha! Okay, he just stopped in the middle of a play."

"Yeah?"

Riley looked into her binoculars, her shoulders shaking with mirth. "Oh, he looks confused. The coach is walking over to him. Lila!" she whispered-yelled, before bursting into laughter. "He's scratching at his inner thighs now. Oh my God, he looks like a monkey. The boys are hollering. Oh, oh, shit. He's walking back this way. Ohhh, he looks pissed!"

Good.

"How pissed?" I demanded, feeling mighty proud of myself. Maddox was made of rock. He was untouchable, and if little ole me, Lila Garcia, could get him *this* pissed off – then I won.

"He's reaaally mad. He's still scratching himself. You should see the look on his face!"

Riley handed me the binoculars, and I looked through them. True to her words, Maddox was marching across the field like a mad bull. His face was filled with rage, his nostrils flaring like a wild beast. He was seething, and I could bet, he figured out what happened. Maybe not *who* was behind the prank, but at least *what* was done to him. It should have scared me, the brutal look on his face, but I couldn't help but chortle with laughter at the way he couldn't stop scratching at his muscled thighs and crotch.

As if he could sense me, his stormy eyes connected with mine through the binoculars, although I was sure there was no way he could see me. Riley and I were hidden perfectly.

But just in case, I lowered myself to the ground. "Hey, are you sure... it's safe? I mean, I wanted to prank him, but what we did isn't too extreme, right?"

Riley waved away my concerns. "Nah. He'll be fine. The itching powder doesn't leave any lasting side effects. It's harmless. I kinda feel bad for his dick though."

My jaw clenched as I remembered the cafeteria scene where he had cornered me. "He deserves it after the comment he made in the cafeteria. He propositioned me for sex, like I'm some kind of paid who–"

Riley slapped a hand over my mouth before I could finish my sentence. "Shh, he's coming in."

We both ducked around the corner, the same time Maddox stormed into the building and right into the locker room.

"I feel like a spy," Riley announced in my ear, giggling softly.

Basically, we were *spying* on him.

Riley and I snuck closer to the locker room. The door was partially opened, and we peeked inside. It was empty, since everyone else was on the field – except Maddox. From where we stood, we could hear the shower running.

"He must be itching really bad right now."

I shushed Riley when she couldn't hold in her laughter any longer.

"Can you see him?"

I stood on my tip-toes, trying to get a look inside. "Nope."

A few minutes later, the shower turned off and then I did see him.

"Oh," Riley whispered behind me.

Yeah, oh.

Maddox was bare chested, with a towel wrapped loosely around his hips. His body was still wet and glistening as if he didn't care to dry himself the moment he stepped out of the shower. He roughly rubbed another towel through his long curly hair, before running it over the rest of his body.

I hated him; I truly did, but there was no denying it; something about his physique was making my lady brain go mushy and all my lady parts tingle. I inhaled deeply as I took in the sight in front of me.

Maddox furiously wiped the ringlets of water from his muscled chest until his skin was glowing pink. I tried to look away – it was the decent thing to do, but I failed miserably. My curious eyes found his torso, and I bit my lip, mentally slapping myself but I. Could. Not. Help. It.

It was like studying an expertly, carved statue in a museum. Beautifully chiseled chest, strong arms and well-defined masculine thighs. Auguste Rodin would have begged to sculpt a man like Maddox Coulter since he was damn near close to rugged perfection.

"Even his nipples are sexy," Riley whispered.

My heart slammed in my chest, and I bumped back into her. I had completely forgotten she was there with me, and she was also getting an eyeful of Maddox.

I watched as he wrenched his locker open and rummaged through it. The effects of the itching powder were still not gone since he was still scratching at his crotch.

I could tell the moment he read the note I left him. His back went rigid, and the muscles of his shoulders clenched tensely. Maddox turned sideways, giving me a perfect view of him as he scrunched my little note in his fist.

How does your crotch feel? – Lila

First rule of enacting a well, plotted out revenge plan: always leave a note behind, so your nemesis knows it's you. Play dirty but don't be a coward.

He muttered something under his breath and shook his head, before he did something unexpected. I knew he'd be furious, and he was, but then his lips twitched. Maddox rubbed his thumb over his full, smirking lips.

"Uh oh," Riley muttered from behind me. "I'm not sure I like the look on his face."

"Ladies, what are you doing here?" Another voice joined us, loud enough to have my heart leap in my throat, and I choked back a gasp.

Riley and I jumped away from the locker room, and we swiveled around to see a teacher giving us *the* look. Oh shit, busted.

"It's late. Why are you two still on school grounds?" She demanded with her hands on her hips.

"Um, we forgot something," I stammered, looking back toward Maddox while contemplating my escape.

Maddox's head turned toward me at the same time, and through the partially opened door, for only a nanosecond, our gazes collided. His deep, ocean blue eyes flared in surprise, and I could swear his stare burned through me, causing a warm flush to spread through my body. Then... the moment was gone.

Riley grabbed my hand, already pulling me away. "Sorry! We're leaving."

We sprinted out of the school, and once we passed through the Berkshire's main gate, Riley and I came to a halt.

"Shit. That was close," Riley panted with her hands on her

knees.

"So worth it though."

She straightened her back, one perfect eyebrow raised. "Are you sure? Maddox is not the type who is going to let you off the hook. Revenge is a dish best served cold. He's going to get you back, probably not tomorrow or the day after, but he will – trust me, and I don't think it's going to be pretty."

"He shouldn't have messed with me. I'm prepared for anything he's going to throw my way," I responded, fighting back a smile of my own.

I remembered the look in Maddox's eyes when our gaze briefly met in the locker room. I didn't admit it out loud, but I wanted to see what Maddox could do and how far he was going to push me. It was too tempting to mess with him, to retaliate after seeing Maddox's reaction – he started this game, and now, I was all in.

CHAPTER SIX

Maddox

The girl on my lap grinded against me. Her tits were practically spilling out of her tight red dress, and she shoved them in my face. I gripped her ass in one hand and smoked a blunt with the other. Miss-Fake-Tits let out a moan, which sounded straight out of a porn video.

Although I've seen better acted porn. She was inexperienced and quite an amateur. Trying too hard, with too little self-respect.

Easy pussy, easy fuck. I didn't have to hunt for them; they landed right on my lap.

"Maddox," she purred in my ear. My jaw twitched as I caught a whiff of her strong perfume and the stench of alcohol was strong on her breath. She was fucking drunk and humping me like a bitch in heat.

Any other day, I'd be all up in her pussy... tonight, my dick was not in the mood.

Or I guessed, I was not in the mood for *her*.

On the opposite couch, Colton had his tongue shoved down a girl's throat. Brayden and Cole were in a heated conversation about this week's football match. We won, big time. Leighton High School wasn't even worth our time. Knox, our best linebacker, was missing, but he was probably in a room lost in pussy.

And I was fucking bored.

Drunk and bored.

The party we crashed was lame, and I needed some kind of action, something to get my blood pumping – something dangerous. I was itching for a fight and a fuck. Too bad the girl on my lap had absolutely no effect on my dick.

Her lips parted, and I felt her tongue on my neck. She sucked on my throat, biting teasingly. "Let's get out of here. Go somewhere quieter."

"If you wanna fuck, we do it here."

She pulled away, her green eyes hooded and confused. "*Here?*"

I lifted an eyebrow, amused. The only reason she was sitting on my lap and humping me was because she needed to fuck a Berkshire football star, so she could go around and rub it in the other girls' faces. I was her ticket to being Miss Popular at Leighton Public High School -- Berkshire's rival.

"Too shy for a little audience?"

She looked around, stammering, "No-o."

I squeezed her ass, not even bothering to be gentle about it. That was a warning. "I don't do sweet girls."

Nah, sweet girls didn't do shit for my libido.

Feisty girls, though, yeah... they made my dick hard.

Full of sass with brown eyes, black hair, curvy hips and a pretty Latina ass that would make any man drop to his knees, begging for a taste.

Goddamn fucking trouble she was, but she was exactly what my dick wanted.

Lila Garcia.

Too bad she didn't want me anywhere near her.

I took a hit off the blunt one last time and exhaled a puff of smoke, not bothering to move my head away. I knew I was being an asshole, but hey… chicks like her wanted jerks like me – so who the fuck cared?

Dropping the now useless blunt onto the ashtray, I leveled her with a look. She scrunched her nose, but her eyes flared with determination. What she didn't realize – I ate girls like her for dinner before spitting them out two hours later, no guilt with one very satisfied dick.

I curled a hand around the back of her neck, bringing her head closer. "You want a taste of me? We do it *my* way."

She looked around again, her cheeks flushed, and she was already a little bit out of breath. "Do you even know my name?"

"Do you know mine?" I threw back, although the answer was obvious. Of course, she knew who I was. Miss-Fake-Tits was only here to use me like I was about to use her. Fair game.

"Who doesn't? You're Maddox Coulter. And for your information, my name is Madison."

She thought she was special. Newsflash – she wasn't the type of girl I'd wake up the next morning with. I arched an eyebrow with a *tsk*. "Here's the thing, I don't need to know your name to fuck you."

Miss-Fake-tits, er… *Madison*, wrapped her arms around my shoulders. Her hips moved in a circular motion, quite tempting as she practically grinded against my dick through our clothes. Any passerby would have thought we were fucking.

She let out a fake giggle. "Didn't your mommy or daddy teach you some manners?"

She was teasing; it was a fucking joke.

But the silent rage inside me bubbled over, threatening to burst through, without any care of the consequences. Fuck her. And fuck mommy and daddy dearest, too. Manners? No, they didn't teach me any – just like they didn't give a fuck if I lived or died, either.

I crashed the party because I wanted to *forget*.

But Madison, aka *Bitch*, right here, just pissed me off even more.

She reminded me of why I was *here*, made me think of my fucked up parents when I was so hell bent on forgetting their existence.

Daddy dearest caught me smoking today, lounging on the couch and watching TV. He walked in with his business associate. Oh, he knew I smoked, except he never cared. But Brad Coulter didn't want me to set a bad example in front of his business partners; his image had always been more important than my health.

"You don't smoke in my house," he hissed in my face, taking a threatening step toward me. There was a time when my father was taller and bigger than me. He used to be intimidating, and his words were law in our house. But that time was long gone.

Now, I was bigger… taller… meaner.

He didn't scare me.

Now, he just pissed me off more often than not.

"I've been smoking since I was thirteen. Never knew we had a rule. You didn't seem to care before, father."

His lips curled up in disgust, and I felt it. I fucking felt it – his anger, his disappointment, his revulsion. My hands clenched into fists, and I exhaled through my nose. At a young age, I had quickly learned how to mask my emotions until I became a solid wall of nothingness. You'd cut me open, and you'd find something hollow inside.

"I constantly question if you really are my son."

When I was seven years old, my heart had frozen in my chest. But his words, to this day, could still fucking burn me like acid in my veins. My father held an arrow in his hand, the tip of it aflame, and it was aimed right at my chest – my goddamn heart was his target.

"Nah. I'm definitely your son. You're an asshole, I'm an asshole. It runs in our blood."

His blue eyes – the same as mine, darkened and his face was vicious.

"Brad." My mother's soft voice interrupted us. "They're waiting. Let's go. Maddox, go back to your room. This deal is important to your father."

I heard her unspoken words. Please, for Christ's sake, don't ruin it.

He took a step back, his jaw hard and twitching. Without sparing me another glance, he walked away. I saw the look in my mother's eyes, her parted lips, and I waited for her to say something. But there was nothing left to say, so she walked away, too.

And so, I'd been dismissed. I saw my parents after three weeks, and without even a greeting, I had been brushed off and forgotten. Yet again.

Just like ten years ago...

When I had needed them the most. I was left behind, locked away in the dark... forgotten.

"Maddox," she purred in my ear again. I blinked, the past going out of focus, and I crashed landed in the present.

I had called Colton after the 'fight' with my father. He didn't have to ask me questions, he *knew* what I needed. So, here we were. Crashing Leighton's party, knowing full well we were about to piss off a whole bunch of people.

Yeah, that was exactly what I needed.

A good fight, a good fuck.

Marley – wait, no – Madison rubbed her hands over my chest and shoulders. "You're so big and strong. So hard, in all the right places."

She was so eager to please me, so eager to be *just* another girl on my list.

My fingers tangled in her hair, twisting the thick blonde strands around my fist. My knuckles dug into her scalp, and she winced, before quickly hiding it with a fake-ass smile. Without care, I pushed her on the ground. She collapsed to her knees with a low whine, her wide eyes blinking up at me, unfocused, confused, and with way too many expectations.

Her pink lips parted, *waiting,* and I figured why-the-fuck-not. With one hand, I unbuckled my jeans. "Let's put your deepthroating skills to good use, shall we?"

Her face lit up, and she scooted closer between my thighs. Maybe she wouldn't be such a bad lay after all. At least she was willing to suck dick. Some bitches thought they were too pretty and fancy to be on their knees.

A loud snarl came from outside, making all of us pause. There was more shouting, and through my hazy mind, I realized Colton was no longer in the same room. Brayden and Cole looked at each other, too, confused.

"Isn't he from Berkshire?" The whispers started to get louder.

Brayden and Cole shot off the couch at the same time as me. Miss-Fake-Tits shrieked as she fell back hard on her ass. "What the hell?"

No fucks were given.

I buckled up my jeans before marching outside, Brayden and

Cole following closely behind. *Ah fuck.*

Colton was standing in the middle of the front lawn, smiling like a goddamn maniac, while he was surrounded by a bunch of Leighton boys.

"Your girl wanted her pussy eaten," he announced, loud enough for all of us gathered to hear. "You weren't doing a good enough job, man."

The girl in question, who was the same girl on his lap a few minutes before, sputtered a half-ass excuse. Her face was bright red, and she hid behind her friends.

I noticed Samuel, Leighton's Quarterback, charging forward. Ah, so he was the boyfriend. This was also *his* party, and *we* weren't invited.

Yeah, we were trouble with a capital T.

Colton was able to block the first punch, which only served to piss off Samuel more. He was livid as he tried to bring Colton to the ground, quite unsuccessfully. *Pussy.*

It was a fair fight...until it wasn't.

The Leighton boys came forward, surrounding Colton until he was trapped.

"Fuck no," Brayden growled.

My jaw locked, and the fire inside me burnt like lava, liquid hot and fiery. We cut through the mass of people, the itching need to fight putting all of us on an adrenaline rush.

Without giving it much thought, I yanked one of the boys away, and he fell backward. Weak and fucking useless.

Samuel spun around, his face red and a mask of fury. My fingers curled into a fist, and before he could blink, my fist made contact with his face. Not so pretty face anymore, huh?

He roared but swiveled back around quickly, blocking my next hit. The alcohol was fucking with my senses now, and he caught me in the ribs. The pain coursing through my body fueled me to fight harder and meaner.

He lunged at me, swinging but missing. I could hear the others fighting, the brawl getting louder and messier.

This wasn't just a fight. It was retaliation. It was a fight based on ego -- who had the bigger balls, who was stronger.

I drove my shoulder into Samuel's chest, slamming him into the ground. He tackled me back, but I was able to land solid punches into his gut. We were both walking out of here with at least one cracked rib.

My father's disappointment – *punch.*

My mother's lack of care – *punch.*

My fucked up childhood – *punch, punch, punch.*

The suffocating darkness, a constant reminder – *punch.*

My knuckles were bleeding and raw, my left eye was swollen shut, but I. Couldn't. Fucking. Stop.

Brushed-off and forgotten.

Enraged and lost.

Through my hazy brain, I heard Colton shouting. My head snapped toward him, seeing him rush toward me. My eyes widened for a nanosecond before the bottle cracked against my temple.

My body slumped forward as the ringing of my ears amplified, my chest caving in as I tried to *breathe.* My heartbeat slowed and the metallic taste of blood filled my mouth.

My vision blurred, and I didn't see the punch coming.

I only *felt* it.

My jaw cracked, and I fell back, my head hitting the ground.

Breathe.

Breathe.

DO YOU DARE?

Fucking breathe.

The world slowed.

I blinked. Once. Twice.

Silence replaced the ringing in my ears as the world went black.

CHAPTER SEVEN

Lila

66 "Y ou're late, Mr. Coulter."

My head snapped up at Mrs. Levi's voice and Maddox's name. Everyone seemed to have the same train of thought since we all looked up at the same time as Maddox walked into the classroom. Contrary to his usual swagger and smirk, he was brooding and quiet.

Except that wasn't what caught my attention.

No, it was the fact that his beautiful face was messed up.

His left eye appeared swollen and that side of his face was heavily bruised. He had a band-aid on his eyebrow, and there was a cut on the corner of his full lips. It looked painful, and even I winced at the sight of him like *this*. Instead of a man bun, his curly hair was left loose, and I had a feeling he was hiding behind them.

People talked; Berkshire's hallways were never without rumors. There was always something going on. A new break-up, a new student, a bully, someone caught cheating. There was always some kind of drama.

Yesterday, when Maddox didn't show up at school, we heard there was a fight between Leighton and Berkshire boys. They said Maddox landed in the hospital with a slight concussion.

I had brushed off the rumors and thought it was a peaceful day – finally.

But now, seeing Maddox like *this...*

He didn't spare me a glance, taking his seat at the back of the classroom. I waited for the warmth that would always accompany his burning stare, but I felt... *nothing.*

Glancing over my shoulder, I took a peek. Maddox stared down at his notebook, a frozen statue in time. He didn't stare back, didn't tease, and unlike the last few weeks, the playful Maddox disappeared. In his place was a bitter, sulking boy.

I turned away and looked at my own paper. Why did I care? I shouldn't be bothered by his change of attitude. He was having a shitty day, so what? Everyone had bad days. Hell, *I* knew the exact meaning of shitty days.

When the bell rang, I didn't move from the chair. I couldn't bring myself to, even though I should have gotten up and walked away. *Like always.*

Instead, I found myself waiting.

Maddox walked past me, without a word or a fleeting look. He didn't bump into me, didn't pull my hair, didn't throw me one of his annoying smirks. *Nothing.*

I blinked, confused at my own mixed feelings.

I didn't care; I shouldn't care.

Any other decent person would have ignored Maddox and moved on – probably be thankful for another peaceful day.

Me?

I found myself following him.

Oh, how the tables have turned.

Maybe it was the fact that I was ready for him today. The last few weeks, Maddox had been a constant pain in my ass, and as much as I hated to admit it, I'd grown used to him being a jerk. The verbal sparring and the pranks became a part of my daily routine, and somehow, I found myself *disappointed* that Maddox wasn't in the same mood.

"You're dumb," I muttered to myself as I followed behind Maddox, only a few steps away. "Stupid, stupid, stupid."

Turn back. Walk away. Now.

You see, there are two sides to Lila. The indifferent side of her and the intrigued Lila – I was currently the latter.

Something about Maddox was different today, and it intrigued me. I had always liked puzzles, and Maddox Coulter was a difficult one to solve.

Maddox stopped by his locker, and he carelessly stuffed his books in there. His irritation was apparent, and he wasn't even trying to mask it. No wonder everyone was keeping their distance from him. The students stared, but quickly scrambled away, when he directed his scowls at them.

I should have kept my distance, too. Ignored him and walked away.

But apparently, I liked to play with fire and to push my boundaries. Maddox and I were playing tug-of-war. It was an everyday battle between us.

Stopping a mere foot from him, I leaned my shoulder against the locker next to Maddox. "Is it shark week?" I remarked with a grin.

He didn't spare me a glance, but his lips had thinned into a hard

71

line, his jaw tensed. Maddox's blue eyes darkened, but he otherwise ignored me. The scowl on his face was intimidating, but it only made me want to push his buttons even more. "Did your period attack you today?"

He blew out a breath before slamming his locker shut. His knuckles were red and bruised. The wounds on Maddox only made him appear more brutal... and slightly *broken*.

Maybe that was why he piqued my interest.

My grandma always said I was fixer. Since I was a kid, I always picked up the stray cats and the injured birds. Our house was a tiny zoo for all my little friends.

Too bad Maddox Coulter was not a friend.

He was my nemesis, and I didn't want to fix him, I reminded myself.

"What do you want?" he asked, his voice low and hard. A shiver ran down my spine, and I stood up straighter, hiding the obvious effect he had on me and my body.

"Just wondering if you need a tampon. Or, do you already have one stuffed up your ass? Is that why you're so grumpy?"

"For fuck's sake," Maddox grumbled.

"Ah. Definitely shark week." I waited for him to snap, but he only gritted his teeth together, so hard I wondered how his jaw didn't crack under the pressure. "It's okay, you'll eventually get used to all the messy hormones. If you need any advice on how to deal with it, I can make a PowerPoint for you."

"Not in the mood for your pranks, Garcia."

"You love my pranks."

My stomach dipped when his chest rumbled with a low growl. "Get out of my way."

He tried to walk past me, but I was having none of that. Could be my curiosity or my stubbornness, but I wasn't ready for him to leave.

I sidestepped into his path. Maddox squared his wide shoulders, standing taller, and his eyes narrowed on me. "*Move.*" There was a warning in his voice, but I chose to ignore it.

"Are you okay?" I asked before I could stop myself.

I told myself I wasn't worried nor did I care, but still... the question popped out before I thought it over.

Maddox leaned down toward me, bringing our faces closer and crowding into me. I fidgeted with the straps of my school bag, holding myself in place and refusing to step back. He didn't intimidate me.

"If I didn't know better, I'd say you *care*, Garcia." My breath caught in my throat when our eyes made contact. He held me there, in the moment, before he flashed me a sardonic smile. "What is it? Finally decided to sit on my dick? I might make an exception for you. I'll tell you all about my day if you let me in your pus–"

"You know, two minutes ago, I actually cared. But never mind, I take it back now. You're still a jerk, Coulter."

Maddox pulled back, straightening to his full height again. "Always have been, always will be. Remember that, Sweet Cheeks. Ain't no pussy gonna tame me and definitely not yours."

Good. Lord.

The urge to smack him was strong, and the urge to slap myself for being stupid enough to care was *also* strong.

I came to a very important conclusion: I preferred Maddox silent. Why did I even try to get him to talk? The moment he opened his mouth, I realized why I *despised* him. He was an asshole, through and through.

I shuffled through my bag and took out two very important

items, shoving them in his hands. His dark eyebrows pulled together in confusion.

"Tampons and chocolate," I explained with a fake smile. "You're welcome. Have a good day, Maddox."

I pushed past him, and just before I walked away, his lips *twitched*.

Did I just get Maddox Coulter to smile?

"Can you stop following me?" I paused and then turned on my heels quickly. Maddox caught himself in time, coming to a halt, so he wouldn't bump into me.

After our 'conversation' right before lunch, the rest of the day took a sudden turn. Maddox decided to follow me around; he was like a lost puppy – Riley's words, although I only found him to be irritating, so maybe more like an *annoying* puppy.

I wished we could go back to 'silent, brooding' Maddox. That version of him was ten times better than *this*.

I looked up at his bruised face, making sure to harden my heart at the sight of him battered and bruised. "Stop. Following. Me."

He shrugged, nonchalantly, and then stuffed his hands into the pockets of his beige slacks. "Can't do that. I'm having fun looking at your ass. By the way, do you mind if I warm my hands up?"

Exasperated, I let out a tiny growl from under my breath before I could stop myself. He was smiling now. As if pissing me off was his favorite fucking pastime.

"That's sexual harassment, Coulter."

"You looking at my dick print is sexual harassment, too, Garcia."

My eyes widened at his words, and I felt the air being sucked out of me. "Wha-at? No...no I wasn't," I sputtered. My gaze fleeted to his crotch before I could stop myself. Shit. Biting on my lip, I blinked and looked away – anywhere but at *him*.

Maddox let out a throaty chuckle, and my eyes snapped back to his. He gave me his signature smirk, his dimple popping, creating a sexy indent into his left cheek. "You were, Sweet Cheeks. You were probably calculating how thick and how long I am, too."

My jaw snapped together, and I hissed through gritted teeth, "Shut. Up."

"Want me to tell you?" He quirked up a mocking eyebrow. "Or, you want to check for yourself? It's a little cold today, maybe you can warm my dick up with your little hands."

He acted as if he was reaching for my hands, but I slapped him away. In a blink, his arm snaked out, and he gripped my wrist, pulling me closer until our bodies were *almost* touching. My neck craned up, so I could stare into his face – he was too tall compared to my own tiny height. The top of my head barely came to his shoulders.

"You are disgusting," I hissed, feeling my cheeks warming up under his dark, teasing eyes.

His breath feathered over my cheek; his lips way too close to my ear. "I am proudly *filthy*, Sweet Cheeks, and so are you. For having these dirty, dirty thoughts."

I suddenly felt hot. Sweat beaded on my neck and between my breasts. My chest heaved with a shallow breath as my insides shuddered at the mere proximity of him.

His lips grazed my earlobe, and my body tensed. I tried to twist my arm out of his grip, but it was pointless. My other hand landed on his hard chest, and I shoved him back. "Fuck off."

He let go of my hand and took a step back, his bruised lips quirking up on the side. "See you tomorrow, Garcia."

I flipped him the finger and started walking away. Fuck. Him. Asshole.

CHAPTER EIGHT

Lila

I felt him before I saw him.

His enticing scent engulfed me as he pushed against my back, barely touching, but still way too close.

"What do you want, Coulter? Was today not enough for you?" I asked with a heavy sigh.

It was not a good day, not after the stupid prank Maddox pulled on me. My wet hair was currently soaking the back of my Berkshire's blouse, the soft material sticking to my skin. I was irritated and absolutely exhausted. One more class left and then it was the weekend. Two blissful days without Maddox.

"Looks like you were able to wash your hair." He chortled at his own lame joke. "Sorry about the feathers, but it was payback. Don't be such a grumpy ass, Garcia. You can be a sweet ass, though. I'll eat it."

I swiveled around and leveled the douchebag with a glare. "You think gluing feathers in my hair is funny?"

I wanted to throttle him and his stupid, smirking face.

"Don't exaggerate. I didn't use glue. I used flour, water and feathers. Simple and harmless. Anyway, you looked cute with a nesting head."

Mr. Asshole here glued, oh wait, my bad – *pasted* feathers into my cute beanie with flour and water. So, naturally, when I put on my beanie, all the sticky feathers transferred to my hair. No, I didn't look at my beanie before putting it on. Who does that, anyway?

My fists clenched and unclenched as I sucked in a deep breath and held back a snarl. Maddox rubbed his jaw, and against my own accord, I took notice that his face was healing up nicely. His bruises were barely noticeable, and his left eye was no longer swollen, black and purple.

He was back to his sexy, irritating self. *God give me patience.*

Maddox closed my locker, leaning against it like he owned the thing. I gave him a blank look, waiting for this to be over. The hallways were empty, except for the two of us.

"The pink hair prank? That was actually a good one, I'll give you that. The feathers were payback for the pink hair you gave me."

Ah, the pink hair. A few days ago, after Maddox left a butt-plug in my locker, *a gift*, he had written in his note – I decided to retaliate. The need for revenge was strong, and it was easy. I had sneaked into the locker room while Riley kept guard outside. I found his personal locker and switched his shampoo with temporary pink hair dye.

"Itching powder though? Lame as fuck, Garcia."

"It was a reminder."

He arched an eyebrow, waiting for me to explain.

"That's what happens when you lay around with whores. You end up with an itchy dick. Also, a reminder that I'm not someone you can fuck around with. *Remember* that next time you proposition me for sex like a paid whore."

"That was a nice thought, except... I don't need to pay someone for sex. My name comes with a label, baby. Maddox-Coulter-Will-Fuck-You-So-Hard-You-Will-See-Jesus."

"Where did you find that definition? Dickpedia?"

"If you open dickpedia to the word *orgasmic*, you'll find my name there."

I rolled my eyes while mentally facepalming myself. Why did I even bother to have a conversation with him? It was completely useless. The only thing that came out of his mouth was sex, sex and more sex. Or something completely dumb.

"You know what your problem is?"

"What?" I raked my fingers through my wet hair, frustrated.

"You want me," he said, as calmly as if he was announcing the weather. *Oh, it's sunny. Oh, you want to fuck me.* This man was mentally unstable, period.

"Excuse me?" I placed my hands on my hips, astonished he could even come to *this* conclusion.

"You want me, but you don't want to admit it. You're fighting the chemistry." Maddox lazily eyed me up and down. There was no embarrassment, no awkwardness from him. He was practically undressing me with his eyes, and he was being so casual about it. When he spoke again, his voice lowered to a deeper tone. "Does fighting with me make you wet? We could fight in bed, let's not waste time here."

"If your brain was as big as your ego, maybe you'd be more appealing."

Maddox grinned harder and then let out a deep chuckle. "I'm not sure about my ego or how big it is, but I can assure you, I got something big here." He cupped his dick and raised a mocking eyebrow.

Annoyed, I pushed away from the wall. He was so goddamn rude, immature and vulgar. "You think every girl wants to fuck you. You really think you're every woman's wet dream, don't you?"

"I know I am."

Maddox moved closer, forcing me to take a step back. He stalked me, coming closer and closer until I was forced to press my back against the wall. I shivered, not because of him, I told myself. Because my hair was wet and cold and now that I was plastered against the wall, it only caused my wet blouse to stick onto my back like a second skin.

He leaned forward, bending his head to be level with me. His lips caressed my ear, and it tickled. I went to pull away, but he was quicker. His arms came up, and he caged me against the wall, his palms on either side of my head. He barely touched me, but his body was so close, his heat pressing into me, caressing me and causing a warm flush to spread throughout my body.

My thighs quaked, and my lower stomach tensed with his close proximity. "And you know what? One day I'm going to be your wet dream, too. Picture this: You'll be alone in bed at night, unable to sleep. My face flashes in front of your eyes and your stomach clenches. Your thighs are spread open and your pussy feels warm but strangely, empty. There's an aching need in the pit of your stomach. You won't be able to stop yourself. Your hands find their way into your panties, and you feel how wet you are with your fingers. You bite on your lip to keep from moaning. You touch yourself slowly, a little confused. A little frustrated. You'll think:

Why can't I stop thinking about him? You're going to hate it, but you'll still love it. And you know what you're going to do?"

My skin was on fire, my body burned, and I couldn't *breathe*. My stomach dipped and twisted as the air felt like it was being sucked out of my body.

My heart stuttered when I felt his body pressing into me, finally *touching* me.

"You'll finger fuck your pussy while imagining it's me on top of you, pressing against you, and it's *my* cock fucking you. Not your little fingers," Maddox breathed into my ear, whispering the dirty fantasy as if he was making dirty love to me.

Horrified, I could only blink, trying to remind myself to breathe. He shouldn't be able to affect me this way, he shouldn't be able to control my thoughts like *this*.

I was not weak, no... Maddox... couldn't...

He pulled away slightly to look into my face. His eyes were so blue, I almost drowned in them. "It won't happen today. Or tomorrow. Or next week. But one day, for sure. And no, I'm not being cocky. Cocky is for boys who don't know what they're doing. Me? I know exactly what I'm doing. I know for a fact it will happen. Fight it if you can."

He pushed away from me, and the cold washed over me as if I had been carelessly dunked into the ocean.

I silently gasped for breath as Maddox walked backward, away from me. The look on his face was something I've never seen before.

"I dare you, Lila."

I padded barefoot into my room, fresh from my shower and still wrapped in nothing but my fluffy towel. My phone pinged with a message, and I walked over to the nightstand to see it was from Riley.

What time are you leaving?

I typed out a quick message back. *I'll catch the bus in 20 minutes.*

The three little dots appeared on my screen, indicating she was typing.

If you want, I can pick you up, and we can go together.

My thumb paused over my phone as I read her sentence. My ears rang with the distant sound of glass shattering and bones crushing. The taste of metallic blood filled every corner of my mouth, and I almost choked on it. Except, there was no blood. I was choking on my own saliva, and the air surrounding me turned heavy, cold… suffocating.

My fingers trembled as I typed back my message to Riley. *I can't. You know I can't. I'm sorry. I'll take the bus.*

She knew the reason, and I also knew she was only trying to help, but there was no need. I was beyond helping when it came to…

I shook my head, clearing out the blurry flashes in front of my eyes and refusing to think of the night my whole life changed.

Grabbing my blow dryer, I leveled it over my head and made sure to work through every tangled strand of hair with my comb. Once my hair was dry and shiny, I made a French styled twin braid on top of my head with twin ponytails. It was cute and made my face look rounder and more symmetrical.

My reflection through the floor length mirror stared back at me. My hand traveled to my chest over my towel, where it was slowly coming undone. The top of my breasts came into view, and my eyes caught the scars. The long, jagged white lines snaked straight down from the middle of my petite breasts.

I let my towel slip through my fingers, the full scar now visible through the mirror. The skin around it was a bit pinker than the rest. It was healed up properly, but I didn't think it would ever completely fade away. Sometimes it ached, like a ghostly echo of the real agony I went through.

Pain washed over me like a raging storm, and my knees threatened to buckle under me. My eyes burned as tears hung on my lower lashes, and I furiously blinked them away, refusing to cry. My heart wailed, but I refused to shed any tears.

I slowly brought my hand up and lightly brushed it down the scar, tracing the pink-white lines. The tips of my fingers barely touched my skin, and I clenched my hand into a fist, holding back my tremors.

They said I stopped breathing on the operating table – I died for a moment before they brought me back.

I wondered... if maybe. . . it would have been easier if I really was dead.

But then I remembered... I was alive for them – my parents.

I averted my gaze from the mirror. It has been four years since I got the scars, but I still couldn't look at them for longer than two minutes. They were a beautiful reminder that I was alive... but also an ugly reminder of that night and all that I lost.

Grabbing my ripped jeans and a matching sweater, I quickly got dressed, so I wouldn't miss my bus. My grandparents were still at their grocery store, so before locking the door behind me, I made sure to turn on the alarm.

The moment I stepped out, I was thankful the sweater was my first option when the cold air hit me. It was mid-October; the sun was already at the horizon, and the Haunted House opened in less than an hour.

The bus ride was short, and Riley was waiting for me outside the main gate of Berkshire. This year, they used the gymnasium and the outer field as the haunted house. Apparently, it was a big project, and I could see that. Everything looked expensive and... creepy.

Creepy and scary things were not my forte. Hell, I didn't even watch horror movies because they would give me nightmares for months.

Shit.

"I'm not sure I like this haunted house idea, Riley."

She pulled at my arm, dragging me across the field and toward the fake mausoleum. "Don't be a scaredy cat. Let's go. I already paid for our tickets, and it'll be fun!"

I dug my feet into the grass right before we could pass through the creepy, wooden door. "Wait, Ri–"

With one harsh tug, she pulled me forward before I could contemplate my decision. *Okay, that's it. I'm going to die.*

The moment we stepped inside, we were swallowed by darkness, and the screams of previous victims who have entered this dark place. "And if I die?"

"You're exaggerating," Riley muttered under her breath.

She wrapped her arm around me and guided us through the darkness. "I can't even see anything!"

"That's the point, Lila! It's called a haunted house for a reason, smartass."

She was laughing now, but there was nothing funny about this situation. A loud growling sound came from behind us, and I jumped at least two feet high. Someone was close, way too close to us. I could feel them stalking us in the darkness, their hot breaths on our neck.

"They're behind us," I whispered, my heart taking a dive into the pit of my stomach. The temperature was cold, but I had stress sweats. The air was thick and almost suffocating, or maybe that was just me. My hands were clammy, and I clenched onto Riley's arm.

She let out a shaky breath. "I can feel them, too. Just keep walking."

We walked further into the labyrinth looking path. Metal chains clanged close to us, as if someone had been tied to them and they were restlessly pulling at the chains. None of it was real, I reminded myself. They were live humans with costumes and wickedly good make-up.

I peeked to my left and wished I hadn't.

One very vile zombie man, his face bloodied and disfigured with his eyes pure white, walked out of the shadow, a mere inch away from me. His mouth was opened, and he snarled right into my face.

My lips parted with an ear-splitting scream. Riley jumped, and she let out a shriek, too. Grabbing my hand in hers, we made a run for it.

At every corner, there was a different horror waiting for us.

A bloody clown. Mass zombies. Ax murderers. A creepy nun with a white face and black, rotted teeth. They were snarling and quite terrifying. Another loud shriek came from Riley and I when they reached out to touch us.

They weren't supposed to get this close, right?

Wrong.

Riley forgot to mention this Haunted House was supposed to give us the real experience. As in, the actors were going to be touching us and getting really close.

"Holy shit balls!" Riley screamed as a seven feet man with a bloody chainsaw came forward. I pulled her arm and guided us to the other corner. We moved from room to room, stumbling through tiny dark hallways as dozens of creepy arms reached out to touch us.

"Are you scared?" I whispered again. The exit was near, I could see the fluorescent light ahead.

Riley didn't respond, but I noticed the change in her. Oh yeah, she was freaked out, too.

My heart was pounding like crazy with my whole body trembling. My knees were weak, and I wondered how I was still standing.

We finally walked through the exit and stepped outside through the backdoor. Riley giggled, although I could tell it was forced. She was definitely scared while we were in there. "See, that wasn't so bad. It was freaky but fun."

The heavy pressure on my chest was still there, but I finally took a deep breath.

Fun, ha. No.

"You look spooked," she teased, bumping her elbow into my hip.

"Shut up." I returned the favor, laying a soft punch on her arm.

We could hear other people screaming from the inside. Poor souls. If I had a choice, I wasn't going back in there. Once was enough.

"Are you happy now?" I demanded with a smile, turning to face Riley. My heart was still racing a mile an hour, adrenaline and fear still coursing through my veins.

My smile froze and died when I caught sight of what – who was standing behind her. Riley's gaze went over my shoulder, and her eyes widened, her lips parting as if to let out a scream.

Chills ran down my spine, my heart leaping in my chest.

Someone was standing behind me, just like the creepy mask man was standing behind Riley, too. His arms reached out for her, and my heart thudded so hard in my chest, it *hurt*.

Bile burned my throat, and I tried to warn Riley. Except, none of that happened.

One second I had my feet planted on the grass and then I felt a pair of hands on my hips, before I was airborne.

He lifted me up, hoisting me over his shoulder. I hung upside down, and I still couldn't find my voice. My breath stuck in my throat, and my whole body went limp in fear. Riley shrieked and from my position over his shoulder, as he strode away, I found the mask man holding and dragging Riley backward.

No. No. Wait!

The man carrying me marched through the field, taking it toward the back of the Mausoleum.

Oh My God. No one was coming to save her, no one could hear us scream. We were alone and…

My whole body was cold and numb… I couldn't feel anything, except fear.

I could be molested or… raped.

He was going to kill me.

This was not part of the Haunted House.

This was not an actor.

My pulse thundered in my throat and my vision blurred with black dots as I stayed limp, upside down over his shoulder.

From the distance, I heard Riley scream again, the sound filled with so much terror.

Alarmed, my body started to prickle with awareness, and I began to struggle against my captor. "Let me go. Let. Me. Go."

He laughed, like a mad man. The laugh sounded right out of a horror movie.

"If... if you think you're going to rape me... think... again. Let me go, asshole."

The hiccups between each word made my threat sound less... threatening. Humiliated and panicked, my eyes burned with unshed tears. The lump in my throat made it harder to speak.

My captor kept marching, my head and arms swinging back and forth as I laid heavily over his shoulder.

"Someone... is going... to come and find us."

He laughed again, his hands clenching over my ass, his fingers digging in my flesh. That did it. I let out a shriek and started to struggle harder. My fists thumped on his back, but he barely even flinched.

Realizing my advantage in this position, I drew my knee back before slamming it forward between his thighs. I missed my target, but he hissed.

His hand came down on my ass, hard. He tsked, taunting me.

I was so close to bursting into tears, dread and horror filling every cell in my body. I continued to wrestle with him.

If I was going to die, I'd die fighting.

When my knee slammed forward again—missing its target once more—he finally relinquished his hold on me. My captor dumped me on the grass, without a care, like a sack of useless potatoes.

He had taken me away from the mausoleum and the haunted house and deposited me behind the school – where no one could see us, no one could come to my rescue.

I inched back, still on my ass. My whole body shook with tremors, and I finally faced *him*.

My chin wobbled at the sight of him, a deep sated fear instilled inside of me. I was going to die tonight. This man was going to hurt me. *That's it.*

I survived on the operating table only to be left to die in the field behind Berkshire Academy.

His face was covered with a black purge mask, with glowing red LED lights. He had a dark hoodie on, with its hood over his head, and black ripped jeans.

The sight of him was right out of my nightmare.

He moved forward, and I put my hands out, as if to ward him away. "Don't come near me. Don't touch me."

Please.

The pit of my stomach quaked, and I really thought I was going to piss myself in fear.

Purge mask man stalked me as I kept inching back. The cool wet grass soaked through my jeans, but I didn't care.

He was having fun, feeding on my fear and silently taunting me.

He stopped a foot away and squatted down in front of me. His arm reached out as if to touch me, and I shrank away. "Touch me and I'll break your dick. I'll do it."

He pulled his hand back, tsking again. He shook his head, as if he was disappointed in my threats. Slowly, he brought his hand to his face and pulled the purge mask off.

Uneasiness tickled down my spine, my body filled with apprehension.

The mask came off and dark blue eyes met mine.

Full smirking lips and a face I knew very well.

"Maddox," I breathed.

"Boo," he rumbled.

All the horror and confusion slipped away, replaced with anger. My jaw snapped together, and I clenched my teeth.

"Are you fucking serious?"

The previous chill running down my spine disappeared as my blood boiled.

"Why are you so set on terrorizing me?" I snarled. Jesus Christ, he almost gave me a heart attack. Fury rolled off in heated waves. Seething, I curled my legs from underneath me, sitting up. I still couldn't stand up, since my legs were still shaky and weak.

He grinned, almost boyishly, except I saw the mischief in his eyes. I was dancing on the edge of danger with this boy. Against my better judgement, my gaze traveled the length of his body as he stayed squatting down in front of my kneeling form. He was hard and sculptured everywhere, in all the right places. *Definitely not a boy. Man. Fuck. Whatever-he-is.*

"It's fun," he finally said, snapping me out of my thoughts and forcing my eyes away from his body. I looked into his icy blue eyes instead.

I was stunned into silence for a second. "It's fun?" I sputtered. "It's fun to scare the shit out of people? Was that your friend who took Riley away, too? This is not funny!"

Maddox shrugged like it was no big deal. I could feel myself glaring at him, my eyes turning into slits as I regarded my nemesis with utter distaste. If I could breathe fire, I would have fumes coming out of my nose.

My jaw clenched at the way he kept grinning. It made me angrier. It unsettled me. "What are you? A fucking psychopath? Because that's the only explanation. No sane person thinks it's fun to scare someone else to the point they thought they were going to die!"

I fought the urge to punch him and claw his beautiful eyes out. What was it about him that make me lose all my control?

Oh right. Maddox Coulter was an asshole.

He cocked his head to the side, one side of his lip turning up slightly. Maddox then released a deep chuckle, his wide chest vibrating with a decadent sound. "That's new," he whispered, his voice raspy. It made the tiny hair on my bare arms stand up.

"What?"

He was still smirking. *Fuck you,* I mentally slapped him. "I have been called many names before. Been swore at so many times, I lost count about three years ago. But being called a psychopath? That's a first."

I gaped at him. Was this guy joking or seriously just insane?

Maddox brought his head closer to me, his body leaning into mine. He brought warmth with him, and I didn't like that. He wasn't supposed to be warm. He wasn't supposed to smell nice. He wasn't supposed...

"I like it."

His lips were only an inch away from mine. His face so close I could feel his minty breath feathering over my skin. I stayed still, completely still. If I moved, our lips would touch.

My fists clenched, and I squeezed them over my thighs. "What?" I breathed.

"I like it. You calling me a psychopath. It's new. It's different." He was still too close. He was still grinning like a fucking loon. He was still so warm...he still smelled so good...

My body seemed to overheat with his presence. My heart thudded in my chest. "You are crazy," I whispered.

His eyes glinted with something mischievous and roguish. "Wanna see just how crazy I am, Sweet Cheeks?"

CHAPTER NINE

Lila

There always comes a time in your life when your tenacity is tested, and when that happens, you have two choices: you either run away with your tail tucked between your legs, or you stand up for yourself.

Maddox has been playing me, pushing and pushing until I reached the end of my rope and snapped. He wanted to remind me he had the power to make me lose control.

He craved the hunt, to be the hunter – the predator, to be at the top of the food chain, doling out punishments as he deemed necessary.

Being an asshole was his way of living, I guessed he didn't know how to be anything else.

He knew exactly how to make his victims feel small to the extent that all you can do is cower away.

My blood pumped hot. Shaking away the terror and fury

coursing through my veins, I stood up. Maddox pulled away and came up to his feet, too, standing to his full height. The crooked grin plastered on his face infuriated me, but I channeled all my frustration.

"What do you want from me, Maddox?"

He raised one perfect eyebrow, without saying a word, shoving his hands in the pockets of his jeans and rocking back on his feet, quite nonchalantly.

"You're the most frustrating person I've ever come across."

"Why, thank you. I take that as a compliment." He was still smirking.

Motherfuck–

My mother always told me to avoid trouble and look away. The least attention you give to bullies, the more disinterested they'll become.

Maybe she was right.

Still staring at Maddox, I took a step back. "Have a good night, Coulter."

I pivoted on my heels to march away, but his taunting voice stopped me. "Giving up so easily, Sweet Cheeks? I must have been wrong about you."

My fists clenched at my side, and I came to a halt. I *really* should have listened to my mother's warning.

But I never, ever turned down a challenge. Maybe that was my mistake…

Show time.

I swiveled around and stalked forward until I stopped in front of him. Maddox's gaze drifted to my mouth, where I was chewing on my lip – not in nervousness, but to put Maddox exactly where I wanted him.

My hand landed on his firm chest. His eyes widened slightly since this was the first time I've touched him willingly. A roguish smile played on his lips, and I *pitied* him.

He thought he won me over. *Too bad, Maddox. Don't play games with a girl who can play them better.*

He should have heeded my warning the first time.

I rubbed my hand over his chest, sliding it down toward his stomach. The black hoodie did nothing to hide all the hardness of him. His muscles tensed under my slow, exploring touch, and his eyes glinted with something devilish.

Down and down I went, until my fingers halted on his hips, right over his belt. I hooked a finger into the belt loop and pulled him closer to me, our bodies colliding together softly. Maddox let out a small chuckle, playing along.

Standing on my toes, I brought our faces closer, bringing my lips mere inches from his squared jaw, and I leaned in, so I could whisper in his ear. "I know what you want from me."

"Oh, do you?"

"You've made it abundantly clear. I can give you what you want. One unforgettable night."

"See? That wasn't so hard. Don't know why you've been playing so hard to get." His hands landed on my hips before they curled around my back, squeezing my ass.

"You want a taste of this ass? You can have it. Fuck me sideways, fuck me front and back, put me on my knees, get between my thighs. Put me on your dick, and I'll ride you until the sun comes up. I'm on the pill. If you're safe, we can ditch the condoms, and you'll feel every inch of me. Have you ever fucked a girl bareback? I can be your first. I'll even show you my deepthroating skills. You want filthy? I can make your *filthiest* fantasies come true,

Maddox. You can have it all, baby."

My teeth grazed his earlobe before I bit down softly. His throat bobbed with a low groan.

"In your dreams," I breathed in his ear.

I released him and pushed away from his body. His eyebrows curled together in confusion before realization dawned in his eyes. He reached for me, but I sidestepped him, tsking. It was *my* turn to taunt him, and by the look on his face, he hadn't expected it.

Oh no, Maddox Coulter underestimated me.

I winked, and my lips curled into a satisfied smirk. "See you tomorrow, Coulter."

I walked backward, enjoying the look of complete shock on his face. My gaze slid over him, from the top of his messy blond hair down to his brown leather boots.

"Oh. You might want to take a cold shower to help with *that*," I said, pointing toward his semi hard-on, which was indecently poking through his jeans.

Whoops.

Maddox

I couldn't remember the last time a girl had knocked me on my ass. Probably never because it was impossible. *I* played the games, and *they* were my catch.

How did the tables turn?

Lila marched away, shaking her plump ass as if to tempt me further, with her long black hair teasing the curve of her hips.

She gave me one last haughty look over her shoulder before she disappeared around the building, and I was left dumbstruck in the middle of the field with a fucking hard-on.

I should have known – she was fierce. I underestimated her, but honestly, I didn't expect her to give me goddamn blue balls.

With pink lips and a sultry voice, she was a siren with a filthy mouth and I. Was. A. Goner.

There was just something about Lila Garcia that I wanted to explore. I thought she was an interesting plaything at first. *Now?* I rubbed my thumb over my jaw, still staring at where she had disappeared. Her scent still lingered around me. It was some sweet perfume, nothing too heavy or cheap like the other bitches I had hanging around me. It was soft and sweet, and my tongue slid out over my lips as if I could taste her.

I was spellbound, my palms twitched and my dick – yeah, that bastard was more than interested.

I wanted to see how far I could push before she exploded into tiny little pieces at my feet.

Sure, Lila was feisty and oh, so fucking sassy, but for how long? How long would it take to break her and mold her into a pretty little thing like I'd done with all the others?

She was fucking trouble.

Guess what?

I wasn't the type to shy away from trouble.

Come at me, Sweet Cheeks.

CHAPTER TEN

Lila

I walked into my grandparents' grocery store early Sunday morning. We weren't opened yet, but they had been here for an hour, getting everything ready for a busy day. I usually came in to help them during the rush hour, but otherwise, they had part-timers helping them daily.

I walked further inside toward the back storage. "Gran?"

"In here, sweetie," she called out.

Smiling, I stepped into the storage room. "Do you need my hel–"

My smile slid from my face as I came to halt at the door, facing the one person I never wanted to see here.

What the hell?

"You," I said, my voice filled with accusation.

Maddox grinned, still holding one huge box in his arms. "Good morning, Lila."

My mouth fell open, dumbstruck. *No way, no fucking way.* "What are you doing here?"

Grandma patted his arm as if she had known him for the longest time. I wasn't sure I liked the way she was smiling up at him. "I hired him yesterday. He came looking for a part-time job, and since we're hiring, he got the job. He said he's from Berkshire. You won't be bored at work anymore since you two are friends."

"Friends?" My jaw went slack, and I couldn't formulate a better sentence. *Friends? What? How? Who? What? When?*

"Yes. I told Mrs. Wilson how close we are. I didn't know this store was owned by your grandparents. What a surprise," Maddox explained, with a shit-eating grin.

Bullshit. The look on his face told me the truth. Maddox knew exactly what he was doing, and he was here on purpose. His mission was to make my life miserable, in every way. I wanted to knock the smile off his face. So, he was stalking me now. Great.

"Yes, what a surprise," I muttered, plastering a fake pleased look on my face. Gran appeared too happy for me to break the news to her.

This is my enemy, and he's an asshole. Don't fall for his easy smile and charming looks. This was what I wanted to say, but I bit my tongue and held back any snarky remarks. I'd deal with Maddox on my own.

"I just need help to organize the inventory. Sven will be here soon," Gran announced, patting me on the back as she walked out of the storage room, leaving Maddox and I alone.

Once she was out of hearing range, I stalked forward. My whole body strummed with anger. I wouldn't say I was a violent person, but I was feeling quite violent at the moment. "What the hell are you doing here?"

He turned his back to me, lifting another box over his shoulder. He carried it into the walk-in freezer and deposited it on the self.

Maddox walked out and went for another box, but I sidestepped into his path.

Leaning back against the wall, he crossed his ankles and his arms over his chest. Today, he was wearing a black shirt and black jeans, ripped around his knees, with brown leather boots like he wore the night at the Haunted House. It was strange seeing him in anything other than the Berkshire uniform.

He looked… *normal*. Instead of the Berkshire star quarterback I despised.

"I asked you a question. What are you doing here?"

Maddox cocked his head to the side, giving me an amused look. "Working, Garcia. Simple as that."

Impatiently, I tapped my foot on the ground, not falling for his stupid games. To work? Yeah, right.

"You don't need to work. Don't your parents give you an allowance? Your credit card is probably unlimited."

For a brief second, I noticed the way his eyes darkened as if he was disappointed in *me*. But it was gone too quickly, leaving me wondering if what I saw was real or just my imagination. He tsked, shaking his head.

"See, that's your problem. You assume too many things."

I wasn't assuming anything. He wasn't just rich; Maddox was filthy rich. He didn't need a part-time job, especially not at my grandparents' grocery store. He didn't *ever* need to work.

In fact, he didn't even need to be here, in *this* neighborhood, where didn't belong.

But no, he had to be here. The only two days I had without Maddox being a jerk every minute – my only two peaceful days, he had to come and ruin.

"How did you get my grandma to agree to this?"

99

"That was really simple. I smiled."

A frustrated sound came from my throat, and I rubbed a hand over my face. "Maddox," I grumbled under my breath.

He pushed away from the wall and walked past me to lift another brown box. His shirt stretched over his shoulders as he placed it on the top shelf and diligently arranged all the boxes in expiration date order. "She thinks I'm charming and sweet. Trust me, this is the first time someone has called me *sweet*. Shocking, right?"

I didn't think that was the correct description for Maddox. He was anything but sweet.

"You need to leave. Now."

He shook his head, his messy hair slowly coming undone from his man bun. "Can't. I like it here, and I like your Gran. Your grandfather, though, he's tough. No worries, I'll figure something out."

I grabbed the box he was holding and slammed it back on the ground. The storage room was starting to feel hot or maybe my blood was just boiling.

"Damn, Sweet Cheeks. It's too early for you to be this angry. Are you always this grumpy?" Maddox mocked with a rough laugh.

Yes, since you came into my life.

I stepped closer, lifting my chin up to meet his eyes. "Listen, Maddox," I said, stabbing a finger into his chest. "This is not a joke. You have a problem with me, then it's only me. I don't know what you want but don't bring my grandparents into this fight between us."

Maddox leaned forward, getting into my face. The laughter was gone, and his face was a blank canvas, devoid of any emotions. The change in him was so sudden, confusion clouded my mind. "Why do you always think the worst of me?"

I could've been fooled, but I knew better.

It was my turn to laugh; as fake as it was, I really was amused by his question. "Probably because you've only ever shown me the worst of you. If there was any good in you, I would have seen it already. Too bad you're only focus is on being a douchebag."

Maddox opened his mouth, probably to rebuke me, but I was already turning away, ignoring anything else he had to say. I lifted the box next to my feet and started organizing the messy shelves. Inventory days were always crazy and busy.

Maddox and I worked quietly. He didn't try to speak to me again, and I wasn't interested in holding a conversation either. The silence was tense and heavy, like an impending thunderstorm looming over our heads, dark and cloudy. An hour later, the storage room was somewhat organized, and all the boxes, old and new, had been put away on their designated shelves.

Lifting one last box, my arms trembled under the weight, but I still pushed it above my head, reaching for the rack. Except, the box was too heavy, the shelf was too high, and I was too short to reach it, even with me balancing on my toes.

Damn it.

I cursed under my breath when the box started to wobble in my hands and a surprised shriek came from me when I could feel it tilting back over my head. The box was going to fall, and I didn't have the strength to keep hold of it.

But before it could slip through my fingers, another pair of hands grabbed the box.

"I got it." His whisper crept along my neck. "You can let go."

I did, and he pushed the box onto the shelf with ease. Maddox was too close, and I didn't like it. Maddox obviously didn't understand the meaning of personal space. His mere presence annoyed me and having him this close had me on edge. I wasn't sure why, but everything about Maddox just made me feel... *irritated.*

I was thankful he saved the box, though, so I uttered a quick *thank you* as my arms fell down to my sides.

His breath was hot on my skin as he pressed closer, barely touching me. I slid away from under his arms before turning to face him. His gaze moved up and down my body, and the burning intensity of his eyes urged me to cross my arms over my chest.

"You're tiny," he grunted.

I hissed under my breath. He insulted my boobs the first time we met and now he had to make me feel *small.* "I'm not. I'm five foot two."

He let out a scoff. "And I'm six foot three. A whole head taller than you. You're literally bite-sized."

"You're just a giant, not average."

His crooked smile should have warned me of what was coming. "You're right. I'm far from *average*, Sweet Cheeks."

Yep, I walked right into that one.

"Wanna see for yourself?" he asked with no shame.

"Keep your dick in your pants and keep your hands to yourself," I warned. Stalking past him, I took the broom and started sweeping the storage room. I expected him to leave now that we were done putting away all the inventory but that wasn't the case.

He leaned against the wall opposite to me, making himself comfortable. Maddox took a small box of cigarettes from his pocket.

My voice was sharp when I spoke, "You're not allowed to smoke in here."

Maddox made a derisive sound in the back of his throat as he flipped the tiny box over his fingers and around in his hand. "I won't disrespect your grandparents like that. I'm just checking how many I have left."

I could almost hear his unsaid words. *Stop assuming the worst of me, Lila.*

Ignoring the silent jab, I continued with my sweeping. Even with me not looking at him, I could feel his stare burning into the back of my head. He was staring *hard.*

Maddox stalked me with his eyes, and I didn't like how he could make me feel... small.

"So, are we not going to talk about the elephant in the room?"

"What elephant?" I grumbled, distracted.

"The hard-on you gave me two days ago."

Oh. I had been trying to forget all about that night, but he had to bring it up. Of course, since I left him dumbfounded. Not a lot of people has the chance to push back on Maddox. I gave him a taste of his own medicine, and he obviously didn't like it.

I stopped sweeping and held the broom up, leaning my arm on it. "Oh that. Did the cold shower help?"

"It didn't. I had to use my hand." If I didn't know better, I'd say there was a note of petulance in his voice.

"I didn't need to know that."

He shrugged, quite nonchalantly. "You asked, I answered. Can I borrow your hand next time though?"

Oh, for fuck's sake. "That's going to be a hell no, Coulter."

His lips twitched, and I *almost* rolled my eyes. "You're boring, Garcia," he taunted once again.

"I'd rather be boring than be your next hookup."

Anything was better than being his next meal. To put it simply, Maddox was a lion – it was quite easy to see the resemblance. When given meat, lions pounce without a second thought. They devour their meal, messy and savagely. Once they're done, they spit out the bones, and with a belly full, they walked away.

That was Maddox.

He devoured anyone in his path, without care of the consequences, and he'd spit out the bones once he had his fun. Guys like Maddox would play with you, tear you apart, layer by layer, piece by piece and then lay you down – fragmented and empty -- because they took everything from you.

Maddox pushed away from the wall and took a step toward me. "You hate me that much?"

He actually looked curious, as if he wanted to pick apart my brain to see inside, to delve into my thoughts. He wanted to see beyond my wall. Too bad, he was the wrong person to break through it.

"It's not about hate. I'm simply not excited about your existence."

It wasn't about hate. That was too black and white. *No.*

Boys like Maddox have already stolen enough from me...

My heart thudded in my chest, and I looked away. Boys like him... they *ruined* me.

Placing the broom back in its corner, I walked toward the door without sparing him a glance. "You should ask Gran what else she wants you to do. I'm going to take a ten-minute break."

Maddox blocked my way out. "Let me change your mind. Spend one afternoon with me."

His words speared me with shock, making me stumble back a step. *What?*

Why would he...

Maddox truly didn't understand the word 'boundaries.' How did we go from enemies to him asking me to spend an afternoon with him?

Well played, Coulter.

He looked at me expectantly, as if he really wanted me to consider his offer.

I scoffed back a laugh that bubbled in my chest and threatened to escape through my throat. Was I a joke to him? Wait... I knew that answer.

"And what? You'll have me putty in your hands?" I asked with a quirked eyebrow.

He grinned, losing the expectant look on his face. He was back to being a jerk. "In my arms and on my dick, yeah."

I leaned forward, pushing my body against his. He never hid the fact that he appreciated the way I looked. My body tempted him; I was aware of that. *So, two can play this game.* "Is this your way of asking me out on a date?" I whispered, my voice sultry but dripping with sarcasm. If he was smart enough, he'd catch that.

Maddox stared down at him, his lips crooked on the side. "I don't date. Ever. My favorite pastime is having girls on their back or on their knees for me."

"You. Are. Disgusting," I growled.

He shrugged.

Pushing away from him, I tilted my chin up, both to look at him and in defiance. He wasn't winning me over. "Tell me something, do your fangirls know how you think of them?"

"Most of them know and don't care. They're using me the same way I'm using them. Sex, fun and popularity. Three things they want and three things I can give them. They're happy with the arrangement. Those who aren't, I show them the door. Simple."

"So, girls get hot and bothered *because* you're a jerk."

"That's the appeal, Sweet Cheeks."

I opened my mouth but then snapped it shut when I couldn't find the appropriate words. I was speechless.

"Lila!" Grandpa's voice broke through our silent battle, and I flinched away. "Can you come and help me with this?"

"Coming!" I called out.

I tried to push pass Maddox, but he didn't budge. On the contrary, he moved forward, forcing me to take a step back and away from the door.

"So, what do you say?" he grumbled.

A frustrated sound spilled from my throat. "What?"

He kept moving forward, and I walked back a step, two... and three. "One afternoon. Give me an hour of your time, and I'll change your mind."

"Not interested, Coulter. You're not even worthy of one hour of my time," I bit out, glaring up at him through my lashes.

He slid closer against me, and I stumbled back into the wall. Shit. "So, you're saying, if I kiss you right now, *really* kiss you... the way you should be kissed and then I slide my hands into your panties, I won't find you wet for me?"

Cocky much? I bristled at his words, and my fists clenched at my sides. He brought his face closer to me, staring into my eyes as his hands landed on either side of my head.

"Lila!" Grandpa called out again, louder this time. He sounded closer than before. If I didn't leave right now, he was going to come and find me in the storage, room and he was going to see Maddox and I... *Oh God.*

"Kiss me and I'll make it so you don't have the ability to kiss another girl ever again," I warned.

"Challenge accepted."

106

Maddox leaned down as if to kiss me, his lips a mere inch from mine. I turned my head to the side, and I could feel his minty breath feathering against my cheek.

"Move," I growled.

"Lila," he breathed, closer to my ear. His voice sounded deeper, edgier... like he really imagined kissing me.

I kept my head turned, refusing to give him access to my mouth. My eyes landed on his forearm as he kept me caged against the wall. I could feel the bulge between his legs pressing against my hips, and I bristled with anger and displeasure instead of being turned on.

I didn't know why, but I expected something better from him. When he asked to spend one afternoon with me, looking adamant... for a brief moment, I almost believed he was serious about changing my mind.

The muscles in his forearm, where he had rolled up his sleeves, tightened, and I struck out, without thinking much about it. I bared my teeth and clamped down on his arm, biting.

Maddox let out a hiss of surprise, and I lifted my gaze to his. He had pulled away, only slightly to stare down at me. I grabbed his outstretched arm and bit down harder when he didn't make a move to pull away. He froze for a second but then stayed still. I continued to put pressure, where my teeth were clamped down on his flesh.

He didn't even flinch. *No*, he did the opposite.

Slowly, his lips quirked up into a tiny smile. His eyes glimmered with amusement, and he cocked his head to the side, waiting... and the bastard appeared not to be bothered by my action.

With an angry huff, I released his arm and pushed away from him. Mr. Pain-In-My-Ass looked down at the bite mark and then grinned a slow, lazy grin. "I always knew you liked it rough... but I would have never guessed you were into biting."

Holding back a frustrated growl, I pushed him hard enough to have him stumble back a step. I shoved my middle finger into his stupid, smirking face before stomping away.

His amused chuckles followed me, even as I left him behind in the storage room.

Don't kill him. That's murder. Do. Not. Kill. Him.

CHAPTER ELEVEN

Lila

Later that day, Riley and I were lying in my bed, going through her Advanced Calculus homework. Riley had planned to major in business and after go to law school, that was her parents' expectations, which wouldn't be difficult for her since she loved Law and Politics.

Her weakness, though, was math. Absolutely everything that had to do with math. It was sucky for her since if she had to major in business, she had to pass her calculus courses with flying colors.

Enter me: Her best friend, her tutor and a genius in math. Lucky her.

"I don't understand shit," she whined, flopping on her back. Riley closed her eyes and threw an arm over her face, hiding from me.

I gave her a gentle nudge with my toes. "Let's try the question one more time."

"That's the third time. I'm a hopeless case. There's no way I'm getting into Harvard if I flunk Calculus."

She was exaggerating. Riley was in no way flunking Calculus. She was currently in the mid-eighties, since she had been busting her ass night and day to practice all her equations and solving extra math problems. Riley Jenson was dedicated to a fault.

"Practice makes perfect, right?" I cajoled, gently. "One more time, babe."

She lowered her arm a bit and peeked at me. "Then we can watch *Riverdale*?"

"One episode," I reluctantly agreed.

"Binge watch the whole season?" Riley gave me puppy eyes, the ones she had mastered, which almost won me over.

I pinched her shin. "Now you're pushing it, Missy."

She hissed, pulling her feet away, and her bottom lip jutted out in a pout.

"Let's go back to the question."

Riley nodded and sat up, focusing back on her notebook. I explained the steps to her again, she nodded along and gave it one more try.

Twenty minutes later, she let out a shout of victory. "I did it!"

Yes, she did. Just like I knew she would.

The happiness on her face was infectious, and I found myself laughing with her as she did half a twerk on my bed.

We spent the next two hours working on our homework. Once we were done and had put all our stuff away, I went down to get us snacks while Riley loaded *Riverdale* on Netflix. She wanted to binge watch while I was settling for only two episodes. It was going to be a battle for sure.

Halfway through the first episode, Riley started to get edgier.

She was sneaking glances at me, and I noticed the way she was practically poking a hole through her blouse.

I knew Riley long enough to know this was a sign of nervousness, and it had nothing to do with *Riverdale*. I waited for her to speak instead of pushing for information. If something was wrong, she'd tell me on her own without me having to force it out of her. It was a silent understanding between us. Riley has never pushed me about my past. I told her bits and pieces, and she accepted them without demanding more. I did the same with her. She only gave me what she wanted; we established this understanding early in our friendship.

Her silence didn't last for more than fifteen minutes. "I have to confess something."

I paused the episode and faced her. We were both sitting cross legged on the bed. "What is it?"

Riley swallowed hard and chewed on her lip, her brows pulled together in nervousness. Her body was strung tight with tension, and I didn't like the dreadful look on her face.

She licked her lips, took a deep breath and started. "On Friday, after Maddox pulled you away and Colton grabbed me..."

The night of the haunted house? Confused, I nodded and waited for her to continue. "Yeah?"

"He pulled me behind the dumpster..." Riley trailed off, her eyes wide and glassy.

"Yeah. You told me. Fucking assholes. Both of them. If I could, I'd report them–"

Riley shook her head and cut me off, sharply. "*No*, listen. I didn't tell you everything that happened."

And then she... blushed. She averted her gaze for a second, and she went back to poking holes in her shirt.

111

"Riley...?" I slowly questioned.

She let out a loud, frustrated sigh. Her cheeks were tinted pink, but there was a guilty look in her eyes. "I messed up. I don't know how it happened but it just... happened. One minute, I was screaming at him and I even punched him; he was laughing like a stupid, madman and then he pulled me close and... it just *happened*. I didn't think. I wasn't thinking."

She was babbling, talking too fast, but I caught the gist of it. For her sake, I carefully concealed my shock. But... oh my fucking SHIT!

"Riley, did you... I mean, you two...?"

"No! We didn't have sex," she sputtered and blushed even harder. "We made out. Oh God, I can't believe I'm saying this. But he pulled me into him and just slammed his lips on mine. I think it was the adrenaline. I was so scared, and then I was excited and like, my heart was beating so fast, I felt dizzy and then I just kissed him back."

Don't freak out, Lila. Don't freak out.

"What happened?" I calmly asked, even though I was anything but calm.

"Colton pulled us down, so I could sit on his lap. And we just... um, kissed."

"And?"

Riley buried her face in her hands, letting out a choked scream. "I'm horrible. Jasper was right. I'm a whore."

"What? Riley!" I scooted closer to her and pulled her hands away from her face, so she would have no choice but to look at me. "Don't say that!"

"We kissed. I don't know when it happened, but he unbuttoned my jeans and put his hand inside and... he *touched* me, and it felt good, Lila. I know this sounds stupid, but it felt really good. It was crazy and everything was happening so fast."

She broke off, looking at me like I could save her from whatever she was going through in her head. My poor Riley. I was shocked, speechless, so I could only pat her arm.

"Ifhame," she muttered too fast for me to catch.

"You what?"

"I came! He was just touching me and... I orgasmed on his lap while we were sitting beside a fucking disgusting, smelly dumpster."

My jaw went slack, and I stared at her. Riley let out a cry, looking so conflicted and heartbroken. "I don't even like him! God, I like Grayson, and I let Colton touch me like that. I'm horrible. Just like Jasper said."

I snapped out of my shock at her words and grabbed her shoulders, shaking her. "Riley, you are not. Stop that."

Her chin wobbled, and she bit harshly on her lip. She was so red now, her cheeks, her ears and her neck were all flushed. "Colton is the first guy... I mean after Jasper. I haven't been with anyone else. I haven't even kissed anyone since Jasper. I couldn't bear it, and then with Colton, it just happened."

"Oh honey. Come here." I hugged her close, and she hiccupped back a sob. Now that she had finally confessed what was eating her on the inside, her mixed emotions had bubbled over, and there was no stopping them.

"He probably thinks I'm stupid and a slut."

"Hush." I soothed a hand down her back, comforting Riley in the only way I knew how. I sucked at comforting people, but I hoped my presence was enough for her.

"He's going to spread rumors like Jasper did. I'm so scared to go to school tomorrow. What if I walk in and everyone stares at me like… before… when Jasper… the whispers, the snickers, the laughs behind my back."

I pressed a firm hand on her back. "Not all boys are like Jasper, sweetie."

"I know…"

"It's okay."

She lifted her face and pulled out of my arms. "He hugged me."

"Colton?" That was… shocking.

"Yeah. After, my… um, orgasm. I think I was in shock. And I teared up. I wasn't crying, but I mean, there were tears. He noticed and broke the kiss. Then, he just hugged me. We didn't speak. That's when you found us. I heard you calling out my name, and we broke apart."

Oh wow.

"He apologized," Riley confessed gently. "Before I left, he whispered he was sorry."

I didn't know what to say. Colton and Maddox were cut from the same cloth. Both were fuckboys, and both were assholes. It was almost impossible to imagine Colton doing something as sweet as to hug and apologize to Riley.

"Not all boys are Jasper," I said again.

She nodded, her eyes glassy with unshed tears. Riley was always so cheerful, so full of life. The conflicted look on her face tore my heart apart. "Does that make me a bad person? I don't like him. I want Grayson."

"No, it doesn't make you a bad person. Like you said, it was the adrenaline and in the spur of the moment. It happens, and no one has the right to judge you. If Colton hugged you and apologized, then I don't think he's going to spread rumors about you. I guess, he's not like that."

As I said the words, I came to a shocking realization.

Maddox and his buddies were one big package of douchebaggery. They were jerks, they constantly played with girls' hearts and all they cared about was sex, sex and more sex. But I'd never seen them spreading any stupid rumors about other students. Sure, they were irritating – but they had never done anything to ruin someone's reputation. Not like Jasper had done to Riley.

I guess... that was one good thing about Maddox and his friends.

Monday morning, Riley's fear was put to rest when we walked through the gates of Berkshire, and everything was normal, like any other day. It appeared that Colton hadn't spread any rumors, and I could tell Riley was finally able to breathe better. She was back to her smiling self in two seconds flat.

We went to our respective classes, and the day continued without any more drama.

Except... with Maddox being a constant presence in my life, I only had three hours of peace and quiet until it was time for lunch.

The hallways were empty as I walked out of Mrs. Callaway's office, my Chemistry teacher. Our meeting ran longer than expected, and everyone was already in the cafeteria, since it was halfway through lunch now.

I made my way to my locker to deposit my textbooks, only to stop dead when I noticed who was standing there. Maddox leaned against *my* locker, looking like he owned it. He was everywhere I went, everywhere I wanted to go – he was *there*. A constant thorn in my ass.

I was starting to believe there was no escaping Maddox Coulter once he checkmated you. And that was exactly what he did to me. He put me on his radar, and then *checkmate*, I became his unwilling prize. No matter how much I fought and pushed back, he was there, pulling me just as hard and pushing back harder. It was a never-ending cycle, and it was starting to get tiring.

Letting out a sigh, I walked forward. As I grew closer, I noticed he had a toothpick between his lips, his dirty blond locks were rumpled and let down, instead of the man bun, and his Berkshire coat was missing. His white shirt was untucked and his tie hung loosely around his neck.

He looked like an imperfect canvas, flawed and wild. But like every piece of art, you couldn't take your eyes off him.

It was my first time seeing him like *this*. His godly appearance had been replaced with something imperfect and... humane.

"What do you want?" I asked, stopping next to him.

He chewed on his toothpick, thoughtfully. "You hurt me," he said, simply, as if he was announcing the weather.

"When? How? Oh right, probably in your nightmare." I punched in the code to my locker, opened it, and slammed my textbooks inside.

He finally stared down at me, his lips crooked and his eyes lit with mischief. "So, you agree, you're a pain in my ass?"

Me, a pain in *his* ass? This was the joke of the century.

"I'm not roses, Maddox. If you're going to make my life difficult, I'm going to be the thorn that pricks you. Don't expect me to be all smiles, hearts and googly eyes. I'm not that girl."

He kept the toothpick in the corner of his mouth as he spoke. "I know you're not."

When I didn't answer, he slowly rolled the sleeves of his white shirt up to his elbow. The same arm I bit yesterday. He shoved his arm into my face and a huge, red bite mark stared back at me.

My eyes widened at the angry looking mark. I grabbed his forearm for a closer inspection. That couldn't be from when... I bit him, right?

"You hurt me," he said again.

I... did.

"Look at it. It hurts so bad; my arm has been aching the whole time."

My gaze flew up to his, and I would have thought he was serious if I didn't notice the twinkle in his eyes.

"I don't remember biting you that hard, and it was yesterday morning. It's been a whole twenty-four hours. It's impossible that the bite mark would still look like this, except if..."

I let my words trail off, and I squinted at him, now suspicious.

"You think I bit myself? Damn, Garcia, you really are cruel. Why would I cause such pain to myself when I have you to do it?"

He shoved his arm in my face again. "Now kiss it better," Maddox demanded, "or, I'll tell the principal you bit me."

Sweet Jesus, he really was impossible.

"Go ahead," I hissed under my breath. "I'll tell him how you've been harassing me!"

Maddox had the audacity to look innocent. He let out a mock gasp before his bottom lip jutted out in a small pout. "Me? You're the one who got physical with me, Sweet Cheeks. Every. Single. Time. If I didn't know better, I would say you're trying to get me to touch you."

My stomach dipped, and my frustration bubbled to the point where I thought I'd do something worse than bite him. *That's it.* I couldn't deal with him anymore.

I threw my hands up in defeat. It took everything in me to

accept it, but I was done. "You know what? Truce. We're even with each other. Let's stop here."

Maddox looked at me for a second longer. His gaze seared into mine, burning through my walls and forcing itself to peek into my soul. I clamped up and met his gaze with a hard look.

He lifted a shoulder, a lazy shrug. "Fine. Truce. But you need to kiss my boo boo better first."

Is he fucking serious?

So, this was his game? He really wanted my lips on him, somehow. Jerk. But fine, I'd play. "Fine. I'll kiss your *boo boo* better before you go running back to your mommy crying."

I brought his arm closer and slowly bent my head down to the bite mark. It did look ugly and painful. For the briefest moment, I felt bad and guilt gnawed at me before I pushed it away.

Before my lips could touch him, Maddox crowded into my space. I sucked in a harsh breath when his arm curled around my waist and he pulled me into him. Our bodies collided together softly and time came to a halt. *Tick...tock...*

His heat seeped through his clothes and mine, and I could feel the flush on my skin. My heart skittered, and I could feel the beat of his own heart against my chest.

Something pulsed between us, electrifying and powerful... a brief moment in time... something that lasted for only a nanosecond.

His other hand came up and his fingers slipped behind my head, curling around my nape.

My brain screamed at me, angry and confused.

His breath feathered over my mouth; I blinked, and his lips crashed against mine.

I gasped into his hungry lips. My hands landed on his chest, and

I *tried* to push him back, but he clutched the back of my neck as he deepened the kiss. With his arm still locked firmly around my waist, he swiveled us around, and my back slammed into the locker. My heart dipped into my stomach when he pushed against me, and he lifted me up, only allowing my toes to touch the ground.

I didn't know if I should kiss him back… push him away…

My mind went blank as he licked the seams of my lips. His chest rumbled with a small groan when his teeth grazed my bottom lip before he bit down. I hissed into his mouth, even though I was trembling in his arms. The gentle bite stung, and I could feel the blood rushing through my ears. Slowly, he pulled his mouth away. The taste of him, mint and tobacco were heavy on my swollen lips.

"Now we're even. Truce, baby," he whispered in my ear, his voice deeper and darker.

My breath caught in my throat as he untangled himself from my body, and I slumped against the locker. I couldn't… *breathe.*

Shock and rage coursed through me, a sea of mixed emotions, too deep while the tides were too violent, I was drowning into the bottomless ocean.

Maddox gazed down at me, and he lazily swiped his tongue over his red, swollen lips as if to taste the remnant of our kiss. "You taste sweeter than I thought."

His lips twitched, and with a ghost of a smile, he strutted backward and away from me. I let out a choked gasp… finally able to breathe.

I inhaled sharply, sucking in desperate breaths as he winked at me, and then rounded the corner out of my sight. My hand slowly crept up to my chest, and I left it there, over my rapidly beating heart.

His lips had tasted like… sin.

And I hated myself for reacting the way I did to his kiss.

CHAPTER TWELVE

Lila

I walked through the door of my grandparents' home and stumbled onto the couch. Gran leaned against the kitchen's doorway, having heard the door open. She watched me closely. "What's with that face, sweetie?"

"Nothing," I grumbled, rubbing a hand over my face.

"That sigh tells me it's definitely something." She took a seat on the opposite couch, waiting for my answer. I knew she wasn't going to rest until I told her what was actually bothering me. "Is someone bothering you?"

Someone? Yes, your precious helper aka Maddox, my enemy.

I groaned in defeat. "There's someone..."

She gave me a knowing look. "A boy."

"Yes, a boy."

"What boy?" Grandpa came down the stairs, and he settled beside me with a hard scowl on his face. He was a tad overprotective.

The last boyfriend I had was two years ago. We dated for about four months before I lost my virginity in the back of his dad's pickup truck in the dark. The next time we made out, he noticed my scar and the look of disgust on his face still burned through my memory. Leo broke up with me the next day. When Pops found out, without any of the nasty sex details, he lost his shit. Since then, he had been wary of any boys who came around.

"It's someone from school," I finally admitted, leaving Maddox's name out, since they both thought highly of him and it'd break my Gran's heart if she ever found who the real Maddox was. Granted, yes, he was the perfect helper on Sunday, and he really did work hard, so I couldn't really ruin his image just because he was an asshole to me in school. Right?

"Is he being rude to you? Do I need to file a complaint to the Headmaster? Molly, where is my rifle?" He stood up, his back straight and his jaw hard as granite. My sweet grandpa, even in his old age, he was fierce.

I grabbed his arm and pulled him back on the couch again. "No, no. He's just... a bit annoying."

"A bully?" Grandpa inquired. His intense stare burned holes through the side of my face. This was his *if-you-lie-to-me-I-will-find-out* look.

"Not exactly. I won't let him bully me. You could say I've been a pain in his ass, too. I dyed his hair pink."

Gran snickered. "Did you know that's how our love story started?"

"You dyed Pops' hair pink?" I gasped, my jaw going to slack.

"Not exactly. It was during summer camp. Your grandpa was a sweetheart, but his friends were vexing. You see, I didn't mean to dye his hair. It was meant for his other friend who stuck gum in my hair."

"She had to cut off her beautiful locks." The forlorn look on his face as he stared at Gran, as if he was remembering that day very clearly, made my romantic heart sing.

"Yes. But Sven went into the shower first and… he came out with white hair."

"Jack Frost," Pops mumbled under his breath.

"A handsome Jack Frost." Gran lifted her chin, a twinkle in her pretty brown eyes. "That's how our love story started. We hated each other until he kissed me at the end of summer. We parted ways, but he followed me. He said he was going to marry me, and he'd win me over. He did."

I was already shaking my head before she could finish her sentence. Love story? Maddox and I? Ha. I refrained from letting out a mocking laugh. "Oh no. There's no love story between us. He's my…."

My what? My nemesis who kissed me? Confused, I couldn't find the right word to describe him. The definition of our relationship was… complicated. He was a jerk, but he wasn't exactly a bully, since I fought back just as hard. Sure, he was my enemy, but he also kissed me, and my treacherous heart had done something weird in my chest. We were both passionate about our ongoing war, but it wasn't *hate*.

Pops patted me on the knee, always on my side, always so encouraging. "If he's making your life hard, make him miserable. Don't be shy. Make him bend the knee," he said fiercely.

I swallowed past the knot in my throat, refusing to admit that Maddox and I had anything more than war between us. It was a battlefield between us. Turning to Pops, I gave him a tender smile. "You've been watching *Game of Thrones* again?"

"It's... *interesting*." He gave his wife the side-eye, his lips twitching with a half-smile. There was something in his look, and when Gran's flushed under his appraising gaze, my own eyes widened, and I fought a gag. Oh shit, I didn't want to know.

"Right. I need to shower, then I'll help with dinner." I got up to kiss Gran on the cheek and Pops on his balding head. They both chuckled as I walked away.

The next morning, I walked down the halls of Berkshire. It was a whole hour before the bell rang, to indicate the start of the school day. There were barely any students roaming the school halls. Berkshire was participating in a science experiment, and if we won Regionals, we would be representing our state. Today was our first meeting. I, of course, joined. Science was my drug, plain and simple.

I was marching down the halls when something caught my eyes, making me come to a halt. Not something: *someone*. Through the window, I caught sight of Maddox sitting outside on a bench.

I didn't even think he'd be up this early since they didn't have football practice today. Why was Maddox here?

He stared at the empty field; his elbows perched on his thighs as he smoked his cancer stick.

It was starting to grow cold in Manhattan, and we now needed a sweater or thicker jacket before stepping out. Maddox was only wearing his Berkshire uniform, as if the cold wasn't bothering him, as if he had grown immune or numb to it.

But that wasn't what made me stop and stare. No, he was *alone*. He was never alone; he was always either surrounded by his fangirls or his friends, or he was annoying me.

I placed a hand over the window as I studied him from afar. There was no reason for my heart to ache, but it did. Something clenched in my chest, like a fist holding my heart tight. Sitting on the bench, in the cold, with a cigarette between his lips, he looked like a sad, lonely god.

Maddox stood up, his longish hair falling across his face, hiding himself from my view. He took one last inhale before dropping the cigarette on the ground and stepping over it.

His hands curled around the back of his neck, and he looked up at the sky. His blond locks fell away from his face as a gust of wind breezed past him.

Eyes closed, he turned toward me and...

The agonized look on his face made me suck in a harsh breath.

His pain was stark and on display for all to see, but there was no one looking at Maddox except *me*.

He looked like a beautiful canvas being torn apart as sorrow bleed through him.

For the first time since I've met Maddox, I felt something other than annoyance. I really shouldn't have cared. I convinced myself I didn't, that I only felt bad for him because I had a habit of tending to strays.

But Maddox wasn't a stray or a wounded animal.

He wasn't mine to soothe.

But still...

"Why do you always think the worst of me?"

For the first time, I decided to not be a judgmental bitch and wondered what his story was.

"See, that's your problem. You assume too many things."

I did assume a lot of things, but that was only because Maddox had only ever showed me one side of him – the asshole side.

This side of him? The pained, broken one – it spoke to the inner part of me, to my little caged heart. Because I remembered staring into the mirror, my own reflection staring back at me, with the same expression on Maddox's face.

Broken.

Lost.

Lonely.

Scared.

His eyes opened, and my lips parted with a silent gasp as our gazes met. He couldn't see me... right?

But oh, he did.

He watched me, silently, as I'd done to him.

Something unspoken crossed between us, something... personal.

He lifted his chin in silent acknowledgement before he walked away, fading out of my sight.

The heavy weight on my chest didn't lift away. My heart cracked for a boy who probably would forget about me soon enough.

My fists clenched. I shouldn't care.

I didn't care.

CHAPTER THIRTEEN

Lila

"I didn't know you were a stalker, Sweet Cheeks." His whisper crept along my neck, causing me to shiver. I didn't hear him approach me. I had been too lost in my thoughts; I hadn't even felt him coming closer.

It was after school; the bell had just rung, and all the students were filing out.

I swung my bag over my shoulder, closed the locker and turned to face him. "I wasn't stalking, Poodle."

"Poo-what-the-fuck-dle?" He asked, confused.

I didn't even know why I said that. Maybe because he caught me off guard, or it was the fact he insisted on calling me *Sweet Cheeks*, and I needed to retaliate. Or maybe it was because I needed to feel in control again after what I saw this morning. I barricaded my heart, feeling the coldness seeping through me.

But one thing was true.

Maddox was definitely a Poodle.

One eyebrow popped up, and I stared at him, watching as realization dawned on him. His hand came up, and he touched his curly hair. "Poodle? Seriously, Garcia?"

"Poodle," I said again.

His nostrils flared in brief annoyance before he turned the table on me. "So, stalking is your new hobby?"

Clutching my bag tighter to me, I repeated, "I wasn't stalking."

"I caught you red-handed," Maddox said, his voice gruff.

"What's your problem, Coulter?"

What I really meant to ask was... what... *who* hurt you?

He cocked his head, scanning me. "You."

"Huh?"

"You're my problem, Sweet Cheeks."

Maddox stepped closer. "That kiss..."

"Won't happen again," I finished for him. "That was your only taste of me, Coulter. First and last. Memorize it and sear that kiss in your brain because it's the only one you'll get."

"Harsh," he mumbled. "I like you when you're a spitfire, like a little annoyed dragon."

I lifted my chin, squinting at him. "I'd like you better if you were nicer."

"Nice?" He let out a booming laugh that had other students turning around and focusing on us. "If you're looking for Prince Charming, you kissed the wrong frog."

Maddox Coulter was neither Prince Charming nor the... villain.

He was something else, and I didn't know where exactly to place him.

"I didn't kiss you. *You* kissed *me*."

"Same shit." He combed his fingers through his hair, pushing the stubborn locks away from his eyes.

"We're going in circles, Coulter." I pushed past him, making sure we didn't touch. "Have a good day."

His hand snaked out, and he grabbed my wrist, pulling me back into his chest. His heart thudded against my back, and I stayed still. The crowded hallway faded away as his voice lowered to a mere whisper, speaking only for me to hear. "Next time, make sure you don't stare at me with such a heartbreaking expression. Anyone would have thought you cared, except I'm no fool."

He was referring to his morning, when he had caught me watching him through the window.

Oh God.

His deep voice rolled down my spine. "Don't fall for me, Lila. I'll break you."

Conceited much? Why would he think I'd fall for him out of all the other options I had? Maddox was the last person I wanted in my heart.

"Falling in love with you is the last thing I want. Rest assured, even if you were the last man on earth, I would neither fuck you nor love you; you're too ugly for me."

"Me or my heart?"

"Both," I breathed. *Lies.*

He let go of my wrist, and I could feel the burn on my skin, where his touch had just been. His breath feathered next to my ear. "Good."

I took a step away from him. He followed, to my irritation. "One last thing. If I can't kiss your lips, can I kiss your pussy instead?"

My... what?

Fucker!

Anger coiled inside me, and I swiveled around, glaring. "Didn't your parents teach you any manners?" I spat out through clenched teeth.

Maddox instantly lost the teasing look, and his face hardened to granite. The change in him was so quick and confusing; it felt like I had been dropped into the rabbit hole.

"No. They didn't. They never cared enough to teach me anything," he simply said, his eyes empty.

My mouth opened, although I didn't know how to respond. My brain stuttered for a moment in shock as my heart dropped to the pit of my stomach. Maddox didn't wait, he walked past me, and I lost him to the crowd before I could call out to him... to *apologize*? For what?

I didn't know. Shit. Fuck.

Shock and confusion coursed through me, and for the first time, I realized that I truly didn't *know* Maddox.

What's your story, Maddox Coulter? Who are you?

"Table eight," Kelly said, handing me a tray of warm food. I nodded, bursting out of the kitchen and going straight to the table she told me.

The soles of my feet were burning and the high heels were not helping. The restaurant I worked at was nice, the ambiance was pretty and welcoming, and because we were the only *Grill and Bar* restaurant for miles, this place could get hectic. I wasn't allowed to work at the bar, though, since I was still underage. I was hired two months ago, and I only served tables. The tips were good enough to keep me here, even though the job was tiring, and some nights, I could feel the exhaustion in my bones.

I swore under my breath when another customer tried to catch my attention, waving his arm with irritation.

It was a busy night, much busier than the last few days, and we were short two servers. Both of them had called in sick last minute.

"Coming," I called to him.

I served table eight their dinner, a tight smile on my face. "Let me know if you need anything else. Enjoy," I said, chipperly. It was fake, I was feeling anything but chipper.

I went back to the man who was waving, fishing out my small notepad from the pocket of my apron. As I got closer to his table, I noticed that he had already ordered and ate his food. The plates were empty in front of him. Ah, so he needed the bill then.

I handed table five his bill and went along to the next table. The rush came and went. Hours later, I was dead on my feet and wishing I was in my bed. Kelly, my co-worker, who was also busting her ass, gave me an exhausting look as she passed me. "Table eleven. Can you grab it for me? I need the bathroom."

I nodded. "I got it."

I straightened my apron, took a last bite of my sandwich, wiped the corners of my mouth and made my way to the awaiting table.

I saw that he had already been served. "Hi, would you like anything else?"

My smile froze on my face, and I choked back a gasp. *Are you fucking kidding me?*

Mr. Stalker aka Mr. Pain-in-my-ass aka Maddox grinned at me, an almost boyish look on his face with decadent mischief in his gaze. The second thing I noticed was that his poodle hair was gone. Holy shit, he cut it? Maddox's long, shaggy dirty blond hair had been cut short. No more man buns, no more surfer swagger. Did he cut it because I called him Poodle? I didn't think he was *that* offended, but I figured it bruised his ego.

"Yes. You," Maddox said.

I recovered from my shock, picked up my jaw from the floor and snapped my mouth shut. "Excuse me?" I asked stiffly, still reeling from disbelief.

He pushed his chair back, extended his legs in front of him and crossed his arms over his wide chest. "You asked if I wanted anything else, I gave you my answer. *You.*" His teeth grazed his lower lips and he eyed me up and down in my waitressing outfit. "I've been wondering if your pussy tastes like cherry, too."

Oh, for Pete's sake.

"Maddox," I hissed.

"Lila." My name rolled off his tongue, like he was tasting it.

"What are you doing? This is my workplace."

He quirked up an eyebrow. "I'm here for the food. I approve, by the way. Five stars for the food, five stars for your service."

"You're stalking me," I deadpanned.

"I am," he admitted, calmly and without any shame.

This was getting out of hand. It was unacceptable, but I couldn't even say anything back. Not while I was still working. My boss was somewhat of a bitch, and I couldn't risk pissing her off, so I bit my tongue and *smiled.*

"I'll give you the bill. We close in thirty minutes," I said, as politely as I could, the corners of my eyes twitching with the effort to keep from snapping at Maddox.

Turning on my heels, I walked away before he could say anything else. I prayed he'd be gone by the time my shift ended.

When the clock struck eleven thirty, I hurriedly fumbled with the strings of my apron. I went into the bathroom and quickly changed out of my waitressing uniform, jumping into my jeans and yanking my beige sweater over my head. Done and done. I had fifteen minutes to catch my bus, and it was the last bus for tonight.

As I walked out of the restaurant, I prayed... and hoped...

But *nope.*

There he was, standing against the lamp post next to the bus stop.

Deep breaths, Lila, I told myself.

My lips tightened into a firm line as I walked to the bus stop, stopping next to Maddox but refusing to acknowledge him. He was starting to become unbearable. Why did I even *feel* something for him before?

The smell of cigarette was strong in the air, and I rolled my eyes. "Smoking is bad."

"Yeah, yeah. I know. Cancer and shit." From the corner of my eyes, I saw him take another long drag before exhaling a puff of smoke through his nose.

My lips curled in revulsion. "I don't care if you die, but you're probably going to give me cancer along the way if you keep smoking around me like this."

It was a horrible thing to say, I knew. But for someone to care so little about their own life and health, it made me pity the poor fool. He really didn't know what it meant to precariously hang between life and death. He didn't know how scary and lonely the door behind death was. I saw it, and it still haunted me to this day.

Maddox let out another puff of smoke before he looked down at me. "Why do you hate me so much?"

A mocking laugh spilled past my freezing lips. It was colder than I anticipated, and I wasn't dressed properly for the weather, stupid me. "Wow. Are you *that* full of yourself you can't figure out why I despise you so much? I thought you were smarter than that."

"Well, I want to hear it from you. I don't like to speculate."

Oh really? I didn't think he was ready for this, but I humored him anyway.

Fighting another shiver from the cold, I hugged my waist and turned slightly toward Maddox. The ripped jeans were a bad idea since my legs were numb now. But I refused to show any sign of being frozen to death, least of all in front of *him*. "First. You still haven't apologized for bumping into me in the coffee shop."

He let out a mocked gasp, filled with disbelief. "What? You're still pissed about that day? It's been two months!"

I locked my jaw, silently bristling. "I don't care how long it's been. I appreciate it when people take responsibility for their mistakes and apologize when they're wrong."

"I'm sorry."

My jaw went slack, and my eyes snapped to his. Wait...did... Maddox Coulter just apologize to me? Was something wrong with my ears? Maybe I was dreaming. Yup, that must have been it. "What did you just say?"

He threw the rest of his cigarette on the ground, squashing it with his leather boot. He kept his eyes on me, his face devoid of any mischief. He looked... serious. What a confusing man. I couldn't tell which side of him was real anymore. "I said I was sorry," he rumbled, the expression on his face genuine.

I narrowed my eyes on him. "Apologies don't count when they're not sincere."

"You confuse me, woman. First, you want me to apologize. Then when I do, you tell me not to. Pick one, Garcia."

"When someone says he's sorry, he should mean it. Apologies need to be sincere or else it's useless and, frankly, a waste of time. Mean it or don't say it at all. I don't accept half-assed apologies."

Maddox brought a hand up, holding it over his chest. "Jesus.

You're harsh, Sweet Cheeks."

"Second, you've been annoying me non-stop, always following me around, and you find every reason to irritate me! Whether it's in class, at lunch or outside of school. You do know that personal space exists, right?"

He looked thoughtful for a second, and I thought he really was considering my words. But then he opened his mouth, and I wanted to smack him. "Girls love it when I'm in their personal space," he admitted as if it was the most obvious thing.

"Full of yourself and absolutely cocky. The list is growing at an accelerating rate."

"So, you hate me because I give you attention?" Maddox took a pack of gum out of his pocket, popped one in his mouth before offering me one.

Against my better judgement, I took it. He was offering; I needed something to keep me distracted. "I *despise* you because I don't want the attention you give me."

"Anything else?" The corner of his lips tilted up, a small grin on his face. There was nothing taunting about it. In fact, he looked *pleased*.

"You keep calling me *Sweet Cheeks* even though I have told you a thousand times to stop. And you keep using vulgar language. You're rude and immature and inconsiderate to other people," I whisper-yelled.

"But you call me *Poodle*." Was that all he got from my rant?

"I call you *Poodle* because you call me *Sweet Cheeks*. I believe everything is fair in love and war."

He stood closer, bending his head, so he could whisper in my ear. "And what do we have between us? Love? Or war?"

"War," I said through gritted teeth.

"I approve," he said too quickly, popping his gum. "Anything else?"

"Yes," I practically screamed now, "You. Kissed. Me."

"Ah. So, you hate me because I stole your first kiss?"

Was that what he thought? That little shit.

A sigh escaped me, and I rubbed a hand over my face, trying to chase away the cold. "That wasn't my first kiss, Maddox. And I despise you because you did it without my permission. That... was unacceptable."

He rubbed his cheek with his thumb and shook his head, still grinning. "Goddamn it. You've got a lot of rules."

My lips curled. "And I guess, you're one who hates rules?"

Maddox flashed me a wicked smile. "I break 'em, Lila. I love to break rules."

"It makes you feel extra manly?" I taunted.

"No. It makes me feel alive." His confession made me still, and I stared up at him, watching his expression for any lies, but all I saw was sincerity.

For a moment, Maddox's pained face flashed through my brain: outside in the cold, sitting on that bench, looking so lost. I didn't want to admit it before, but there was *something* about Maddox that really intrigued me.

I couldn't forget that look on his face, it was tattooed in my memories. Maddox Coulter was more than Berkshire's star quarterback. He was a complicated puzzle, and I wanted to tear him apart, layer by layer, so I could study him, delve into his soul and learn all his secrets.

A gust of wind breezed past us, and I quickly patted my hair down. This time, I couldn't hold back the involuntarily shudder that racked through me. Maddox took notice, and he frowned, his eyebrows pinching together. "Why don't you have a proper jacket on?"

I hugged myself, rubbing my hands up and down my arms. "I didn't think it was going to be this cold. I thought the sweater would be enough."

Before I could finish my sentence, and before I knew what was happening, he shrugged off his jacket and pushed it toward me.

I eyed the jacket, suspiciously. "What are you doing?"

Maddox circled my wrist with his finger and dragged me closer. He placed the jacket over my shoulders and gave me a pointed look, his face hard, until I succumbed and placed my arms through the sleeves. "Keeping you warm. I'm a man, Lila. I know you don't like me and think I'm an absolute asshole."

His lips twitched when I scoffed. "Fine, I'm an asshole sometimes."

I gave him *the* look. *Are you serious?*

"Okay, all the time. But I still know how to treat a lady right."

Treat a lady right? What a joke.

But still… my heart warmed. His scent was still heavy on the jacket, and I chewed on my lip when I noticed how good the smell of him was.

Maddox buttoned up the jacket for me and tugged the collar higher and closer, so my neck was covered. "There. Cozy enough?"

My lips parted, but I didn't know how to answer, so I only gave him a tiny nod.

He pulled back and looked me up and down, a frown appearing on his face. "Jesus Christ. You're so tiny."

I rolled my eyes. "Thanks."

I expected another joke coming from his lips. Instead, he looked tense and his brows were curled with a frown. "Are you sure it's safe for you to be out here like this, so late?"

Huffing in response, I rolled my eyes again. As if he cared. "I don't need a knight in shining armor. I can take care of myself."

His blue eyes were so bright and vivid under the moonlight. It was tempting to get lost in them. But when he opened his mouth, he squashed down all the effects he had on me. "I'm not going to be your Knight because I know you aren't a damsel in distress. You're more like the dragon in the fairy tale."

My lips curled and against my better judgement, I found myself smirking. "If I could fry you right now, I would."

It was easy to get lost in the easygoing expression on his face What were we arguing about before? Shit, I got sidetracked.

His devious grin was back, but there was something... pleasing about it. He was mocking me like before, being a bully, but this was a war with no venom. "I bet I'd taste good as an omelet."

"Do you always have a reply to everything?" I asked, not expecting a particular reply since I already knew the answer.

Now, he was smirking like the devil. As if he had won this round. "Were you born this sassy or do I bring the sass outta you?"

I blinked, my brain stuttering at his question.

I was petty, yes. I never backed down without a fight, yes. But this newfound sass...

Swallowing past the heavy ball in my throat, my gaze skittered away from him. Maddox tended to make me feel on edge, like I was about to jump off the cliff. He irritated me, non-stop. But as bad as it sounded when I admitted it, I had grown used to him being a jerk. The ongoing battle between us was exhausting, but it had been something I started looking forward to. Our pranks and verbal sparring had become something I had grown used to.

The realization had me taking a step back.

I had always been competitive, but I had never found a proper opponent.

Not until Maddox.

His gaze shifted behind me, and his smile slid off his face. "Your bus is here," he said, breaking through my muddling thoughts.

The bus came to stop in front of us, and I started forward, leaving him behind. My hands were shaking as I tried to take off his jacket. He held my hands in place, over the buttons. "Keep it. You can give it back later," he said, his voice gruff and thick.

"Have a good night," I breathed, stepping into the bus.

"Oh, Lila?"

I peeked at him over my shoulder. He had his hands shoved into the pockets of his pants, a few stubborn strands of hair falling over his eyes. "You don't hate me," he stated firmly before cracking a smile. "Sweet dreams, Lila. I might visit you there."

My lips twitched, and I turned away before he could see it. If you google Maddox's name, Cocky will be his definition. Maybe that should be his middle name. Maddox 'Cocky' Coulter.

I swiped my card and took a seat at the back of the bus. As it drove past where we had been, I saw Maddox still standing there, staring at the bus as I left him behind.

He was right.

We were at war, two very fierce opponents.

But...

I didn't hate him.

Realization dawned on me that I didn't loathe Maddox as much as I thought I did. Things just turned out to be a bit more complicated because it would have been easier if I hated him.

CHAPTER FOURTEEN

H ate is a strong word.
It's a bitter but sweet fucking poison. It's like cocaine, and once you've had a taste, it's damn addictive. It becomes something more. It infiltrates your system, running through your veins, until you can't see anything other than red rage.

Hate kept me going.

Rage kept me alive. It became the oxygen I breathed.

See, I didn't hate my parents.

I *loathed* them.

I wasn't angry at them. No, it was something more. The rage festered over the years. I tended to it, watered it and watched it grow into something nasty and ugly.

Years ago, I found out it was easy to hate but so damn difficult to love.

But no matter how deep my hatred ran for them; I still looked into their eyes and hoped to see something *more*. Love for the child they brought into this fucked-up world and forgot to look after. *Me*.

My mother and I stood opposite of each other in the hallway of our home. She had a cashmere shawl wrapped around her shoulders and the moonlight shone through the window, casting a glow on her face. I was the carbon copy of my father, but I had my mother's eyes. I waited for her to acknowledge me, I waited for her to smile and say a few words. I waited to see if she'd ask me if I ate today or if she wondered how school was. Something simple, something small... but something other than silence.

It had been two weeks since we saw each other. We lived in the same goddamn house, but my parents were never here.

She clenched her shawl tighter to her body and walked toward me. It was way past midnight; I had come home late, yet again, after partying with Colton and the boys. I smelled of alcohol, weed and the scent of cigarette was heavy in the air, clinging to my clothes.

Her eyes met mine for a half second before she averted her gaze. Her lips parted as if she wanted to speak, and my heart thudded so hard in my chest as I *waited*.

The look on her face told me she didn't *hate* me, maybe she even cared... but when she closed her mouth and walked past me, I realized... she didn't care enough.

My heart plummeted to my feet, bloody and weeping, as mommy dearest walked over it and walked away from me.

I marched to my bedroom and slammed the door close, knowing full well my parents wouldn't hear. I was on the opposite side of the house, the distance between us too big.

The bottle of liquor, sitting patiently on my nightstand, called to me.

I wasn't an addict, but I *needed* it. Tonight, at least.

Grabbing the bottle, I sank into my couch and watched the shadow dancing over my walls in my dark room. I took a long swig of the bottle, feeling the sweet burn in my throat. Fuck yeah.

Rage... Hate... I *breathed* it in.

My head swam, the air was thick and hot.

To everyone, I was Maddox Coulter – the golden boy, star quarterback and Berkshire's king.

To my parents, I was a disappointment.

To myself? I was just the boy trapped in the closet.

Hate was cold fire; there was no warmth from it.

My eyes fluttered close. Before I became lost in the space between sleep and consciousness, a mouthy girl with pretty brown eyes and black hair came to haunt me.

I slowly smiled.

Fuck, she was something else.

Lila

The next day, I walked through the halls of Berkshire as if I was on display. If I didn't know better, I would have thought I forgot to wear clothes this morning, but no, I was definitely dressed. Their eyes burned into the back of my head, and the whispers followed me. They made no attempt to hide their curiosity; some of them – Maddox's fangirls -- even looked at me with open distaste.

Shit. Now what?

Riley popped next to me out of nowhere and gripped my arm.

"You owe me an explanation," she hissed in my ear.

Confused, I looked down at her. "Why? What did I do?"

"The rumor," she started, but then trailed off as her gaze skirted over my head. Riley scowled hard, and I turned around to see Maddox and Colton walking through the entrance.

I stayed rooted on the spot as he sauntered toward me. My brain told me to run. The look on his face was anything but *nice*. Mischief glimmered in his blue eyes, and a smirk twisted his full lips. Uh-oh.

The hallway became quiet, as if awaiting a long, overdue dramatic scene. I could feel everyone holding their breaths, anxious and curious as they stared back and forth between Maddox and me.

I tried to backpedal out of his way, but he ate up the distance between us with three long steps, stopping right in front of me. "Coulter," I said in greeting, eyeing him with suspicion.

Maddox dipped his head to my level, breathing against my lips. My heart stuttered, and I froze on the spot. His lips skated over my cheek in a chaste kiss, and he lingered there for a second too long. "Good morning, Lila," he said, his breath warm against my skin.

I felt the stares on us, the silent gasps coming from the others at Maddox's public display of affection, even though it was anything but affectionate. He was teasing me, making me the center of attention because he knew how much I despised it. Fuck, this wasn't good.

I pulled back, glaring up at him through my lashes. Without a word, I stalked past him, but his voice followed me as he called out across the hallway. "Don't forget to give me back my jacket, *baby*."

Double shit!

I snuck a quick look to my left to see people staring at me with open-mouthed expressions. Holding back a growl, I didn't spare Maddox a glance as I stomped away with Riley at my heels.

When we rounded the corner to a fairly empty corridor, she grabbed my arm and pulled me to a stop. "You kissed him!" she whisper-yelled, her face a mask of astonishment.

A groan escaped me. "Is this why everyone's staring at me like I've grown two heads?"

"Someone saw you two kissing at your locker two days ago, and you know how quickly rumors spread," she admitted.

The rumors in Berkshire spread like a wildfire, untamed and unstoppable. The people were hungry sharks in the tank full of blood. They probably thought Maddox and I were dating now due to the kiss and then the jacket comment made by Maddox.

"Well, here's one important fact. I didn't kiss him. He kissed me."

"He kissed you?"

I threw my hands in the air. "Yes," I growled. "Why is this such a big deal?"

Riley's eyebrows popped up, giving me a look that said the obvious. "You kissed Maddox Coulter after declaring war on him. Yeah, babe. It's a big fucking deal."

"Whatever. It won't happen again."

She followed me, hooking her arm with mine. "Is he good, like the rumors say? I heard some girls say he can tongue-fuck your mouth like he'd tongue-fuck your pus–"

"Riley!"

She let out a smothered giggle, and I instantly knew she was teasing me on purpose. Such a brat. "Sorry, but you should see how you're blushing right now."

Ignoring the warm heat against my cheeks, I leveled Riley with a glare, and she pouted, but, thankfully, chose to remain silent.

I left Riley at her Calculus class before making my way to

English. When I walked inside, Maddox was already there, sitting in his usual spot. He had his legs thrown over his desk, his ankles crossed. Two girls surrounded him, and they were giggling at something he must have said, except he didn't look interested in the conversation; in fact, he looked like he needed to be saved from them. Why couldn't they see that?

A little self-respect would go a long way. He didn't want them; it was as clear as the sunrise in the morning and the moon in the night sky. The thing about Berkshire was that everyone wanted to be on top of the food chain. The only way to get there? Date a popular jock, it was as simple as that.

Maddox was the biggest fish in the tank, the best catch, and every girl wanted to get her hooks in him.

His gaze slid to me and the corner of his lips quirked up into a small smile. Maddox gave me his signature smirk, followed by a wink that had dozens of girls melting at his feet.

I lifted my chin in silent acknowledgment before taking my seat.

Soon enough, class started. Mrs. Levi began her Shakespearean lesson for this semester; we were studying *Hamlet*. She wanted to start the lesson with a *Hamlet* movie, the popular one with Robin Williams.

"It's the best adaption," Mrs. Levi explained. "But the projector isn't working. So, I'm going to need someone to get the TV from the storage room. Lila, do you mind?"

She looked at me expectantly, and I nodded.

"Any volunteer to help?"

I held back a groan. *No, no, no…*

"I'll go with her," Maddox said smoothly.

Mrs. Levi clapped her hands together. "Oh, great."

I marched out of the classroom, making my way to the storage room at the end of the hall. Maddox caught up with me easily. "You don't look happy, Garcia."

"Oh look, you're back to your annoying self," I countered.

From my peripheral vision, I saw him give me a lazy shrug. "You shouldn't be surprised."

Actually, I wasn't.

"Did my jacket keep you company last night?" He said the words like he was whispering a dirty secret.

Of course. Everything had to be dirty with Maddox. He probably thought I sniffed his jacket while I masturbated. Fun fact: *I didn't.*

I huffed. "I have it in my locker. I'll give it back to you after school."

"Are you asking me to meet you after school? A date?" A shocked gasp spilled from his lips, but it was fake. I could easily sense the mocking smile in his words.

"No," I growled. "Come to my locker. I'll return your jacket to you, and we both can go on our merry ways, *separately.*"

He didn't have a chance to refute me since we were already standing at the storage room.

A note glared back at us, and I rubbed a hand over my face. "Great," I muttered under my breath. "The light isn't working."

I snuck a glance at Maddox, and he looked a bit... apprehensive. Hmm. "Can you keep the door open for me while I get the TV?" I asked.

Maddox shrugged.

The door was heavy as we pushed it open, and I walked inside. It was dark, but the lights from the hallway illuminated the inside enough for me to spot where all the TVs were kept against the back corner of the room. Aha, there it was.

Each TV was sitting on its own small four wheeled shelf, and all I had to do was roll one out. Easy peasy. *Not*.

When I tried to pull, it didn't budge, not even an inch. Goddamn it.

I took a peek behind the TV and saw that there was no way I could roll it out of this storage room. All the cords were tangled up together.

"Maddox, can you help me with the cord? It's stuck, and it's dark in here. I can barely see anything."

"Just pull it," he rumbled, impatiently.

"If I could, I would," I hissed. "It's stuck. Help me."

He was silent for a moment before uttering, "Ask nicely."

"Are you fucking serious?"

"Say please.

"Please," I said through clench teeth.

He tsked. "Say the full sentence."

I straightened, bringing my hands to my hips, as I rolled my eyes. "Maddox, can you help me with the cord, please?"

"Good girl," he praised.

He pushed the door wide open, holding it against the wall, and stared at it for a second, waiting. "It's not going to close. Hurry," I called out.

When Maddox was sure the door wasn't going to close and lock us into the storage room, he sauntered inside. He looked behind him once, staring at the open door for a second longer, before coming to stand beside me.

"Move aside," he demanded.

I rolled my eyes, again, but still did as I was told. Maddox reached behind the shelf, trying to find the cord. "Fuck, what is this?"

"Exactly. It's all tangled up with the others." There were four TVs in all, and they were pushed together into a tiny corner. We hadn't used them in the longest time, since we got the new projector screens, so they had been sitting here, collecting dust.

He let out a frustrated groan before starting to untangle the cords, which would take a lot of patience to do. The space between the rack and the wall was too tight, and I could see he was having trouble. "Here, let me get my flashlight. That might help," I suggested.

I fished out my phone from my pocket, but before I could turn it on, a loud banging sound echoed through the room. We both flinched, and Maddox lifted his head in surprise, hitting the top shelf in the process. He let out a string of curses.

Before I knew what was happening, we were surrounded by complete and utter darkness.

Shit, the door closed.

And... double shit, we were locked inside; the note had said that the handle was broken.

"No...no... No!" Maddox bellowed, rushing for the door through the dark. Huh? Was he scared of the dark? Who would have known Maddox Coulter, with his cocky smirk and eyes that could melt you on the spot, was scared of a little darkness?

I successfully turned the flashlight on, already thinking of teasing him like he would have done to me. My gaze slid to Maddox just in time to see him bumping against a shelf in his hasty attempt to reach for the door. The metal rack crashed to the floor with a loud, booming sound, and Maddox fell to his knees before he scrambled up again. He slipped over the broken shards and fallen liquid, crawling toward his escape.

No, wait. *No*... he wasn't just scared of the dark. This was something more.

A heavy weight settled on my chest, my throat closed and my breath stuck in my throat. Shocked, I stayed rooted on the spot as Maddox came completely undone.

Cool, collected and flirty Maddox was replaced by a stranger. He blindly reached for the door, grabbing the broken handle and pulling himself to his feet. Maddox hit the heavy door with his palm. "No, no! Please! No, no, no. *Please*," he repeated under his breath. "Don't do this, please Let me out of here! Don't leave me here. Don't do this. No, no, please! *Don't*."

He repeatedly hit the door, his open palm connecting with the surface with such hard slaps that it should have hurt him. "Help me, help. Please, don't leave me here."

Maddox scratched at the door, as if he was trying to rip it free from its hinges. He was trying to break through. His fingers clenched into tights fist as he started banging on the door, violently. His screams echoed through my ears, and my heart thudded hard against my ribcage, I felt his *pain*. His agony was a reminder of my own silent suffering.

"I can't... I can't breathe. I *can't*," he whimpered, his voice cracking.

Thump – thump – thump.

"This is what death feels like, and you're going to die alone," a voice whispered in my ears.

My lips parted with a silent cry as I fought to breathe, but I couldn't. I really couldn't.

My breath came out in sharp, hallow panting, and my vision grew darker and blurred. I squeezed my eyes shut and pressed down on my eyelids. A kaleidoscopic of stars fluttered behind my closed eyes. Help me, help. Please, help me.

I thought maybe I was having a heart attack; yet, there was no physical pain. But my whole body vibrated, my skin crawled like I was picking apart my flesh and trying to jump out of my skin.

"This is what death feels like."

I can't breathe.

Help me.

"Help me," Maddox screamed.

My thoughts fluttered away, and my heart kicked in my chest, pushing me forward. I snapped out of my frozen state and rushed to his side, my own hands trembling. "Maddox," I said softly, trying to break through his madness. "Maddox, please."

He banged on the door harder, and I noticed his knuckles had been split open from his attempts to break free from the storage room. Oh God, he was hurting himself. "Maddox!" I said louder, grabbing his arms and trying to pull him away from the door. He resisted and shook me off him.

"Maddox, no! Please. Don't do that. You're hurting yourself. Just..." I scrambled, trying to figure out what to do, what to say, so I could break through to him, reach Maddox in the place where he was lost. I had to pull him out.

"I need to get out. I need to get out. Get me out of here!" His fist pounded continuously on the door, a sob racking through his body. His voice was hoarse as he screamed brokenly. "Get me away from here. Get me out of here. I need to get out... I can't breathe! I need to get out."

He went to punch the door again, but I grabbed his fist, holding his hand in my own. It was a risk. I knew he was so lost in his head that he could have hurt me. Unintentionally. But it was important for him not to hurt *himself*.

It was becoming clearer that he was suffering from a panic

attack. I knew exactly what it looked it, what it *felt* like.

"Please," he whimpered. "Get me out of here. Please. Please. Please. *Please.*"

I held back a choked sob as he started pleading, each word spilling out of his mouth like a goddamn arrow straight to my heart. I bled *for* him.

He started mumbling something I couldn't hear, his breathing ragged and loud as he struggled to breathe.

When he realized he couldn't break free, Maddox crouched down, his head dropping to his hands as he fisted his hair, pulling at the strands. The mumbling under his breath grew louder as he shook his head back and forth. "Please, please. I need to get out. Help…Help me…Please."

My chest grew tight at the sight of him like this.

My knees weakened. When I couldn't hold myself upright any longer, I knelt down beside his trembling form. My hand landed on his chest to feel his heart pounding, hard and erratic, as if it was beating right out of his chest. His shirt was drenched with sweat, sticking to his body like a second skin.

I knew what it felt like to suffer like this. Chest caving in, all the air being sucked out from your lungs, a fist clenching your heart so tight, blood rushing through your ears, your lungs can't seem to work properly and then it happens… *suffocation.* The need to crawl out of your skin, as if your body is not your own anymore, chasing an escape you couldn't even see through the fog.

The tremors kicked in and Maddox started shaking. It started with his hands before his whole body quaked as he struggled to do a simple thing as inhale and exhale.

I had to get him to breathe first, it was the only way to ground him into the present, to bring him back from wherever he was lost inside his head.

Maddox held his head in his hands, his body rocking back and forth. "No, no, no. Please. Please," he begged.

"Maddox," I spoke softly. "Maddox, I'm right here. It's okay."

A tortured sound came from his throat, and my eyes burned with unshed tears. This was... hard. So fucking hard.

This wasn't Maddox.

This was a boy, frightened and lost.

I gripped his hand and pulled it away from his face, holding it with both of mine "I'm right here, Maddox."

His eyes were squeezed shut; his eyebrows pinched and his face... it was a mask of raw pain. He was tormented by something, his past... maybe, I didn't know, but whatever it was, Maddox was still hurting. I could almost taste his suffering in the heavy air surrounding us.

Squeezing his left hand, I spoke firmly. "Look at me, Maddox. I'm right here. Look at me, okay? Please."

When he kept his eyes closed, I changed tactics. "Breathe with me, baby. Can you do that? Can you breathe with me? I'll count. Maddox, you can do it. I know you can."

He sucked in a ragged breath, his chest rattling with the effort. "There you go. Slowly. Breathe with me. I'm right here. I'm not leaving you. It's going to be okay."

I squeezed his hand again, counting to three out loud. "Inhale," I instructed.

He did. He slowly sucked in a breath.

I counted from four to six now. "Exhale."

Maddox let out a harsh breath.

Squeeze. Inhale. Squeeze. Exhale.

One. Two. Three. Inhale. Four. Five. Six. Exhale.

When his breathing slowly became less ragged, I whispered, "I'm proud of you. That's good. Do it again, Maddox. Breathe with me. Stay with me."

His eyes opened, and I realized whatever I said had gotten through to him, so I repeated it again. "I'm proud of you. Stay with me."

I inhaled, showing him how to do it, and Maddox breathed in a shaky breath. Somewhere in his tortured blue eyes, I saw him trying to hold onto his own sanity. I stared into his dark and bottomless eyes, seeing something I had never seen before. Fear and misery consumed every part of him.

I saw myself in him, and we bled together, our pain seeping through us, similar to how tears would leak from our eyes. Maddox looked at me as if he was staring at something he was about to lose.

"I'm not going anywhere," I soothed gently, rubbing my fingers over the back of his knuckles.

He was still shaking, but he wasn't struggling to breathe anymore.

I remembered my mother singing to me when I was a child, a sweet lullaby as she'd put me to sleep. When I'd suffer from my own panic attacks, my therapist told me to play the lullaby on YouTube. It had helped calm me down. I knew everyone rides out their panic attacks differently, but maybe... maybe I could...

Right now, Maddox looked like a child who needed someone to hold him.

So, I did.

I knelt between his thighs, so I was close to him, and held his hands in my own. I continued to rub my fingertips over his bruised knuckles, letting him feel my touch.

My lips parted, my heart *ached* and I sung him my favorite

lullaby.

"Lullaby and good night, In the sky stars are bright, May the moons silvery beams, Bring you sweet dreams, Close your eyes now and rest, May these hours be blessed, Till the sky's bright with dawn, When you wake with a yawn."

I saw brief recognition in his gaze. His eyes turned glassy, and he had a faraway look, like he wasn't seeing *me*, because Maddox was somewhere else.

"Lullaby and good night, You are mother's delight, I'll protect you from harm, And you'll wake in my arms, Sleepyhead, close your eyes, For I'm right beside you, Guardian angels are near, So sleep without fear," I sung gently.

His lips quivered, and panic welled up inside me. I fucked up; I shouldn't have sung to him. He was just starting to calm down and now...

Maddox curled his arm around my waist, and he pulled me against him, his head dropping to my shoulders. The world stilled except for our pounding hearts, beating together like a broken violin, shrieking with violent, pained sounds. A silent sob racked through his body, and I felt wetness on my neck where Maddox had his face hidden.

He was *crying*.

In silence.

He suffered in silence.

His tears carried the weight of his pain.

My emotions became jagged as my chest ripped open, a knife digging itself into my little, fragile heart. It was so hard to swallow past the heavy lump in my throat. Emotional pain bore invisible scars; yet, these scars could be traced by the gentlest touch, I knew that.

Breaking apart was hard. It stung with every breath taken.

Recovering from it was the hardest.

Sometimes, the pieces can't be put back together because they're mismatched, missing or completely shattered, making it an impossible feat.

Tears slid down my cheeks, and I choked back a cry. My own voice cracked as I continued to sing the rest of the lullaby.

He pulled me tighter into his body, and I wrapped my arms around his shoulders, holding him to me. I remembered how it was, coming out of my panic attacks, the adrenaline rushing away as I came back to the present. Everything would hurt, and I'd always feel so lost.

This was Maddox right now.

So, I held him.

Because he needed to be held, even if he didn't say the words.

He needed me.

Maddox trembled in my arms, his whole body shaking with his silent cries and tremors. As the lullaby came to an end, I pressed my lips against his cheek. "You're going to be okay, Maddox. I got you."

Thump – thump – thump.

There was a hollow ache in the pit of my stomach.

I embraced him.

He didn't let go.

His breathing smoothed out, and his pounding heart slowed.

"I got you," I soothed, running my fingers through his soft hair.

His arms clenched around me, and he nuzzled his nose into my neck. *Hold me tighter*, he said without any words.

I got you.

CHAPTER FIFTEEN

Lila

Maddox and I were still wrapped in each other's arms when the door of the storage closet opened, and the janitor peered inside with a look of horror on his face.

"What are you two doing in here?" He held the door open, and the light from the hallway bathed the inside of the dark room.

Maddox's grip on me tightened at the new voice, and he kept his face buried in my neck. His silent tears soaked through my blouse as I smoothed a hand down his back. "I'm right here," I whispered in his ear before looking up at the janitor, who was limping inside. He had a bad leg, the rumors said it was from a military accident. He had been working for Berkshire for fifteen years now, and he was loved by everyone. Sweet Mister Johnson.

"We got locked in by accident," I explained, motioning toward the TV with one hand. "We had to get the TV, but the door closed on us."

Mr. Johnson looked down at Maddox and I, where we were still kneeling. I was practically sitting on his lap, and his arms around me were tight. Maddox was a sinking ship; he was drowning in the wreckage of a wounded heart, and I was the anchor holding him together.

I got you.

My heart couldn't bear to let go, even though I knew I had to. Eventually.

"Is he okay?" Mr. Johnson looked mildly curious, but mostly worried.

I nodded. "Could you grab the TV for us, please? The cords are all tangled up together."

"Of course. Let me get it. Which class are you guys in?"

"Mrs. Levi."

"I'll bring it. Get back to class." He waved, shooing us away.

"Thank you, Mr. Johnson."

My nails grazed Maddox's scalp in a soothing manner as I ran my fingers through his hair. "Maddox?" At the sound of his name, he pulled away from me and stood up. I could tell he was still shaky, his body swaying before he found his footing again, and he refused to look at me. Still holding onto his hand, we walked out of the storage closet. His breathing has evened out now, and his face had hardened, his eyes lifeless.

Maddox was shutting down... shutting *me* out.

"We can grab a bottle of water from the vending machine," I suggested, gently.

When I tried to squeeze his hand, he ripped it away from me. Like I was some kind of disease and he didn't want to be infected. "Madd–"

"Stay away from me," he said, and it sent chills down my spine. His voice was like a thunderclap, furious and strained.

"Maddox," I started, but he cut me off.

"Don't." That was a warning, and I should've listened; I really should have because for the first time, I saw a different Maddox.

A boy filled with rage, but blue eyes that held a broken song.

When I tried to grab his hand again, to stop him from walking away and shutting me out, he swiveled around without warning, and I almost fell into him My lips parted with a silent gasp when he grabbed my arm in an unyielding grip and slammed me against the wall. Maddox towered over me, his jaw clenching and his eyes darkening. He looked like a raging warrior, riding into battle with the promise of death in his gaze.

His head lowered, and his breath caressed over my lips. "Tell *anyone* about this and I. Will. Ruin. You. Lila," he warned, his tone thick with threat.

"I would never…" I breathed as my body went cold.

He bared his teeth with a low growl, silencing me. "It's been harmless fun between us, but, trust me, breathe a word about this to anyone else, I will make sure you're never able to walk through the halls of Berkshire again without wanting to cower and hide away in fear."

"Maddox, listen. I–"

My heart stuttered, and I forgot what I was about to say when his hand slid up my arm, and he wrapped it around my neck. His fingers tightened around the base of my throat, but it wasn't a punishing grip. It didn't hurt, but it was a silent promise, a warning, a deadly threat.

"I will ruin you. You'll beg for mercy, and I will show you none, Lila." His voice was a sharp sword carelessly slicing through me.

Maddox pushed away from me as Mr. Johnson walked out of the storage room.

"Everything okay here?" he asked, his gaze going back and forth between Maddox and I.

Maddox swore under his breath, loud enough for me to hear before he stomped away.

In the opposite direction of the class.

He was... leaving?

My voice caught in my throat as I watched him walk out of the building, the double doors closing behind him with a loud bang. I flinched as he disappeared out of my view.

Clearing my throat, I gave Mr. Johnson a tentative smile. "He just needs... a minute by himself."

"He's an angry young man," he commented. "Reminds me of myself after I was discharged from the military."

"He just..."

Mr. Johnson waved me away. "No need to explain. Here's the TV."

I swallowed past the burning lump in my throat, mumbled a quick *thank you,* before grabbing the TV stand and rolling it toward the classroom.

I expected him to come back later, but he didn't.

There was no glimpse of Maddox for the rest of the day. I walked through the halls of Berkshire, looking for him, but he was... gone, and I felt his absence like a sharp sword slicing through me.

Maddox's mixed emotions might have been justified in the moment, but not toward *me.*

I hadn't done anything to deserve being on the receiving end of his anger. Especially not after the time we had spent in that dark storage room.

My gran always told me I was a curious little thing, but this wasn't just about curiosity. This was the *need* to know the real

Maddox, the one he hid behind a cool façade and a bad boy mask.

Because the Maddox in that closet, the one I held in my arms... he was a lost boy, and he reminded me of myself after I had woken up from my coma.

Maddox

The scent of a heavy cheap perfume touched my nostrils, and I almost gagged at how strong the smell was.

My head hurt.

My body ached.

What the fuck?

My eyes split open, and I stared at the ceiling of... *not* my room.

Ah fuck. Why couldn't I remember anything? There was an empty hole in my memories, and all I remembered was...

The pounding headache had me wincing as I rolled over to my side as my stomach twisted with nausea. The bed shifted with another weight and a low moan came from the person beside me.

I let my head drop to my pillow and closed my eyes as the memories came flooding back.

The fucking storage. A reminder of my fucked-up past, carelessly thrown into a living nightmare. *Lila.* Fucking hell, Lila. She was with me. She held me.

She goddamn held me in her arms and rocked me like I was a child.

Lila... sang to me.

A lullaby.

The same one my mother used to sing to me. She had a habit of coming into my room to put me to sleep. She'd sing to me and kiss me on the forehead before turning off the lights and closing the door behind her.

Good night, Sweetheart. Sweet dreams.

Good night, Mommy.

That was all...before.

Before things changed, and I became a stranger to my own parents.

And Lila...

Fuck! I remembered walking away from her, threatening her.

A pained groan escaped me when I realized what a shithead I was. Lila was the one good thing in that moment, and I ruined it with my anger and ego.

No, I had been...*scared.*

"Hmm," someone mumbled next to my ear. My eyes closed as I remembered the party.

I had been drunk and needed to fuck the anger out of my system. It led me to this... grabbing a bitch at Brayden's party. The hotel. Alcohol and sex, then I passed out.

"Hey babe." Her hand smoothed down my naked chest, and my skin crawled at the touch. None of the girls I slept with were allowed to stay after a fuckathon. I hated the after-sex-talk, and I loathed sleeping beside them. It gave them unnecessary expectations that I wanted *more* than just sex.

I grabbed her hand and pushed it away. The mattress shifted again and another weight beside me rolled over, throwing a leg over my hips.

Wait... another?

Ah fuck.

I guess I didn't grab a bitch, I picked two.

"Get out," I growled.

The one to my left let out a sleepy snort. "Excuse me? It's four in the morning."

"Yeah, get the fuck out." I threw an arm over my face, waiting for them to do as they were told.

"You're a fucking asshole. We're not leaving." This one was from the woman to my right. I could imagine the haughty look on her face without even having to look at her.

I sat up in bed without sparing the two of them a glance. I pushed Miss-Right-Bitch out of the way and climbed out of the huge, king-sized bed. She let out a nasty snarl, and from the corner of my eye, I saw her grabbing the bedsheet and trying to cover up her naked self.

Miss-Left-Bitch was silent but still sitting in *my* bed.

"I paid for this room. So, either you leave, or I call security to have you thrown out. I'm saving you some grace and keeping your dignity intact by only kicking you out and not having you thrown out. Now, Get. The. Fuck. Out," I warned while putting on my boxers.

I turned around, giving both of them a pointed look. "I'm going to take a piss. You have two minutes to leave this room before I have you thrown out. You wanted a taste of Coulter? You got it. Now, shall we go on our merry ways? In case you're wondering, no... I'm not putting a ring on your finger."

Blondie's eyes turned into slits as she glared at me. "Are you always like this?"

The bedsheet was still scandalously wrapped around her curvy body. It was tempting, I had to say. But my dick didn't rouse at the sight, so that would be a no for me.

"I don't even remember your name."

She let out a gasp, her hand flying to her tits in shock. Way overdramatic. This wasn't some goddamn soap opera.

The pounding headache was making it difficult to focus, so I blinked several times, trying to clear my blurry vision. How much did I drink? I couldn't remember shit.

"Two minutes," I snapped, before walking away. The bathroom door closed behind me, putting the lock in place, in case either of them had the stupid idea to join me. I didn't usually say no to shower sex, but I wasn't in a mood for another fuck session. My head was killing me, my body was sore and so was my dick.

After taking a piss, I walked out of the bathroom to see that Blondie had left, but her 'friend' was still here. Black hair, exotic sun-kissed skin and brown eyes, she looked like she had just walked out from a magazine.

And those chocolate brown eyes reminded me too much of Lila.

"My name is Tammy," she introduced, breathlessly, with a thick British accent. "I mean, you didn't ask for our names last night."

That was because I didn't need to know her name to fuck her. Nameless and faceless. There were countless women before her; she was just another lay. I was probably just another man on her list, too.

She only had her skimpy panties and bra on, her big tits practically spilling out. Any man would take their time with her body, but I wasn't that man.

Tammy sauntered over to me, stopping an inch away. Her tits brushed against my chest, and she smoothed her palm over my abs, sliding down toward my dick. She cupped me in her warm hand, rubbing me through my boxers. "C'mon, babe. Don't be like this. I thought you said we could go all night. We barely just started. Now that Jenna is gone, it's just us."

My patience was thin, and I snapped, roughly grabbing her arm and pulling her toward the door. On our way, I grabbed her black dress off the couch and dumped both outside the door.

Her face was a mask of fury, her lips parted, probably to curse me, but I slammed the door before she could go on a rage-filled rant. What a typical scene.

Yeah, I was being an asshole.

But fuck, I didn't have the strength to deal with girls like her right now.

I sank into the bed with my head still throbbing.

Sleep took over within a minute, but it was no beauty sleep.

"Run and hide. I'll count to twenty before coming to find you,"
Nala said to me with a giggle. We were playing hide and seek. It was
my favorite game to play with Nala because I was smart, and she could
never find me.

Mommy said I was the smartest.

That was why I always won our games.

Nala started counting, and I ran to the basement. She wouldn't find
me there. I had to find the perfect hiding place. Our house was huge, and
there were corners to hide, but Nala knew almost all of them by now.
We had been friends for a few weeks, and she discovered all my hiding
spots. So, I had to find a new one.

The closet!

I closed the door behind me and snuck under the shelf. Perfect spot.
I was going to win again. Mommy showed me this spot when we were
playing last time.

I waited and waited...and waited for Nala to find me.

It must have been a long time because my knees were starting to hurt from staying in the same position for too long.

I crawled from under my hiding spot and went to the door.

My heart froze when the door didn't budge.

I pulled harder.

It didn't open.

"Mommy," I called out, but then I realized…

My parents weren't home. Daddy said he had a business meeting, and they would be home late. They were always busy, always leaving the house in the morning before I woke up and coming home later, after I'd gone to bed. That was why Nala was here to keep me company. She was Mrs. Kavanaugh's daughter, our maid.

I pulled at the door even harder.

It wouldn't open.

No, no, no.

"Nala! Nala, I'm here. In the basement. Nala, come find me!"

I slapped the door, punched and kicked and screamed. My throat started to feel dry, and tears slid down my cheeks. I didn't like crying. I had to be strong, like daddy. He never cried.

But I couldn't… stop… the…tears…

"Daddy," I yelled, feeling myself go cold.

Scared… I was so scared and cold. Why was I so cold? My teeth rattled, and I shivered, feeling more tears slide down my cheeks. My face was wet as I cried more.

I didn't like this.

Why couldn't I open the door?

Why? Why?

I pulled and pulled, but the door was too heavy for me, and it wouldn't open.

"Mommy, please! Mommy! Daddy!" I screamed.

Why couldn't anyone hear me?

Maybe... maybe... they'd eventually realize I was missing, and they'd come find me later. Mommy knew of this hiding spot; she'd know where to find me.

I sank to the ground, bringing my knees to my chest.

Mommy and Daddy would find me, I knew they would.

"When they come home, they'll search for me," I murmured.

I had to be strong. Strong like Ironman. I had to be strong like Daddy.

I didn't know when I had fallen asleep or for how long, but when I opened my eyes again, it was dark.

So dark, I couldn't see anything.

The lights, what happened to them?

Oh no.

I couldn't see...

I couldn't breathe...

"Mommy!" I scrambled up, searching for an escape.

I punched the door, but my hands were too small, and they started hurting.

But I didn't stop.

I punched and screamed louder. "Mommy! I'm here. Daddy!"

It was so dark. I didn't like it; I didn't like the darkness. I never did. It scared me, that was why mommy always left my night light on.

"Help! Help me! I'm in the closet... help... me..."

I couldn't breathe...

I couldn't breathe....

"I can't... help.... I can't... breathe... mommy..."

My heart was beating too fast.

I couldn't see anything.

It was dark, so so dark.

My body shuddered, and I stumbled on the floor, next to the door, still scratching and punching.

"Can't... breathe... daddy... please... please... come find... me! Please..."

I cried.

I didn't want to; I had to be strong, but I couldn't stop.

I cried harder.

"I'm... scared..."

My hand went numb until I couldn't feel it anymore. "Don't... leave me here... mommy. Help," I whispered when I could no longer scream.

Everything hurt.

My head. My throat. My hand. My body.

Everything.

And it was so dark. There was a monster in the dark, like in the movies. I could feel it watching me, and my skin crawled.

The monster kept watching me; I couldn't see it, but it was there.

I still couldn't breathe.

"Help..."

Mommy and Daddy had promised they'd always find me wherever I hid. They said they could **feel** me because I was their baby, and they'd always know where I was.

They... lied.

They didn't find me.

"Don't... leave... me alone," I begged, but I could barely hear the words.

"Please."

My body swayed sideways, and I fell to the ground, my head touching the cold tiles of the closet. I curled into a small ball, trying to chase the cold away.

Come find me, mommy.

Don't leave me, daddy.

"Please... I'll be... a good boy. I... will... never ask... for another toy... or chocolate. I will...never cry again... I promise. I promise... I will... be good, a good boy... promise, mommy. Please, daddy... please..."

They lied.

They didn't find me.

"Help me."

They left me with the monster in the dark.

"Please."

They forgot me.

"Mommy... daddy..."

I jerked awake, gasping and breathless. My body was so cold; I was numb and shaking like a fucking leaf during a storm. The bedsheet was soaked with my sweat, and I swallowed past the heavy lump in my throat.

It was just a nightmare.

Lies.

How could it be *just* a nightmare if it followed me when I was awake?

My heart pounded in my chest, and there was dull pain.

The world spun, and I wanted to vomit as my stomach churned with nausea. The pain in my head flashed hard and heavy.

Breathe. Fucking breathe. Goddamn it.

Slamming my fist into the mattress, I let out a snarl. Hate. Anger. Self-loathing. Pain, so much fucking pain clashed together, and my head swam with all the emotions. Fuck this, FUCK!

I rolled over and grabbed the bottle on the nightstand.

I convinced myself I wasn't an alcoholic, but tonight... I had to drink, had to forget.

Taking a long sip, I felt the alcohol burn down my throat, and I winced, my brows furrowed tight with pain. My temples twitched, and it felt like I was sticking hot needles into my eyes as I continued to drink from the bottle.

My stomach heaved as I remembered how I called out for my parents, but they never came... and then I remembered crying on Lila's shoulders, like I had done before in that closet when I was seven years old.

Lila saw me at my weakest, and I hated her for holding me like that, as if she cared.

She didn't.

No one did.

My heart thumped harder, almost angrily, and it pumped acid through my veins, except I was...drowning.

It was then I realized that you didn't need water to drown.

Just like there hadn't been any real monster in that closet when I was seven years old, but the monsters had been in my head, and to this day, I couldn't escape them.

My body swayed, heavy and lethargic, as I took one last gulp before throwing the empty bottle on the floor. I fell back on the bed, sinking into oblivion.

Sweet fucking silence.

CHAPTER SIXTEEN

Lila

Gran pushed a box in my hand. "Storage, please."

She patted my cheek affectionately before rushing away to help the customer waiting for her. Gran was always on her toes. That was exactly why I told them to hire more people to help in the store. Old people were stubborn to the bone.

My gaze slid over to the windows as I walked out of the storage. When I caught sight of who I was looking for, my heart skittered a beat.

Black hoodie, ripped designer jeans and leather boots.

Maddox looked almost too good to be true. If I didn't know better, I'd say he was some kind of fallen angel. But he was anything but.

Maddox stood outside, his hood over his head as he smoked his cigarette in the cold. He had his hands shoved in his pockets, and his head bent low, staring at the ground.

Something had shifted between us since *that* day.

A week had gone by. Maddox was still his usual asshole self, but sometimes, I got the feeling he was purposely avoiding me.

The only time I saw real mirth in his eyes was when I hid a pink, glittery dildo in his locker. It was during lunch, the hallways crowded and bustling with students, when Maddox opened his locker. Mr. Big Ben aka Mr. Dildo slapped him square in the face while everyone around him gasped and promptly started laughing.

I had winked and sashayed away, satisfaction coursing through my veins, after seeing the look on his face. I made him grin, a real smile since that day we had been locked in the storage room.

The dildo prank was two days ago.

Yesterday, he retaliated with fake cockroaches in my bag and my sweater. I remembered throwing my bag on the ground, screaming bloody murder, while the students burst out laughing like it was the best joke of the century.

It was humiliating to say the least. I wanted to be mad. I had every right to be, but the moment I had spotted Maddox laughing, all my anger faded away.

Poof, just like that.

"He doesn't look very cheerful, does he?" Gran came to stand beside me, watching Maddox through the window. "He came in early today to help with inventory, and he hasn't eaten anything yet."

"He didn't have lunch?"

It was almost three in the afternoon.

A customer called for Gran, and she patted me on the arm before walking away.

Before I could think through my actions, call my instinct to help, I had grabbed a wrapped sandwich from the fridge and was walking out of the store.

Maddox looked up as I approached. He took one last inhale of his cigarette before throwing it on the ground and crushing it under his feet. He blew out a cloud of smoke before licking his lips, eyeing me up and down. "What's up, Garcia?"

Silently, I pushed the sandwich toward him.

He quirked up an eyebrow. "Is this a peace offering?"

"Gran said you didn't eat," I said as an explanation. I was just being... *nice*. There was nothing to it.

Maddox grabbed the sandwich from my hand, our fingertips touching briefly, before I quickly pulled away. "Careful there, Lila. You're starting to look like you care."

My eyes snapped to his, and I glared. "I'm being a decent human being. Give me back the goddamn sandwich if you're going to be an asshole."

Maddox was already ripping through the wrapping before I could finish my sentence. He took a huge bite, chewing hungrily. "Sorry, Sweet Cheeks. You can't give a hungry man food and take it away. Just like you can't put a pussy on display in front of a horny man and expect him not to devour you."

I blew out a breath. He was absolutely impossible. "Does everything have to be sexual for you?"

Maddox took another bite of the sandwich. "We were born to be sexual beings. Why not embrace it?"

I leaned against the window, watching the cars drive by, as Maddox devoured his sandwich in big bites. He was obviously hungry. Once he had polished the last bite, I broached the forbidden topic.

"That day... in the storage room," I started.

I didn't have to look at Maddox to feel the change in him. When he spoke, his voice said it all. "Speak of this again, and I will mess you up so fucking bad–"

"Why are you so full of anger?" I cut him off before he could finish his threat. "I'm not your enemy."

He let out a humorless laugh. "That's a pretty ironic thing to say considering our *relationship,* if you'd even call it that."

"It is ironic, isn't it?" I finally turned to look at him. He had a shoulder against the window, facing me. His eyes were bright blue in the sunlight, glimmering and hiding something darker.

Who was the man behind this mask?

"But I'm not going to hurt you. That was never my goal. I've only been trying to get even with you."

Maddox and I had been playing a game of cat and mouse. It was infuriating but harmless.

He cocked his head to the side. "So, you're saying, you won't hurt me unless I hurt you first?" he questioned with a rough, gravelly voice.

"Yeah, it's only fair. If you hurt me, I'll make you regret it."

"You're the first girl who hasn't fallen at my feet and begged me to fuck them."

"What does that make me?"

He grinned, wolfishly. "My prey."

I let out a laugh, instead of being offended like I would have been two months ago. "You have a one-track mind, Coulter."

"You're running circles around my head, Garcia."

Was that a… confession?

I backpedaled away from him. "Gran will expect us back to work in two minutes."

Swiveling around, I went to walk away but then stopped. There was a sinking feeling in my stomach, a gut-wrenching feeling that I was about to do something so fucking stupid. But I couldn't stop myself. I had always been a girl who planned ahead, never doing something so... reckless. After life punched me in the face and left me scars, I vowed I would never be foolish.

Always in control.

Always cautious.

But apparently Maddox's reckless habits had been rubbing off on me.

I marched back to Maddox, standing a mere foot away. So close I could feel his warmth.

"You know what? I think me and you can be really good friends," I announced, the words spilling out before I could stop myself.

Yeah. Stupid, right?

His eyes widened a fraction before he scoffed. "How does me wanting to get in your panties equal to us being good friends?" He eyed my hand, the one stretched out between us. "And are you really waiting for a handshake?"

Goddamn it, what was I thinking?

Heat burnt my cheeks in embarrassment. "I'm trying to be civil here," I said through clenched teeth. "I just think... if we're so good at being enemies, imagine us being on the same side?"

It was true. I was tired of fighting with Maddox, day after day, over and over again. It was time to call truce, to end this war and to start over.

There was an unreadable gleam in his eyes when he spoke. "You'll bring Berkshire to its knees, Sweet Cheeks."

I'm going to bring you to your knees. I kept that tidbit to myself.

Maddox looked thoughtful for a second. He rubbed a thumb across his square jaw before giving me a simple nod. "Fine."

Wait...really? I blinked, waiting for him to laugh and call me pathetic.

He didn't.

Maddox stared at me expectantly.

Holy shit.

I swallowed past the nervous lump in my throat, and this time, I showed him my pinky. "We solemnly swear to not share any animosity between us anymore and we'll play nice."

If Maddox thought I was being stupid, he didn't show it on his face. "I solemnly swear not to be an asshole, but I'll still think of sixty-nine ways of how I can dick you down every time you look at me or shake your ass my way."

"Maddox!" I hissed, heat blooming in my cheeks at his crude words. I was no saint, but damn it, he knew how to make a girl blush.

He let out a throaty chuckle, the sound coming deep from his chest. Maddox wrapped his pinky around mine, squeezing it the slightest bit.

My lungs burnt, and I realized I'd forgotten to breathe.

This is it, I reminded myself.

The end of something; the beginning of something else.

I didn't know how serious Maddox was or if he'd keep his words... I didn't know if he knew the meaning of *friends*, I didn't know what tomorrow would bring us, if he'd be back to his usual asshole self, but I knew one thing – I no longer wanted to be on the opposite side of Maddox.

"Friends?" I breathed.

"Friends," he agreed.

Maddox

I watched Lila walk away, back into her grandparents' store. I scratched my three-day old stubble over my jaw, thoughtful.

The door closed behind her, hiding the perfect view of her ass from my feasting gaze. I had to remind myself to look away because, fuck me, Lila could bring any man to his knees with an ass like that.

Our eyes locked through the glass window, and she was *smiling*. A genuine fucking smile.

Lila waved at me to come inside, and my feet followed. If I was a puppy, my tail would be wagging back and forth.

Ah, for fuck's sake.

Friends?

Friends.

I paused at the door, blinking as I came to a sudden realization.

The moment Lila aimed for my dick in that coffee shop, I was fascinated. Girls were usually on their knees for me, worshipping my dick like it was the best meal of their lives. I never had a girl who wanted to cause Maddox-Junior pain instead of pleasure, until Lila.

When she had smirked over her shoulder before walking away, I was instantly intrigued. Who was this girl?

I made it my mission to find more about her, to study her... and to break her. She was my pet project, and I had wanted to bring her to her knees. Someone feisty as her? It would be sweet when she'd finally *beg* me.

Two months later...

Lila Garcia just fucking friend-zoned me.

Well, shit.

A laugh bubbled from my chest. Little Miss Perfectionist was ballsy, I had to admire that. I never had a girlfriend before. If someone had a pair of tits, Maddox Junior had a one-track mind. Sex. Plain and simple.

Lila had three things that made me weak: tits, pussy and ass big enough for my greedy hands.

I scoffed at the thought. This was going to be interesting. I wondered how long she'd last. The games have changed; the tables have turned, and I was going to play her game now.

Who was going to break first?

The player or the prey?

Fuck, this was going to be fun.

CHAPTER SEVENTEEN

Lila

A firm hand landed on my ass, squeezing the soft flesh like its personal stress ball. The warmth of his body radiated against my back and the familiar, spicy scent of his cologne filled my nose.

"Take your hands off my ass. We're friends, Coulter."

When he didn't let go, I elbowed him, and he let out a small *ouf*. Maddox came to my side as we walked to our English class. "Wait, I thought you meant friends with benefits. Because that's the only type of *friends* I do."

I rolled my eyes. Day three of us being friends, and Maddox was still an asshole. A somewhat bearable jerk, but still a jerk. Apparently, he couldn't grasp the concept of *just friends* and was still trying to cop a feel.

Well, I couldn't really fault him since he caught me eyeing his dick print again yesterday. He didn't say a word, but his stupid smirk was enough.

"No. I meant normal friends. As in, you respect my boundaries, and I respect yours. Stop. Getting. So. Touchy."

"So, you mean, I can't slam you against the wall and fuck you?"

Sweet Jesus, help me, or I was going to murder this dude.

Exasperated, I gave him a look that said it all. "That's the opposite of friends, Maddox."

"Well, that's disappointing. You've seen how good I am on the field, but I was looking forward to showing you how good I am at thrusting."

There was a flash of mischief in his eyes, and my lips twitched. He was being annoying on purpose, the dumbass. Sure, we were still stumbling over this new friendship thing, but it wasn't so bad. At least, I didn't find any more cockroaches in my sweater today and no pink dildo for Maddox.

As expected, when we walked into Mrs. Levi's class, all eyes were on us. The attention had me on edge, but with Maddox constantly at my side, I was starting to get used to it.

People always stared, after all, Maddox was the center of attention. He loved it, practically feeding off it. His chest puffed out like a proud peacock, eyes gleaming, and his signature smirk plastered on his full lips. Girls fawned, and guys burnt with jealousy.

Now that I was on Maddox's side, more like he kept me next to him all the time, we turned heads wherever we went. People assumed we were fucking, and I was his latest conquest. Some said I was his girlfriend.

No one believed we were just…friends.

Even Riley was suspicious at first, but she finally understood the nature of our relationship when Maddox stole my apple, and in revenge, I sprayed ketchup on his crotch. Childish and stupid, right?

But there was just something about Maddox that made me feel…carefree.

I ditched the front row and followed Maddox to the back of the classroom, where he always sat. Settling next to Maddox, which put me in the middle of him and his friend, I gave Colton a nod in greeting.

He smiled and fist pumped Maddox. "The whole school is talking."

My lips flattened in a straight line. "They need to stop gossiping."

"That's their job. To gossip," Maddox said with a lazy smile. "What's so bad about being my girlfriend, Garcia?"

"Because I'm *not*."

"You sure?" Colton shot back.

There was one thing I learned during these three days.

Colton and Cole were twins, but they were nothing alike. Cole was more reserved, the quiet type. He didn't always hang around with us, and he was less of an asshole and more of a gentleman. In fact, you'd think Colton and Maddox were twins because… they were both pompous jerks. Attitude and personality, both were fuckboys and infuriating.

Now that Maddox and I were *friends*, that meant his friends were mine. Poor Riley got dragged into this mess, too.

Riley was ready to deck Colton any time now, and I wanted to raise my white flag in defeat, but refrained from doing so. My mama didn't raise a quitter.

"If you two are going to gang up on me, I'm going back to the front row." I went to stand up, grabbing my bag with me.

Colton raised his hands up in mock defeat, and Maddox grinned. "Keep your ass seated on that chair, Garcia. I'll drag you back if I have to."

I plopped back on the chair. "I'm not your pet, Coulter."

He leaned closer, his lips next to my ear, so he could whisper while Mrs. Levi started her lesson. "You're kinda cute when you're pissed off."

"Shut. Up."

He sat back in his chair, looking quite satisfied with himself, like he had just tamed a dragon. As if. I ignored him and focused on the lesson instead. Sure, he was distracting, but I wasn't going to let him affect my perfect GPA.

Hours ticked by, slowly... so goddamn slow...until the final bell rang. It was a long day of being scrutinized and glared at, and the whispers followed everywhere I went. It didn't matter if Maddox and I were enemies or friends; I was an outsider, always had been and always would be.

Some were curious, some were just plain mean about it.

I heard she's poor. She's probably just fucking him for money. Desperate whore.

She's not even that pretty.

Do you think she's fucking Maddox's dad, too? I wouldn't be surprised if she has a sugar daddy.

Oh my God, that's so funny! Both father and son. Her hole is probably so stretched out.

She might be fucking her way through the whole football team.

They didn't understand why Maddox was so fascinated by me, their words, or why me and not them. Honestly, neither did I. Maddox was somewhat a mystery even to me. Why did he put me on his radar?

Riley let out a huff, her face red with anger. "What the fuck is wrong with them?"

"Just…ignore it," I said, breathing out a tired sigh. "They'll eventually grow bored and choose another victim."

"It's not fair."

No, it wasn't, but I was learning to accept my fate.

Riley, bless her heart, looked ready to attack someone, but I pulled her back.

"You have dance practice, right? Don't be late." I nudged her toward the door.

She let out a sigh and gave me a sad look. "You can't them walk all over you, Lila. I did that. I let them bully me to their satisfaction and they took everything from me. My friends, my popularity, my pride… until I had nothing left. They are like vultures. They won't stop until they break you apart. You need to show them who's boss because *you are.*"

After all, I had nothing to be scared of. Maddox was on my side now. His friend. His only friend who was a girl. I had more power than any of the girls he slept with. He was king, and as much as I hated it, that made me the unofficial queen. Berkshire Academy was my kingdom.

But no one wanted a cold queen. The last thing I wanted to do was have them despise me any more than they already did.

Once Riley left, I walked into the bathroom since my bladder was close to exploding. The bus wasn't going to be here for another fifteen minutes, so I had enough time.

I was washing my hands when it happened.

When they rounded up on me.

In the mirror, I caught sight of four girls. I recognized two of them. Bethany, probably the most popular girl in Berkshire, and her best friend, Suraiya. The other two girls were familiar, but I didn't know them well enough to know their names.

They circled around me, and I shut off the tap, shaking away the droplets of water from my hands.

"Can I help you?" I asked, suspicious of their sudden appearance.

"She can speak," Bethany mocked, with a fake innocence.

"If you've got nothing to say, I'm leaving." I walked past her, and she grabbed my arm, digging her long nails into my skin. I didn't flinch, but it stung like a bitch.

"Not so fast, *Garcia*." She said my name like it was a stain.

"What do you want?" I wasn't scared, but I didn't like how there was one of me and four of them. They crowded around me, trying to be intimidating.

Bethany smiled, though it looked every bit as fake and malicious as she was. "I just wanted to give you a little…warning."

I laughed. "Maddox? Right, of course. Go ahead, give me your warning."

I tried to appear unfazed, but I knew what was coming. They were here for a reason. The fact that I wasn't cowering or begging for them to spare me angered them.

"Let's just say, I'm trying to save you some face. Maddox will grow tired of you, soon enough, and he'll drop you like yesterday's trash. You're going to be hurt because that's what he does. He breaks girls like you for a hobby."

I returned her fake smile with one of my own. "Oh, like he grew tired of you and threw you out like yesterday's trash?"

The corners of her eyes twitched, and her smile slipped off her lips.

I wasn't done yet. If she wanted to be a bitch, I was going to show her how to play the game right.

I shook her hand off me, tsking under my breath. "I remember that day. Gossip tends to travel fast."

Last year when I was still the new girl, Maddox and Bethany slept together. The next day, she publicly claimed she was his girlfriend, but he turned her down in front of everyone by saying: *You were a good lay but not good enough to earn the title of my girlfriend.*

It was harsh, and things turned ugly that day.

But Bethany was rich and spoiled as well as the cheerleading captain. She was Miss Popular and gossip like that didn't affect her. Sure, her pride was wounded, but she bounced back quickly and kept the title of queen bee.

She growled and lashed forward, backhanding me in the face. I didn't see it coming, and it *hurt.* The metallic taste of blood filled my mouth when I tried to lick my aching, bruised lips. Her friend kneed me in the back of my legs, and I fell to my knees.

"You're easily disposable, Lila. I claimed Maddox a long time ago, and all the girls of Berkshire know he's my property. That's the same as playing with fire."

Maddox... her property?

Oh fuck. My stomach cramped, and I busted out laughing. This was probably the most hilarious shit I've heard in this decade.

They looked at me like I was a maniac. Maybe I was.

I was about to get my ass beaten, and here I was laughing at my assailants.

Bethany hissed, her face growing red. Poor little, insecure Bethany.

She pressed her thumb against my bleeding lip, and I forced

myself not to flinch. She smirked and pressed harder. It hurt so much that unshed tears burnt the back of my eyes. "You're as pathetic as I thought. Dirt poor, not beautiful enough, so easily forgotten and so easily replaceable that you had to grab onto the richest and most popular guy."

Her voice told me everything I needed to know.

I was poor and beneath them. Maybe I wasn't as pretty or as rich as Bethany and the rest of Berkshire, but... Bethany, she felt *threatened* by me.

"I don't slut shame, but I can smell a bitch from a mile away," I said lazily. "You smell of jealousy. Very stanky. Go take a shower, sweetie."

Bethany gave me a disdainful sneer, her face twisting, and I saw all the ugliness she hid beneath the sweet girl mask that everyone loved and bowed down to.

She was Berkshire's official Queen, a pretty face with a nasty soul and a hideous heart. Her minions still had their hands on me, holding me in place and keeping me from attacking them. They had successfully trapped me; my arms twisted painfully behind my back and their knees were pressed into my shoulder blades, keeping me close to the ground.

Bethany crossed her arms over her huge tits, smirking down at me. "How would your grandparents feel if they lost their grocery store? Their only income and source of survival? They've had the store for fifteen years now, right? I guess, it's time to close down."

So, she did her research on me.

Bethany brought her face closer to me, and I saw the evil glint in her eyes. "Tsk, how sad would it be to watch them beg my daddy? I can ruin you and your little family. All I have to do is snap my fingers, and I'll watch you burn to the ground."

Rage bubbled over. She thought I was weak. She and her minions thought I was helpless.

Bethany gripped my jaw, her long nails digging into my sensitive flesh. "Where's Maddox now? Your hero is not here to save you."

I let out a small laugh.

Maddox, my hero?

She was mistaken.

I was my own hero.

I didn't need him to protect me or my family. I was my own protector in this story. Like Maddox once said, I didn't need a prince charming or a knight in shining armor.

Bethany's first mistake was standing too close to me. She had underestimated me. Once again.

My head reared back before I brought it forward, slamming my forehead into her nose. Hard.

She screamed, her wails piercing, as she pushed away from me. I twisted my arms away, kicked back at my attackers before standing up on my feet again.

I wasted no time and grabbed Bethany by the throat before she could escape and slammed her against the bathroom's wall.

"Don't. Fuck. With. Me," I hissed. Blood gushed from her nose; it wasn't broken, but I knew it was probably painful as fuck.

She glared at me, but too bad she was no longer in control. Her friends tried to grab my arms, to pull me away from their queen bee, but I held her tighter. Her throat was small and delicate in my hand.

"Don't fuck with me," I repeated. "You won't like the consequences. You might not like to get your hands dirty, but I don't mind. After all, I'm a poor, dirty rat, right? You don't threaten my grandparents. You don't threaten me. Because trust me, I will destroy you. I have my ways, Bethany Fallon. That's your first and only warning."

I pushed away from her, and she gasped for breath, wheezing. "You... fucking... bitch."

Suraiya tried to grab me, but I sidestepped out of her way. "You'll end up with a broken nose, too," I warned.

She smartly took a step back, and I *smiled*. Yeah, maybe I did look like a maniac in the moment, but Riley had been right. I couldn't let them walk all over me.

Bethany's minions surrounded her as she moaned and cried about her nose. I gave them a final glance and walked out of the bathroom.

I wasn't Miss Popular; I wasn't rich or the cheerleading captain... but the lack of these titles didn't make me weak because I was no doormat.

The next time they threatened the people I loved, I'd show them my teeth and claws.

CHAPTER EIGHTEEN

Lila

I stumbled out of school, my legs feeling a bit shaky. My knees were bruised from where they had slammed me on the bathroom floor. My lips throbbed, and I could feel a headache coming. That was one hell of a slap, kudos to Bethany.

As I walked through the main gates, the bus drove past me, and I stood there, dumbfounded. Damn it, I missed my bus. Fists clenched, I held in the urge to cry because now was not the time for it.

It was cold. I was moody and in pain.

But I. Would. Not. Cry.

"Lila!"

My steps faltered at the sound of Maddox's voice. Huh.

"Lila, what the fuck?" he called out. I looked over my shoulder to see him running toward me. His mouth was curled in a dark scowl as he approached me.

My dark hair fell as a curtain around my face, and I looked down at my feet. I didn't want him to see the bruises, didn't want his pity or his stupid, mocking laugh.

But Maddox, being Maddox...

He crowded into my space, his front pressing against my back. His arm curled around my waist, and he pulled me into his body.

"How did this happen?" he asked, his voice low and serious.

"What do you want?"

"The back of your skirt is ripped. Doesn't look like an accident. Who did this?"

What?

I pushed away from Maddox and reached behind me to realize that he was right. There was a large tear in my Berkshire skirt, big enough for my panties to be visible and everyone could see it. No wonder I felt the cold breeze on my ass.

Anger flared up inside me, and I let out a shuddering breath.

I didn't want to cry because I was hurt or humiliated. They were tears of outrage, and I swiped at my cheeks, refusing to let Maddox see them.

"*Lila*," Maddox said slowly. The sound of my name came from his lips so softly, as if he cared. It was stupid, but my heart still did a silly jump.

He grasped my shoulders and turned me around to face him. I kept my face lowered, but he was having none of that. His fingers grazed my cheeks, and he brushed my hair away from my face.

When he let out a string of curses, I knew he saw the bruises. His hand clenched my arm, and he dragged me to the bench. I tried to pull out of his grip, but he held tight.

He sat me down and knelt in front of me, looking like a dark, angry warrior. He was...pissed?

"Who did this?" he asked, his voice hard and strained.

"Your girlfriend," I shot back. I wretched my hand from his grasp and crossed my arms over my chest. "She isn't too happy about our friendship status."

His eyes turned into slits, and he gave me a hard look. "Bethany," Maddox hissed under his breath. "She's going to regret this."

I scoffed at that. "I don't need a protector. I can take care of myself."

His lips twitched. Even though his expression was hard and serious, the humor was back in his blue eyes. "No, you're right. You're the dragon."

Ha. Very funny.

I rolled my eyes and looked around us. Most of the students had gone home already, and I was probably two or three of the few who took a bus, since everyone had a car or a driver to pick them up. Perks of being rich, I guessed.

"What are you doing here?"

Maddox dragged his fingers through his hair, still short since his last haircut. I couldn't decide if I liked the long hair better, but I missed his poodle hair.

"Coach needed to speak to me. I was about to leave when I saw you walking out of the building and noticed the tear in your skirt. Nice panties, by the way. It reminds me of your cherry lips."

Mental facepalm incoming: 3...2...1.

Maddox brought his hand up, his thumb brushing over my sore lips. "Are you going to tell me what happened?"

I gave him a sheepish grin. "I can tell you about the part where I broke her nose and choked her."

"Atta girl," he praised out loud. "I was almost worried you were going to tell me you didn't fight back."

He grabbed my water bottle from my bag, and I watched as he wet his handkerchief. Against my nature, I stayed silent and *watched* him. His eyebrows furled in concentration, his lips in a firm, straight line, and his eyes darkened as he studied my bruises.

Maddox pressed the wet handkerchief over my lips, rubbing gently to clean the dried blood. I flinched but stayed still for him. He then swiped it over my cheek, which was almost on fire. Bethany's ring must have caught my skin. I let out a sigh when I realized it would be a nasty green or purple shade tomorrow.

"I don't like how you got hurt because of me," he finally admitted. Maddox touched my cheek, his thumb hovering over my wound. His touch was gentle and soothing.

"Feeling guilty, Poodle?"

His eyes snapped to mine, glaring. "It's not funny."

"What's not funny, *Poodle*?"

"Lila," he warned.

"Yes, Poodle."

"You're hurt!"

I pressed my finger over my cheek and winced, then gave him a nod in confirmation. "Yup, I can feel that."

He fumed, silently. His jaw clenched, and I swore I heard his teeth grinding together. Finally, I let the poor guy out of his misery. "I don't blame you. Bethany was a bitch. I dealt with it, and it's over now. Little scratches can't hurt me because they don't leave permanent scars."

Maddox stood up and offered me a hand. I grabbed it, and he pulled me up to my feet. "Fine. Let me drive you home."

The world came to a halt at his words, and my knees weakened.

I suddenly forgot how to breathe as my eyes watered. Sweat trickled down my forehead and between my breasts. I choked on my saliva as the gut-wrenching feeling in my stomach had me wanting to throw up.

The long, jagged scar between my breasts throbbed with a ghostly ache, a reminder. It wasn't painful anymore, but my body and my mind remembered the pain.

"No," I choked out.

Maddox gripped me by the elbow. "For fuck's sake, Lila. Just let me—"

"No!"

He didn't understand; he didn't fucking understand.

I stumbled back and away from him, desperately trying to count backward.

Ten... nine...eight...

"Lila."

His voice sounded so far away, as if I was submerged under water, and he was yelling at me from the sky.

Seven...six... five...four...three...two...one.

I opened my eyes and took a shuddering deep breath. Maddox was staring at me with an unreadable expression, and it angered me, not knowing what he was thinking.

Was it pity? Or was he judging me? Did he even notice I just had an anxiety attack?

"I'll take the bus... thank you for the...offer though," I spoke, trying to hide the tremors in my voice.

He took a long moment but finally gave me a slow nod. Maddox silently peeled his blazer off his body. I didn't expect it, but he stepped closer to me, his body flush against mine. He was a whole head taller, so he towered over me. He wrapped his arms around my waist, and I stilled, my lips parting in shock. When I looked down, I saw him tying a knot with the sleeves of his blazer around my hips.

It laid heavily against the back of my ass and legs.

He was… covering up my ripped skirt.

"I got you," he breathed in my ear, before pulling away.

I opened my mouth to say thank you, but I couldn't find the words. Maddox looked over my shoulder and gave me a small smile. "The bus is here."

I nodded, still stupidly silent. *Say something, damnit. Anything.*

His hands were shoved in his pockets as he watched me climb into the bus. I settled in the back, like always. Maddox was still watching me.

I pressed my palm against the window, and he grinned, boyish and sexy.

Thank you, I mouthed as the bus drove away.

The next morning, as I stepped out of the house, Maddox and his car were there waiting. He rolled down his window and beckoned me over.

"What are you doing?" I asked. "Stalker much, Coulter?"

He handed me a brown paper bag. "Good morning to you, too, Sweet Cheeks. You look better today. No bruises, I see."

My bruises, which I had successfully been able to hide from my grandparents, were covered with makeup. I shrugged and took whatever Maddox was offering me. "Makeup did the trick."

I peeked inside the bag. Mint. Chocolate. Muffin. Oh my God! "You–"

"You're welcome," he said.

I let out a laugh. "Seriously, what are you doing?"

"I thought you said we were friends."

I eyed him suspiciously. "We are."

"So, I'm getting you breakfast. You and Riley tend to share lunch, right?"

I couldn't decide if this was sweet or dorky, neither of which suited Maddox Coulter. I gave his SUV a once over. "I'm not getting in your car if you're trying to bribe me with my favorite muffin. For all I know, you could be a kidnapper or an axe murderer."

Maddox winked. "I'd make a sexy axe murderer, admit it."

I rolled my eyes, for the umpteenth time, and took a bite of my mint chocolate muffin. "My bus is here," I muttered around a mouthful. I bent down, so we were eye-level and gave him a smirk of my own. "You can follow me to school. Like you followed me home yesterday. You need to improve your stalking skills, Coulter."

The look on his face was comical. Busted, Poodle.

I winked and sashayed away.

We rode to Berkshire separately, although it didn't quite feel like it. The muffin he gave me kept me company. I tried to devour it slowly, but mint chocolate was my one and only weakness.

Maddox was waiting for me at the gate when I stepped off the bus. He hoisted his bag on one shoulder and gripped my hand. Surprised, I looked down at our interlocked fingers as he pulled me into the building. Wh-what?

"What are you doing?" I asked with caution.

"Holding your hand."

His hand was warm and strong. I wasn't sure how to feel about it, but I didn't pull away. "Why?"

His eyes briefly met mine before he went back to staring everyone else down. "Because I need the world to know they can't mess with what's mine."

It was on the tip of my tongue to rebut him. I didn't need a savior, didn't need to cower behind Maddox's back because I could handle all the haters on my own. Yesterday, I let my claws out and I was no longer worried about using them.

But when I saw the look on his face, hard and serious—I swallowed the words.

Something in his eyes told me he wasn't going to budge on this matter.

I didn't know *why* I kept silent and let him hold my hand. It bugged me why I did it, but then I pushed the feeling down.

We marched through the halls, and the students stepped out of our way, like the ocean parting in half for us to walk through.

I bit my tongue, held my chin high and kept my hand in Maddox's. His grip was firm, but comforting. I expected the whispers to follow us but was met with...*nothing*.

By lunch time, I couldn't bite my tongue any longer. The day went on just like this morning. The other students avoided eye-contact, no one glared or sneered at me and no one dared to approach me. Even Riley found it odd.

When Maddox reached for my fries, I slapped his hand away and leveled him with a look. "Did you do something? Did you threaten people? They're acting weird."

Riley gave me a grunt of agreement.

Maddox took a bite of his sandwich, simultaneously throwing an arm around the back my chair, before glancing around the cafeteria to give his *kingdom* a once over. "I think you were threatening enough for both of us."

"Huh?"

"Bethany's nose isn't broken, but you did a number on her. Gossip travels fast."

"They're scared of me?"

"They're scared of *us*," he amended.

I picked at my fries, no longer hungry. "Am I going to get in trouble... for hurting Bethany?"

Colton pushed back against his chair, rocking on the two back legs. "No, you won't. We took care of that already."

My eyes snapped to Maddox, frowning. "So, you *did* threaten someone."

The side of his lips quirked up. "I have my ways."

I should've been mad; I should've told him to mind his own business.

I really should have.

But then I had a brief moment of realization – he was *protecting* me. Even though I told him numerous times that I didn't want him to. It was a very different Maddox, from the one who was jerk to me and it was shocking to the say the least. I was curious how far he'd go... to be my friend.

The moment Maddox and I did that pinky swear outside of my Gran's grocery store, it became obvious that my business was his and his was mine. It was an unspoken understanding between us.

We both shared a smile.

And that was it.

The beginning of something Maddox and I weren't ready for.

That day, we somehow sealed our friendship.

Friends?

Yeah, friends.

CHAPTER NINETEEN

Maddox

Three weeks later

Lila slammed her thick textbook closed and growled low in her throat. If she thought she was being intimidating, she was highly mistaken. That was a kitten growl, cute and harmless.

"You're distracting me. Stop!" she said through clenched teeth, keeping her voice low since we were both huddled in a corner of the library.

"What am I doing?" I feigned innocence because, seriously, my favorite pastime was annoying her.

She was studying for our upcoming calculus test while I was watching… porn. Okay, fine. Not exactly porn. But Tumblr was *nasty*, and I was making a habit of showing Lila all the videos I came across. Miss Garcia didn't find that amusing, but it was hilarious to me, so she was growling and hissing. Like I said, a kitten.

I didn't know if I had a semi-boner because of the videos I was watching or because Lila was sitting across me. Probably a bit of both.

"Do you realize you're the most frustrating person I've ever met in my life?" she finally snapped. I bit my tongue to keep from laughing.

I'd give her credit, though, for lasting three weeks as my *friend*.

I thought she would break, but no, Lila was fierce, something I greatly admired about her.

She plugged her earphones in and went back to her textbook. Her notebook was filled with equations as she did the practice questions over and over again. Over the past few weeks, I've learned a few things about Lila:

    1. She was a perfectionist.

    2. She wanted to get into Harvard and was still waiting on her confirmation letter to come through. Every day, she grew more anxious, although she tried hard to hide it. Since I got a football scholarship, I already had an early acceptance to Harvard.

    3. She loved her grandparents dearly.

    4. She was competitive as fuck.

Two minutes later, Lila gave up. She snatched her earphones out and glared at me. I tried to wipe the grin off my face, but damn it, it was hard when she was being so... *cute.*

"I know you're getting into Harvard with a football scholarship but don't your marks need to be just as good, or you could lose your scholarship?"

I swiped out of Tumblr as she ranted. My textbook and notebook laid in front me, untouched. "Yeah."

"Then, why are you not taking any of your classes seriously?"

Ah, so she was on my case. I refrained from rolling my eyes and shrugged instead. "I don't care."

"So, you're okay with not playing football after high school and losing your scholarship?"

That made me pause.

I didn't care about school or Harvard... but football was my fucking kryptonite. Similar to how Lila was my favorite drug of choice, sweet and so fucking addictive.

I was MC–Maddox Coulter, Berkshire's reckless quarterback and Casanova.

But there was just something about Lila that kept me... grounded. It wasn't exactly a bad thing but it wasn't a good thing either. I didn't like how she could get under my skin, and I didn't like how she could read me so easily. It made me feel... weak, like that time in the closet. She saw everything I didn't want anyone to see. And even now, she could see through me.

"It doesn't matter. I'm getting into Harvard either way."

"Because your parents are going to buy your way into Harvard. Gotcha."

My head snapped up at the tone of her voice. She sounded... *disappointed*. In me.

My parents were on the Board of Directors for Harvard. It didn't matter if my marks weren't good, I wasn't going to lose my scholarship. They'd make sure of it. After all, that was all they ever did for me. Pay my way through Berkshire, throw a cheque at me, give me a fancy car for my birthday although they were never actually present on the day... it was all ever materialistic to them. Harvard was no different. Maybe paying for me to get in Harvard would actually remind them they did in fact have a son.

"You're getting into Harvard because of your parents." She

paused, giving me a look as she studied me. "How about for once in your life, you don't depend on your parents' money and reputation. Why don't you do it for *you*? On your own. Through your own hard work and failures... and success on your own merits."

Her eyes bore into mine, looking...searching into my soul.

My jaw clenched and the muscles in my cheeks twitched. "Thanks for the pep talk, Garcia. Do I need to slow clap?"

"Still an unapologetic asshole," she whispered. Lila looked thoughtful for a second before she leaned closer, her face a mere inch away from mine. *"I dare you..."*

Bewildered, I let out a laugh. "What?"

Lila didn't laugh. In fact, I'd never seen her more serious. The look on her face made me capitulate, and my laughter turned into a coughing fit as she waited, patiently.

When I cleared my throat, she nudged her chin high and gave me another one of her I'm-serious-right-now looks. "I dare you to get into Harvard on your own, to keep your scholarship without your parents' help."

I blinked.

Then blinked a-fucking-gain.

She was kidding, right?

"Chop chop. Gotta work your ass off, Coulter." Lila paused and gave me a mock gasp. "Oh wait... don't tell me, are you chickening out? Gonna lose this dare? Tsk, so disappointing. Here I thought *the* Maddox Coulter will never turn down a dare."

She was goading me, waiting for a reaction.

Fuck it.

She got me.

Lila got the reaction she wanted.

I gripped the back of her neck and brought her face closer to mine. She had to lean forward, half of her body bending over the table. Her lips parted with a silent gasp, and her eyes darkened. "I accept this dare."

Her lips twitched, and she smirked. Yeah, I was definitely rubbing off on her. Miss Perfectionist was now a she-devil.

"Good luck because you're about to get your ass kicked. First level of this dare, you have to pass this calculus test."

"Easy fucking peasy."

"Really?" She raised an eyebrow, not at all convinced.

"I'm a genius, Sweet Cheeks."

Little did she know…

She cocked her head to the side, her hair falling over one shoulder. Lila looked every bit the wet dream she was —sexy, smart as hell, bold and passionate.

And my friend.

My dick was regretting this and begging for mercy.

Goddamn it.

She gave me a sugary smile. "Game on."

Four hours later, Lila closed her textbook. She leaned her head back against the chair and stretched, a small groan escaping her lips. I didn't know how she did it, but Lila barely came up for air in those four hours. Her eyes barely came off her textbook.

I closed my own notebook and studied my little friend. "Ready to go home?"

"Yeah, I'm exhausted." She piled her things in her shoulder bag and stood up.

"Will you let me give you a ride this time?" I asked, even though

I already knew the answer.

Lila paused. "No."

I didn't push because the day she lost her shit on me was still a vivid memory in my mind. She panicked when I asked her to get in the car; I saw it in her eyes, on her face and the way her body trembled.

My fists clenched at my sides. The question was on the tip of my tongue as her lips pursed.

"The bus will be here in ten minutes. You can leave now if you want."

I stood up next to her, and we walked out of the library. "I'll wait."

Because...

Just... *because.*

We waited at the bus stop. Lila shivered, and I could hear her teeth rattling from the cold.

"Lila," I started.

"Hmm?"

My lips parted; I went to ask the question that has been burning inside me for the longest time, but I couldn't form the sentence. Lila lifted her head up and stared, waiting.

"You refuse to get in a car... is it because of your accident?"

Lila gave me a wide-eye grimace, and I instantly regretted probing. The crestfallen look on her face, as if she had been sucker-punched and viciously thrown into a lake where she couldn't swim back up for oxygen – *that* almost gutted me.

Her eyes were tortured, and they reminded me of myself when I looked in the mirror.

"Your parents..."

"They died in that car accident," she whispered. Each word felt

like they had been torn from her throat, raw and painful. "I was...
I was the only one... the only survivor. They... died...they didn't...
pull through."

I cupped her cheek. "Is that why you can't get in a car?"

She nodded, one slow nod. Lila silently spilled her secrets, so
trusting of me, and my heart thudded in my chest.

From the corner of my eye, I saw the bus approaching. She
must have noticed it too because her eyes darted that way, and she
quietly sniffled.

Lila looked like she was swallowing a bitter lump of tears. My
fingers brushed against her cold cheeks, and she gazed at me with
burning eyes, her chest heaving.

One single tear trailed down her cheek, and I caught it before
swiping it away.

I'm sorry, I wanted to say.

She gave me the tiniest smile, so strong yet so delicate. *It's okay.*
Thank you, her eyes told me.

Lila took a step back, and my hand fell away from her face. I
wanted to keep her pinned to me, wanted to hug her... but when
she nudged her chin high and regarded me with red eyes, shining
with fierce intensity, I let her go.

She didn't need me to swoop in to be her hero or her protector.

Long after the bus had disappeared from my view and she
was gone, I stayed at the bus stop, with an overwhelming set of
emotions swimming inside of me.

What started out as a game for me was not a game anymore.

Lila was truly and honestly my...friend.

The last thing I wanted to do was hurt her. In fact, I didn't like
the thought of her hurting at all. I didn't know when or how it
happened. But too soon, Lila became someone important to me.

Maybe it was when she hugged me in that dark closet and sang me a lullaby.

Or when she had offered me that tuna sandwich.

Or maybe it was when I wrapped my pinky around hers and did that silly pinky swear.

But somehow, Lila Garcia became more than just my prey.

She was someone I wanted to protect.

From the world.

From *me*.

CHAPTER TWENTY

Lila

Two months later

I stayed by my locker after the last bell rang, keeping a close eye on Riley and Grayson. She approached him, blushing and stuttering as she asked him about yesterday's homework. It was an excuse to talk to him. They chatted for less than five minutes before Riley gave Grayson a warm smile and bounced away.

It was so quick; anyone would have missed it. But I was looking and I caught Grayson watching her leave, his stare intense and his lips twisting with amused smile. Grayson rarely ever smiled.

From the corner of my eyes, I noticed someone else watching the encounter. Colton had his hands shoved in the pockets of his beige slacks as he leaned against his locker. His jaw clenched, and I swore the corners of his eyes twitch. No, that must have been my imagination.

But something was up with him, and it piqued my curiosity.

I snuck a glance at my phone, half expecting a text to pop up, but... nothing. Damn it, I was starting to worry now.

"Colton," I called out as he walked past me.

He paused and jerked his chin up at me in greeting. "Sup, Lila?"

"Did you see Maddox today? He's not replying to my texts or answering my calls," I asked cautiously.

An unreadable expression passed over Colton's face, and he scratched his chin before looking down at his own phone as if waiting for it to light up with a text, too. "No. He's not replying to mine either."

That was weird. Maddox never went radio silent on us, well... *me* before today. In fact, he was always the first to pester me in the early morning and until late at night with his horrible and silly jokes.

Maddox: *What's black, red, black, red, black, red?*

Me: *Idk. Let me sleep.*

Maddox: *A zebra with a sunburn.*

He always found a random joke to tell me at night; that was our goodnight. At first, I didn't know if it was weird, annoying or... sweet. But after a few weeks, I'd grown used to it and had come to expect it every night after I climbed into bed.

Maddox: *What's green and sits crying in the corner?*

Me: *Bye.*

Maddox: *The Incredible Sulk. C'mon, admit it. This one is funny.*

Me: *Ha. Ha. Ha. G'night.*

Maddox's face faded into the background as I focused my attention on Colton again. "Is something...wrong? What about the surprise party we're throwing him later today?"

Two months after our truce and the beginning of our friendship, Maddox had successfully passed the semester with good enough marks to keep his scholarship at Harvard.

I knew Maddox would never back down from a dare because he was no loser. But Maddox Coulter forgot to mention he was a genius. Not Einstein genius, but we all thought he was never paying attention to his classes. Apparently, he *was*, and he wasn't braindead like I believed. In fact, Maddox was probably smarter than me, and this was something I begrudgingly admitted. His brain was working overtime to catch up on his classes, and he did it. Quite successfully.

One semester down.

One more to go.

After our exam marks came in, we decided to throw Maddox a little surprise party. Just his close friends, nothing too big. That was supposed to be tonight.

Except Maddox was nowhere to be found.

"Sometimes..."

I looked at Colton, waiting for him to continue. "What?"

"He likes to disappear for a day or two," Colton slowly admitted.

"So, something *is* wrong?"

He must have seen the alarm on my face because he was already shaking his head. "Not exactly. It's just... some days, Maddox gets low. He doesn't like to be around people when he's feeling like that."

I grabbed my shoulder bag and slammed my locker close. "Do you know where he is right now? Where he goes when he's like this?"

Colton gripped my shoulder, his face intense as he pinned me with a harsh stare. "Listen, Lila. It's best you leave him alone when he's like this."

"He's my friend," I claimed out loud.

Colton let out a humorless laugh. "He's my best friend. So what?"

"I know him." I wrenched away from his grasp and glared.

"I know him better than you," he said simply. "I've known him since we were kids."

But he hasn't seen Maddox like I had… trapped in that broom closet, screaming to be let out… crying and begging for someone to save him.

Colton didn't see that Maddox. I had. I held him and sung to him.

I gnawed at my lower lips, Colton's warnings ringing in my ears, but my need to run to Maddox and to make sure he was okay was strong.

"Don't do it, Lila. Leave him alone. He'll come back when he's ready."

I hefted my bag over my shoulder and stepped away from him. "Here's something you need to know about me, Colton. I don't listen well to warnings."

"You can't fix him," he said to my back.

No, I couldn't.

But that was the thing… I didn't want to fix him.

I wanted to hold his hand.

Nothing more; nothing less.

So, I did the opposite of what Colton told me. I took a bus to Maddox's house, er… mansion. That would be my first stop, and I hoped he was there. If not, then I was about to go on a wild goose chase. If he didn't want to see me, I'd leave – but after making sure he was *alive*.

The Maddox I knew didn't disappear and go radio silent on his friends.

No, the Maddox I befriended was an annoying, pestering jerk. Like the time he gave me roses.

Maddox was walking toward me with... flowers? What the hell?

I leaned against my locker and gave him a look, a look that said— what are you up to now?

He halted in front of me with a smirk I wanted to smother with a pillow. I raised an eyebrow and nodded to the flowers in his hands. "What are those?"

"Roses," he said, looking mighty proud of himself.

"For you." I rolled my eyes.

"They're dead, Maddox."

He gave me a petulant look, like a child who had their favorite toy taken away. "Yeah, dead like my heart because you won't let my dick anywhere near you because you friend zoned me. So here you go. Roses for you, Garcia."

"You need to see a shrink. I don't think you're mentally stable," I announced, already walking away from him.

He fell into step beside me. "You won't accept my roses? I'm hurt."

My lips twitched. Okay, it was really hard to stay serious when Maddox was in one of his pranking moods.

"You're so fucking silly. I don't know if I should laugh or... be concerned."

"Anything to see that smile on your face," he said with a grin.

And it was then I noticed, I was smiling. It had been a frustrating day, one of those days where nothing seemed to go my way. I was feeling moody and a tad bitchy, but here I was...

Instead of being annoyed with Maddox like I would have been before our truce, I was smiling. Fuck, this wasn't good. He couldn't have me smiling so easily.

"Are you flirting with me, Coulter?" I still couldn't wipe the grin off my face.

"Are you falling for it, Garcia?" He shot back, his eyes dancing with

mischief.

"No," I deadpanned.

"Good. The harder you play to get, the more fun this game is."

"I'm not playing hard to get. We're friends," I stretched out the last word, putting more emphasis on it. Because obviously, Maddox didn't understand the meaning of 'just friends.'

Maddox let out a small chuckle. "Oh, I know. Besties forever. I'll do your nails and you'll do my hair type of shit." He paused, glancing down at me with a wicked smirk that should have warned me of what was about to come out of his mouth. "That won't stop me from trying to slide into your ass though."

I missed a step and stumbled forward before quickly regaining my footing. Sputtering, I glared at him. "My... ass...?"

Why did my voice come out like a squeak? Damn you, Maddox. You and your filthy mouth and dirty thoughts.

Maddox put himself in front of my path, so he was walking backward, facing me. "I'm an ass man, baby. You got enough to fill my two hands. And my hands are big enough to handle you."

Hmm. Oh really? He was almost too easy because I just found the MC's weakness.

"My ass makes you weak?"

He nodded. "Weak to the fucking knees."

I paused, lifted my chin up and regarded him with a regal look. If I made him weak in the knees, then...

"Great. Get to your knees and beg for it then. You might change my mind if you ask nicely."

He blinked, looking bewildered. "Wait, really?"

"Try and we'll see."

I forced myself not to laugh at the hopeful expression on his face. Poor baby. Maddox quickly got on one knee, in a proposal stance and presented me with the bouquet of dead roses. He gave me his most sincere look and asked, "Can I please fuck your ass?"

He said the words as if he was asking me to marry him, and this was some grand proposal. Don't laugh, Lila. Don't. You. Dare. Laugh.

I brought a hand up, tapping my index finger against my jaw in a thoughtful manner. His eyebrows furrowed, and he started to look suspicious.

I let my own smirk show. "Hmm. Not nice enough for me. Sorry, try again next time."

"What?" He let out a mock gasp, but I caught the grin on his face before I stepped around him.

Giving him a final glance over my shoulder, I winked.

"What a man would do for a piece of ass," he grumbled loud enough for me to hear.

I marched away, and maaaybeee, I put an extra sway in my hips—giving him a good look of the ass he wanted so much but couldn't have. What could I say in my defense? It was fun teasing a man like Maddox.

I smiled as the memory faded away, and the bus came to a stop at Maddox's place. I had been here a few times, even got to know his butler, Mr. Hokinson. I didn't know people in this day and age had butlers, but apparently, people as rich as the Coulters did, in fact, have butlers.

I waved at the guard and walked through the gate. Mr. Hokinson was already at the door, as I expected. He must have been alerted by the gatekeeper the moment I stepped foot onto the property.

"Good afternoon, Miss Garcia," he said politely with a slight southern drawl and a little bow. Cute, old Mr. Hokinson.

"Is Maddox home?" I asked, sounding hopeful even to my own ears.

He gave me a tentative nod, as if this was a secret. "He is, Miss Garcia. But he hasn't left his room since this morning. He didn't come down for breakfast or lunch, so we know to leave him alone."

My fists clenched at my sides. "And his parents?"

Mr. Hokinson swallowed, averting his gaze from mine, but didn't answer. Ever so loyal, what a fucking joke.

"I wish to see him."

He sidestepped into my path when I tried to walk around him. "I'm sorry, but I can't allow you."

I raised an eyebrow and gave him a polite smile, even though I was feeling anything but. "Please tell me, Mr. Hokinson. Did Maddox tell you to keep me outside? Has anyone specifically said I'm not allowed into this house? Because from what I remember... Maddox said I can come and go any time I want. I have free rein, don't I? Even you're aware of that."

The old man blinked and pursed his lips in silence. "Are you going against his words? I'm not sure he's going to like that."

"He—"

"I just want to know if he's okay, and I'll leave," I interrupted before he could give me another excuse. Before Mr. Hokinson could stop me, I walked around him and into the house.

I took the stairs two at a time to his room. His door wasn't locked, but I still knocked. Once, twice... four times, but there was no reply.

With caution, I opened the door and peeked inside. Nothing. Empty. Bare. No Maddox.

I walked inside to find the heavy drapes still down, blocking any sunlight from entering the dark room. There was something gloomy about the atmosphere. His bathroom's door was open, though, and I could hear the water running.

There he was...

My brain stuttered for a moment and a shocked gasp escaped me. The sight of him had me stumbling and rushing into the bathroom. "Maddox!"

No. No. Please, no.

I fell to my knees beside the overfilled tub. He sat inside, fully clothed with an empty bottle of...

God, no.

Maddox stunk of alcohol and cigarettes. I almost gagged at how heavy the smell was. His eyes were closed, his head barely staying above water. My heart fell to the pit of my stomach, cramped and twisting with nausea at the distraught look on his beautiful face. There were shadows under his eyes, as if he didn't sleep the night before.

I cupped his cheek. "Hey, Maddox." I gave him a gentle shake.

His bloodshot eyes fluttered open, and I could see the naked pain in his eyes. Maddox, strong and carefree Maddox, looked... beaten. Not physically. There were no injuries marking his body, but he looked wounded in spirit.

"Oh, baby. What happened?" He didn't respond, not that I was expecting a reply.

"Go away," he grumbled under his breath. God, he was pissed drunk. How many drinks did he have?

"And leave you in the tub like this?" I asked gently. "I can't leave you now, Maddox."

Maddox closed his eyes, his shoulders slumping further into the water. "Don't... need a... lecture."

There was a strain in his voice—a voice that used to be full of warmth – now so cold and... empty.

"We need to get you to bed. You can sleep this off, but you need a bed. Not a tub full of ice water."

Maddox was stubborn, but so was I.

He gritted his teeth, a storm flashing across his face. "Fuck...
off. *Leave.*"

"No."

He let out an empty laugh. "Then how about... you shut the
fuck up... and sit on my dick instead? Be a nice... give me good...
pussy and cheer me... up, why don't you?"

That was drunk Maddox speaking, I reminded myself. He was
barricading himself against me, trying to be hurtful and mean–to
push me away.

I blew out a frustrated breath and reached under his armpits,
pulling him up. He sat forward, and the water sluiced onto the
sides. I turned off the running tap with one hand while supporting
Maddox's limp body against the crook of my arm. "I'm going to
ignore what you just said. But still, you need to get out of this tub
before you catch pneumonia," I mumbled. "Don't be a jerk."

His clothes were soaked through, and I couldn't get him in bed
in this state. Shit.

His eyes closed, and his head slumped over my shoulders, with
his nose buried in my neck. A shiver racked through my body
because Maddox was practically freezing as I dragged him out of
the tub.

"I'm sorry," I said in a low voice. "But I'm going to have to get
you out of these clothes."

Maddox was going to catch a cold if I left him like this. He
mumbled something under his breath as a response. He settled on
the edge of the tub as I peeled his wet shirt over his head. It wasn't
my first-time seeing Maddox shirtless, but I still found myself
pausing to stare.

Maddox was ripped, sculptured and…

No, stop! Don't look.

I averted my gaze and worked efficiently, trying my hardest not to stare longer than I needed at his naked body. He slurred more profanities at me, but I chose to ignore all of them. Once he was clad in his grey sweatpants and a shirt I found lying on the floor in his room, I dragged Maddox out of the bathroom.

My knees almost buckled under his weight. "Jesus, you're heavy."

He snorted in response as his body shuddered violently.

I *hated* this. So fucking much.

I was angry, so goddamn furious, that nobody thought to check on him. His parents or Mr. Hokinson. Anyone, damn it! What if I hadn't found him when I did? He could have accidentally drowned himself or… worse.

I was livid and fuck…

My heart *ached.*

How could Maddox be so careless? Didn't he understand how precious life was… and how easily it could slip out of our grasp? In a blink of an eye… everything–*gone.*

Tears burnt the back of my eyes, and I sniffled. "Why, Maddox? God, why?"

"Stop being a bitch… come and sit on my dick if… you won't stop yapping…" he slurred.

"I'm going to throw you on your ass if you throw one more insult at me, Maddox," I warned him. He stumbled and jerked out of my grasp, swearing under his breath.

"You're all bark and no fucking bite, Garcia," Maddox snarled, his eyes opened into slits.

He was angry – about something. I didn't know what, but if I

215

could take a lucky guess, it had to do with his parents.

I understood that. But he didn't have to be an asshole.

When he stumbled again, his legs giving out under him, I grabbed his arm and hauled him to bed. Once he settled on the mattress, he swatted my hand away. It didn't hurt, but it still stung.

With my hands on my hips, I squinted down at him. "Don't do this, Maddox. I'm going to walk away."

The warning gained me a reaction, a small one. He opened his bloodshot eyes and stared at me, his expression a mask of unfiltered pain. "Then go. That's what they always do anyway. Walk away."

Goddamn it, did he have to hurt my heart like this?

I rubbed a hand over the ache in my chest, attempting to relieve the dull pain there.

"There is no reason for you to be mean to me when I'm only trying to help," I said softy, running my fingers through his wet hair. "Don't push me away."

Maddox let out a mocking laugh and closed his eyes. So be it.

I got off the bed and was only able to take a step away before he grabbed my hand. Firm and strong, even in his state. "Don't go. Don't leave...me," he croaked. The cracks in his voice made me pause. "I'm scared... scared of being alone."

I settled back on the bed again, all fight leaving me in one breath.

Maddox wasn't complicated in ways everyone liked to believe. Once I got to know him, I really saw him, the real *him*, and realized that he only hid behind a mask.

"You can't do this, Maddox. You can't be an asshole and then ask me to stay with that look on your face." Like a kicked puppy, a lost boy, a broken man. My sweet Maddox, with a heart of gold.

"Don't wanna lose you," he mumbled. Maddox grasped my hand

in his, albeit clumsily, because he was still really drunk. Our fingers interlaced together, and his hold tightened.

I gave his hand a squeeze in comfort and in warning. "I don't do toxic relationships."

His eyes cracked open, and he gave me a small smile. There was something melancholy about it. He had the appearance of a desperate man, starving and reaching blindly toward *something*, but it always escaped out of his grasp before he could grab hold. Maddox was breaking my heart, and there was nothing I could do to end this suffering.

"We're not in a relationship."

I knew that but I still asked. Maybe I was a glutton for pain. "Then, what are we?"

His gaze fixated on me again, eyes so blue they looked like the midwinter sky – beautiful yet dreary. "You're... more," he whispered the confession. "Don't leave, *Lila*."

He said my name like a prayer, as if he was whispering all his hopes to heaven.

With that said, he closed his eyes again, and this time, he was no longer conscious. I looked down at our hands, and I swallowed back my tears. "What are you doing to me, Maddox?"

Before I could think twice about my actions, I climbed under the comforter and joined him. His body was still cold, but slowly regaining its warmth. Under the strong smell of alcohol and tobacco, his scent still lingered. Warm, rich and earthy...

I didn't know when it happened or why I didn't realize it until now, but Maddox's familiar scent brought me comfort.

I curled into his side; our fingers still intertwined. He needed me; he needed his friend. "I'm not leaving. Pinky swear."

Maddox was bad.

There was a boy once, a boy just like him, who ruined me and left me scarred.

Maddox was everything I stayed away from; he was everything I didn't need in my life.

I told myself... never again. I'd never let myself be weak around men like Maddox.

But no matter how much I tried to walk away, to put distance between us, to somehow end this *friendship*... he wouldn't let go.

He was bad. He smoked, he was too hasty about life, he liked to break the law, he broke girls like me – he left a trail of shattered hearts behind him, and he didn't care about anything. I thought... maybe it was because no one taught him how to care for another human being.

I saw a few glimpses of the Maddox he tried to hide from everyone, the Maddox who just wanted his parents' approval – *that* Maddox was starving for attention.

There were a hundred reasons why he was bad for me.

But all those reasons became insignificant when I realized he didn't want to hurt me. At first, I was skeptical. I was waiting for Maddox to do what he was best at – break hearts.

But he didn't.

Weeks went by.

Two months passed.

I realized Maddox Coulter was a little bit ruined, a little bit messy, a little bit broken -- a beautiful disaster.

Like *me*.

All those reasons were no longer important, because every morning, he'd wait outside my grandparents' home, he'd hand me a muffin and follow my bus to school. Every afternoon, he'd sit with me and *study* – something he hasn't done in years. He hated studying, he hated opening a textbook, but he did it anyway. Because of a dare, because of me – he did it for me.

It was silly, it was something so little, yet…

I couldn't let go of my friend.

He was annoying but hilarious. He was the world's biggest asshole – a douchebag by definition. In fact, he'd take that trophy home. Asshole of the decade.

He angered me, made me want to scream in frustration, he drove me utterly crazy, but as much as he had me sighing in exasperation and rolling my eyes… he made me smile.

Maddox was out of his mind: too careless, too reckless, too foolish.

But he was the chaos to the perfect world I had built around me – a world where I kept my heart carefully guarded.

Miss Perfectionist, he liked to say.

Hmph. Maddox made my world a little bit less… perfect. Was she okay with this? Is this the realization she came to here?

CHAPTER TWENTY-ONE

Lila

As I came awake again, for the fifth time this night, I realized it wasn't night anymore. The heavy curtains were still drawn, but I could see the sunlight through the slits.

My hands landed on a wall of muscle, warm and strong. I could feel his heart beating under my palm. My gaze slid up his chest, neck, squared jaw and finally, his eyes.

I realized two things.

One – I spent the night with Maddox, and I slept for over twelve hours, and he had slept even more.

Two – Maddox was awake, and he was staring down at me with an unreadable expression.

"Hi?" I mumbled.

Shit, shit. Shit!

I meant to leave in the middle of the night, after making sure Maddox was alright.

But I must have passed out and now…

This wasn't my first time sleeping next to a man. Well, my ex-boyfriend and I shared a bed a few times. But he was a boy. A lanky, inexperienced boy. Maddox was not a *boy*.

I wasn't shy or inexperienced, per say.

But I wasn't sure I liked the way Maddox was staring at me. The expression on his face made my stomach flip and clench. A shiver racked through my body; except, I wasn't cold. In fact, I was very, *very* warm. Maddox was a human heater.

His eyes were dark and intense, no longer dull or bloodshot.

"Stop looking at me like that," I grumbled, pushing away from his body. The sight of his dirty blond, disheveled hair, eyes glinting with something unspoken, full lips slightly parted, wide and strong shoulders—there was a masculine aura around him. He made me feel small and... feminine.

"What are you doing here?" he finally spoke.

I sat up, chewing on my bottom lip. "You don't remember..."

Maddox rubbed a hand over his face and rolled over onto his back. "I do. But, I mean, in my bed. Not that I mind, but I just didn't expect it when I woke up. Nice surprise there, Sweet Cheeks."

Ah, so he was back to the normal Maddox.

"I fell asleep," I admitted. I didn't know how to make this not awkward. "But I should probably leave now."

I got off the bed, but the sound of my name from his rough, sleepy voice made me pause. "Lila."

"Yes?"

I glanced back at him. Maddox was on his side, facing me and propped up on one elbow, \casual and at ease. There were so many differences between the two Maddoxs I had seen in the last twenty hours.

"Thank you," he said. There was something akin to *affection*

221

in his voice. My chest tightened with an unfamiliar emotion. My mouth opened, but I never got a chance to tell him it was okay.

A knock sounded on the door, and Mr. Hokinson's voice came through. "Your parents are asking you to come down for breakfast."

There was a flash of annoyance and twisted fury on Maddox's face. "You can tell them to fuck off, thanks."

"Good morning to you, too," Mr. Hokinson said before his steps faded away.

"Maddox–" I started.

"No, Lila," he growled.

He climbed off the bed and went into the bathroom, slamming the door behind him. I flinched at that and stood where I was, waiting for him to calm down.

Ten minutes later, he was standing in front of me again. Arms crossed, he leveled me with a warning. "Stay out of this."

"What happened yesterday?" I shot back.

He surprised me by answering. "Bad day."

I took a step forward, reaching out to him. "Maddox..."

In a moment of renewed anger, his chest vibrated with another threatening growl. His jaw clenched, and I wondered how it didn't crack under the pressure. "I called my father to tell him about my final marks."

Oh no. No, I didn't like where this was going.

"He hung up on me because he was too busy. When he came home, I mustered up the courage and told him. You know what he fucking said?"

I shook my head. *I'm sorry.*

His lips curled up into a snarl as he mimicked his father's voice. "Who did you bribe for those marks, Maddox?"

Hot, nasty fury coursed through my body. *For* Maddox. He

continued, spitting out the words like they burnt him from the inside.

"He doesn't believe in me. Father dearest probably thinks I fucked my way through my teachers to pass my exams. So, you see? Lila, it doesn't matter. If I get into Harvard on my own or if I passed my semester. None of this fucking matter!"

My heartbeat pounded in my chest. "Yes, it does."

"No," he hissed.

I stalked over to where he was standing and cupped his cheeks. "Look at me! It does matter, Maddox."

He tried to jerk away from me, but I didn't let go. "I don't care what your dad says, but you worked your ass off for this. I saw it with my own eyes. You should be proud of yourself. And if you can't believe it, then let me tell you. I am so proud of you. Got it?"

His lips thinned into a straight line, his eyes going distant. "Lila–"

"I'm proud of you," I whispered, rubbing my thumb over his clenching jaw, the muscle relaxing under my touch.

His eyes squeezed close. "Fuuuuck," he muttered under his breath.

I let out a small laugh, hoping it would rub off on Maddox. "Well, Poodle. That's one way to put it."

His eyes snapped opened, clear as the sky, and he grasped my hand, pulling me toward the door.

"Where are we going?" I asked.

There was a renewed urgency in his voice when he spoke. "Breakfast. Let's go."

Well shit...

"Um, can I brush my teeth first?"

Fifteen minutes later, we were sitting at the table with his parents. It was my first time meeting them, and his father barely gave me a once over before going back to his tablet. His mother sent me a tentative smile before avoiding eye contact. She munched on her toast while an awkward silence fell upon us.

"We didn't know you had *someone* over, Maddox."

His father's voice was deep and uninviting. There was a harsh coldness to it. Mr. Coulter gave me an unappreciative glance, and I frowned. Did he…?

Holy shit, he thought I was Maddox's fuck buddy or last night's conquest.

And he probably though Maddox brought me to the table just for the sake of causing a ruckus. Well, that explained one thing. Maddox got his assholish ways from his father.

I cleared my throat. "My apologies, we haven't met before. I'm Maddox's friend."

"Friend?" His father gave me a dismissive flick of his hand.

"Brad," his wife warned in a low voice. The tension in the air was palpable, so thick someone could choke on it. My throat went dry, and I tried to swallow several times.

"What's your name?" Mrs. Coulter seemed to be more… approachable. The lack of judgement in her eyes had me relaxing, a tad bit.

"Lila. Lila Garcia."

She gave me a half-smile. "You can call me Savannah. How did you and my son meet?"

I took a small bite of my toast. I had been hungry before, although I was not anymore. My stomach twisted with knots, and I knew I couldn't have more than a few bites. "Maddox and I met in Berkshire Academy."

His father's head snapped up, and he speared me with a look. "Berkshire, you said? I don't recognize your last name. Who are your parents?"

He thought I was one of them... the wealthy and the corrupted. After all, Berkshire Academy was a tank full of those.

I took a slow sip of my water, trying to soothe my parched throat. "I live with my grandparents."

I jerked my chin high and returned his look with one of my own. I wasn't ashamed of who I was.

"Lawyers?"

Was this a goddamn interrogation?

I shook my head, pursing my lips in displeasure. "No, they own a grocery store."

"That's nice," Mrs. Coulter jumped in before her husband could utter another hateful word. He was staring at me as if I was a pest. As I stared at Brad, I could see the resemblance. Maddox was a carbon copy of his father. The same hair, same eyes, same angry look on their faces.

"So, have you gotten any college acceptances yet?" Savannah tried to break through the tension, looking back and forth between Maddox and me.

I nodded, chewing on the bite I just took before answering. "Yes, to Princeton, but I am hoping for Harvard."

Maddox's father let out a huff. "Harvard? It's not easy to get in."

My shoulders straightened, and I gave him a tight smile, trying to look polite. If Brad saw the irritated look on my face, he ignored it. "Oh, I know, but I've been working for this for years now," I told him. He didn't scare me, not with his judgmental stares or his cold smile.

Maddox finally spoke. "Lila is one of the top five students at Berkshire."

There was a hint of pride in his voice, and my cheeks heated. I quickly took another bite of my toast before swallowing it down with the tea I had in front of me.

Brad tsked, looking only slightly impressed. He regarded me with a curious look as if he was finally seeing me in a different light. He gave me a sharp nod before his gaze focused on Maddox. "Well, that's good to hear. Maybe you can teach my wayward son how to be responsible."

I wasn't touching Maddox, but I *felt* it as if it was my own—his muscles tightening, his body rigid as a bow—he was ready to sprint away or lunge at his father's throat. There was fire in his eyes and ice in his veins. My hand slid over to him, and I placed my hand on his thigh, holding him down, even though I was no match to his strength. His muscles rippled beneath my touch, and his own hand landed on mine. His breath expelled in a jerky rush.

I got you.

I leveled Brad with a cold stare of my own. This was a battlefield. Maddox and I on one side, his parents on the other. Our words didn't cause any physical wounds, but fuck, our looks and the words spoken were sharper than any knife.

I'd go to war for Maddox.

And *this* was war.

"Maddox is working really hard," I started, my eyes flickering from his father to his mother. "He passed this semester with high marks."

Brad looked incredulous. "Oh, did he?"

I held onto my temper and gave them a smile. "Yes. You should be proud of him since he did it all on his own."

Savannah perked up. She was obviously trying to break the ice, but this situation was already too frosty. "That's good to hear! Maddox, why didn't you tell us?"

He tensed, his fork clanking against the plate. "I did."

Her smile dissolved. "Oh."

I realized one thing in that moment. Savannah wasn't ignoring Maddox's existence, although it appeared like that on the outside. But now that I really *looked* at her, I realized she was scared of her son. Maddox intimidated her, and knowing him, he made himself less approachable around his parents.

Maybe I was wrong. Savannah was *trying*, but it was too little... too late.

"We're done here," Maddox announced. He stood up, roughly pushing his chair back and dragging me with him.

"Maddox," Brad called out after his son, his voice threatening and so... cold. "You will show respect."

Maddox wasn't listening. We were already marching away. He didn't stop, even after we were the through the gates of his house. We walked for an hour, side by side. There was an unspoken understanding between us as we walked in silence until we reached Berkshire.

Today was Saturday, so the building was closed. I snuck a glance up at Maddox. He was breathing hard, his lips curled back, and his eyes dark.

He held so much anger inside him, so much disappointment. I could *feel* it, deep in my bones. Maddox felt betrayed, hurt and deceived. He held more pain than he showed to the world.

I gave his hand a squeeze. "You have to train your mind to be stronger than your emotions or else you'll lose yourself every time," I said softly.

His eyes locked with me, and the intensity of his gaze caused my stomach to flip. "Why are you here?" There was a sudden harshness in his voice that had me flinching.

My lips parted, confused. "What?"

"Here," he gritted out. "With me. Why? Why didn't you walk away?"

"Because you're my friend," I simply replied. *Because I care.*

Maddox released a shuddering breath as if he needed that confirmation. So young and so angry. If only I could make him smile again.

A sudden spark of an idea had me silently gasping. Of course, I could make him smile. I knew exactly how.

I let go of his hand and pointed at the building next to Berkshire Academy, opened every day, even the weekends. The library.

"I dare you," I started.

"For fuck's sake."

"I dare you to go in there, no clothes except your boxers."

He paused, watching me with his mouth agape. "Are you serious?"

"Dead serious." I crossed my arms over my chest.

"Naked?"

I nodded, fighting back a smile. "Only your boxers."

Oh, this was going to be a sight to see.

"They'll call the police," Maddox said, still looking at me as if I had lost my mind.

"That's the point, Poodle."

He blinked, still looking surprised. "Holy shit, I corrupted you," he gasped.

My lips quirked up. "Do you dare, Coulter?"

Maddox smirked, a playful and sinful as fuck smirk. "I accept this dare."

He quickly pulled his clothes off his body and handed them to me. He was partially... naked. His Calvin Klein boxers hung low around his hips, the crevice of his ass visible and my throat was suddenly parched. Fully clothed Maddox was... sexy.

Partially naked Maddox was... *gulp*

We were just friends, but damn it, I was a hormonal teenager who wasn't scared to appreciate a fine specimen like Maddox Coulter.

"Stop looking at my ass, Garcia."

"Stop prancing around me naked, Coulter."

He sneaked a glance over his shoulder. "I've a feeling this was your way of getting me naked. Are you feeling tempted, Sweet Cheeks?"

"Tempted to kick your ass to Mars, yes."

He grinned. "Liar."

Fine, I was a liar.

"Damn, it's cold!" His teeth were chattering as he rubbed his hands up and down his arms.

I stuck my tongue out and waved toward the library. "Off you go."

He jogged toward the entrance. "Do a little twerk," I yelled after him.

His warm laughter was heard through the cold breeze. I stalked after him and waited at the entrance, watching Maddox's spectacle through the large glass windows. He pranced around the library, completely at ease and with a cocky smirk. He was completely comfortable in his skin. The people stared, speechless and in shock. A girl had her phone out, probably filming him. Some laughed, others looked outraged.

Maddox paused in front of the old librarian, who was blushing and sputtering, bent down and did a half twerk against the granny before running off.

I couldn't hold my laughter in anymore. My stomach cramped, and I wheezed as he sprinted out of the library, the librarians and security guard at his heels.

"Run!" he hollered at me, his smile wide and infectious.

I took off, and we ran.

We didn't stop until we lost them. Hiding behind the dumpster, I tried to catch my breath.

"Fuck, you're crazy," he gasped through his laughter.

I elbowed him, grinning. "We make a good team, don't we?"

He smiled.

A real fucking smile.

My chest tightened, and my stomach did a crazy flip, like little butterflies dancing around in there.

Maddox might seem like he had the world at his feet. He was Berkshire's king, and he ruled with a cocky grin, though no one saw the pain behind that playful smile. To the world, he had everything everybody else wanted: money, status, friends, a scholarship and two beautiful, successful parents. He was untouchable.

But he was still human.

Maddox Coulter wasn't invincible. He had multiple cracks and scars in his soul.

He was a simple, seventeen-year-old boy, who only wanted his parents' approval, with a little messy childhood and now, he starved for attention.

I made him smile.

I did it. And I'd continue to do so.

One dare at a time, I'd chase his smiles—because I realize Maddox needed someone who cared enough about his happiness and his anger. And I did.

CHAPTER
TWENTY-TWO

Lila

The crowd cheered so loudly that I wondered if my eardrums were ever going to be the same. Excitement bubbled in my chest, and I felt giddy as the players strode out of the tunnel, leading to the football field. Maddox liked to have me accompany him to his practices but this was my first actual game. I knew absolutely nothing about football but I had to be here for Maddox. This was important to him, hence it was important to me.

"MC! MC! Go Berkshire!" the girls screamed from behind me.

Holy shit, this was huge and it was exhilarating.

The cheerleaders were doing their own thing as the game started. All eyes were on the Berkshire players. I held my breath, and I couldn't tear my eyes off the field. Riley grasped my hand in hers, and she was screaming at the top of her lungs.

Maddox probably just scored a point because the crowd went wild, batshit crazy wild. I knew it was him because of the swagger as he trotted around the field, soaking up all the attention. He banged his fist against his chest, and our cheerleaders cheered even louder. I was too far away to see his face, but I could imagine the cocky grin. Yeah, this was definitely MC—Maddox Coulter, all macho and arrogant.

Tonight was the last football game of the season. Due to the snow in January, the game got pushed back a few weeks. It was still cold as fuck, but our Berkshire boys were crushing the other team. I didn't understand much about football or any sports for that matter, but when Riley and our people cheered, I did too.

I tried to keep an eye on Maddox, but everything was happening too fast, so I had no idea what was going on.

The audience hollered once more, "MC! MC! MC!"

They were calling out to Maddox. He was the star football player, after all.

There was one last touchdown before the field and crowd erupted. We... won?

Holy shit, we won! Not that I was surprised or anything, but WE WON!

I was never much of a sports fan; I didn't much care about football, but this was Maddox's passion—his whole fucking life. He was happy, which made *me* happy.

Riley jumped, and I danced in my spot, laughing. "We won!" she shrieked.

My heart thumped so loudly that I could hear the beats in my ears. What a night.

Maddox paused at the edge of the field, and I was standing in the front row, courtesy of being the quarterback's friend. He took off his helmet, smirking. His breathing was ragged, but the expression on his face was one of pleasure and bliss.

Maddox wiggled his eyebrows at me as the girls surrounded him.

A cheerleader rubbed herself against him, grabbed his face and landed a big kiss on his lips.

Okaaayy then.

More girls joined the group, all of them trying to cop a feel of Maddox. I sincerely worried for his ego. This couldn't be healthy for a seventeen-year-old boy. So much arrogance and cockiness.

He spared me a glance, challenging me with his gaze. I remembered the words he spoke to me before the game.

Riley stood beside me, completely oblivious of what was about to happen. Maddox waited, giving me an infuriating look, as if he expected me to lose this stupid dare.

Sincerely, fuck you, Maddox Coulter.

As another girl wrapped her arms around him, I lunged into action.

Do you dare?

Ha. Ha. Ha.

Riley let out a shocked gasp as I grabbed the back of her neck and pulled her forward. My mouth landed on hers, and her eyes flared in surprise. I pressed my lips harder against hers before pulling away.

She wiped her mouth, sputtering and glaring. "What the *fuck*, Lila?"

Shrugging, I gave her a sheepish look. "Maddox dared me, sorry."

"If I win the game, I dare you to kiss Riley," he said, amusement *flashing in his eyes. This was probably some woman on woman fantasy for him.*

"You can't be serious!"

His lips quirked up. "Do you dare?"

I turned to face Maddox again, and he was chuckling. I flashed him the middle finger, and he laughed even harder. Maddox pulled away from all the girls as they tried to grab him, vying for his attention, but he shook his head.

He said something to them and pointed at me. Everyone turned to stare at the same time.

Suspicious, I squinted at him as he made his way to me.

"What did you say to them?" I asked with my hands on my hips. My eyes narrowed on him.

He smirked. "Told them my girlfriend was getting jealous."

Huh? Wait... what?

I was in too much shock from his words that I didn't see it coming until I was flung upside down and over his shoulder.

"Maddox!" I screeched.

He swatted my ass. "Be nice. These girls are driving me crazy, and you're my escape plan."

"Let me down. Now!" I banged my fists into his back, feeling his muscles clench under my attack.

"How about you be docile for five minutes?" He rumbled with a chuckle.

Docile? Excuse me, DOCILE?

I hit him with my fist again, although I was pretty sure he didn't feel anything. "What am I? Your pet?" I snapped.

Maddox hummed, thoughtfully. What a douchebag.

"You're such a wild chihuahua," he said.

"Careful, or you'll end up with a nasty bite, Coulter."

His shoulders shook with silent laughter. "Bite me then, Garcia."

I rolled my eyes as he stalked away from the crowd with me over his shoulder, caveman style.

Once we reached the boys' locker room, he let me down, and I blew my hair out of my face. "Why are we here?"

"I need a shower and then we'll be on our way to the bonfire. Berkshire is celebrating tonight. I need my favorite person there."

I crossed my arms over my chest as he sauntered toward his locker. "You do realize if you keep grabbing me and throwing me over your shoulder like this, they will never believe that we're just friends."

We were already getting weird looks. No one believed we were just friends. Maybe that was partially our fault.

Maddox and I spent way too much time together. He'd hold my hands, kiss my cheek or throw an arm over my shoulders while we walked down the halls. He stole bites of my lunch, and we continued to play silly pranks on each other. At first, I hated the public displays of affection, but they grew on me, just like the rest of Maddox's quirks. He still made inappropriate jokes, but he never tried to do anything... more.

Maddox gave me a nonchalant half shrug. He removed his shoulder pads and stripped off his jersey before throwing it my way. "A souvenir, Sweet Cheeks."

"You really don't care?" I asked.

He didn't bother to hide his amusement at my question. "Lila, people's opinions don't matter to me. You shouldn't care either. They live to gossip while we're living our lives to the fullest. So, who the fuck cares if they think we're friends or we're fucking?"

Okay, true. Point taken.

Two hours later, we were celebrating with the rest of the Berkshire students around bonfire. There was a lot of us here but the open field was big enough so it didn't seem crowded. Bottles and cans of beer littered around us. A few guys were already a tad drunk, and they were laughing about something, pushing each other around.

Maddox walked over with a beer in his hand and a paper plate in the other. "Got you some Hawaiian Teriyaki Chicken skewers."

I smiled, taking the plate from him. "Thanks." I looked around, seeing all the smiles. "They sure love celebrating."

He took a long pull of his beer before wiping the corner of his mouth. His legs were lazily spread apart, and he was wearing black ripped jeans, expensive leather boots and a hat that probably cost more than my bra. Maddox looked like he owned the world—a god amongst us mere mortals.

He licked his lips, grinning. "This is nothing. The real celebration is at Colton's house next weekend."

My brows furrowed at that. "I don't want to know."

I munched on my grilled skewers while slowly nursing my own beer. A moment later, Maddox tsked. "I'm bored. Let's cause a little trouble."

He stood up and went to the middle of the field. He spread his arms out, smirking. "Let's play a game," he announced.

The others hollered in agreement.

Oh, no.

His gaze found mine, mischief flashing in his eyes. I glared, trying to look severe, but my own lips twitched with a smile.

Here comes trouble.

CHAPTER
TWENTY-THREE

Maddox

I glanced down at my phone for probably the hundredth time, waiting for a text back. She wasn't replying. I left school early today when Lila missed the first two classes. Now, I sat in my car in front of her grandparents' home like a goddamn stalker. Worry gnawed at me because it was so unlike Lila to ghost me, and she never missed her classes.

I did the same shit a few weeks ago. Bailed on her and ghosted everyone who tried to reach out to me. I didn't expect her to turn the tables on me, and I didn't like it, not one bit. Now, I understood how she felt when I wasn't answering her phone calls and she found me in that tub, freezing and pissed drunk.

Was she hurt?

Did something happen?

Why. The. Fuck. Won't. She. Reply. To. My. Texts?

Goddamn it!

I slammed my fists against the steering wheel, slightly unhinged at the mere thought of Lila being hurt.

I went to their grocery store today and found out that her grandma was home. Sure, I could have spoken with Sven, her Pops, but I'd rather not. He liked me enough, but he didn't seem to trust any boys around his little Lila, even ones who were her friends and didn't want to get in her pants.

Okay, that was a fucking lie.

I still wanted to get in her panties.

Maybe he could read me better than I thought. Was I that obvious?

Oh, she was my friend, but I still wanted to fuck your granddaughter. Up and down, sideways, on our knees, every fucking position.

Well, yeah. No wonder he didn't like, *like* me.

I rang the doorbell, and Lila's grandma opened the door, a pensive look on her face. She looked tired and weary. At the sight of me, she smiled a little. "Maddox, what are you doing here?"

"Hi," I said, peering behind her shoulder, expecting Lila to pop up. "Is Lila home? I tried to contact her, but she isn't answering, so I grew worried."

She was silent for a moment, her eyes turning glassy. "You don't know?" She spoke the words so softly that I almost missed them.

My heart skittered a beat, and I started sweating. The blood rushed through my ears and my heart hammered in my ears. "Is… something wrong? Did something happen to her?"

She shook her head. "You don't know what today is?" she questioned, but then answered her own question before I could say a word. "She didn't tell you. I'm not surprised. My Lila always suffers alone."

Suffers… alone?

239

Fuck, no. She would never. Not alone.

Lila had *me*.

True, she didn't need a hero to save the day, but the more I got to know her, the closer we grew—I wanted, no —I *needed* to protect her. Maybe it was to return the favor since she took care of me when I was at my weakest or simply because I…cared. I'd ever confess that out loud to her. She'd sock me in the face because Lila Garcia hated to be pitied.

Except, I didn't pity her.

I just wanted to… protect her.

"What are you saying? Is she hurt?"

Her grandma gave me a heartbroken smile. "She's been hurting for a long time."

That… hurt. Right there, in my fucking chest.

Mrs. Wilson leaned against the doorframe, looking more haggard than her age. "Did you know that Lila never cries? Never, except one day of the year. On that day, she cries alone; she hides her tears from everyone. That's the only day she lets herself feel pain."

My heart nearly spilled out, and I rubbed my chest, trying to alleviate the ache. It didn't stop the pain. It infiltrated my veins and my blood, for *her*.

Her shoulders shook and slumped, as if she had finally been released from a heavy burden she carried. "My Lila is strong with a fragile heart," she whispered.

"Where is she right now? Where can I find her?" Even I could hear the urgency in my voice, the desperation.

And I was not a desperate guy.

But Lila made me feel many things I'd never felt before. Not for any other girl.

"Lila left this morning. She's at Sunset Park. You'll find her sitting on a bench."

I nodded my thanks and took a step back, clenching my car keys in my hand. Sunset Park, I'd find my Lila there.

"Maddox?"

I paused and glanced over my shoulder. "Yes?"

"Are you Lila's friend?"

Confused, I blinked, and my brows furrowed. Grandma was well aware we were friends; we had been for months. But she stared at me, expectantly, as if her question held more meaning behind those simple words.

And I realized they did.

That question was powerful because it made me *think* about how important Lila was to me, how close we were and how much she meant to me. One simple question, and it put our whole relationship in perspective.

Yes, I respected the hell out of Lila. She was smart, funny, wild and... caring.

Yes, I still wanted a taste of her. Wanted it since I first laid eyes on her.

But she meant more.

We had each other—she got me and I got her.

Suddenly, the idea of us being more than friends became taboo. Because if we were ever more than friends, we risked losing what we had now. A silent understanding. A friendship based on honesty and loyalty. Lila saw behind all my bullshit and didn't let it deter her. She pushed and pushed until I cracked open in front of her. Lila and I were alike in so many ways, yet still... different. Maybe that was why we suited each other so well as friends. We balanced each other.

She was the calm in my reckless life.

I was the chaos in her peaceful one.

"Lila's my best friend," I finally confessed, with a curl of my lips.

Grandma looked thoughtful for a moment before she gave me a melancholy smile. "Take care of our girl. She refuses to let any of us lend her a shoulder. Maybe you'll be different."

Thirty minutes later, I was sitting in my car at Sunset Park. My gaze found Lila the moment I parked and turned off the engine. Like her Gran said, I found her sitting on a bench, alone. Sweet Lila was cuddled up in her winter coat, trying to stay warm against the cold. I couldn't see her face from where I was, but I didn't like what I was seeing.

She was hunched over the bench, her legs up on the seat with her arms wrapped around her knees. Lila looked... lost.

I stayed in my car for a few more minutes, giving her some time by herself. I knew *why* she was here. Sunset Cemetery Park.

Her parents were here.

Did you know that Lila never cries? Never, except one day of the year. On that day, she cries alone; she hides her tears from everyone. That's the only day she lets herself feel pain.

And I knew what that day was, what today was, and why it was so important for Lila.

Sweet Lila—the fiery dragon with a fragile heart.

I stepped out of the car when I couldn't stay away any longer. The cold wind blew hard, and Lila hugged herself tighter. There was a magnetic pull between us, and I walked toward her without even realizing my feet were taking me to her side.

She didn't move when I settled at her side on the bench, didn't look up, didn't even acknowledge my presence. Silently, I grasped her hand and pulled it away from her knees. She clutched my hand, and I squeezed hers in return, a silent vow.

I'm not letting go, Lila.

She didn't speak, and I didn't dare break the silence. Lila quietly sniffled and dashed away her tears with her other hand, but she couldn't keep her cries in. She cried her little heart out, a desolate sob coming from a person drained of all her hopes and dreams.

As if realizing now that she was holding onto my hand, she tried to wrench it away from me. I held fast, squeezing her hand in comfort. "Go...away," Lila murmured.

I stayed silent, refusing to utter a word, but also refusing to leave.

Minutes probably turned into hours as I sat with her. She cried until I thought there would be no tears left, but she still cried. She didn't speak again and neither did I. Lila needed to grieve in silence, but I'd be there with her. I was staying, and I'd fight any motherfucker who'd try to make me leave.

Each sob that racked through her body wrecked my stupid heart even more. A whimper escaped her, a tortured sound, and she gripped my hand harder, her nails digging into my skin. Her other hand came up, and she clutched her chest, a broken sob slipping past her lips. Her whole body was shaking, whether it was from the cold or the force of her tears, I didn't know.

The sound of her struggling to breathe through her crying decimated me.

"*It... hurts,*" she whimpered. "*It... hurts... so much,* Maddox."

Her breathing was ragged, gasping, and her body slumped forward as if all the strength had left her body. She shouldn't be able affect me so strongly, but wild emotions swirled inside me as I breathed in her pain and suffering.

Watching the Lila I knew, the strong and confident Lila, break apart like this…

Fuck!

There was a phantom ache in my chest, like an invisible knife digging and twisting viciously into my flesh – the pain becoming unbearable.

I grabbed her before she could slide off the bench, her body weak in her grief. Our knees dug into the damp mud, but I didn't care as I pulled her into my arms. She was half sitting on my lap, her face buried in my neck as her tears soaked through my shirt and against my skin.

"Why doesn't it… stop? Why? Why? *Why*!?" She wailed. Her tiny fist clenched around my shirt. "It hurts… even more. Every time… every year. The… pain… just never goes… away."

I didn't know what to say, didn't know what to fucking do, so I just held her. I was never good with words of condolences, never had anyone to comfort until Lila.

For fuck's sake, the moment a girl started shedding a few tears, I'd be running the other way as far as I could go. Girls and tears were the one thing I didn't do, nope… never.

Until Lila.

Life had broken her.

Just as it had broken me.

Maybe it was why we found each other.

Call it fate, kismet… or maybe it was God's doing…

Lila was meant to hold my broken pieces together; just as I was meant to hold the shattered pieces of hers.

No, she didn't fix me, and I didn't fix her. We just… held each other; it was that simple.

"I got you," I said softly against her temple.

She trembled in my embrace. "They didn't deserve... to die. They didn't!"

I murmured soothing words to her as she wailed her agony. "Why did they... die... and why... me... why am I... *here*? I want... to go... to my mom and my... dad. I don't... want to be here. I don't!"

I'm sorry, so so sorry, baby girl.

The pain flowing from Lila was as palpable as the frigid wind around us. Such agony and such a lonely, broken soul.

More time went by, and eventually, her sobbing turned into hiccups and quiet sniffles. Lila was still on my lap, face still tucked into the crook of my neck and her fingers still clutching my shirt as if her life depended on it.

I brushed her hair out of her face, my thumb rubbing over the trail of her tears. "I got you."

She hugged me tighter.

"Can I meet your parents?" I asked.

Lila gave me the tiniest nod. She stumbled out of my lap and stood up on shaky legs. I did, too, trying to ignore the tingles prickling through my legs after sitting in the same position for too long. She took my hand in hers, and we walked toward her parents' headstones.

"Hey, mom," Lila said, her voice cracking. "I've got someone for you to meet."

Catalina Garcia.

The sun shines brighter because she was here.

Beloved mother, wife and daughter.

She pointed at the tombstone beside her mother. "And that's my dad. Dad meet Maddox, Maddox meet Dad." A small, wobbly smile appeared on her lips. "And no, daddy. He's not my boyfriend."

Zachary Wilson.
A gentle man and a gentleman.
Loving father and loving husband.
What a beautiful memory you left behind.

My throat clogged with emotions, so I nodded in greeting. "It's good to finally meet you, Mr. and Mrs. Wilson."

Lila knelt down in front of the headstones. She brought her legs to her chest and wrapped her arms around her knees again. I realized, now, that she was trying to physically shield herself from the pain. I joined her as I tried to understand what I was feeling. There was a heavy weight on my chest, and it almost made it harder to breathe. Lila was eerily quiet for the longest time before she finally spoke.

"You scare me," she whispered.

"Why?" *You scare me, too.*

"Because I trust you. Because I want to tell you what I've never told anyone before."

Same, Lila. Fucking same.

"Do you know what hurts the most?" Lila said, sniffling. "The regret."

I waited for her to continue to tell *her* story.

Lila

"I think I'll always carry that regret in my heart because the last thing I said to my parents was that I hated them. I remember whispering it in the back of the car, but I don't know if they heard it or not. Because right after I had said those words, I heard my father scream, and my mother cry out. Then... the car... I was in the air... and the next thing I knew, everything hurt. So much pain."

A single tear escaped and slid down my cheek. I dashed it away, almost angrily, because right now, anger tasted bitter on my tongue while the pain laid heavy on my heart.

"I was only thirteen, well... almost fourteen. So young, so foolish, such a stupid, stupid brat. They wouldn't let me attend a birthday party that all my friends were attending. Mom said they didn't know the girl whose house I was going to, so they didn't feel comfortable with me going. Dad didn't think it was safe because it was too far from our neighborhood, and they didn't know the parents. I wanted to go. I wanted to have fun with all my other friends. But they refused, and I was so, so angry. We were in the car, and we were arguing. Then I said... *I hate you.*"

The memories were vivid in my head, as if it were just yesterday. I could almost hear my parents' voices, and if I closed my eyes, I could see them.

I looked away and blinked away the burning sensation in my eyes, but the tears didn't stop. "I didn't mean it. I *didn't*. I just said it because I was angry, but I didn't mean it, Maddox. I... didn't. Those were the last words I said to my parents. That is my deepest regret," I broke off, letting out a pained whimper. I choked on my shame. "It... hurts because I will never get to tell my parents how much I love them. I will never feel my mother's arms or my dad's warm hugs again. My mom will never sing me happy birthday in her silly voice, and my dad will never tickle me because he loved to hear me laugh. He said my laughs sounded like a chipmunk."

I ducked my head, hiding behind the curtain of my hair.

247

"Sometimes, I forget what it is to feel okay, to feel normal because I'm filled with… so many unspoken emotions."

Maddox was silent, and I wondered what he was thinking about. Did he pity me? Could he feel my shame? I didn't want to be pitied, though… for the first time since my parents died, I just wanted to be held.

I'd been pushing the people who cared about me away: my grandparents and Riley. They tried, but I always shut them down because I hated being pitied, I hated the sympathetic look on their faces. When Gran suggested therapy, I refused to see any shrink. Talking about my feelings to a stranger? Letting them see me at my weakest? No way.

Realization dawned on me, and I choked back a sob. By pushing them away, I was causing myself more pain. I needed someone to talk to.

I needed to be held.

I needed to cry and have someone tell me it was going to be okay.

Sniffling back a cry, I dabbed my tears away. Maddox was here, and it was ironic because of how much I despised him when we first met.

"Do you know why I hated you so much before?"

He let out a dry laugh, without any humor. "Because I was an asshole?"

If only he knew the truth…

Maybe it was time.

I took a deep breath and let it out. "No, I despised you, hated the mere idea of you, because you reminded me of my parents' murderer."

His head snapped up, and I could almost hear his heart beat rattling through his chest.

Thump.

Thump.

Thump.

There was a moment of silence, his lips parting as if to speak, but he couldn't say a word. His eyes bore into me, searching, and I saw matching pain in his. My words hung heavily between us, and we both bled from the invisible gunshot, a festering open wound.

I swallowed past the heavy lump in my throat, my whole body shaking with tremors. "We wouldn't have gotten into an accident if we hadn't been hit by a drunk driver that night."

Four years had gone by, and I was still haunted by the memory.

"He was seventeen and very drunk, way above the limit, especially for someone underage. The road was slightly icy, so he lost control of his vehicle. Our cars were travelling the opposite direction, and he hit us from the front. I still remember the bright headlights flashing in front of me as his car crashed into ours."

"He–"

"He should have been jailed for a long time. He should have been punished, right? Maddox, right?"

He nodded, his eyes red. *Don't give me such a tortured look, Maddox. My heart is already breaking.*

"He didn't," I said, hugging myself tighter. "He didn't even spend a night in a cell; he wasn't punished, and he walked away from the accident, unscathed. Do you know why?"

"Why?" Maddox whispered, but he already knew the answer.

"He was the rich and spoiled son of a wealthy and influential attorney who had the whole world at his feet. His dad swept the accident under the rug and was able to get his son out of trouble. I was in a coma for a few weeks, and when I woke up... I found out the case was closed and had been filed away. We were told the chauffeur took the blame and had been pardoned by the law; except, he wasn't the one driving that night... *that* boy was. I know because I did my research after I woke up. My grandparents helped, and we tried to open the case again."

"Lila," Maddox breathed. His head fell into his hands. "Goddamn it."

"I was in the hospital, still recovering from my injuries, when the dad walked through the door. The look on his face, God, I can still see it so clearly. There was no remorse, Maddox. *Nothing.* He didn't care that I just lost my parents because of his son. He didn't care that I was practically crippled in a hospital bed, in pain, in so much fucking pain. He took out a check..."

"No," Maddox let out a curse. "Fuck, no. Lila, *no.*" He banged his fists against the wet, muddy grass.

I laughed and laughed, dry and empty and cold. Yes. He offered me one million dollars to stay silent. He said he'd give me more if I'd just shut up and leave his family alone."

Then I cried.

And cried... and cried.

"We... lost...the... case," I hiccupped back a sob, but I was only choking on my own saliva. "Money and power and too many connections, he had everything, and we stood no chance against him."

"He paid off the judge?" Maddox growled, his words laced with anger.

"I assumed he did or he didn't have to. They were buddies."

I tried to breathe, tried to stay alive, forced myself to survive. *Inhale, exhale.*

I wanted to scream until I pass out and forget all of this happened. Maybe when I'd wake up, I'd find myself in a world where my parents were still alive, and we were living happily ever after.

"When you're rich, you can pay for someone's silence, buy life and death, play god and win. That's what he did. I'm a mere mortal... I lost."

"I'm sorry."

I am too.

"I hated you because you were a reminder of the boy who ruined me and stole my life from me," I croaked, my ability to speak fading. I rubbed my chest, over my scars. "So rich, so spoiled. Such a brat with so much arrogance."

Maddox made a sound at the back of his throat; it sounded almost like a silent cry before he spoke. "I'm sorry," he said again.

With all my strength gone from my body, I couldn't sit up anymore. My body swayed, and I fell onto my back and closed my eyes. I was drained of everything, all the pain, all the suffering... my past and all the memories.

I felt... empty.

And numb.

I didn't have to open my eyes to *feel* him. Maddox settled on the cold grass and laid down beside me. I felt his warm breath against my neck. He was really close.

I breathed in the fresh air, and there was a comfortable silence between us. It lasted for a long time, and I soaked it in, the warmth from his presence. Until Maddox broke the silence.

"Tell me about your parents. How did they meet?" he asked gently.

So, I did.

I told him about an unlikely love story.

"My mom was the only Hispanic in their neighborhood, and all the other kids would pick on her. My dad was apparently one of her bullies until she grabbed him one day and slammed her lips against his then pulled back, looked him straight in the eye and told him, 'If you can't shut up, I'll shut you up.' He said he fell in love with her right then and there. My father always told me to be with the person who makes your heart beat a thousand miles an hour," I told Maddox.

We stared at my parents' headstones, and I wondered if they could feel me since I was so close to them? Were they watching over me?

There was a dull ache in my chest, but I didn't feel like crying anymore. Maybe I'd finally spent all my tears; because even though it *hurt*, the urge to cry was gone.

Until next year, until I allowed myself to break down again. I hated being vulnerable. The last time I was; I had been in a hospital and I couldn't give my parents' the justice they deserved.

I didn't know why I let Maddox see me like this, why I allowed him to see my weakness... but all I knew was the moment he sat on that bench next to me and held my hand, I didn't want him to let go.

I didn't even cry at parents' funeral until everyone was gone, and I was alone. Except the moment Maddox touched my hand – the dam broke, the cage around my heart shattered, and I hadn't been able to stop crying.

We sat there for a long time. The sun was starting to go down, the sky turning a bright orange. I guess this place was called Sunset Park for a reason; it had the best sunset view.

"Do you believe in love?" Maddox asked, roughly.

What a strange question in a moment like this.

"Yes. But I've long decided that it's not for me. Not anymore."

"Why not?"

"Because I don't want to lose anyone else." I've suffered enough loss for a lifetime, and I survived it, but I didn't want to test my luck.

How much pain can a person bear before they break down completely?

I was stronger than the magic of love.

I wrapped my arms around my knees and brought my legs closer to my chest. I laid my head over my knees and turned to look at Maddox. He was staring at my parents' headstones, looking thoughtful.

"Do you believe in love?" I asked him back. My cheeks felt tight from the cold and my dried tears. My face was probably blotchy and red, but I couldn't find myself to care in the moment.

This was Maddox, my best friend.

He blinked, as if he wasn't expecting the question. "I don't know."

Curious, I pushed for more. "What do you mean?"

"I used to think love was fake. It didn't exist. Love is too complicated and shit. No one belonged to me before. I was never close enough to love someone or to even understand the meaning of it."

Wild emotions clogged my throat, and my heart flipped like a caged bird, beating its wings, looking for an escape.

"And what do you think now?" I whispered the question.

Maddox faced me, his blue eyes staring into mine, looking right through my cold exterior, pushing right through my walls and knocking at my caged heart.

When he spoke again, his voice was deep and rough. His words were a silent confession.

"Now, I have someone to lose, and I know it will break me. I know what it means to fear losing the person who means the most to you. That person has the power to destroy me."

Silence fell upon us, and I couldn't find the words to convey what I was feeling. I turned my head away from his probing gaze and went back to staring at the headstones.

Seconds turned into long minutes, but we sat there in comfortable silence.

"Maddox?"

"Yeah?"

I took a deep breath and made my first promise to Maddox. "You won't lose me. Ever."

He was quiet for a moment, and I thought I fucked up, until his hand came into the line of my vision, and he showed me his pinky.

"Promise?" he asked softly.

I hooked my finger around his. Maddox was warm and familiar. He felt solid and safe. I wanted to cling to him and never, ever let go. "Promise."

He flexed his pinky around me and then he smiled.

For the first time today, I smiled, too.

Pinky swear, me and you... forever.

CHAPTER TWENTY-FOUR

Lila

"So, is it like…a date?" I asked. "A real date?"

I couldn't see Riley's face through the phone, but her giddiness was apparent as she let out a small squeal. "Well, yeah. I mean… he called, and he asked if we could grab dinner, and he told me to dress warm since it tends to get a bit colder at night," she breathed, each word laced with excitement. "And Lila, his voice… over the phone… I think I almost orgasmed. Holy shit."

I fell back on my bed, a wide grin spreading over my lips. "Honestly, I didn't think Grayson was going to do it," I said. "I mean, ask you out."

He was so reserved, so quiet and didn't mingle with the rest of the Berkshire students.

In fact, he was a loner.

Riley didn't give up though.

She giggled, and I heard some rustling in the background. "It's been three months. It's about time he breaks down and ask me out. I can't decide what to wear. Jeans or a dress? He said to put on something warm, but maybe a dress is fitting? Something cute or something sexy?" She paused, thoughtfully. "I don't want to come across as easy or trying to fuck on our first date. But I also want to feel pretty and sexy."

After Jasper, Riley had sworn off any Berkshire boys. She said they were all the same, and the pain of what Jasper did was still too fresh, even though it had been over a year since their breakup. It was the first time I'd seen her *this* excited; I just hoped Grayson didn't end up breaking her heart.

Although, I liked to believe that he was into her as much as she liked him. He was always subtle about his feelings but I had seen him sneaking glances at Riley and trying to hide his smile. There was a look in his eyes when he watched her–something akin to adoration.

The same look I had seen in Colton's eyes, too.

I wasn't sure if I should've talked to Riley about Colton, but she was happy with Grayson and that was all I wanted. He was a good guy, and Riley liked him. The end.

She made her decision. Colton would just have to accept it.

"Remember the black dress you wore last Christmas? The mini one, V cut? You looked cute but smoking hot," I offered.

Riley made a sound of agreement. "Oh, that one! My boobs look nice in that dress. I can wear those new high heels boots I got!"

"Atta girl. There you go. What time is he picking you up at?" I looked at the clock and saw that it was almost six pm.

"Umm… an hour. Shit, I gotta get ready. Talk later?"

Her happiness was contagious. "Yeah, babe. Text me when you get home. I want to hear all about it."

Riley let out a small giggle before she mumbled. "He better kiss me, or I'm going to be reaaally disappointed."

Oh yeah, he better.

Because I wanted to know all about that kiss.

We said our goodbyes and hung up.

Riley was happy...

The ringing of my phone jostled me out of my thoughts, and I stared down at the screen. Maddox. His name flashing on my phone screen reminded me that I was supposed to be angry.

I answered the phone, and Maddox cut me off before I could say anything. "Come outside. Now," he demanded. The low rumble of his voice had my stomach fluttering before I remembered to hang onto the anger.

Ugh, asshole.

"What do you want?" I shot back, rather rudely. What he did was... unforgiveable.

"Lila." There was a warning in his voice.

"Maddox," I hissed.

"I'm outside. Come out. *Now*."

"Maybe if you say please." The sarcasm dripped from my mouth easily. *Watch out, I got my sassy pants on today.*

There was a frustrated growl before I heard him sigh. "Please."

Huh. That was shocking.

My lips flattened in a straight line. "No."

"For fuck's sake! Are you still pissed because I ate your muffin?"

"You stole my muffin!" And it was the last one.

"I thought you didn't want it. You left it on the table."

I growled in response. He was silent for a second before he laughed. The jerk actually *laughed*. "Are you on your period?"

"Fuck you." I ended the call with a growl.

Yes, I was on my period.

Yes, I was cranky. Because this asshole, aka my best friend, ate my mint chocolate muffin.

A second later, my pinged with a message. *Come out, please. I'm sorry about the muffin.*

I typed a quick text back. *Why?*

My screen flashed with another message. *Just trust me.*

I rolled of my eyes and bounced off the bed. Maddox wasn't going to give up. For all I knew, if I didn't come out of the house, he was going to come in and get me.

I stepped out of the house to find Maddox leaning against his car, arms crossed. At the sight of me, he licked his lips and winked. My breath caught in my throat because he was so sinfully handsome. Then I remembered he was my best friend... and I was supposed to be mad, right?

I crossed my arms over my chest and glared. "What do you want?"

Maddox crooked his index finger at me, beckoning me to come closer. I did.

"Come closer. I'm not going to bite, Garcia."

"You're annoying me, Coulter," I snapped.

He tsked before he looped his arm around my waist and pulled me closer. I stumbled against him, and our bodies clashed together.

A cocky grin spread over his lips. "I can't decide if I like you feisty or I like you quiet."

I huffed and blew my hair out of my face, before squinting up at him. He sobered, the mischievous glint in his eyes gone. My heart dropped to my stomach, and my palms started sweating.

"Lila, do you trust me?"

My eyes flared in surprise. "Why are you asking?"

"Answer the question." His gaze didn't waver from mine, absorbing me and holding me captive.

I shook my head and tried to move away from him. "What's going on?"

I didn't like the look on his face. Something was up, and I wasn't going to like it.

"I want to try something with you," he slowly explained.

"Jump off an airplane? Scuba diving? Bungee Jumping? Rafting? Something stupid and thrill seeking?"

Maddox loved the adrenaline rush, loved any outdoor activity that would have my heart spilling out through my mouth. We went mountain biking a few weeks ago. Well, *he* did, and I watched from the sideline, convincing myself not to pass out.

It was too dangerous, too reckless... everything that Maddox needed in his life. The thrill and the rush through his veins. He *lived* for it.

Maddox shook his head, the expression on his face still too serious. "No, this isn't about me. This is for you. But I want us to do it together."

"Maddox, spit it out." Nerves gnawed at my gut as I waited for him to speak.

Still holding me in his arms, Maddox turned us around, so I was facing his car, with my back against his front. I was trapped between him and the car.

My breath expelled through my lips with a harsh exhale, and my knees quivered. His hands landed on my hips, and his breath feathered next to my ear. He reached around me and pulled the passenger door open, his intention clear.

No. No. No.

I was already struggling against him before he could say a word.

"Maddox—"

"Do you trust me?" He said in my ear.

"No, I don't." My throat convulsed, and every muscle in my body turned to ice. There was a roaring in my ears, and my heart pounded so hard it felt like it was about to beat right out of my chest. "I... can't," I wheezed. "Don't make me do this."

"Lila, do you trust me?" The baritone of his voice reverberated through my bones, commanding and strong—grounding me and forcing me to face reality. My hands shook, and I started sweating, even though the spring air was cold against my skin.

I swallowed. "No."

"Don't lie, Lila." His hands tightened on my hips.

My lungs burned, and I couldn't *breathe.*

The panic began with a cluster of sparks in my abdomen. My skin itched, feeling too tight around my flesh. My own body was causing me to suffocate. Chest heaving, breath coming out in gasps and tears threatening to fall, I crumbled to the ground. Maddox came with me, not letting go. My heart jumped in terror, in fear, and each breath I pulled into my body became painful.

Why? Why was he doing this to me? Why, Maddox?

There was a hurricane of emotions coursing inside me, threatening to burst through. I couldn't stop shaking, my mind playing continuous tricks on me.

"Breathe," Maddox said, his voice breaking through the chaos in my head.

"I... can't."

Breathe! Damn it, I told myself.

I clutched my chest and gasped. Ten... nine... eight...

The world around me slowed and became a blur, my blood turned to ice and my body felt... *numb.* There was a vicious pounding in the back of my head and the veins in my neck throbbed.

"I believe in you," he whispered.

Seven... six... five... four...

"Breathe, baby."

Three... two... one.

For the longest time, we stayed just like this.

My head lolled backward onto his shoulders. "Is this fun to you? Seeing me like this...?"

His lips brushed my temple, softly. "No. But I'm about to help you conquer your fear. You only live once, Lila."

"I... can't do it today," I confessed.

Maddox shook his head. "Not today, not tomorrow... but maybe next week. We're going to keep trying."

My chin wobbled, and I nodded my head.

I did try. For five days, I tried. Maddox successfully got me closer to his car. Every day, he opened the passenger door, and I'd crumble to the ground, shaking and gasping.

Day by day, I tackled my past and pushed past my fear until my body threatened to give out.

On day six, I could barely step out of my grandparents' house. My legs were shaking so badly that Maddox had to help me walk down the gravelly path to his car.

Again, my knees weakened, and I slumped forward.

A sob escaped past my lips as the crushing anxiety made its way into my body once again.

"I'm... sorry," I choked.

Maddox waited for my panic attack to recede, his presence commanding and his hand steady on my back. He dominated my panicking, soothing me with a gentle touch.

I lifted my head from his shoulder, and his intense, beautiful eyes locked with mine. Panic coursed through me, making my eyes wild and my face white as a ghost, but he didn't stare at me like I was some pathetic loser.

Maddox waited patiently. Because he believed in me.

I chewed on my lip as I tried to calm my breathing. The muscles in my body spasmed, but I fought to stay conscious.

"Put me in the car, Maddox." I tried to sound firm, but my voice only came out as weak as the cries of a newborn kitten.

He pressed his lips together, searching my eyes. Maybe he saw the resolve in them because he nodded. We got to our feet, and I struggled to stand upright. This time, when Maddox opened the passenger door, I climbed into the car on unsteady legs. I slumped into the seat, my heart banging viciously against my ribs.

He placed the seatbelt around me as I held onto my seat, knuckles white, fingers aching with how tight I was holding on.

He pressed his thumb over my full lips, putting them away from my teeth. "Trust me," Maddox rasped.

Trust him? I did, wholly and truly, with all my heart.

That was the scariest part.

"We're doing this."

He grinned. "No, *you* are doing this."

Maddox closed the door, and I watched him move around the car to the driver's seat. He climbed in, and I took a deep breath. His hands were on the steering wheel, waiting.

"Do it, Maddox." *I trust you.*

"Before we do this, I need to tell you something," he paused. I cocked my head, waiting. "Those yoga pants you're wearing should be illegal, Garcia."

My lips parted, and a sudden laughter bubbled up from my chest.

"Maddox!" I was still laughing when he turned the ignition, and, without me realizing, the car started rolling forward.

My smile slipped off my face, and I *gasped*.

"Oh God." My breath stuttered.

That night... the memories...

Everything hit me at once, and I was drowning, sinking... dying. *I can't breathe.*

Maddox grasped my hand. "I got you." His deep voice was soft but powerful, with a rich silky tone. "Lila."

My eyes closed, and I breathed through my nose.

Ten... nine... eight... seven... six... five... four... three... two... one.

I was dying.

"You're not dying," a voice said to me.

His voice.

Maddox.

"I am." *Mom... dad... I love you. I love you so much. Can you hear me? I'm sorry.*

A warm hand folded around mine. "I'm right here. You're not dying."

So warm, so strong, so familiar.

Cold wind brushed against my sweaty, overheating skin.

"Open your eyes, Lila." *No.*

"Trust me," he said.

Anguish twisted my stomach. I pressed a hand over my chest, trying to rub the ache away. My eyes fluttered open as I wheezed through each breath.

My window had been rolled down, hence the breeze brushing up against my hair. And...

Oh my God.

"Beautiful, isn't it?" Maddox spoke.

I couldn't blink, couldn't take my eyes off the pink and orange sky. The sunset. We were apparently driving over a hill, and I recognized that it wasn't too far from my house. I never knew the sunset could be so beautiful up here, like this…

I couldn't stop the tears burning my eyes and threatening to spill. They slid down my cheeks, and I choked back a cry.

"Maddox," I breathed, my hands shaking in both fear and… something else, I didn't know. Maybe in relief?

"Look out and feel the wind, Lila. I got you. You're safe."

I brought my head closer to the window and felt the breeze against my face. More tears spilled down my cheeks. My stomach churned with an anxious feeling. Panic and fear thrummed through my veins.

But…

I was in a car.

Maddox was driving.

I was… alive.

My lips wobbled with a smile. "Hey, Maddox?"

"If you're about to confess your undying love to me, I'm going to tell you to stop right there, Sweet Cheeks," he rumbled.

"Still an asshole, I see."

Maddox chuckled, and my stomach fluttered. *Thank you.*

"Friends?" I asked, showing him my pinky. It was something so silly to do, but it was *us*.

He grinned and hooked his finger around mine. "Friends."

Maddox drove for hours, until the sunset disappeared and the stars came out in the dark sky. He eventually stopped the car over a hill and cranked up the radio, which was ironically playing Lauv's *There's No Way*. He reached behind him to the backseat and handed me a small brown paper bag.

I peeked inside and smiled. A mint chocolate muffin. I took a bite, my eyes going to Maddox to find that he was already looking at me.

I didn't have to confess my undying love to Maddox. What we had; it was an unspoken understanding with unsaid words and a feeling we couldn't explain. Love was too simple a word to describe it because love was black and white. Love or don't love – there was not really an in-between.

What we had... it was a kaleidoscope of colors.

CHAPTER TWENTY-FIVE

Maddox

"I don't like him," I growled, folding my arms over my chest. I stayed rooted in front of the door, as if I could somehow stop her from leaving.

Lila rolled her eyes, bent over and touched her toes. She stretched, and I had to look away because, goddamn it, her ass looked good in those jeans.

I was pissed at my own reaction and this whole situation. And I didn't exactly know *why*.

"It's not up to you," she said in a sing-song voice. Somedays, I wished she was intimidated by me. It'd make this whole friendship thing easier, but nope. Lila Garcia was fucking feisty, and she constantly butted heads with me. "You're not going on that date with him. I am."

Yeah, that was exactly my problem.

She was going on a date.

With someone. Grayson's friend. A fucking date that Riley set up. Now that she had a boyfriend, she was under the assumption that Lila needed a man in her life, too.

Well, too fucking bad, she already had a man. *Me.*

"I don't trust him," I said again.

Lila faced me, hands on her hips. She was wearing makeup, which she rarely did. Ripped jeans, ankle boots and a black tank top that should be illegal. Sure, Lila didn't have big boobs, but her tits looked juicy in that tank top. Juicy, sinful, forbidden... and–

Fuck, she even painted her nails. She looked... beautiful. For *him.*

"You never even met him," she argued. My jaw clenched, and I was about to pop a vein.

"He could be a fucking murderer for all we know!" He could hurt her...

And he wasn't *me.*

Lila's eyes turned to slits, and she nudged her chin high, giving me that haughty look of hers. She really mastered that look that says – You're not the boss of me and I can do whatever I want.

"I've met him twice, and he's a gentleman, Maddox. Stop it."

"I don't like it. I don't like him," I said for the hundredth time tonight. "What if he touches you, and you don't want him to?"

Touch... her. He could touch her and fucking kiss her...

She rubbed her forehead, her eyes looking bleak. Lila was already tired of my bullshit. "Maddox, stop it. You're not going to ruin this date for me."

"He could... hurt you."

A smile ghosted her lips. "Daren can't and won't hurt me."

Daren? Even his name sounded dumb. I imagined Lila moaning out that name, and the urge to pummel his face, someone I had never met before, was strong.

"Can you give me a guarantee that he won't hurt you?" I shot back in my defense. "I won't complain and let you go on this stupid date if you can give me a hundred percent guarantee."

I was playing dirty because I knew she couldn't.

I didn't know why I was reacting this way when Lila told me she was going on this date. There was an uneasy feeling in my stomach and a heavy weight on my chest.

"You're acting like a jealous boyfriend, Maddox," she warned, her lips twisted in displeasure. Her words were laced with a warning.

Jealous... boyfriend?

Jealous... me? Ha.

"I'm acting like a caring *friend*," I amended.

She snorted, quite unladylike. I loved that about Lila. She wasn't fake around me, and she wasn't vying for my attention. Lila didn't mold herself to fit my standards. She stayed true to herself and gave whoever dared to douse her fire the middle finger.

Lila fixed up her winged eyeliner and glanced at me through the floor length mirror. "No, you're being a child. A petulant, bratty child. You went on a date last week, and I didn't stop you. Does that make me any less caring?"

"I didn't go on a *date*," I mumbled, fighting back a grimace. She didn't need to know the details.

Her eyes hardened. "No, you're right. You don't date. You fucked her."

I rubbed my forehead and sighed. This was getting us nowhere, and I was only growing more agitated as the seconds ticked by. Dickass-ren or whatever his name was, was about to pop up any minute now, and Lila would be on her way... to her date...

Jealous?

No, that wasn't it.

Lila and my relationship was clear—there were no hidden feelings and no secrets. We cared for each other, deeply, but that was it. The mere thought of us being anything *more* was a forbidden idea, and my stomach churned.

I'd rather have Lila like this, than risk losing her later because our feelings were fucked up. There was no going back if we crossed that line.

"He'll hurt you," I said one last time, hoping it'd change her mind.

It was just the idea of her being with another guy, as close as she was with me, that didn't sit well with me. I wasn't jealous.

I was just a bit territorial of my best friend.

Lila stared at me for a moment, the expression on her face unreadable. Her gaze was unflinching, and her small fists clenched at her side. She looked like she was having an inner debate with herself.

She swallowed, her throat bobbing with the small action. Then she did something I least expected and sure as fuck wasn't ready for it. Not at all.

My eyes widened as Lila dragged her tank top over her head, letting it slide through her fingers. She stood in front of me in her jeans, boots and bra. Lila wasn't shy, never was. In fact, she could be as crass as me if she wanted to, and most days, she was. She had always been bold and confident.

The determined look on her face should have warned me, but I was too focused on her... chest.

I inhaled, and my dick twitched, straining against my jeans. Shit. "What the fuck?"

"What do you see?" she asked calmly.

269

I see… tits. Titties I could fuck. "What are you doing?" I groaned. "Lila?"

She took several steps forward until we were standing toe-to-toe. Lila was my little midget, so tiny that the top of her head barely came to my shoulders. She had to nudge her head back to stare up at me because I basically towered over her.

Her gaze was somber as she waited. "Maddox, look at me."

My fists clenched and unclenched. I kept my eyes on hers, refusing to let my gaze wander… down. I'd probably bust a nut if I did. "I am."

"No, you're not. Look. At. Me. Look closer," she persisted in that same soft voice.

I did… and I finally saw what she wanted me to see.

"Do you see now?" she breathed.

My heart stuttered, and I lost my breath as my stomach tightened. My eyes fell to her chest, where her breasts were clad in a lacy, black bra.

And I saw…

Pink and white jagged lines… scars…on her beautiful pale skin. Right at the center of her chest and between the two heavy mounds.

"No," I choked. Jesus Christ, sweet Lila.

Before I could stop myself, my hand came up as if to touch her. When I realized what I was about to do, I stopped an inch away from her skin.

Lila took my hand in hers and placed it on her chest, right in the middle, where her scars laid. She let out a shuddering breath the moment I touched her. Her heart thudded hard against my palm.

"Is this–?" I couldn't finish my sentence.

Lila nodded. "From the accident."

My shaking fingers brushed over her scars, feeling the slight bumpiness on her skin, whereas the rest of her was soft and smooth. "It's ugly," she whispered, trying to hide a grimace, but her face said it all.

"You're beautiful," I confessed, my voice strained.

And she truly was.

Lila had been through hell and back. That was the most beautiful part of her; she was a woman who wore her pain like a diamond choker around her neck. Strong, unyielding... a survivor. Lila Garcia straightened her own crooked crown because she didn't need anyone else to do it for her.

Lila let me in, not because she *needed* me.

It was because she wanted me—as a friend, a companion and a partner.

She gave me a bittersweet smile. "Daren can't hurt me because I'm already hurt. He can't break my heart because it's already broken. Do you understand now?"

I nodded. Lila exhaled in relief.

I stepped closer, our bodies pressing against each other. Mine—fully clothed. Lila's—in a state of half dressed. Her skin was warm underneath my touch. She peeked at me through her thick lashes with a look in her eyes that should have told me *something*... but I couldn't understand what she was trying to convey.

She breathed.

I breathed.

The world came to a stop, and the colors faded away, leaving us in a state of black and white.

Lila shivered, a silent tremor running through her body. It wasn't from the cold because her room was hot, and I was sweating. Her gaze fell to my lips before they wavered, and she looked back at my eyes again.

My head descended toward hers, and my lips brushed against her forehead, a simple kiss. Lila sucked in a harsh breath, and her eyes closed.

I'd never given a girl a forehead kiss before. That shit was cheesy as fuck, but it came natural with her. It wasn't like I could kiss her... lips. Lips that looked so soft, so kissable. She'd sock me in the face if I ever tried.

So, we settled with a forehead kiss. That was safe and friend-like.

"Lila?"

"Hmm?"

"You're a beautiful dragon," I said.

Her shoulders shook, and a small laugh escaped past her lips. "Dragon, eh?"

"Dragon," I agreed. "Daren should be worried because you'll probably eat him for dinner if he accidentally steps on your tail."

I closed my eyes and breathed in her scent— she smelled of peaches from the shampoo and body lotion she used.

Lila slowly pulled away, and I let her go. She grabbed her tank top, and once she was dressed again, she checked her phone. "He said he's on his way to the restaurant."

"Can I chaperone?" I asked, only half joking. Actually, I was serious.

Lila wasn't amused. "No, Maddox," she said. There was a note of exasperation in her voice.

She walked past me and out the door; I watched her go with a sinking feeling in my stomach.

I considered following her to the restaurant and keeping an eye on them, just in case, Dickass-ren tried to do any shit to my girl-*friend*. But Lila would never forgive me, and I'd rather stay on her good side. She could be brutal, and she had sharp claws.

I never thought of myself as a possessive person... but apparently, I was.

Of our friendship.

Well, fuck.

CHAPTER
TWENTY-SIX

Lila

I watched as Pops let out a robust laugh at something Maddox said. Grandpa said something else of his own that had Maddox shaking his head and grinning. Sure, Maddox worked for my grandparents, but only Gran had welcomed him with open arms. Pops was a little apprehensive; he always had been with any boys hanging around me.

He said he didn't trust them, and he was right.

But Maddox and I had been friends for months now, and Pops slowly started to warm up to him. In fact, if I wasn't mistaken, they were on the same team now.

Project: Don't let Lila date and protect her at all costs.

It only took two weeks for me to realize my best friend had been right about Daren. Dickass-ren, as Maddox liked to call him, was indeed an asshole who was only interested in sleeping with me.

Grandpa was a hard man to win over, but I wasn't surprised Maddox did. He was… genuine, and even Pops could see that. I was just glad that the two men in my life were finally getting along, well enough for them to share a beer and watch a football game together while discussing sports.

Oh, you know. A usual Sunday night.

Maddox had spent the day with us. Gran even dragged him to church, and he went without complaint. I never pegged Maddox as a religious person and neither was I, but I humored Gran every Sunday and let her drag me to church. Sure, I did believe in God, but if He really loved me, my parents would have still been alive. So yeah, God and I didn't share an amicable relationship.

We had brunch together, then went over to the grocery store for inventory day. After we closed for the night, Pops invited Maddox over for dinner and football. If I had to guess, Pops was a tad lonely, missing a buddy to talk with and he was making a truce with Maddox.

"I think they're best friends now."

My eyebrows rose, turning to Gran as she helped me put the dishes away. "They are?"

"Your Pops doesn't laugh like that with just anyone." She smiled, glancing back at them. "Trust me, I've known him for too long time and been married to him for decades."

Well, yeah, it was Maddox after all. He could easily win anyone over. That was my best friend, ladies and gentlemen.

The men hollered from the living room, and I was guessing it was probably a touch down for their team. I grinned, watching the two most important men in my life finally bonding. Maybe if my dad was here too...

My chest ached, and I rubbed the spot, trying to alleviate the pain. Somedays, the skin around my scars would itch and the scar itself would *hurt*, like I was pouring kerosene on already burning skin. The doctor said it was all in my head. The pain wasn't physical anymore, but my brain and body were used to it, and sometimes, they liked to remind me of the pain.

I thought of the day I showed Maddox my scars. It was weeks ago, although it felt just like yesterday, the memory still fresh in my head and my skin still burning from his touch.

Maddox had brushed his fingers over the marks left on my body, touching my past, lingering over the jagged and ugly lines, tracing the dents of my soul and the rough edges of my heart.

He didn't run away, not like Leo did after taking my virginity. I didn't see the look of disgust or revulsion on his face. Maddox didn't flinch.

He stayed and called me a *dragon*–that was Maddox's way of telling me what I needed to know.

And when his head had descended toward mine, I thought he was going to ruin everything by kissing me that night. For a brief moment, maybe I had wanted him to, but then I felt an immense rush of relief when he didn't.

My phone pinged with a message, snapping me out of my thoughts. It was from Riley.

Quick question. Does this make me look slutty?

She had a tight black dress on – one that molded to every curve of her body. Her boobs were practically slipping out, and she had on red lipstick. Her blond curls bounced off her shoulders, in a Marilyn Monroe style, since she cut them last week. Riley was pouting in the picture.

Slutty and cute. I texted back. **He's gonna be shooketh.**

If he doesn't fuck me tonight, I'm going to taser his dick.

I choked back on my laughter and disguised it with a fake cough before Gran could ask me what I was laughing about. Poor Riley was dickprived, or in Riley's words, she was suffering from dick deprivation. Grayson was being a thorough gentleman and courting Riley, his words, because she doesn't deserve anything less.

I agreed, but apparently, he was withholding sex because he thought Riley wasn't ready yet after the fiasco with Jasper. They were doing everything else, except sex—well, a home run. Riley did say they were on third base. She spared me the explicit details except she mentioned how good Grayson was with his tongue, and she saw Jesus. Lucky her.

They had been dating for a while now, and Riley... well, she was deeply and irrevocably in love with Grayson. I didn't doubt Grayson's feelings for her because it was apparent in the way his eyes followed her every move, the way his gaze searched for her in a crowded place and how he always had a possessive arm around her hips. Sure, he was *gentle*—but it was obvious he was trying to tone down his territorial instincts. Anyone could see that.

Especially after all the testosterone went flying across the room last weekend at Colton's party. That was... intense, to say the least. They both wanted Riley. Riley already made her choice, but Colton was having trouble accepting that.

You should just tie him to your bed and sit on him. Problem solved.

I was only half joking when I sent the text, but then... apparently, Riley didn't get the joke. ***Holy shit. That is the best idea.***

I quickly typed back a message. ***Wait! I wasn't serious.***

My phone pinged with a message a minute later. ***I am. Thanks, babe (;***

Oh God. Grayson had no idea what he was about to walk into.

"Is that Riley?" Grandma asked. "Tell her I'm sad she didn't

277

come over for brunch today."

I nodded, fighting back a giggle. Sorry, Gran. Riley was a tad busy right now. Busy convincing her boyfriend she was ready to be dicked down.

As I put the last plate away, my eyes found Maddox. He was intensely focused on the football game, a pleased smile on his lips. The indent in his left cheek, a small dimple, winked at me as he let out a laugh at something Pops said.

He looked... at home with *my* family. Like he belonged here, with us, not in the cold and sterile Coulter Manor, alone with his dark thoughts.

"Lila," Gran said softly. I looked back at her, and her eyes were glassy as she watched Pops and Maddox, too. "He does a good job of hiding it, but that boy needs a family; he needs love. He's far too young to hold such pain in his eyes."

She patted me on the arm and walked away to join them in the living room, leaving me alone with my thoughts.

He had *me*.

Some days, I wondered if *just friends* would ever be enough for us. We friend-zoned each other; well, basically, *I* friend-zoned *him,* but he eventually went along with it, which means I've tried to date other guys and he still fucked around with some girls, but they never lasted for more than four days. The last one only made it three days; he kicked her to the curb because she called me a bitch for accidentally cockblocking them.

It only made me roll my eyes, but I had never seen Maddox drop a girl so fast. He was pissed, although that was an understatement.

That night when I showed him my scars, we had a moment. Maddox and I had looked at each other a little too long to be *just friends*. That eye contact was more intimate than any words or

278

touches would ever be. There was something unspoken between us, and in that moment, I almost thought he was going to... kiss me. It was both mixed signals and my own overthinking.

He didn't kiss me.

I had been both relieved and... disappointed.

Although now that I thought about it, it was better this way. Just friends. He was safe and familiar. Being anything *more* would ruin what we had, and I wasn't ready for that.

Our eyes met as I walked into the living room and joined him on the couch. Folding my legs under me, I leaned against his side and sipped my tea. Maddox casually looped his arm behind my shoulders, probably doing it without realizing. His fingers drummed against my biceps as he continued watching the game.

As the football game came to an end, Gran and Pops retired upstairs for the rest of the night. Maddox searched Netflix, and we settled on watching *Anabelle*. Maddox loved horror movies; I hated them.

"I'll keep you safe." He grinned with a mischievous glint in his eyes.

I popped a tiny pretzel in my mouth from the bowl of party mix chips. "Actually, I think you're going to use this to your advantage to scare me, aren't you?"

Maddox gave me a half-shrug, but he pressed his lips together to avoid smiling. Jerk.

Halfway through the movie, I realized Maddox was handing me the pretzels and ringolos because those were my favorites while he ate the other chips.

Yeah, it was the little things. I needed my partner in crime. I didn't need a lover in Maddox. Friends were better than a boyfriend, right? Too much drama came with a relationship. Whatever

Maddox and I had, it was safe from any unnecessary drama.

My eyes fluttered close as I fought to stay awake. Before I lost consciousness, I felt his lips brushing against my forehead.

"Sweet dreams, Lila."

Just friends, I reminded myself.

CHAPTER
TWENTY-SEVEN

Lila

I stood on the stage, the light in my eyes blinding me for a moment, before I blinked away the blurriness. My gaze found Maddox in the crowd. He was dressed in his graduation cap and gown, a lazy smirk on his lips. He winked, which helped with my nerves.

We were graduating today.

We fucking did it, as Maddox would say.

I shook hands with the Headmaster as he handed me my diploma. My hands trembled, and I smiled as pictures were taken. I walked down the stage, my stomach twisting and feeling beyond exhilarated. I was excited but I also hated having everyone's attention on me.

This was my dream—everything I had worked my ass off for in the last few years.

I remembered the day I received a white envelope—an envelope that held the fate of my future in it.

"I don't know… I mean… what if… it could be a… rejection letter," I stuttered, my heart galloping a mile an hour. "Do… they send out… rejection letters?"

"You're freaking out, Lila. Calm down," Maddox said in his smooth voice.

"Calm down?" I screeched. "This," I waved the envelope at his face, "is everything I ever wanted, and what if it's not what I think it is?"

He raised his hands up in mock surrender, and I plopped back on my bed. My whole body was shaking. "I can't open it, Maddox."

"Lila," he started.

"No, I can't." My stomach twisted with nausea. I think I'm going to be sick."

"Lila, I don't think they send out rejection letters." Maddox rubbed a hand over his face, and I could tell he was fighting back a smile. What an asshole. He was laughing as I freaked out. I was a little miffed.

"How about I open it?" he suggested.

I popped up and bounced off the bed like a jack-in-the-box. "Yes! You do it!"

Shoving the envelope in his hand, I paced the length of my room. Sweat beaded my forehead, and I swiped it away.

Maddox tore open the envelope, and my stomach churned harder. Oh God, I really was about to throw up.

My eyes closed, and I reminded myself to breathe.

The sound of him opening the envelope filled the room. My heart thudded, and I inhaled… exhaled…

"Open your eyes," he said, his voice sounding closer to me. He was standing right in front of me because I felt the heat coming off him. The closeness of him helped… calm me.

I squeezed my eyes close.

"Eyes on me, Lila," Maddox demanded more forcefully, his voice *deep and thick. "Now."*

Helpless against his command, my eyes snapped open, and I tearfully stared up at him.

He was... smiling.

My knees weakened, and I grasped his arm to stay upright.

"Congratulations, Lila Garcia."

The breath I'd been holding shuddered out of me. Maddox waved the letter at me. "You're about to go to Harvard."

A loud squeal left me, taking Maddox by surprise. I launched myself into his arms, unable to contain my excitement. He hefted me up, and I wrapped my legs around his waist, laughing. "I got in!"

His arms came around me, one hand on my back and one hand planted firmly on my ass as I clung to him.

"You did it," he murmured in my hair, with such pride in his voice that my heart nearly burst out of my chest.

I breathed in his musky scent before pulling my face away from his neck. Our faces were mere inches away from each other. His prominent Adam's apple bobbed in his throat as he swallowed. Maddox nudged my nose with his, and his minty breath feathered over my lips.

"You did it," he said again.

"Thank you. For opening that letter, for not leaving my side, for holding me, for forcing me to face my fears... and for being my friend."

Maddox hugged me back. "You're welcome."

I untangled my legs from his waist, and he settled me back on my feet. "You need to tell your grandparents."

I licked my dry lips and nodded.

Harvard, here I come.

I had gotten my acceptance letter two months ago, a little later than usual, but when I found the envelope in our postal box, my heart had dropped and the first thing I did was call Maddox. I didn't understand *why* I did it, but I knew I needed him with me.

He was at my house in less than ten minutes, out of breath and smiling.

Maddox never left my side as I freaked out, and he didn't leave when I told my grandparents the news either. It meant a lot to me, that he stuck by my side. I never expected us to go from enemies to friends...to best friends.

The rest of the graduation ceremony was a blur. Soon enough, we were outside under the blue sky with the sun shining on us.

Grayson had Riley in his arms, and they were laughing and kissing. Each student found themselves surrounded by their family. My gaze lingered over the crowd, looking for Maddox's parents.

Please be here, please be here. Don't hurt him anymore.

They were nowhere to be found.

I seethed, anger simmering through my veins and gut. How dared they? They should have been proud to have a son like Maddox.

Yes, he was a troublemaker–a total misfit.

But damn it, he was sweet, and his heart was pure. He worked his ass off to graduate with honors. Time and time again, he proved himself to the world that he wasn't just a rich and spoiled kid.

My fists clenched at my sides, and I growled. Fuck it, fuck them! They didn't deserve to share this day with Maddox.

There was a tap on my shoulder, and I swiveled around, coming face-to-face with Maddox. He stood tall, his shoulders squared, and I had to admit, he did look hot in Berkshire's navy-blue graduation gown with his cap on top of his head.

His lips curved in an easy smile, and I searched his eyes, looking for the disappointment I expected to see. But there was none.

It was then I realized that he no longer expected anything from his parents. They were strangers to him, not a *family*. Because they had never been here for Maddox for the most important days of his life – his football games, his birthdays, his graduation.

"What's up with that kitten growl, Sweet Cheeks? Did someone step on your tail?" he teased.

I swatted his arm. "Watch it, Coulter."

"You don't scare me, Garcia."

"I'll bite you."

"Bite me then," he dared.

I snapped my teeth at him, and he threw his head back, chortling. My anger at his parents melted away at Maddox's laughter. I refused to bring up the topic of his parents not attending the graduation ceremony. He was happy, right here and right now, and that was all that mattered.

I crossed my arms over my chest, pouting.

His laughter died, but he was still smiling. Maddox shoved his hand in his pocket, and he fished out a teal Tiffany box. What...?

My lips parted in surprise as he snapped open the small box. No way!

Shock coursed through my body. "Maddox," I breathed, shaking my head. My cap slid down, and I fixed it on top of my head again, still staring at the box he was holding.

It was a necklace, exquisite but simple, with only a sterling silver charm.

"A dreamcatcher," I whispered, my fingers brushing over the intricated webbed floral centerpiece and the delicate feathers attached to the round center.

"Now, we've got matching dreamcatchers."

I let out a laugh at that. The memory from a few months ago flashed in my mind.

"What is this?" Maddox asked, giving the object in my hand a weird look. He appeared unimpressed.

"A dreamcatcher, silly." I gave it to him, and he looked even more confused.

"Why are you giving me a dreamcatcher?"

I realized Maddox sometimes had bad dreams.

We fell asleep together last night, on his couch, while we were studying, and he had woken up from a nightmare. He didn't speak of it, but the bleak look in his eyes broke my heart. He couldn't go back to sleep and ended up going to the gym that was open twenty-four-seven.

Maybe it was fate or just pure coincidence, but as I was scrolling through Instagram, I found an ad for dreamcatchers.

Sure, it was a silly thing to give to him, but I remembered the dreamcatcher my mom used to hang on my headboard when I was a kid. She said it'd keep all my bad dreams and monsters away.

I didn't really think much of it when I ordered it. True, Maddox and I were too old to believe in this, and he was obviously too macho for something so childish, but maybe…

Damn it.

I didn't even know why I got this dreamcatcher, and now, I was doubting myself. The first gift I ever gave Maddox was a dreamcatcher. Oh, what a story to tell the world and our friends.

His eyebrows rose. "You seriously expect me to hang this on my bed?"

It wasn't the response I was hoping for. My shoulders slumped, and I chewed on my lips, the feeling of bitter disappointment gnawing at my stomach. I thought maybe he'd be a bit more… appreciative?

I rose to my feet and squinted down at him, hands on my hips. Fuck him. "Look, if you don't want it, you can throw it away. It was cheap anyway, so I don't care."

Maddox didn't say a word. He just went back to looking at the dreamcatcher as if it was the weirdest thing he had ever seen.

I had thought he threw it away, like I told him to.

Except the next day, when I walked into his room... there it was.

The silly dreamcatcher I gave him, hanging onto his headboard. It looked so out of place in his bedroom, but Maddox kept it, close to him, right next to him while he slept.

We never spoke of it again, but every time I'd walk into his bedroom, that was the first thing my eyes would notice, and it'd always be there.

And months later, Maddox still had it. It was my first gift to him.

The dreamcatcher he didn't want but never threw away.

I flipped my curled hair over my shoulders and stared up at Maddox. "Can you put it on me?"

He took the silver necklace out of the Tiffany box, and my throat went dry as his hands slipped around the back of my neck. He stood close, crowding into my space, but I couldn't complain. His body heat caused me to flush, and his fingers were warm against my skin—a teasing touch, so featherlight that I barely felt it.

Maddox placed the necklace around my neck and the dreamcatcher charm laid on the base of my throat where it belonged.

"Beautiful," he rasped, his breath caressing the tip of my earlobe. It made me warm and breathless, though we had been this close so many times: we hugged, we slept in the same bed, and Maddox would give me piggyback rides. We were always touching, one way or another, but some days... it felt more than just a friendly touch. Like today.

My eyes fluttered shut as his thumb brushed against the pulsing vein in my neck. His touch lingered there, feeling my heartbeat through my throat.

"The necklace or me?" I asked, my eyes still closed. Why... did I just ask that?

"You," he said. "Always you." His voice was soft and hot, leaving me feeling things I couldn't explain, couldn't put into words.

I leaned into him, my palms landing on his chest. The hard thump of his heart had my eyes snapping open. Maddox's gaze flickered to my lips. His hands fell to my curve of my shoulders, sliding down my arms, and his fingers curled around my hips.

A single heartbeat passed between us.

I pulled back, breaking the moment between us. Maddox blinked before releasing a shuddering breath. My skin still burnt from where he had touched me, and I hated how cold I suddenly felt from pulling away from him.

Maddox took a step back, too, pulling us farther from each other. He ran his fingers through his hair, which he kept short since the first time I called him Poodle. He thought it'd make me stop calling him that stupid pet name if his hair was no longer long and curly like before.

Ha, he *thought wrong*.

Once a poodle, forever a poodle.

"Pictures!" Gran said. She waved Riley over, who came forward with Grayson.

"Closer everyone," Pops demanded as he held a camera in his hand.

Colton and the boys—Brayden, Cole and Knox—all whom were Maddox's teammates and close friends, surrounded us. Riley stood beside me, with Grayson on her side, while I stood next to Maddox. We formed a semi-circle and Gran was smiling from ear to ear.

"Say cheers!"

"Cheers," we called out and the camera's shutter clicked.

Picture perfect.

The moment our circle broke apart, we were surrounded by the other Berkshire students. I lost Maddox in the crowd, all the girls vying for his attention one last time. They were probably hoping he'd take one of them home for a graduation fuck fest. Colton and the boys had their own little harem around them, too.

I found Grayson and Riley, holding hands as they stood under a tree, watching from a distance. Grayson looked slightly relieved that Colton's attention was no longer on his girlfriend.

Riley was convinced that Colton didn't have any feelings for her. She was either in denial or she truly was blind to the tension between Grayson and Colton, which was extremely palpable.

Gran came to my side, pulling my focus away from the lovebirds as she hugged me, surprising me by her strength. "So proud of you, Lila. Your parents would be, too."

I blinked back the tears at her words. "Is it weird that I felt like they were with me during the ceremony? Like they were right there, watching me?"

"No, sweetheart. It's not weird because I know they're watching over you." Pops rubbed my back. "You've grown into such a beautiful and smart young lady."

"I'm going to miss you two when I go to Harvard," I confessed, choking back my tears. My heart was heavy in my chest as I realized I only had a few weeks left with my grandparents before I moved away to a whole different state.

Gran cupped my cheeks, smiling. "You have Maddox and Riley with you."

In the end, Riley, Maddox, Colton and I were going to Harvard.

Cole got accepted to Yale and that was where he was going. The other boys were leaving for Princeton or Dartmouth.

I sniffled, nodding. "Yeah, but they aren't you."

Even Pops looked crestfallen–I was his little girl–the one he raised and his only grandchild. Pops was rarely emotional but times like this reminded me just how much he loved me and Gran. He placed a chaste kiss on my forehead. "You're going to be okay," he said with strong conviction.

Hours later, I found myself in Maddox's car. We no longer had our cap and gown on, but instead, Maddox was wearing a white buttoned up shirt, black slacks and a black tie. He was... in other words, sinfully sexy, but I wasn't about to tell him that. He rolled up his sleeves to his elbows and flexed his forearms, his hands on the steering wheel.

"Where to, Sweet Cheeks?" he asked, flashing me a half smile. There was light in his blue eyes, and it glimmered with teasing mischief. "The world is ours. Let's cause some trouble."

My lips curved upward. "You've got a bad reputation, Coulter. Stop trying to corrupt me. I'm a good girl."

Maddox didn't give a damn about his bad reputation. In fact, he loved being a bad influence. Such a rebel and a troublemaker.

"Good girls do bad things sometimes," he drawled. "It's me and you, Garcia."

"Me and you?" I breathed.

Maddox and I against the whole world. Partners in crime and best friends.

"Me and you," he agreed, starting up the car. "So, where to?"

I raised an eyebrow, smiling because there was only one answer to that question. "I have a dare, but it's dangerous."

I loved the way his eyes lit up to the word *dangerous*. Such a rulebreaker.

"Do you dare?" I asked.

Maddox grinned, a devious grin, and I had my answer.

Who would have known it end this way? From that day in the coffee stop, to us being enemies… and then calling truce, being friends… and to *this* moment? Maddox and I had come a long way *together*. Fate really had a way of playing with us.

I used to despise him.

And now he was the most important person in my life.

CHAPTER
TWENTY-EIGHT
THREE YEARS LATER

Lila

I tapped my foot against the asphalt, waiting for Maddox to show up. I shot Riley a text, letting her know I was going to be late for dinner. She was cooking tonight, her infamous ravioli dish. We were celebrating since she finished her thesis last night. We were currently halfway through our second semester in our third year at Harvard.

While I had gotten accepted into Harvard for Chemistry, Riley was studying Sociology. She was planning to pursue a post-graduate degree in Criminal Law.

Colton was majoring in Statistics while Maddox was studying Business, although he wanted to pursue a football career. Him getting a business degree at Harvard was just to appease his parents, although he did say he enjoyed it. At the end of the day, football was where his heart belonged and he was really fucking good at it.

I still couldn't believe it had been three and half years since that day in the coffee shop—the day I spilled my ice coffee on Maddox and the rest was history. I tried to think of a moment when I hated him, but although we had been enemies for a short period time, I never truly *hated* him. Sure, I had despised his arrogance and douchebaggery attitude, but it wasn't hatred.

Maybe that was the reason why it was so easy for us to go from enemies to friends to best friends.

Such a strange twist of fate—from that day to now, almost four years later.

There was a tap on my ass and I rolled my eyes, knowing full well who it was.

"You got to stop touching my ass, Coulter," I warned.

He chuckled and walked around me, coming into view with his glorious self.

A lot had changed in three years. Maddox, for instance, had grown *bigger*. He was already brawny in high school from playing football and working out, but now, he had packed on extra muscles. His shoulders were half a size bigger than before and now twice the size of my own. His biceps bulged, his arms full of veins and muscles. He filled out the black shirt he was wearing, the fabric stretching tight over his wide chest. He had a six-pack before and now he had eight. His abs were hard and cut. My fingers itched with the memory of touching them. I had seen him shirtless countless times and had seen his progress from seventeen-year-old Maddox to twenty-year-old him.

Me? I was still the same. Same height, same weight – still a midget compared to Maddox, and he took great pleasure in reminding me of that fact every time he manhandled me and put me where he wanted.

His blue eyes glimmered in the sunlight. He eyed me up and

down, his gaze lingering longer on my bare legs. I wore denim shorts that were frayed at the end and a black long-sleeved shirt with a brown leather jacket over it and ankle boots. It was March, and the weather was slightly hotter than normal. To our surprise, spring came early this year.

"My eyes are up here, Maddox," I teased.

He glowered, and I fought back a smile. I stuffed my hand in my bag and pulled out his phone charger. "Here you go. Thank you for letting me use it."

I handed him the charger and waved for him to go. "I'll see you tonight. You're going to be late for your next lecture. Go!"

"I'm always coming to your rescue." He tsked with a slight grin. Maddox gave me a finger salute as he started to backtrack. "Always at your service!"

"I don't need a knight," I said, loudly enough for him to hear a few feet away.

"I know you don't. You're not the damsel in distress who I need to save."

My heart warmed, and my lips twisted in a smile. "You're right. I guess I am more like the dragon, eh?"

"A cute and sexy dragon," he called out.

Maddox jogged across the open field toward his building. Since our programs differed greatly, his classrooms were on the opposite side of the campus while mine were on this side.

He faded away in the distance, and I strode away to our apartment building, which was only about a ten-minute walk through the campus.

I took the elevator up to our apartment, which was on the third floor. I found Colton at the door with a girl in his arms. They were kissing, and by the look of it, they were about to fuck in the corridor.

I cleared my throat, and he peeled himself away from the chick, his eyes hooded. "Sup, Lila?"

My eyes narrowed on the girl beside him. Her mocha skin glistened with a sheen of sweat, and she flushed. It appeared like they had clearly already fucked on the way here.

"Are you coming over for dinner or...?" I asked.

He gave me a half shrug, his gaze moving to the apartment next to him. "She didn't invite me."

I grimaced and smiled sheepishly at him. Things were tense between Colton and Riley—well, tense was an understatement at this point in their 'relationship' or whatever they had.

To put it simply, they... *hated* each other.

But that story was for another time.

I opened the door to my apartment, the one I shared with Riley, which also happened to be next to Maddox and Colton's; we were neighbors.

"Baaabee, is that you?" Riley called out.

Colton's jaw clenched at her voice, and he grabbed the chick, pulling her into his apartment. The door closed with a bang behind him.

"It's me," I said, walking inside.

Her back was to me as she stood in front of the stove, humming a song under her breath. She had sweatpants and a shirt on, her blond hair up in a messy bun. Riley spared me a look over her shoulder. "Did you get the garlic sticks I asked for?"

I lifted my arm up, showing her the grocery bag I was holding. "Gotcha. It smells good in here."

She brought the spatula to her lips and blew on it. "Wanna taste?" she asked, cheekily.

I nodded, and she offered me the spoon. The richness of the sauce hit every one of my taste buds, and I moaned. "Yummy!"

We set up the plates, and she placed a bottle of wine on the table. "Is it just us? Is Maddox coming?" Riley asked as she took her seat at our small dining table, opposite of me.

I shook my head, piling some ravioli on my plate. "No, he missed his lecture this morning, so he's attending a later class today. Isn't it too early for wine? It's not even six yet."

Her lips curled up. "Lila, it's always time for wine, and we're celebrating today."

Riley loved to drink—wine and margaritas in particular. She had been obsessing over red wine lately. It was her favorite and now my favorite as well. We were besties for a reason, right?

Riley swallowed a bite of her dinner and then gave me an inquiring look. "How's it going with Landon?"

My heart stuttered. Landon, my boyfriend of five weeks.

"Good," I said, moving a piece of my ravioli around in my plate.

Riley sighed, carefully placing her spoon on her plate, before leveling me with a look. "Lila, don't give me that shit."

I chewed on a piece of ravioli before swallowing it down with red wine. I drank half of my glass before slamming it back on the table. "He's not replying to my text."

Riley let out a curse. "Did you call him?"

"I'm not that desperate," I snapped.

"Lila," she sighed. I refused to look at her because I didn't want to see the sympathy on her face.

Landon pursued me for three months before I finally gave in. He was a good guy: smart, sweet and nice. At first, I refused to give in since I thought I was his rebound. Landon had broken off with his long-term girlfriend four months before he turned his attention to me. But he courted me, flowers and all, and he was different than the other guys.

Maddox was hellbent on keeping us apart because he believed Landon was no good.

But then again, that was his excuse for every guy I dated over the years.

Granted, none of them really lasted for long—four months maximum.

Sex wasn't some sacred thing to me. I wasn't a virgin; I had a few hook-ups here and there, but I never had a one-night stand. I need the intimacy before and after sex, and one-night stands don't give me any of that. I've had a few boyfriends over the years, but Landon was the one I felt... comfortable with, enough for me to give in and have sex so soon into our relationship.

That was three days ago. And he was acting weird since then.

Leo was the first guy to turn away with disgust when he saw my scars. Since then, I either had sex while half-dressed or when we were in the dark—dark enough they couldn't see the jagged, pink lines between my breasts—just so I could spare them the disgust or shock they'd feel if they saw it. I didn't need or want their sympathy either.

My scars never bothered me, and I wasn't really embarrassed of it.

But maybe I was lying to myself.

Landon... he saw my scars. He didn't really flinch away, but I noticed the way he kept his gaze averted during sex. He didn't look at my boobs and kept his eyes on my taunt stomach or the spot between my legs instead.

I'd be flattered... if I thought he was focusing on my pussy, but I knew he was just trying to avoid looking at the marks on my chest.

He didn't act weird afterward, so I believed everything was okay. Until yesterday.

Landon wasn't replying to my texts, which was unusual. He had always been very attentive... until now.

"Damn it," I growled and poured more wine in my glass. "Maybe he's just busy."

"Too busy to send you a single text?" Riley stabbed her ravioli with too much aggression. She was a tad bit overprotective of me. Maddox was probably rubbing off on her. "It'd take him two seconds," she added.

I cleared my throat and took a slow sip of my wine. Drinking too much and too fast would have me tipsy in less than an hour. "It doesn't matter."

She made a face at me. "He's an asshole."

I shrugged and continued with my dinner, shoving a spoonful into my mouth.

"You don't care... if he breaks up with you?" she asked slowly.

"I'm not in love with him if that's what you're asking," I said around a mouthful.

It was true, I didn't love Landon. He was nice, and I *liked* him. But that was it.

"Maddox—"

I cut her off. "He doesn't know and you won't tell him." I leveled Riley with a hard look, and she leaned back against her chair, looking only a bit intimidated. "If he finds out Landon is ghosting me or if he thinks I'm hurt over this, which I'm *not* honestly, he's going to kill Landon."

Riley cocked her head to the side, thoughtfully. "Didn't you... um, spend the night over at Maddox's last night?"

"We fell asleep while binge watching *Friends*," I amended. I woke up in *his* bed in the morning; he carried me to bed after I had fallen sleep, and I had been all cozy against *his* pillows and *his* blankets while Maddox slept on the couch.

"Do you think maybe the issue is Maddox? Not that I'm saying he is, but you know how all your exes were sensitive about him. Maybe Landon is too?"

She raised a good point.

Maddox *loathed* every guy I dated.

Consequently, they hated him, too. And none of them were too happy of my relationship with Maddox. They didn't like that we were *that* close. They didn't approve of Maddox having access to my apartment. He could come and go freely and vice versa. They didn't like that I attended all of Maddox's football games and some of his practices.

It was a lot to juggle, and granted, yes, it made sense why they didn't approve of Maddox's relationship with me.

But none of them came close to what or *who* Maddox was to me.

I wasn't going to fix what I had with Maddox to suit these guys. Maybe that was the issue in all my past relationships, but I wasn't willing to change anything between Maddox and I.

My stomach twisted at the thought of losing Maddox. The mere idea of being without him made me sick.

We were best friends; no one and nothing was going to change that.

Not Landon... and none of those girls Maddox fucked around with.

"Lila!" Maddox called out from the bathroom.

I settled back into the couch and stuffed a handful of sweet caramelized popcorn into my mouth.

"What?" I responded, before taking a sip of my energy drink. I was a bit tipsy from all the red wine I had tonight with Riley. She was passed out in our apartment, and I had come over to our neighbors' place to bring him dinner.

Colton and his fuck buddy had disappeared when Maddox came home.

Maddox walked out of the bathroom with only a towel wrapped low around his waist, bare chest and his v-line teasing me. You see, I've seen Maddox half naked many times over the years. But each time, my mouth watered at the sight of his wide, muscled chest and washboard abs and that nipple piercing. He had gotten it one night when he was out partying with his football team. They had been pissed drunk and they went into a tattoo and piercing shop. The rest was history.

I never considered a nipple piercing sexy, but on Maddox? *Puuurfect.* Yes, I just purred.

I was his best friend, but I wasn't blind, and I had a pussy, which meant that I appreciated the male species. A lot. Including my best friend.

Was I drooling? I wiped the corner of my mouth just in case.

Maddox huffed and gave me a look that bordered between comical and exasperation. "Did you get in my phone and change your name to *My Main Chick*?"

Oh.

I had been a bit drunk when I did THAT a few nights ago. And then I had been too lazy to change it back.

I shrugged, trying to act nonchalant. "Well, yeah. Because I am your main chick. All the other girls are just your side chicks."

Maddox opened his mouth and then shut it, falling silent. He blinked and then just shook his head.

I gave him a cheesy smile. Fuck, maybe I was more than just tipsy.

"It's okay, though. You can fuck around with them. At the end of the day, you come back home to me. And I know I'm better," I muttered around another mouthful of popcorn, sending him my best smile.

He growled and the sensitive area between my legs clenched. Shit, this was bad.

Abort mission, abort mission.

Maddox ran his fingers though his wet hair, exhaling sharply. "For fuck's sake, woman! My only side chicks are your other personalities. And there are like twenty-five of them."

I paused midchew. Ouuh-kaay.

He showed me his hand, ticking off each list with his fingers. "Grumpy Lila. Lazy Lila. Pouty Lila. Funny Lila. Lila when she's sleep-deprived. Sugar high Lila, like right now. On her period Lila. Normal Lila."

My mouth opened then closed. My lips parted again, trying to say something. When I found nothing to say, quite speechless, I stuffed another fist of popcorn in my mouth and chewed in mock aggression.

"Do you want me to go on?" He paused, giving me a blank look as if daring me to argue with his claims.

I had no legit argument, and I had lost this round.

"Whatever," I mumbled. "Go shower. You stink."

"You're impossible." Maddox shook his head with a slight curl of his lips. He walked back into the bathroom.

"You love me," I yelled loud enough for him to hear even with the door separating us.

"YOU ARE A PAIN IN MY ASS."

"You still love me, though," I whispered, once I heard the shower turn on, with the silliest grin on my face. I knew he did because if he didn't... we wouldn't have lasted this long as a friend.

CHAPTER TWENTY-NINE

Maddox

As I walked out of my class, my phone pinged with a message. It was from Bianca. *R u coming over tonight?* Did I want to? No. I'd rather be home with Lila, watching some stupid Korean series with her, which most of the time were cliché as fuck and too cheesy for my taste. Riley was obsessed with anything Korean: K-POP and K-Dramas. She made Lila watch one of the shows *once* and then...*BAM*, Lila was now a K-Drama obsessed, too. We were currently watching some period/historical drama called *Scarlet Heart Ryeo*.

I had to admit, though, that shit was good.

So, did I want to go over at Bianca's tonight? No, I didn't. Bianca was too...clingy. I didn't even go on any dates with her. We fucked a few times, and she declared herself my girlfriend.

I didn't correct her. She was now going around the campus, telling everyone she was Maddox Coulter's *girlfriend*–flaunting our relationship status in everyone's face. Including Lila's.

Lila would just roll her eyes and subtly put her hand in my back pocket, which would make me *smirk* because, damn it, Lila sure knew how to push all these girls' buttons. They were jealous of Lila and my best friend? She firmly believed none of these girls were ever good enough for me.

So, Bianca, my girlfriend?

Ha.

More like recent fuck buddy—but okay, I'd humor her. For a while.

I typed out a one-word response. **Yes.**

After all, it was Friday. Lila and Landon were supposed to have date night.

My jaw clenched at the thought, and my teeth gnashed together. Why couldn't Lila see he wasn't the man for her? There was something off about him, and apparently, I was the only one who could see that. I didn't like him, period. Why? I didn't know.

I just didn't want him anywhere near my Lila.

"Yo, Maddox!" Turning around toward the voice, I saw Jaxon jogging over. He was Harvard's linebacker, one tough motherfucker. He was a beast on the field.

His dark skin glistened with a sheen of sweat, and he flexed his neck left and right. "Can I crash over at your place tonight... and the rest of the week?" His brown eyes pleaded with me.

"Let me guess, Rory kicked you out? Again."

Jaxon grimaced. "She's pissed because she found a lipstick mark on the collar of my shirt. Told her I didn't fuck around with any bitches," he sighed, rubbing a hand over his tired face. "It was before the game when I was hugged by one of the cheerleaders, but Rory doesn't believe me. I'm no cheater, man. But she's driving me fucking crazy."

Jaxon was faithful to his girlfriend of five years. They were high school sweethearts and shit, but Rory was one fucked-up bitch who had major trust issues. I wasn't about to tell Jaxon that, though, because he'd pummel my face into the ground.

"Yeah, you can crash at my place," I said. *Oh, the drama.*

He slapped me on the back and nodded. "Thanks, man. I owe you one."

"You owe a lot. Pretty sure you live at my place more than yours."

He grinned. "I'd say you were goddamn lucky you didn't have to deal with a psycho girlfriend, but I can't complain. She's the best thing in my life."

I didn't need a girlfriend.

Lila Garcia was already the best thing in my life.

As Jaxon jogged away, my ringtone blasted through the pocket of my black slacks. I held back a growl of annoyance and checked the screen. I picked up the phone after seeing it was Riley calling. "What?"

"Lila has been locked in her room for the last two hours; she won't come out, and I think she's crying. That motherfucker. Landon, it's him. You need to come because Lila isn't opening the door for me," she rattled out in one breath. "Maddox! Are you listening?"

I was already sprinting toward our apartment. "I'm coming," I growled.

Red, hot anger coursed through my veins, and I swallowed it down, but it grew in my belly. I felt it pounding through my blood, vicious and brutal.

If Landon had caused my Lila any pain... if he hurt her...

I took the stairs two at a time, stumbling in my haste, but I couldn't find myself to care. The door to her apartment was opened, so I hustled inside. Riley was pacing the length of their living room, worry etched over her face. Colton was leaning against the wall, also looking a bit pensive. That was the only time I had seen the two of them in the same room without being at each other's throat.

"Maddox," Riley said, looking relieved at the sight of me.

I walked past her and stood in front of Lila's bedroom. The door was locked, like Riley said.

"Lila?" I called out, pressing my ear to the door. There was a sound of her sniffling.

She was... crying?

Fuck, no.

FUCK, NO.

My gut churned as my fist pounded on her door. "Lila, open the door."

There was no response from her. "Open the fucking door or I'm going to break it down. Trust me, I will."

"Go away," she called out weakly.

My heart stuttered. "Lila," I said, trying to keep my voice gentle. "Baby, open the door. *Please*."

"Just... go away, Maddox."

My eyes pinched close, and I rested my forehead against her door. "Don't do this to me. Don't shut me out. Don't hide from *me*. I'm not going to walk away, and you damn well know it. Let me in, Lila."

Whatever Landon had done to my girl, he was about to regret it for the rest of his fucking life.

"If you don't open the door, I'm going to think the worst, and I'm going to hunt down Landon... and I might end up in prison tonight."

I didn't give a fuck if I was about to spend the rest of my life in jail because I was still going to hunt down Landon either way, even if she did open the door.

He made her cry–*that* was a death penalty.

"You're not killing anyone," she mumbled through the door.

"Open the door then," I pushed.

There was some shuffling around and then she unlocked and opened the door. Lila came into view, but she kept her head casted down, her black hair covering half of her face.

I placed my finger under her chin and nudged her head up. Her eyes were red, but there was no sign of tears. "I'm not crying," she said, begrudgingly. "I don't cry."

That was right.

Lila never cried, except for one day of the year. She hated being vulnerable and the only time she ever allowed herself to be, was on the date her parents died.

Her cheeks were flushed, and her eyes were red, a clear sign that she wanted to cry, but she was holding her tears in.

Lila pressed her palm over her forehead and squeezed her eyes close. "I'm just... God, he made a fool out of me."

"What did he do?" I asked through clench teeth.

"I was his rebound," Lila said, her voice small. She swiped at her cheeks even though there was no evidence of any tears. "And he has been cheating on me... with his ex. I guess they're back together now, but he was a coward and didn't tell me. I don't understand. Why did he... why did he fuck me... if he was already back with *her*? I mean, he basically cheated on both of us."

Riley let out a curse under her breath from behind me.

Colton hissed. "He's dead meat."

Anger simmered in my gut. The more she spoke of her situation, the angrier I became.

It consumed me, and my skin itched with the need for revenge, to *hurt* him, like he hurt Lila.

My Lila.

My fingers curled into fists as the fury slid through me like acid, burning inside the pit of my stomach.

Riley pushed past me and enveloped Lila into a hug. She whispered something to her, and Lila nodded. They talked quietly to each other. "I'm more angry than hurt. Embarrassed, too, because I let him touch me... we had sex... because I *trusted* him."

Lila's head came up, her gaze finding mine instantly. "Maddox–" she said, but her eyes flared, probably from seeing the look on my face. "Maddox, no."

Lila came forward, her arms out as if to grab me, but I sidestepped her reach.

She called out after me as I stalked out of the apartment. "Maddox!"

I wasn't listening; I was too far gone to stop now.

I charged down the stairs, faster than I knew I could and climbed into my car. The passenger's door slammed shut, and I looked up. Colton settled in the seat.

"You're not stopping me," I snarled.

"No, I'm coming *with* you." He cracked his knuckles, his lips splitting into a deadly grin. "He fucked with one of ours."

After breaking every known traffic law, we were at Landon's apartment two minutes later.

"You stay out of it," I warned Colton. My Lila, my fight.

"I'll let you beat the shit out of him, but I'm just here to keep you from killing him."

Colton rang the doorbell. I heard a high-pitched giggle through the door—a woman—and anger boiled deep in my veins. It churned with the hunger for destruction.

I wasn't thinking clearly, I fucking couldn't.

All I could *see* was Lila's sad eyes and blotchy cheeks as she tried to keep her tears inside.

The door opened, and there was Landon.

His eyes widened in shock, and I pushed forward. He stumbled back inside his apartment, gaping like a fish out of water.

"What the fuck?" he sputtered. "You can't just push your way inside like that."

"We can't?" Colton taunted.

"What's going on?" the woman asked. She was partially naked, the look on her face telling me she had just been fucked, multiple times.

Landon pointed toward the door. "Get the fuck out of my apartment. Now."

I took a step forward, a promise of violence. He saw through me, and his eyes darkened. He shoved at my shoulders, wanting to assert his dominance in this fight, and I *snapped*.

Lunging forward, I grabbed him by the throat. He retaliated quickly, landing a punch in my gut. I quickly threw my weight on him, sending both of us crashing into his glass table in living room.

"Oh my God!" A shrill voice screamed.

I felt his nose crunch under the force of my punch. It was so loud, it vibrated through my ears.

Grabbing his hair, I pummeled his face over and over again. "You," *punch*, "don't," *punch*, "fucking get," *punch*, "away," *punch*, "so easily," *punch*, "after hurting," *punch*, "Lila."

He broke Lila's trust and embarrassed her by cheating on her. *Motherfucker.*

Landon struggled against me, and he knocked me in the jaw, hard enough that I stumbled back. The sound of fists against flesh was all I could hear. Blood leaked from my nose, and I punched him in the ribs again and again.

"Stop! Help! Someone help!" The stupid voice was screaming once again.

I drew my fist back and ploughed it into his stomach. He coughed and sputtered blood. Stars burst in my vision when he got me in the head, but I shook it off.

There was blood on my knuckles but I. Could. Not. Stop.

"Maddox! Maddox, no."

Lila. Her voice broke through the red haze, and I blinked, seeing Landon's bloodied face.

Hands grabbed my back and arms, trying to pull me away from Landon. My eyes connected with Lila's brown ones, and she looked completely… distraught.

For Landon? For this fucking asshole?

Lila whimpered. "You're hurt. Oh God, Maddox. Oh no."

Me?

"Ah fuck," Colton roared. "She called the police. Shit!"

Lila's face crumpled, and she pushed her face into my neck. "No, no, no."

I stumbled away from Landon, and his bitch came forward, falling to her knees beside him.

"Maddox," Lila said softly.

"I got you." I wrapped my arm around her, lifting her so her feet were dangling an inch from the ground.

She let out a choked sob. "No, you don't. They're going to take you away. Landon is probably going to press charges. *Why?*"

Why?

Fucking why?

Because I can't bear the thought of you hurting. Because watching you hold back your tears for an asshole like Landon has me losing my mind. BECAUSE HE FUCKING HURT YOU.

I never got a chance to say any of that to her. Glancing up over her shoulder, I saw the cops walking inside the apartment. They looked around, studying the mess.

"That's him, Officer," the woman cried, pointing at me.

Lila was shaking her head, holding onto me tighter. I had Landon's blood on my hands; I broke into his house... there was no getting out of this. And I wasn't the least bit sorry for turning Landon into my punching bag.

"Colton will take you home, Lila," I rasped in her ear.

She gave me a stubborn shake of her head. "I'm coming with you."

"No," I deadpanned, with my hand gripping her chin. I made her look at me. "Colton will walk you home, and I'll see you in the morning."

"But–"

"No, Lila."

Her face hardened. "You don't tell me what to do."

"I am, right now. Do as you're told." She glared. Lila was stubborn as fuck, and I knew she'd sit with me in jail if I didn't get her home. There was no goddamn way I was letting her spend the night in a cell, even if it was with me. "*Please.*"

I placed her back on her feet, and her chin wobbled. She turned to face the cops. "It's only a misunderstanding, officers. It's my fault."

"Misunderstanding or not, you're under arrest." One of the officers was staring directly at me. I nodded, compliant. There was no point arguing with them.

Colton had to drag Lila away from me as I was handcuffed, my hands behind my back.

"Please," Lila pleaded. "Can I just... hug him?"

The officer who handcuffed me beckoned her over. She slid closer to me, pressed her nose against my throat. "I'm sorry. This is my fault."

Lila sniffled, and my heart twisted. My lips brushed against her forehead, and she hugged me tighter. "I'm sorry."

"I got you," I said again.

Her teary eyes were the last thing I saw as they pulled me away from her. Lila brought her hand up and she touched her dreamcatcher necklace at her throat, as though it soothed her.

It gutted me, because she was crying for *me*.

CHAPTER THIRTY

Lila

I couldn't sleep, there was no way I could when Maddox was in jail, and here I was, in my nice and cozy bed.

He was locked away in a cell because of *me*. My gut twisted with guilt, and I stared at the ceiling through the darkness. Colton had to drag me home with Riley right on our heels.

After convincing me to get in bed while he handled the matter, Colton left.

Why didn't he stop Maddox from getting into a fight?

Why wasn't I fast enough to stop him?

Why… why… *why?*

I always knew that as much as Maddox was laid-back and easy-going most of the time, he was also short-tempered and easily triggered.

The guilt became harder to bear because if I only had put on my big girl pants and didn't cause a scene, Maddox wouldn't have run off to beat the shit out of Landon.

But I had been *hurt* and embarrassed.

Not that I cared much about Landon. I wasn't heartbroken, but I felt... *used.*

Used and discarded after he had his fun with me.

If Landon didn't want to be with me, he could have easily walked away. I wasn't clingy; I had no expectations. But he cheated on me, after I let him inside my body.

That hurt me.

And I had been furious.

I wasn't 'crying' because he broke my heart. They were angry tears, at him... and myself, because I trusted the wrong guy.

I felt foolish, but I didn't think Maddox would react the way he did. Everything happened so fast, and before I could have grabbed him, he was already out of the door.

Then I walked in on him beating the shit out of Landon, not that I cared if my ex was hurt or not. But Maddox was wounded too and that guilt became much harder to bear.

When the cops came, it took everything in me not to beg them to take me with them. Goddamn it, I'd sit in a dirty cell with Maddox if it meant he wasn't alone behind those bars and I was with him.

Landon was pressing charges. His precious girlfriend attacked me after the cops left and her sharp nails have left a nasty mark on my arm. I returned the favor by punching her boobs before Colton pulled me off her and dragged me out of the apartment as I cursed them through their next lives.

My door creaked open, snapping me out of my thoughts, and I squeezed my eyes shut. There was a relieved sigh, and I peered at the door from behind my comforter.

"She's asleep," Riley said softly to the person behind her. Probably Colton.

I was right, because a second later, his hushed voice came through. "Good. It's been a long night for all of us."

The door closed, and I sank back into my soft mattress. My body was still tense, and I couldn't find a comfortable position.

It was a long time before I fell into a restless sleep.

Hours later, I jolted away when my bed dipped under a heavy weight. Someone settled behind me and a strong arm slid around my hips, pulling me back into *his* body. Hard and familiar... warm and solid... strong and safe.

Maddox.

He curled his body around mine, and my ass was nestled indecently against his groin. He didn't shift away like I expected him to. He kept me there, my back against his front, so close not even a string could fit between us. We'd laid in bed many times, but this was... *different.*

More intimate, less 'friendly,' and there was an unspoken tension between us. I licked my lips and cleared my dry throat, feeling the way my stomach dipped and fluttered as he touched me.

Maddox pushed his other arm under my neck and tucked the back of my head against his shoulder. I released the breath I was holding and inhaled his familiar scent, also catching a whiff of alcohol. Did he drink before coming home?

"Landon dropped the charges?" I asked in the dark.

I felt him shake his head. His arm tightened around mine, as if making sure I couldn't escape or maybe he was scared I would.

Little did he know...

"Then?" I pushed for more.

"My father handled it," he confessed, his voice a raspy croak.

Ah, so his father bailed him out. Shit. He found out. *Bad. Bad. Bad.* Colton and I thought to keep this incident lowkey and hoped

Brad Coulter wouldn't find out his son was in jail.

I guess Maddox's father had eyes and ears *everywhere.*

"Was he pissed?"

"He didn't message me, didn't call me either. Didn't even talk to me. He handled everything behind my back and without talking to me. I only knew he did it after I was released, and Colton came to pick me up."

Oh. So, his father hadn't even bothered to speak to him, to ask what happened, why it happened or how his son was even doing. Fuck him.

I snuggled deeper into his embrace and slid my hand into his, the one on my hip. I squeezed his fingers. "I'm sorry."

He expelled a long breath. "I'm not. He deserved every fucking punch I threw at him. I think I broke his nose. Nobody makes my Lila cry. No one. I won't fucking allow it." He slurred his words a bit. Yeah, he was definitely a little drunk.

My eyes filled with tears. I didn't peg myself to be an emotional person, but Maddox made me *feel* so many things at once.

Sorrow... fear... anguish... hopelessness...

My heart thudded in my chest

"Maddox?"

"Um, yeah?"

"I love you," I whispered.

His arm flexed around my hips. "I know." His hold tightened around me in the slightest bit. His lips feathered over my forehead in a whisper of a kiss, before he placed his cheek on top of my head again. "I love you, too."

It wasn't the first time we had said those words to each other but my heart danced in my chest. Without lifting my head, I brought my hand up, showing him my pinky.

"Friends?"

Maddox hooked his pinky around mine, and I could feel his smile without even having to look at him.

"Friends," he said.

My eyes closed, and I fell asleep to the sound of his heartbeat.

In the morning, I woke up to an empty bed. For a brief moment, I wondered if it was all a dream, and Maddox hadn't come home. But when I breathed in, I caught the familiar, musky scent that he left behind. My body still tingled from where he had touched me.

After quickly freshening up, I walked out of the bedroom to find Maddox sitting at the kitchen table, staring out the window. The morning sunshine shone through the glass, and Maddox looked beautiful sitting there. He was shirtless, with only his grey sweatpants on. It was the perfect sight...but my chest tightened at the look on his face.

My wounded warrior.

He had a black eye, and his lips were cut and swollen. His ribs were turning into an ugly shade of purple and green.

"Want some coffee?" I asked, hoping to get him to talk and lighten up his mood. Last night was hell for all of us. I needed to make sure he was okay.

But his next words were not what I expected.

"Am I a disappointment?"

I flinched. "What!? Maddox, what are you—"

My next words caught in my throat when I saw the expression on his face. Utterly defeated, a look that could only be described as *heartbroken*. Like a beaten puppy, whimpering silently as it suffered.

My heart caved inside my chest at that look, and I walked over to him, kneeling between his legs. He spread his thighs wider, encasing me against his body.

"Why is it that whatever I do is never enough?" he said, his words choked.

"Maddox," I whispered.

I saw the phone in his hand and finally put two and two together. Grabbing the phone from him, he didn't stop me, I searched through his messages. The most recent message, two hours ago, was from his father.

You keep disappointing me over and over again. I can't believe I almost thought you had finally been redeemed from your messy ways. This is the last time I will bail you out from things you fuck up.

Oh Maddox. My poor, sweet Maddox.

"I'm sorry," I breathed, looking down. This was all my fault. Why did I ever let Landon in my life?

I grabbed his hands, holding onto him, letting him know he wasn't alone. It was then I noticed his knuckles were bruised, and there was some dried blood left on it.

Shit. That was from last night. He didn't clean himself up.

I got up and quickly and went to get to first aid kit to clean his wounds. His knuckles were slightly swollen, but thankfully, not broken. I attentively cleaned his bloodied knuckles, wincing as I brushed the antiseptic wipes over the broken skin. Maddox showed no outward emotion. He was silent until I finished with his left hand and grabbed his right hand to do the same task.

I kept my movements slow and careful as I cleaned his wounds and wrapped a bandage around his hands. He probably didn't need them, but the bandages would keep them clean, so there would be no infection.

His eyes raked over my face before his gaze slid away—looking bleak and distant, lost.

"I got into Harvard. I worked for it. I worked so fucking hard that I was able to keep my full scholarship for three years. I'm on top in my football career. Why is it not enough? Everything I do... it's *never* enough. I always, somehow...end up lacking somewhere. Always somehow disappointing him. It's never enough, Lila."

"No. No. *No!*" I rushed to say. "Baby, no. Maddox, everything you do is enough. It's more than enough. You. Are. Enough. Please don't say that. I'm sorry about last night. I'm sorry your father is an asshole. I'm sorry he never told you he's proud of you. But *I* am. I'm so proud of you, Maddox Coulter. Everything you've done, everything you do... it's enough," I said in urgency.

He leaned his head back and closed his eyes as if soaking in my words. He entwined our fingers together and clutched onto me. I squeezed his hands back. *I'm here, Maddox. I'm here, and I'm not leaving. Me and you, forever.*

I wanted to ask him what he needed right now. From me. If I could lessen his guilt, his suffering in any way, I would do it. Without a second thought.

As if he could read my mind, his eyes opened, and he leveled me with those beautiful blue orbs. I saw everything I needed to know.

"Can you..." he paused and swallowed. "...hug me? Please?"

He whispered those words so brokenly, like he was scared I'd refuse me, like a child begging for affection. To have someone *just* hold him.

I nodded, mutely, because my throat was closed up as I choked back a cry and forced my tears away. I couldn't let him see me cry.

I stood up, and he pulled me into his lap. Maddox buried his face in my neck. "I got you," I said, softly in his ear.

His grip tightened on me.

Maddox got hurt because of *me*; he got into a fight for *my* honor. The realization was overwhelming because I had underestimated his protective instincts for me and how much he actually cared.

I felt him breathing against my throat, and under my palm, his heart slowly started to beat at a calmer pace. His lips brushed against the pulsing vein in my throat and maybe he hadn't meant to do it or he didn't want me to feel it, but I did. My body was hyperaware of his touch.

"I got you," I said again, as a reminder. My fingers combed through his hair, and slowly, he started to relax in my arms. The tension left him, and my aching heart soothed itself at the fact that Maddox was going to be okay. He was strong enough to be okay.

Once he lifted his head up, I smiled at him. "Okay now?"

His lips curled up in a half smile, and he nodded. "I guess I just needed a hug from my Lila. I swear you're my goddamn therapy. Why waste money on a shrink if there's a Lila in your life?"

I let out a laugh and smacked his arm. "Oh, shut up."

He was grinning now, his eyes lighter, his expression calm.

"So, how about I make you pasta?" It was his favorite thing to eat whenever he was feeling low.

"Woman, you know I'd never say no to your pasta."

"Okay, sit tight then."

Pasta for breakfast. Hmph. Who cared? If that shit made my Maddox smile then we'd have fucking pasta for breakfast. Every. Damn. Day.

CHAPTER THIRTY-ONE

Lila

*S*end me a picture. Wanna see your sexy face.
   I opened the text from Riley and then stared around the
   loud club. We were sitting at a corner booth with pretty bad
lightning.

   Still, I humored Riley and brought my phone up, deciding to
please her with one picture. She wasn't able to join us for a night
out since she had an essay due tomorrow morning. Riley pouted as I
left our apartment with Maddox, Colton, Jaxon and Rory. She made
me promise to send her photos of us being pissed drunk, so she
could live vicariously through us.

   I ruffled up my hair a little, then pursed my lips in a sexy pout.
Just when I was about to click the perfect photo, I was suddenly
jostled. Something wet touched my cheek, and I reared back in
shock. Maddox's head fell into the crook of my neck, and he inhaled
deeply before pulling away, giving me panty-melting smile.

   "Eww, did you just lick me? What the fuck, Maddox?" I

growled, slapping his chest and shoving him away. But he was a wall of muscles so moving him was an impossible task.

He gave me a mock pout. Yeah, he was a little drunk already. "I thought we were supposed to lick the ones we love. I licked you, so you're mine."

I blew out an exasperated breath before hissing. "Are you a dog?"

Maddox paused, as if he really was thinking about my question. And then he shrugged. "Doggy style is my favorite position to fuck. And I'm also your Poodle."

Before I could have stopped him, he leaned forward and licked my cheek once again, leaving a wet trail behind.

His mouth moved to my neck, licking me there, too. Against my own accord, my thighs trembled, and my core clenched as his lips brushed over my throat. "Maddox!" I whisper-yelled. "Stop licking me!"

He leaned back, and his lips quirked up dangerously. "Why? It gets you wet?"

"No," I barked, suddenly feeling the urge to smack him. "Because your *girlfriend* just walked in, and she's coming our way. Oh, she doesn't look very happy."

Maddox looked toward the entrance before sinking more into his seat, as if trying to hide from the raging chick coming his way. "Ah. Shit," he whispered.

Bianca wasn't exactly his 'girlfriend' anymore. They broke up when Maddox didn't show up the night he was supposed to go over to her house. The night he got into a fight with Landon and ended up in jail.

The next morning, Bianca threw a huge tantrum and even called me a 'homewrecker' and 'bitch' for trying to steal her man. Maddox dropped her so fast I thought she'd suffer a whiplash.

Her man? Yeah, right.

Maddox was never hers in the first place.

A week after their breakup, she still didn't grasp the idea and has now turned into a stalker. Bianca stopped at our table, hands on her hips, and glowered at Maddox. "I need to talk to you."

He lifted a shoulder in a shrug. "I'm busy, as you can see."

"Now," she snapped.

My eyes widened at her tone, and Maddox tensed. "You don't get to come here and make demands. I'm not your boy toy, Bianca."

She tapped her foot, impatiently. "You owe me a better explanation for breaking up with me, Maddox."

Maddox rubbed his eyes and slurred a bit as he spoke, "I don't owe you shit. And we were never together in the first place. We *fucked*, that's it."

The distaste was clear on her face as she gave me a nasty look. "It's because of her, isn't it? You're choosing her?" Bianca said in a shrill voice, pointing an accusing finger at me.

Here we go again.

Another 'girlfriend,' same drama.

Maddox growled low in his throat, the sound so threatening even I winced. "Listen–"

My phone rang, breaking through the tension, and Maddox stopped mid-sentence. I gave him a sheepish look and slid out of the booth, phone to my ear.

I walked away from Maddox and Bianca as they continued arguing with each other.

"Hey, Bea?" I answered the call.

"Lila, shit. We're in trouble," she gasped.

"What? What is it? What happened?" I strode out of the club since it was too loud to hear anything Bea was saying over the phone.

Bea was a professional dancer, and my chorographer of the dance club at Harvard. Two years ago, I joined the club as a hobby and soon realized that I enjoyed dancing. It was therapeutic.

I wasn't the best dancer, but I also wasn't too bad. In between my studying and waitressing part-time, I needed something to do to relax and just unwind. Dancing seemed to do that for me.

"Owen is hurt. He broke his leg from a biking accident. He. Can't. Dance," Bea said, out of breath. I could feel her freaking out through the phone.

"Owen is hurt?" I asked, because I couldn't believe what I just heard. "How bad is it?"

"He's okay. He's home, and he just called me. Owen isn't in a lot of pain, but it's bad enough he won't be able to dance for the next three months. *Oh God.*"

Oh shit.

That didn't sound good.

A month ago, our club partnered up with a non-profit organization that put on charity events for people with disabilities. This year, the fundraising event was for blind people.

Our small group of dancers were supposed to present a show for the attendees at the event who would be contributing to the charity.

Owen was my dance partner.

Shit!

"There's no backing out now. This is top-notch, Lila. The organization, the event–*everything*–has to be perfect. We're representing Harvard. We no longer have a dancing partner for you anymore, and *you* open the show!"

My throat went dry, and I tried not to panic, but Bea freaking out like this was causing *me* to freak out. "Bea, you need to calm down. We can figure it out."

"The event is in a week!" She screeched loud enough I had to pull my phone away from my ear.

She was right though. We couldn't mess this up. Every dance number at the event was a couple's dance; the organization specifically asked for a partner dance since they thought it would be more attractive to the attendees.

I took in a deep breath, trying to calm my rising panic. I was used to perfection—my grades and my work. I was obsessed with it, although I wasn't always like that.

My therapist said it was my way of dealing with the death of my parents—chasing perfection and wanting to always be in control.

Right now, everything was happening the opposite of what I wanted.

"So, we need to find me a new dance partner?" I questioned Bea.

"Even if we do, who's going to learn the dance in less than seven days?" She took a shuddering breath and let it out. "It's not possible."

"Nothing is ever impossible," I said.

"Your optimism is admiring but not suitable for the situation since we are thoroughly fucked!"

"I'll find a dance partner," I announced with conviction. There was no giving up after we'd come this far. The event was happening. Owen was hurt, but we had to find a way to make it work.

And I knew exactly who was going to help me.

Even if I was about to hear him grumble about it for the rest of our lives.

"Lila—"

"I know someone."

"Who?" she asked suspiciously.

My corner of my lips curled up. "Maddox."

I had struck Bea into silence, only her breathing could be heard over the phone.

"You're serious?" she whispered, as if we were sharing a secret.

"Yup."

"Holy shit. You mean, *The* Maddox, right?"

"Yup." I grinned harder.

"Holy shit," she said again.

We said our goodbyes, and I walked back inside the club. Maddox was going to hate it, but I knew he'd never say *no* to me.

Back at our booth, I saw that Bianca was nowhere to be seen, and Maddox was nursing a beer. "Where'd she go?"

"I handled her," he said, not giving me any more details. "What's up?" Maddox seemed to have sobered up a bit.

"I need to talk to you about something."

His eyes narrowed on me. "Is it bad?"

I half-shrugged. "Not exactly. Do you want to go home?"

Maddox stood up without saying a word, and I guessed I had my answer.

Maddox

"No," I calmly stated. "Not happening."

"But Maddox," she dragged out my name, pleading with her eyes. When I shook my head firmly, she stomped her foot.

She peeked at me through her lashes. "This is really important to me."

Then Lila got a look on her face, a look that should have warned me of what was coming.

"Lila—"

"I dare you."

Jesus Christ, this woman!

"Take that back," I warned, my voice low.

Lila smirked. "No." She crossed her arms over her pert tits, pulling my attention to her chest.

I was a goddamn weak man.

Weak to my fucking knees for Lila Garcia because she was the one temptation I couldn't have.

She was wearing a crop top that should've been illegal. Her dreamcatcher necklace hung around her neck; Lila never took it off after I put it on her three years ago. Her stomach was taunt, and her belly button looked cute, and as fucked up as it was, a brief image of me licking her belly button and her giggling flashed through my mind. My mouth watered at the thought.

I shook my head and cursed myself. No, I *couldn't*.

This was... not happening.

Never, fucking ever.

Even though it grew harder every year to remind myself that we could only ever be friends and nothing more.

Every time she smiled at me, it became harder not to kiss her.

Though, I had refused to admit that even to myself. I refused to even entertain the idea of touching Lila in a manner other than 'friendly.'

But fucking hell, I was little drunk, and I couldn't get the image out of my head. She was standing in front of me with a crop top and shorts that hugged her curvaceous ass like a second skin, her pink lips glistening and her black hair falling over her shoulders.

Lila looked like a Rated-R Snow White. I wanted to slide between her thighs and make us both forget that we were best friends.

No. FUUUCCCK. NO!

That was drunk me thinking of that shit. Sober Maddox would never think of fucking his best friend, I told myself.

"Maddox, are you listening to me?" Her voice broke through my burning thoughts.

I swallowed and forced myself to look away.

"Yeah," I said, my voice deeper, hoping she didn't notice the way I strategically adjusted the pillow over my lap.

"Do you dare?" she asked cheekily.

I sighed, running my fingers through my short hair and pulling on the strands. "This isn't going to be fun, Lila."

She was asking me to be her dance partner. I wasn't much of a dancer, but I wouldn't say I completely sucked. This was important to her; I was well aware of that fact.

It was the fact that I was going to be too *close* to Lila for a whole week, especially since it had started to become harder for me to control my urges–my dick–around her. *That* bothered me. After the incident with Landon… there had been an unmistakable tension between Lila and I.

We both refused to acknowledge it, going on with our lives, but it was there, and it was becoming harder to ignore.

I didn't know why… I was feeling *this* way.

And I didn't understand what it was.

Angry at myself, I held back a growl, and my eyes snapped to Lila's. She was waiting for an answer, oblivious to my inner turmoil.

Lila Garcia was my best friend, and the last thing I wanted to do was lose her because I couldn't keep my dick in my pants.

I'm drunk, this is why, I convinced myself.

She tapped her foot impatiently. Any other girl doing that would have annoyed me, but *Lila* tapping her foot was cute as fuck.

"C'mon, Coulter. Are you about to lose to me?" She tsked. "It's a simple dare."

Simple?

Little did she know…

She grew cocky when I didn't reply, her competitive nature shining through. Lila knew I'd never turn down a dare, and she knew exactly how to get her way.

"Fine, I accept the dare," I said, my teeth grinding together. "You're going to regret this, Garcia."

Lila pressed her lips together to keep from smiling, but she lost the fight. A beautiful smile spread across her lips, and she laughed a bit, the little happy sound shooting straight to my heart.

My fingers curled and uncurled at my sides.

What in the fuck is wrong with me?

CHAPTER
THIRTY-TWO

Lila

My body was on fire.
I fought back a shiver, and my pulse throbbed in my
throat.

His hands traveled up my arms, slowly… taking his time, as if
he was memorizing every inch of my exposed skin. His touch was
so soft, so featherlight, but it felt as though he was writing a word,
painting a picture or playing a song on my skin. My breath caught,
and my heart raced, tripping over itself because it could longer beat
in a normal rhythm.

Our eyes connected through the floor length mirror. The
intensity of his gaze made my stomach do a crazy flip, and my
thighs trembled.

Maddox was wearing a black sleeveless shirt, the muscles in his
arms on display, and they clenched and tightened with every move
he made. His whole body was a work of art. I wore a tank top and
shorts, comfortable enough for dancing.

His blue eyes smoldered with *something* I couldn't read–dark and intense.

Friends, I told myself.

We were best friends.

But friends didn't look at each other the way we did.

The past five days had been sweet torture.

Sweet because I spent every waking hour with Maddox.

Torture because I spent every waking hour with Maddox.

Dancing… touching… breathing so close to each other's lips… but reminding myself to pull away.

I refused to acknowledge what I was feeling. It was *forbidden*.

Or maybe I didn't really comprehend my own wayward emotions.

Why does my body react the way it does when Maddox is close?

Why does my heart hurt… when he's hurt?

Why does my stomach flutter when he's touching me?

We were friends, weren't we?

Being anything more than friends could risk what we had for the last three years and whatever we had was *beautiful* the way it was.

"Lila?"

His voice, a deep timbre that traveled down through my body and all the way to my toes, snapped me back into the present.

"You just stepped on my toes," he mumbled, his breath against the tip of my earlobe.

I quickly apologized and went back into the position I was supposed to be in.

Our eyes locked, and I moved my hips against his. He followed my movement, and his grip tightened on my waist, his fingers almost digging into my flesh, and it didn't seem like he noticed.

Our height difference had the curve of my ass right at his groin, and my eyes fluttered close, my cheeks flushing in embarrassment and... something else.

Maddox made a sound at the back of his throat, and I looked at him through the mirror. His face hardened, and his eyes grew darker, his pupils dilating.

He grasped my hips and spun me around, taking me by surprise. He pulled me closer, our bodies clashing together. His hand skimmed over my bare thighs, right where the shorts ended, and he slowly lifted my left leg up, hooking my thigh around his hip. Fire licked its way through my veins, and I burned hotter.

Maddox dipped me low, and his warmth seeped through my clothes all the way through to my bones.

"You look a little red, Garcia," he rasped. "Am I too hot for you?"

He pulled me back up, and my heart thudded in my chest. I turned around and rolled my eyes, trying to look indifferent to his stupid remarks and his close proximity.

Maddox chuckled low, his chest vibrating with the sound, and I felt the vibration against my back. "You're rolling your eyes at me, I know. I can see your reflection in the mirror, Lila."

My eyes narrowed on him, and I swiveled around again, swatting his chest. "Concentrate on the dance, Maddox."

His arm snaked around my waist, and he pulled me hard into his body. I stumbled into his chest. "I have you," he muttered softly, and his arm tightened around my waist.

Maddox fished out the white blindfold from his pocket, and he covered my eyes, stealing away my ability to see. I was supposed to be blindfolded for half of this dance, making it trickier. It was all about trusting your dance partner.

It forced me to feel every one of his moves, his steps, our

matching rhythm, our shuddering breaths and the heat coming off him. My body was even more hyperaware of Maddox's closeness to me.

His warmth left me for a brief moment and our song, the song we were supposed to be dancing to, filled the tiny dance studio.

"Time of my Life."

There was no way Maddox and I could compete with the original dance and actors from the movie *Dirty Dancing*; they were legends, but it was my favorite movie and song and it was perfect for *this* dance.

Blindfolded, I waited for Maddox to return to me.

I could feel him somewhere around the room, *watching* me. The heat of his gaze had my stomach clenching.

The longer he took, the more nervous I became. Tick, tick, tick.

His body brushed against my back, and I sucked in a breath. I squeezed my eyes shut behind my blindfold and reminded myself to breathe. His hand drifted down, his fingers whispering over my body. My ribs, my stomach, my hips. Maddox touched me like I was a made of glass, fragile to his exploration.

Maddox pulled me into him, and he started to move. I followed his steps through our mixed tango and contemporary dance.

He gripped my hips and twirled me left and right before I fell back into his arms. My heart raced faster, and his breathing was ragged. I imagined his hard face and eyes that were so blue I drown in them. Beautiful.

Mine.

Oh, I wished.

I embraced the music and swayed with the flow, matching Maddox's rhythm and letting him lead me through blindly. I was at his mercy.

After spinning me around and with my heart in my throat, Maddox pulled me back into his body. With one hand on my waist, he grabbed my thigh and slowly brought my leg up to his hip. I hooked my ankle around his thigh, right under his ass. I was breathing hard now, and I wished I could see his face.

His breath brushed my nose. "Is this right? That's the correct move?" Maddox asked, his voice deep and gruff.

I nodded, mutely. Then, he slowly dipped me low. I released myself into his arms and let him move me. With me bent backward, his body molded over mine. He pressed his face against the crook of my neck. It was just part of the dance, I told myself.

Maddox inhaled.

I exhaled.

He brought me back up, and my leg fell from around his hip. He spun me around to the right and then one quick twirl to the left before Maddox brought me closer to him again. Our movements were synchronized.

I lifted my arms up, and his hands slid down my waist, just below my ribs. I swayed and moved my hips to the music. His fingers tightened on my waist before he lifted me up. My feet left the floor, and I wrapped my legs around his hips before he bent me backward again.

When we were finally standing straight up, I hugged him close, burying my face in his neck. I felt slightly dizzy, my heart beating too fast. But so was his.

Body against body. Chest to chest. I felt his heart beating to the same maddening rhythm as mine. Maddox twirled both of us around once.

My stomach tightened as I slid down his body, and my feet touched the ground once again. His fingers grazed my flushed cheek, and I wondered if he could feel how hot I was. Maddox removed the blindfold as he was told to do during our dance practices.

I blinked, and our eyes locked together.

His face shone with sweat, and my hair was sticking to my sweaty forehead and cheeks. His eyes narrowed on me, hungry and searching. Blazing with *something* – I didn't understand, I couldn't explain.

The expression on his face... I wished I knew what it was.

Maddox took a step back... then another and another, walking backward from me. The song was coming to an end; this was our final move.

Once there was enough distance between us, he crooked his finger at me, beckoning for me to come to him.

I did.

I walked, and then I took off running, one final lift, the same climatic lift as the one in the movie.

Once I was close enough to Maddox, I jumped. His hands gripped my hips, and he lifted me up and over his head. Strong and firm, he kept me steady.

Oh God.

Every muscle in my body tightened. I released a shaky breath as I slowly slid down the length of his body, feeling every hard inch of him. My palms pressed over his chest, sliding down his ribs and abs.

"I got you," he rumbled.

Do you?

Once I was touching the ground again, I curled my arms behind his neck, and our foreheads pressed together. His lips brushed against the tip of my nose, and my eyes fluttered close.

I can't breathe.

I swayed, dizzied by the mere proximity of Maddox. My heart

hammered in my chest. He exhaled, and his minty breath was on my lips.

Don't kiss me.

Kiss me.

No, don't ruin this.

A loud clap against the silence of the room had me flinching away. My eyes flew open, and Maddox's darkened as he pulled away.

I swiveled around and faced Bea. When did she get here?

"Lila!" she squealed, clapping her hands. "That was amazing... explosive! Oh my god!"

Bea walked further into the room, looking quite pleased. If there was any tension in the air, she ignored it.

She fanned herself. "The chemistry... Sweet Jesus, have mercy on us. Just wow! No one would believe you two are just friends. That was... yeah, wow." Bea pointed at Maddox and I. "This is exactly what I was looking for. You need chemistry with your dance partners. You need the audience to *feel* your dance even though they aren't dancing."

Her smile widened. "Oh, I'm so excited. Thank you, Maddox. For doing this on such short notice."

"Lila asked," he grumbled, running his fingers through his hair. "I couldn't say no."

Bea turned to me. "Are you guys hungry? We can grab lunch."

Maddox took a step back, pulling further away from me. He grabbed his duffel bag, his jaw clenching and his body tensing. "No. You go ahead. I'm leaving."

"Maddox–"

But he was already stalking away without glancing back at me. Without a goodbye.

My heart dropped to the pit of my stomach.

The moment between us was gone, the spell broken.

It was better that way, before either of us made a mistake we'd both regret for the rest of our lives.

Friends?

Friends.

CHAPTER THIRTY-THREE

Lila

I walked in on Riley and Colton. They both looked furious, glaring and spitting venom at each other. He had her caged against the wall, and their heads snapped toward me as I walked inside the apartment. Colton pulled away from Riley as though she burned him, and Riley was glaring daggers at his back.

Without a word, Colton left and slammed the door behind him. Welp, this wasn't looking too good.

The animosity between Colton and Riley was getting out of control.

I cleared my throat, and Riley sniffled. Her face crumpled, and she choked back a cry. "I hate *him.*"

"Colton or Grayson?" I asked, already knowing the answer.

"Both," she hissed, fury burning in her eyes. She stomped into the kitchen and filled herself a glass of water.

"What happened?"

"Grayson called," she deadpanned.

Oh. Shit.

She made a sound at the back of her throat. It sounded like a whimper. "Why did he call? After so long... *why*?"

I placed my shoulder bag on the counter and sat on the stool. "What did he say?"

Riley huffed, her lips twisting with a sneer. "Nothing."

My eyebrows rose, and I waited. "He called, I picked up. He didn't say a word. I could hear him breathing over the phone, but he's such a damn coward. I hung up."

Poor Riley.

Three years ago, I thought Grayson was the best choice for her.

Two months after graduation, he broke her heart.

Grayson wasn't going to attend any universities. Riley wanted to do a long-distance relationship. Hell, she even thought of quitting Harvard and moving back, just so they wouldn't have to break up. She was ready to put her heart on the line for him.

But Grayson was adamant and said it wouldn't work out. He wasn't willing to do long distance, but Riley knew it was a bullshit excuse. Something had been up with him, something he had been hiding from all of us. We figured it had something to do with his adoptive parents and his past, but he wouldn't say a word.

She wasn't ready to give up on him though. After going back and forth, making things difficult on Riley, he left. Grayson broke up with her right before the start of our first year at Harvard.

Grayson was back in Manhattan, and Riley was *here*.

She was still very much in love with him, and I knew, if Grayson showed up now, she'd give him another chance.

Enter Colton—who thought after Riley's break-up, he'd have a chance with her.

Oh boy, did he try. He cared for her, any one could see that clearly. If there was someone who could heal Riley's heart after Grayson broke it… it was Colton.

But Riley refused to give into his advances. Tension brewed between them, growing much volatile every day.

"I miss him," she confessed, her voice barely a whisper. "If only he had given us a chance."

I grasped her hand in mine and squeezed. "I'm sorry, Ry."

She swiped away a tear, almost angrily. "Do you think maybe… Grayson has a good reason for staying away?"

Something bothered me about that day.

The frantic and desperate look in Grayson's eyes as he pushed Riley further away from him. And the words he roared.

"I'm protecting you, damn it!"

Protecting Riley? From what? From who?

She let out a humorless laugh; her eyes glistening with unshed tears. "He's had three years, Lila. Three years I've been waiting for him, three years for him to realize we could have been so good together, but he gave up on *us*."

I hugged her, and she fell into my arms, crying softly. She had been holding it in for so long. My heart ached for her.

For all three of them.

Once her cries turned into tiny hiccups, Riley pulled away and rubbed a hand over her face, as though getting rid of any evidence she had been crying over Grayson.

She half-smiled, the corners of her lips twisting slightly. "How was the event? Where's Maddox?"

I left the stool and went to the fridge, taking out last night's leftovers. "The event was great. It was pretty… exhilarating, and they loved the dance. The fundraising part of it was a huge success, too," I told her. "It was fun."

And it truly was. The whole night was pretty epic until...

Riley appeared curious when she asked, "Maddox didn't come home with you?"

No, he *ran.*

The moment our dance ended, Maddox left. He didn't even stay for dinner, and with him gone, just like that, without so much as a word, I could barely eat. My food stayed untouched in front of me, and for the rest of the night, I *smiled* while my heart was breaking– hidden from everyone's eyes. I suffered while they enjoyed the rest of their night.

How could he? Why did he leave?

Why didn't he say goodbye?

Why?

A subdued anger burned in my stomach, threatening to break through. I couldn't understand why Maddox was acting the way he was – why he was running away from me, pulling further and further away from me.

Anger and... fear.

Because it felt like we were hanging on by a thin thread, and it was about to snap, catapulting us into two different world and away from each other.

Maddox and I... if we weren't careful, we were about to *break*, to shatter, and there would be no turning back once that happened.

Me and you, he had promised.

I hoped he was keen on keeping his promises.

My chest tightened. *Don't break me, Maddox.*

"Lila?" Riley's soft voice broke through my stormy thoughts.

"He left. I don't where he went," I admitted out loud, the words tasting bitter on my tongue.

Riley stared at me, her eyes searching. "You don't see it, do you?" she said gently.

"See what?" I shoved a piece of roasted chicken in my mouth.

Her lips twisted. "Nothing. When you see it, you'll know what I mean."

"What—"

Riley shook her head and stood up. "I've had a long day. I'm off to bed. Are you going to sleep soon?"

I nodded. "Probably."

Riley paused at the door of her room and glanced back over her shoulder. "Stop hiding and stop ignoring it. You know what you feel. You're just refusing to acknowledge it."

Without waiting for a reaction, she closed her door. I stood there, mutely. What was I supposed to do with her cryptic words?

It felt like there was a hole in my chest, and I was bleeding out. There was no way to stop the flow of blood. I *bled,* the knife digging into my heart carelessly.

Drip. Drip. Drip.

The dam broke, my blood flowed, and I lost those pieces of me I had carefully glued together.

Tears of frustration blurred my eyes.

I was so...*confused.*

Between wanting Maddox and not wanting to lose him.

For years, I'd swallowed down my confusing feelings and kept them locked away in a forbidden place, refusing to acknowledge them. My throat itched as I forced back a cry, and my lungs seemed to collapse.

You know what you feel.

No! I didn't!

I couldn't.

Never.

Stop hiding and stop ignoring it.

I... couldn't.

I chewed on my lip until it bled, and my knees buckled from the realization – what I felt for Maddox, it was so much *more* and I was damn afraid to acknowledge it.

Why was this so hard?

Maybe I was stupid.

Maybe I had completely lost my mind. It was the only explanation to why I was in Maddox's apartment, waiting for him to get home. It was almost midnight, and the last time I had seen him was...

When he had left the event right after our dance.

Maddox still hadn't come home yet.

I wrung my hands in nervousness, the feeling of anxiety pooling in my stomach. God, what was I doing?

Why was I even... here? At his place, waiting for him.

Stupid, stupid Lila.

What was I going to do when he came back? Hug him? Kiss him?

Nothing.

I'd stare at him, and he'd look into my eyes, that would be it. Because we were... friends.

Such a brutal lie it was. Friends...

The closer we became, the more I noticed smaller things about Maddox. What he loved, what he enjoyed, what pissed him off or annoyed him, his quirks and his ticks, and with every new thing I learned about him over the last three years, it became harder to pull away.

To ignore whatever was brewing between us; yet, we refused to acknowledge it.

He fucked other girls.

I dated other men.

We were best friends.

It was simple to the world, to *him*, but I was battling a war on my own.

My head fell into my hands and a choked sound escaped me. *What am I doing?*

The clock ticked with every second that went by, and when I finally couldn't take it anymore, I snapped to my feet. No, I shouldn't have been here.

This was a… mistake.

I was confused and…scared…and feeling *too* much.

The last thing I needed was to be this close to Maddox if he came home. I had to leave. Shaking my head in desolation, I strode for the door.

I never reached it because the door swung open and Maddox entered his apartment, stumbling inside drunkenly. Sweet Mother Mary, he was out… drinking?

He halted at the sight of me, and his lips curled. "Lila." He breathed my name like a whispered prayer to the heavens above.

Was he praying for absolution or destruction? Because whispering my name like *that* could only destroy us.

He slammed the door closed behind him and stalked forward.

"You're drunk," I accused, taking a small step back.

He hummed, smiling. He stood in front of me, our chests barely touching, and my gaze met his. "You're so beautiful," he blurted out.

God, he was completely out of his mind. Maddox wasn't just

drunk; he was *really* drunk.

He bent his head and stuck his nose against the crook of my neck, inhaling sharply. Was he…sniffing me?

"*Beautiful*," he breathed, before his body slumped forward into mine.

"Maddox!" He was so heavy, my knees almost buckled under his weight. "Maddox?"

Did he just… pass out?

I took his shoulders in my hands and tried to shake him awake. He groaned, but otherwise, didn't move. Shit.

With the rest of my strength, I dragged his heavy body into his room. Maddox barely made any effort, because he was practically dead to the world. How much drink did he have? And why?

God, I was so tired from asking that question–*why?*

I pushed him on the bed, hating that he drank so much in one night. Before I could pull away, his arm curled around my waist, and he tugged me forward, and I fell on top of him.

His throat bobbed as he groaned. I shifted over his body, trying to break free, but for someone as drunk as Maddox, he was still too strong for me. His arm was a band of steel around my hips, keeping me locked against him. He wasn't letting go.

I shifted away but then sucked in a harsh breath when I felt…

My throat went dry. This wasn't happening.

His cock strained through his jeans, the bulge pressing indecently into my stomach.

"Lila." My name on his lips sounded like poetry. So right, so perfect… so filthy.

I pressed my hands over his pecs and pushed. "Maddox, let go."

He did the opposite.

Maddox rolled us over until I was underneath him, trapped

against his body. My legs fell open, and I gasped as he settled between my spread thighs. His eyes split open, hazy and filled with... *hunger.*

His gaze fell to my lips, and he lingered there, his eyelids hooded.

"Maddox," I whispered.

"Say it... again. My... name."

I was utterly helpless in his arms. "Maddox." His name echoed from my lips.

"Again," he demanded.

"Maddox."

He released a shuddering breath before bending his head, pressing his face into my throat. He nuzzled me, his lips caressing my skin. I trembled, goosebumps breaking over my flesh.

He ran his lips down my collarbone, his teeth grazing the sensitive skin there, and I let out an involuntarily shudder. "Don't," I warned, but it was a weak attempt.

Maddox hummed low in his throat, his chest vibrating with the sound. He lowered his body over mine, forcing me into the mattress. He wrapped around me like a cocoon.

We were chest to chest, hips to hips, his hardness against my heated core—so fucking close. There was not even an inch of breath between us.

The area between my legs throbbed, and I clenched, seeking for something but feeling... *empty.*

Maddox was still nuzzling my throat, kissing me as if it wasn't atypical, as if we weren't best friends, as if everything around us would crumble as we remained intimately wrapped in each other's arms.

"Fuck," he grunted against my skin, and his hips jerked, pressing against the most sensitive part of me. My lips parted, shocked, and a silent gasp escaped me.

My hands fumbled toward his shoulders, and my nails dug into his back.

This was so wrong.

Stop.

Don't stop.

Maddox swiveled his hips before grinding against my pussy. We were both fully clothed, and my best friend was humping me like a horny teenager.

And I didn't want to stop him.

How long had I forbid myself from imagining *this*? Too long.

He was drunk; it wasn't his fault. I was fully aware, and it would be my guilt to bear.

We should have stopped.

No, don't stop.

Maddox grinded his erection against me. He was so hard; I could feel him through the layers of our clothes. My core grew hot and wet. Molten desire spread through my veins, and my stomach dipped to my toes.

His breath hitched, and I let out a moan when his hips jerked again, the zipper of his jeans pressing hard against my pussy through my shorts. The friction left my body wanting more, and I became needy. My pussy clenched as the need to be filled became strong.

Maddox thrust into me, again and again, the motion too similar to fucking.

My thighs trembled, and my heart seized.

He kissed his way down my throat, biting and sucking softly at my skin. His palm caressed the curve of my breasts, feeling the heavy mounds in his hands. His grunts and his groans were music to my ears, even as I tried to remind myself how wrong this was.

It's wrong. I released his shoulders and pushed a hand between us.

This is wrong. My fingers traced my wet slit through my shorts.

Maddox rubbed against me again, and it was a delicious sensation that had my eyes fluttering closed.

I shoved a hand into my shorts and tugged my panties aside. My eyes blurred with tears as a whimper echoed from my lips. It felt so good, even though it was so fucking wrong.

"Fuck, goddamn it," he cursed, the muscles in his neck corded, and his face tensed.

His thrusts grew jerkier and faster. He was chasing his orgasm, climbing toward something forbidden between us.

My thumb slid over my swollen clit, and my hips jerked up. I was so hot, and my fingers glided over my wetness. My knuckles brushed against my pussy lips, feeling the way my core contracted. I was so turned on; I'd never been this wet before. I gathered my wetness with two fingers and rubbed my pulsing clit. Pleasure spiked through me and my back bowed.

The feel of Maddox's lips against my throat and his hands kneading my breasts had my eyes rolling back into my head. His thumb skimmed over my hardened nipple through my top, and I shuddered. My body easily responded to his touch, and I realized I had been craving *this* for the longest time.

"Lila," he groaned out hoarsely. "Fuck, Lila. My Lila."

Maddox humped me, thrusting, and I rocked my hips against his in unison, finding a rhythm between us. I imagined he really was *fucking* me. No clothes, no barrier between us, and our bare bodies pressed together in the most intimate way two human beings could be together.

The image of us fucking was so decadently sinful and filthy. My calves tightened, and my whole body clenched as I climbed up and up toward my release.

I rubbed myself faster before sliding my thumb over my clit and pinching it. My vision blurred, and my whole spasmed as I choked back a gasp before biting on my lip. Wetness pooled between my thighs, coating my fingers and panties with my shameful release. Wet and sticky, I continued to rub myself in leisure strokes, feeling the little twitches of my pussy after my orgasm.

Maddox thrust *hard*, and I gasped before a moan spilled past my lips. He tensed above me, and his hips stilled, his head thrown back with a low, deep grunt. Warmth spread through his jeans, and I could feel it through my shorts. He just came.

Maddox's eyes pierced me for a second and then he slumped over my body.

The moment was gone, and I was instantly filled with shame and immense guilt. My stomach twisted, bile coating every inch of my mouth.

What have I done?

There was absolutely no excuse. Maddox had been drunk, and I took advantage of the situation for my own pleasure. He probably wasn't going to remember this tomorrow morning…

But what if… he did?

My heart thudded in my chest, and I swallowed back a sob. I removed my hand from my panties, the stickiness on my fingers a harsh reminder of our actions. I stretched my arm out and kept the hand I pleasured myself with far away from us.

Maddox buried his face in my shoulder. His body went slack, and I felt him soft snores against my skin. The heaviness of him sank into me like a warm blanket, and for a brief moment, I imagined how it'd be to fall asleep in his arms every night and to wake up next to him, just like this. As much as the fantasy was sweet, it would only have a bitter ending.

My fingers slid through his hair, my nails grazing the back of his neck softly, just the way he liked it. My lips parted, wanting to whisper my secret, but I felt choked. The heart is a traitor, and, in that moment, I could feel all my defenses crumbling to the ground.

Maddox grumbled something under his breath, and it sounded like my name. His arm tightened around my hip, and my arms curled around his shoulders as a lone tear slid down my cheeks. I didn't want to let go... but I had to.

"If I love you, I give you the power to destroy me. I'm not strong enough for that. I can't be just another girl to you, Maddox. I need to be more; I deserve more, and I don't think you can give that. I can't risk *us* and what we are. We're beautiful... just like this. Friends."

I prayed Maddox woke up in the morning with no memory of what we had just done.

I'd take this secret to my grave, and I would bear this guilt on my own.

CHAPTER THIRTY-FOUR

Maddox

A week later

My fingers drummed over my thighs as I waited for Lila to come down the stairs. I left her an hour ago to get dressed, and if we didn't leave in five minutes, we were going to be late to the gala.

I was in a tuxedo, which was appropriate for the evening gala we were attending. It was an auctioning event and dinner, my parents being the guests of honor. My dad called me last night and *demanded* me to be present. I told him to fuck off and hung up with absolutely no intention to attend the gala. I didn't give a fuck if this was important to him or that it was appropriate for me to be there to show my face and support to my parents.

It was Lila who convinced me.

The gala was being held in California, and she wanted to visit the beach. Lila said it was a great opportunity for a small vacation after such a long semester, and I couldn't say *no* to her. I could never refuse her of anything.

So, we took a plane here. We'd go to the gala tonight, and tomorrow, I was going to teach her how to surf.

The sound of heels clicking against the hardwood brought my attention to the stairs. Lila came into view, and my breath caught in my throat.

Breathtaking.

She descended the stairs carefully, a silky black off-the-shoulder dress clinging to her slender curves and fluttering around her feet, which were adorned with glittering silver heels. It was plain and simple, yet elegant with a thigh high split. Her creamy thigh was visible through the gap as she walked toward me, a silver clutch in her hand.

Her hair was piled up on her head, in a bun, with a few curly strands of black hair fanning her cheeks. Her dreamcatcher necklace hung between the valley of her breasts, and she wore a smile that made my knees weak.

She did a slow spin. "So, how do I look?"

Her pouty red lips had my dick straining against my black slacks and I stifled a groan.

"Pretty," I rumbled.

Lila pursed her lips, pouting. "Just pretty?"

I took a step toward her, unable to stop myself. "Gorgeous. Beautiful. Exquisite. Stunning. Lovely. Angelic. Breathtaking. Ravishing. Elegant. Bewitching. Alluring. Heavenly. The angels would bow to you because they can't compete. So. Fucking. Exquisite."

Her lips parted, a hitch in her breathing, and she blinked at me through her long, thick lashes that should have been unnatural but everything about Lila was natural. "You said exquisite twice," she breathed.

My fingers skimmed over her bare arms. Her skin broke into goosebumps and a small shiver racked through her small frame. "Because you're twice as exquisite," I confessed, in a raspy croak.

My body burned with a sensation I knew too well, and my pants grew tight around my groin as my dick became harder in her mere presence. I didn't even have to touch her, and I was already leaking cum at the tip.

It was lust, I told myself.

But I lusted after other women before, and whatever I felt for Lila didn't come close to *lust*.

And I hated myself for feeling this way.

Just like I hated myself on that morning, a week ago. I woke up to be an empty bed, but I still felt Lila's presence next to me. It was a dream; though, it had seemed so real, so vivid.

And my boxers had been sticky with my release. I couldn't remember the last time I had a wet dream and spilled cum in the middle of the night like a horny teenager, but Lila... *fuck*, she invaded even my dreams with her sweet voice and sinful touches.

I dreamed of fucking her... my best friend. The same friend I made countless pinky swears with.

Friends?

Friends.

I destroyed the innocence of our relationship–the sweetness of our friendship. I made it into something... dirty, and it was no longer pure and no longer untouched by my forbidden desires. It was my guilt to bear for the rest of our lives.

Little did she know...

Sweet Lila, I fucked up.

Her lips curled. "Such a sweet tongue. I'm almost jealous of all the girls you've said those things to."

My heart squeezed at her words. "Your jealousy is not needed because I've never called another woman those words."

No one had ever measured up to Lila since she came into my life. No other woman had ever been... beautiful or *exquisite*.

Her eyes widened before she quickly tried to mask her surprise. "Liar."

I cupped her elbow, steering her away from the stairs. "I don't lie."

Lila mumbled something incorrigible under her breath before she rolled her eyes. We walked out of the beach house, which was owned by me—well, my parents. We had a caretaker who cleaned up and kept the house safe while we weren't here. My parents and I used to spend a lot of time here when I was younger, a child.

Before everything changed and I became a stranger in my own goddamn house and to my own parents.

A limousine was waiting for us outside. Lila let out a breathy laugh. "Seriously, a limo?"

I shrugged, halfheartedly. "The host for the gala tonight arranged it. Apparently, he sent a limo to all his guests."

Her eyes crinkled to the sides as her smile broadened. "Damn. I don't what it means to be *that* rich. Pardon me for being a lowly peasant."

We climbed into the limo, and the driver peeled out of the parking space, taking off through the neighborhood I was familiar with. The drive to the gala was short, and we were only about fifteen minutes late due to traffic.

We walked into the ballroom, and all eyes fell on us. Lila's fingers tightened around my elbow, gripping me hard, as though her life depended on it. *I got you.*

I met my father's gaze with a hard one, and he jerked his chin at me in greeting. My mother smiled, though it was tight. Probably fake, too, but I didn't know any longer since I long stopped caring if it was real or fake.

The moment we descended the stairs, I was surrounded. I was Brad Coulter's son—prestigious, important and held in high honor.

The night ended before it started. My bow tie suddenly felt like it was restricting my air flow, and my skin itched. This was exactly why I didn't want to attend this gala because all they were talking about was when I'd take over my dad's company—asking about the future. He built an empire, and I was the only heir.

I was approached by businessmen left and right. They laughed, and we shared a drink, appearing as courteous as I could be.

I *loathed* it.

Lila stayed by my side until she was pulled away by the wives. I kept my gaze on her, watching her every move. She didn't know these people, and I knew this was beyond her comfort zone.

But she was here for *me.*

My date for tonight, my friend and my ally.

A slow song came up, and the couples spilled onto the dance floor. This was my chance. I nodded at the gentlemen and made my brisk escape, stalking toward Lila. Her head snapped up as if we were connected by an invisible thread, and she could *feel* me coming for her.

Her brown eyes brightened, and a small smile twisted her lips with relief.

"Maddox." My name spilled from her lips, and my chest squeezed.

"Sorry, ladies. Can I steal my date away for a dance?" I asked, offering Lila my hand. She giggled and took my hand, and I whisked her away.

"My savior," she whispered as we joined the other couples on the dance floor.

"I thought you didn't need a savior or protector."

Her eyes narrowed on me, and she pinched my bicep. I swallowed back my laugh. "Forget I said that. I take it back," she grumbled.

Beautiful Lila, sweet Lila.

My hands landed on her hips and hers curled around the back of my neck. The second her soft skin touched mine, I realized what a mistake it was.

We were *too* close, after I'd been trying to put distance between us.

Her body pressed against mine, and my fingers teased the top curve of her ass before I gripped her hips again. She swayed to the music, and we slowly started dancing.

This was a bad decision, and my dick was pissed at me.

Her cheeks were flushed, and I wanted to ask her what she was thinking about.

Was it as forbidden as my own thoughts?

Did her desires match mine?

I shook my head, trying to clear my mind.

"What's wrong?" Lila asked, her voice delicate. She tilted her head to the side, her eyes sparking with curiosity.

My eyes swept over the ballroom, and my gaze landed on my father's. He was watching us dance, an unreadable expression on his hard face.

Anger burned like acid in my veins at the fact that we were in the same room. Fuck, I didn't want him anywhere near my Lila.

I bent my head, my nose brushing over the tip of her ear as I whispered, "Let's get out of here."

CHAPTER
THIRTY-FIVE

Lila

His voice was gruff when he spoke, "Let's get out of here." Maddox dragged me out of the ballroom, and I tried to keep up in my heels. I knew he was going to hate tonight. As much as he was cocky and arrogant and he loved the attention from the chicks, he loathed being surrounded by people like his father–talking business and mingling with them.

The subject of him taking over his father's empire one day as the only heir was something we never discussed. He refused to talk about it, and I knew he had no intention of taking over.

Instead of waiting for the valet, he took me around the building to the parking lot. "There's our ride," he said under the moonlight of the California sky.

I halted in my step, forcing Maddox to pause, too, as I took in what was in front of me. Maddox chuckled, and he let go of my hand, striding over to his motorbike. His bike?!

I gaped as Maddox climbed onto the beast of a bike – one that was similar to the one back home -- and offered me a helmet. He looked sinful in a tuxedo, with disheveled hair, straddling a bike. I licked my lips, hating the feeling of my heart racing at the sight of him being so devilishly handsome.

I had never seen a man so overtly masculine, so confident in his own skin and with such a dominant aura. The sensitive area between my legs pulsed with need.

"You coming, Sweet Cheeks? Or do I need to steal you away?"

I blinked, still shocked. "*How*...where did you find this bike? We came in a limo."

A crooked smile graced his perfect lips. "I was already planning an early escape." He winked.

I strode over and took the heavy helmet he offered. Maddox helped me buckle the chin strap, his fingers lingering longer at my jaw.

I swallowed and let out a nervous laugh. "Why does it feel like we're doing something very, very bad? Like we're some naughty kids... when in actuality, we have done much worse than running away from a stupid charity gala?"

"Because if my father finds out we ran, he's gonna skin me alive," he said with a slight twist of his lips.

My eyes narrowed on him. "Ha. Funny. Very funny."

I looked down at my long dress and figured this could be a problem. We weren't really clothed for a bike ride. But thank God for the thigh high split. It allowed me to bunch my dress up and tie a knot at my thighs; this way, the fabric wouldn't get trapped in the monster wheels.

"Where are we going?" I asked, curiously.

His gaze fell to my bare legs, and I could swear he swallowed, his eyes darkening in the slightest bit.

"Some place not *here*," he announced smoothly, the deep baritone of his voice vibrating through my bones, all the way down to my toes. My body temperature spiked, burning with unspoken and forbidden need.

He offered me his tuxedo jacket, and I took it, pulling my arms through the sleeves and wrapping myself in his smell–his cologne and his familiar manly scent.

"Well, let's go. Steal me away, Coulter." I pulled down the visor of my helmet, obscuring my face from his gaze, a perfect hideaway for my flushed cheeks.

I straddled the bike behind him and wrapped my arms around his middle. It wasn't the first time he took me on a bike ride. We had plenty of those during our times together.

We rode for a long time, the breeze in my hair and Maddox's warm body against my front. It was… comforting.

This… this was exactly why I didn't want to risk losing him.

This was why I kept my secret and locked away the night we spent together, the heated moment between us. Maddox didn't remember our time together, and it was better this way. Even though I was the only one left haunted by the memories of us, me fingering myself as he humped me through our clothes.

Every time I stared at him, I remembered the look on his face as he orgasmed. My body tingled at the memory of his lips on my throat and his palms kneading my breasts.

It became harder for me to keep my untamed desires in check.

Maddox eventually came to a stop and the sound of crashing waves filled my ears. "We're at the beach?"

He helped me off the bike, before straightening up to his full height. Maddox unbuckled the chin strap and pulled the helmet off. Once the weight was gone, I almost groaned in relief.

His thumb stroked my collarbone in a delicate manner before he caught himself and pulled away. "I brought you to my favorite spot. Let's go."

He grasped my hand in his and pulled me forward. My heels sank into the sand, and I stumbled forward, a surprised giggle spilling from my lips. Yeah, that wasn't going to work. I kicked off my heels, my bare feet sinking into the soft sand. It felt so nice.

We walked closer to the waves, hand in hand. I could see the reflection of the full moon in the ocean, and the sound of the waves were melodious to my ears. We came here last year, with the rest of our friend group, on our summer vacation. It was good to be here again, but this time—just the two of us.

I didn't want to admit it... but it was intimate.

Maddox and I settled on the sand, watching the waves crash against the shore. We fell into a comfortable silence, and I watched him from the corner of my eye. His face was hard and pensive, with shadows under his eyes. Maddox was okay without his parents in his life, but every time they made their presence known... I've seen Maddox retreat within himself—a place filled with anger and hate. He battled his inner wars on his own and in silence.

My heart ached because I wanted to hold him.

I wanted to soothe him, save him and to love him in ways he has never been loved before and in ways only I can love him.

If only he'd let me.

If only he was mine.

If only...

"Are you cold?" His voice echoed through my ears, and I shook away the muddling thoughts.

"No, not cold." I went back to staring at the ocean. The urge to dip into the water was strong. "I want to take a swim."

"We can, tomorrow."

"Or…" I left the sentence hanging.

Maddox read my mind, and his eyes narrowed on me. "Lila," he warned.

"Troublemaker. I learned from the best." I blinked at him in fake innocence. "I dare you to go skinny dipping. Right now."

He gave me a blank stare, before releasing a sigh. "What am I going to do with you?"

"Well, I don't think this is that big of a deal. You dared me to wear a fucking potato sack to the club last week! Do you have any idea how embarrassing that was?"

The tension in his shoulders unraveled. Maddox half-shrugged. "Can't be as embarrassing as you making me wear a fake pregnant belly. I was waddling around campus all fucking day, Lila."

I pressed my lips together to keep from laughing. Oh, that was a sight to see. I'd never seen Maddox so offended in his life, and Colton still wouldn't let him live down that fateful day.

Over the years, Maddox and I have done countless dares. Some of them wild and crazy. Some just plain… stupid and embarrassing.

Maddox taught me how to enjoy life, how to let go of fear and the need for control and to just… *live.*

I wasn't just surviving any longer or simply going through the motions of life after the death of my parents.

I was… living and breathing life.

"So, do you dare?"

Maddox stood up and slowly unbuttoned his white shirt. He tugged at his bow tie, and it fell on the sand beside me. He peeled off his shirt, and my mouth went dry.

His stomach clenched, his abs rippled, and my stomach pooled with heat. My eyes traveled up the length of his torso up to his chest. His strong pecs and his nipples...

My pussy tightened. The silver nipple piercing shone under the moonlight.

I had to remind myself to breathe. My gaze slid up to his face. Chiseled jaw. Full lips. Nose that was slightly crooked, but it was only noticeable if someone paid close attention and his eyes blazed a deep blue—as deep as the ocean--eyes that could see inside my soul.

"I'll get in the water on one condition. You have to do it."

"Is that a dare?"

"No, I'm not wasting a dare on that."

"You think I'll get in just because you asked?"

He smirked. "Yes."

"So cocky." I rolled my eyes and crossed my arms over my chest.

Maddox toed off his black, shiny dress shoes and kicked off his slacks. He left his boxers on and strode toward the waves. "Don't be a chicken, Garcia," he called out over his shoulder.

Oh no, he *didn't.*

I held back a growl and came to my feet, glaring at his muscled back. I should have thought more about it... skinny dipping with Maddox was a bad idea, but I didn't think.

I made silly decisions around Maddox.

I shrugged off my dress and my bra. Covering up my breasts with one arm, I left my lace panties on and jogged toward the water.

Maddox was already waist deep, wading through the cool water, before I jumped on his back. "Boo," I said in his ear.

It was too late to realize my mistake.

My bare tits pressed against his back. Skin to skin. My eyes widened, and my breath stuttered.

Maddox tensed, inhaling sharply, as my puckered nipples rubbed against his shoulder blades. I squeezed my eyes shut, silently berating myself.

"Troublemaker," he grumbled without any heat. Maddox reached behind him and grabbed my thighs, keeping a hold of me. I loved swimming, but it was night, and I couldn't see a thing. The water was too dark, and the ocean wasn't a place to trust. There could be *anything* in this water.

I clung to Maddox, already regretting my dare.

Maddox chuckled, his back vibrating with the sound. My nipples hardened into two aching tips, and we both ignored it. I told myself my nipples were only reacting to the cold ocean, not because of Maddox.

"Don't be a chicken." He was keeping this from being awkward.

"Asshole," I hissed, swatting his bicep.

Slowly, I untangled myself from his back and waded through the water, away from him. I kept afloat on my back, looking at the dark sky.

How did this happen...?

How did Maddox and I go from being enemies to friends... to best friends... to *this*?

Something slimy touched my feet, and I jumped, snapping out of my thoughts with a terrified squeal. Maddox swam over to me, and he pulled me into his arms. "What's wrong?" he asked urgently, his hands sliding down my bare body, searching for any injuries.

Whatever it was slid over my foot again, and I shuddered. "Something just touched me!"

I wrapped my legs around his waist, peering into the water, as if I could see something, but it was too dark.

Maddox stroke my back. "It might just be a fish, Lila."

"Um, I want to get out. Now."

My thighs tightened around his waist, and it was then I

realized...

Fuck.

Maddox's eyes darkened as if he just came to the same realization. My core was seated right above his dick, the thin layers of our underwear the only barrier between us. Chest to chest, hips to hips, skin to skin.

My lungs squeezed, and I forgot how to breathe. My hands curled around his shoulders.

Time halted, and the world came to a stop.

The look on his face was something I'd never seen before, and I wished I knew what he was thinking. His jaw ticked, the muscles twitching. His pupils were dilated and dark, his blue eyes stormy with unreadable emotions. We looked at each other a little too long to be *just* friends.

"Lila," he rasped. His head descended toward mine, his breath feathering over my lips.

I saw it in his eyes; Maddox was going to kiss me.

No, don't.

Yes, please.

His lips parted, captivating me. He pressed me closer to him.

My heart stuttered, and my stomach twisted, butterflies raging inside. I could feel his hardness between my thighs. Maddox, of course, wasn't unaffected. He was a guy, after all. His dick jerked, pressing against my pussy through the layers. I was hot, my core molten lava, and aching.

He just had to slide my panties to the side and thrust into me. He could...

I was open to him; my thighs were spread around his hips.

As though unable to stop himself, he rocked against me, slightly thrusting up against my pussy.

A small whimper echoed through my lips, and my eyes fluttered close.

It was then he snapped.

Maddox roughly pulled away, the water rippling around us harshly. He slipped out of my embrace, forcing my legs to fall away from his waist. "It's cold. We should get out," he said, his rich voice hoarse. It sounded like he was swallowing the words and having difficulty speaking.

My chest cracked open and a searing pain racked through my body as Maddox swam away from me without another word.

Feeling more alone than ever, I ducked my head under the water and came back up for air, hoping the coldness would ease the heat of my body and clear my mind.

It didn't work.

Slowly, I got out of the water. Maddox was sitting on the sand, still half naked, with his back to me. My throat seized with emotions I couldn't explain, and I settled on the sand with him. Back to back, facing opposite directions. I watched the waves, letting it soothe my bleeding heart.

After a while, our breathing had evened out, our bodies no longer wet from our skinny dipping. Maddox cleared his throat. I turned my head to the side, keeping our backs pressed together. His hand came into view.

He was showing me his pinky.

God, Maddox.

Unshed tears blurred my vision.

"Friends?" he asked in a low voice.

I hooked my pinky around his. "Friends."

We both lied to ourselves, but it was better that way. It had to be

Maddox

A low groan escaped me before I could stop myself. Grabbing my pillow, I stuffed it over my face as my hand strayed toward my cock. This was so wrong; I shouldn't want her. Not like this. Never like this.

So. Fucking. Wrong.

Last night, our bodies pressed together in the water under the night sky – I almost lost control. I almost fucked her, right there.

And for a brief moment, I thought Lila was going to let me.

We were both edging toward something dangerous, and I didn't know how to stop.

Because all I could think about were her lips–the way they part when she says my name; her eyes–the way they darken when she stares up at me. Her smooth neck – the way I wanted to bite her soft flesh and leave my marks there. Her hands... the way I wondered how they'd feel around my cock. Her goddamn tits, small and perky, perfect for my hands. She was made for me.

Fuuuuck.

I palmed my cock, squeezing at the base before pumping my length in my fist.

She was in the room adjacent to mine. The walls were so thin, she could probably hear me jerking off. But I couldn't stop. I tried, goddamn it. I tried.

I was hard, aching and... I wanted her. More than I had ever wanted anything in my life.

I shuddered as I imagined thrusting two fingers into her sweet cunt. She would clench around me, moaning, and I'd pull out, teasing her until she was writhing with need, before pushing the same two fingers inside her mouth and demanding she taste herself.

Such dirty, filthy thoughts.

Ragged, guttural groans spilled from me, and I muffled them with my pillow. I pumped my cock with my fist, angry for feeling this way but filled with so much need that I couldn't force myself to stop. The muscles of my thighs tensed, my dick heavy and swollen in my palm as I got closer to my release.

So. Fucking. Wrong.

So. Fucking. Right.

Thick ropes of cum sprayed my stomach and coated my palm as I came, spurt after thick spurt, and I kept fisting my cock, pumping it, until my body twitched and a ragged, breathless groan came from my lips. *"Lila."*

CHAPTER THIRTY-SIX

Lila

The unmistakable pressure between us was becoming harder to ignore. A month after our time in California, which was tense and awkward, the situation between Maddox and I was still same.

Maddox had become rigid, and the distance grew between us.

I wished there was a way to fix this, but it was clear there was no going back, no matter how much either of us wanted to.

I was sitting on my couch, staring at the TV, although I wasn't really watching the screen, when Maddox walked inside my apartment. He wore a blank expression and had a piece of paper in his hand. The last time we saw each other was two days ago, after our last exams. This semester was officially over.

"We're going to Paris," he announced. "Me and you."

Me and you. I almost laughed, a cold-humorless laugh. It used to be cute when we'd say that, but now, it *hurt*.

Me and you. But for how long, Maddox? We were already at the breaking apart.

"Paris, why?" I croaked, before clearing my throat. I didn't want him to read the emotions on my face.

"It's my birthday in four days. Daddy dearest gave me tickets to Paris as a present. Well, he mailed them to me."

This meant his parents, obviously, weren't planning to spend Maddox's birthday with him. In all the years we'd known each other, I'd never seen his parents celebrate his birthday. No hugs, no love, no affection. It made me angry, so furious with the way they always treated Maddox.

He deserved better.

He wasn't as complicated as everyone thought. Maddox Coulter was just a misunderstood boy who needed and deserved someone to fight for him–to show him that he was worth it.

And I was going to be that person. Even if I couldn't do it as his lover, I was going to do it as his best friend, at least.

Because, truly, he was worth all the love–all the love he never had but deserved.

"I've never been to Paris," I finally confessed.

Maddox finally cracked a sincere smile. "I know, and you're going to love it."

City of love. And two best friends who didn't have the courage to acknowledge whatever this was between them.

What were the odds? Fate really did like to play cruel jokes on us.

I dragged my nails over my thighs. "When do we leave?"

"Tomorrow night. That's enough time for you to pack, right?" Maddox asked, walking further into my apartment, but still keeping a distance between us.

I nodded and then patted the couch. "Join me. I'm watching

Friends. It's the pivot scene."

Maddox looked indecisive, a troubled tension hanging between us.

Please say yes.

Please don't leave me. Again.

He swallowed, his Adam's apple bobbing with the movement, and his eyes flickered to me and then the TV. Relief coursed through my veins when he took a step toward me and settled on the couch beside me, not saying a word.

A moment passed between us, I smiled – almost a timid smile, and we turned to face the TV at the same time.

A few minutes later, the brutal tension dissolved, and our shoulders shook with silent laughter at the scene we were watching. Our knees were touching, the briefest touch, but my skin tingled. My pulse raced like a freight train, and my heart palpitated; he was laughing, and I was laughing, and the world had never felt so right in that mere second.

I wanted to cherish this moment, so afterward, years later, when Maddox and I had been torn apart by our unspoken feelings, I'd remember what it felt like to be this close to him.

Later that night, sleep didn't come easy. I tossed and turned, thinking about Maddox and our upcoming trip to Paris. Was this going to be a mistake? Maybe. Probably.

But I couldn't say no, and I wanted to spend this time with him. Just the two of us.

The ache between my legs was back again, my body tensing with frustration.

Ever since that night – the night Maddox was drunk, my body had been on fire, burning, skin tight with need and aching.

And no matter how much I masturbated, I still felt so *empty* after, never fully satisfied.

My clit swelled and throbbed. Reaching over, I grabbed my second pillow and pressed it between my legs. My eyes squeezed shut as I rocked my hips, back and forth, against the pillow, trying to alleviate the pulsing ache in my pussy. I underestimated how much I wanted Maddox.

My need intensified, and I throbbed harder. Pushing a hand between my thighs, I shoved my panties aside, and my fingers grazed my folds, pushing my wet lips apart and then moving higher to my swollen clit. I rubbed and pressed against the bundle of nerves there, while grinding my pussy faster against the pillow, rubbing my exposed, sensitive flesh against the soft fabric. The friction almost had me losing my mind, but it still wasn't…enough.

My hand matched the rhythm of my hips. My index finger probed my entrance, and when my pussy clenched, seeking to be filled, I slowly thrust my finger inside. Oh God, oh God!

My breath hitched, and I grew hotter, my sticky wetness dripping between my legs–a reminder of how wrong this was, but I still moaned out Maddox's name.

I pinched my clit, rocking my hips faster. I imagined it was Maddox between my legs. I imagined it was his cock pushing against my entrance, not my small fingers.

I imagined him pulsing inside me, filling me… thrusting inside… grunting out my name.

My body tightened, and my hips jerked against the pillow as I rode out my mini orgasm; my panties were drenched and my fingers wet and coated with my release. A low whine spilled from my lips,

"Maddox."

I rubbed my finger over my pussy-lips, imagining it was his lips on my pussy, before I pulled my hand out of my panties. My legs were slack against the pillow; my inner thighs still sticky with my release.

I didn't have the energy to get up and change. My eyes fluttered close, and I fell into a restless sleep.

Maddox invaded my dreams. I felt his kisses... saw his handsome face... felt his touch sliding down my body.

Hot tears slid down my cheeks, because it was only a dream, only my fantasy.

CHAPTER THIRTY-SEVEN

Maddox

I was angry. At myself, at Lila, at everyone… everything and at fate.

I'd lost my way with Lila, and I didn't know how to pull her out from under my skin.

We landed in Paris, and my stomach twisted with fury and unwarranted possessiveness as men stared at Lila. Their gaze followed her, lingering over her ass. I told myself I wasn't jealous – just protective of her. These assholes wouldn't know how to handle a woman like Lila.

By the time we reached our hotel, frustration gnawed at my gut, and I was just so fucking angry, I couldn't think straight.

Nothing made sense – not my reaction to Lila or the stormy emotions I couldn't understand why I was feeling.

Friends didn't think about fucking each other.

But that was exactly what I wanted to do. I wanted to hear her moan my name, I wanted her to whimper as my dick stretched her tight cunt, I wanted... *needed*... Lila.

This wasn't just lust. I craved her lips and the sound of her voice. She made me feel unhinged, my emotions too wild to control. I loathed how easily Lila could break through my barrier–she could rip me apart and put me back together, again and again–I was her more than willing victim.

I wanted to possess her. And I *couldn't.*

Lila was sunshine mixed with a little hurricane, and I was getting swept away. I was going to put a stop to it.
It had to come to an end and soon, before we both did something we'd regret for the rest of our lives. I was willing to peel Lila off from under my skin, even if it left me bleeding and mortally wounded.

My eyes flickered to Lila, watching her smile at the receptionist. Sunkissed skin, soft lips, pinkened cheeks and brown eyes that captured me since that day at the coffee shop, almost four years ago.

"Bonjour," a voice broke through my thoughts. "How are you doing today?"

A man appeared at Lila's side, suited and standing tall. His gaze landed on her tits first before they lifted to her face.

Lila nodded in greeting, and they shook hands. He introduced himself as the owner of the hotel, the corners of his eyes crinkling as he smiled at Lila. It was written all over his face.

He wanted her.

My blood boiled, and I swallowed down a growl.

His hand brushed against Lila's arm. "Please, if you need any help today, you can come and find me. A lady like you shouldn't have to go through any trouble alone."

Lila let out a small laugh. "Oh, I'm not alone." She stepped closer to me and place a hand on my arm, smiling. "Maddox is with me."

Mr. Owner, I didn't catch his name nor did I care, eyed me up and down. "A friend, I see?" he asked, with a thick English accent.

He was checking to see if I was his rival. Fuck, if he only knew...

Lila, oblivious to what was happening, replied, "Yes, a friend. We're so excited to be visiting Paris together."

The moment Lila admitted we were *friends*, his eyes lit up with triumph.

I instantly hated him.

He was practically undressing Lila and fucking her with his eyes, and she had no idea. Or she was playing coy...

My chest tightened. Was she interested in him...? Lila was smiling, her body relaxed, and she *giggled* at something he had said.

Motherfucker!

By the time we got to our rooms, I was seeing crimson red. I'd never been so angry in my entire fucking life.

"He said they have a fancy bar. Maybe we should go tonight after we've rested?" Lila asked, rubbing her tired eyes. "I need sleep right now."

She stifled a yawn and peeked up at me through her lashes. I nodded, mutely, and walked into my room, closing the door behind me.

My skin prickled with the need to hit something. I ripped my shirt off and quickly undressed, getting in the shower. I turned the water to cold, letting it seep through my bones. My body numbed, but my mind was still a storm of mixed emotions. It was that feeling when I didn't know what the fuck I was feeling.

I quickly soaped up my body, my hand drifting to my dick. I stroked myself once, and my eyes squeezed shut. An image of Lila drifted behind my eyelids.

Perky tits, pink nipples, cute as fuck belly button, taunt stomach, curvy hips, and an ass I wanted to sink my dick in.

My cock jerked as I put more pressure on it, fisting the length from base to tip. My hand glided over my dick easily through the cascading water. Pre-cum covered the tip, and my balls grew tight between my legs.

Sometimes, as messed up as this was, I wondered if I could just fuck her and get rid of this itch. But Lila wasn't someone I could fuck out of my system. It was years of built-up tension and sexual need between us. One simple fuck, one hot night... would never be enough.

Because the moment I had one taste of her... I'd need more...I would never be satisfied.

My stomach caved, and my thighs tightened as the pressure built, and it finally released. My knees weakened, and I pressed my forehead against the tiles, thick ropes of cum spilling over my hand instantly washed away by the water. I fisted my dick until every last drop was spent and then I cursed. So. Fucking. Weak.

This had to end, now... tonight...

CHAPTER THIRTY-EIGHT

Lila

His presence was a warm heat behind me as we walked into the bar. He was close, really fucking close. I could *feel* him. I could *smell* him. He was so close, yet so far out of reach. A dangerous temptation dangling right in front of me.

I wanted to turn around and wrap my arms around him, bask in his warmth. We'd hugged and cuddled plenty of times before, but since the Charity Gala, everything had been different.

He had been different.

Somehow, there was a wall between us now. I couldn't break it or walk around it. It was exhausting and scary – watching the change in him, seeing him so...cold and withdrawn from me. Sometimes, it felt like he was battling something inside his head. I waited silently for him to come to me, to speak of his worries, so I could find a way to soothe him. Like always.

Except...it started to feel as if *I* was the problem. As if he was hiding from *me*.

A week in Paris. This was supposed to be fun and exciting. An adventure for us, but it was day one and it was already going to waste.

I chewed on my bottom lip as we walked further inside the dim room. It wasn't overly crowded, but everyone here looked fancy. After all, this was one of the most famous hotels of Paris; wealthy and posh people came here often. "I didn't think the hotel would have its own bar. Fancy. I like it."

"It's nice," he replied. There was a roughness in his voice, except his tone was robotic. No emotions whatsoever.

I paused in my steps, expecting him to bump into me. He didn't. Instead, I felt his arm slide around my waist as he curled it around me. Our bodies collided together softly, and I sucked in a quiet breath. His rock-hard chest was to my back, pressing against me, and I could feel every intake of breath he took. His touch was a sweet, sweet torture.

Fuck you. Fuck you for making me feel this way. Fuck you for tempting me and leaving me hanging. Fuck you for making me fall in love with you...

"This way." His lips lingered near my ear as he whispered the words. He steered me toward the bar stools.

We sat side by side. From the corner of my eye, I watched him as he ordered our drinks. His voice was smooth, and it slid over my skin like silk. Soft and gentle.

Lost in my thoughts, I didn't notice the man standing next to me until his hand touched my shoulder. I swiveled to the left, my eyes catching the intruder. Yes, intruder. He was interrupting my time with *him*.

Maddox Coulter – the balm to my soul but also the stinging pain in my chest. He was a sweet heaven but also the of my existence.

"Remember me?" the man in the suit asked with a tiny grin.

Yup, I did. He was the owner of the hotel. We met him when we checked in yesterday.

"I saw you across the bar, and I knew instantly, you had to be the pretty girl I met last night." His English was perfect, but it was laced with a husky French accent. I had to admit, it was kind of sexy. Mr. Frenchman stood between our stools, separating Maddox and me. He blocked my view of Maddox and I. Did. Not. Like. That.

"Thank you for helping us yesterday," I replied sweetly, masking my irritation.

His emerald eyes glimmered, and his grin widened. Mr. Frenchman was your typical tall, dark, and handsome eye candy. And he wore an expensive suit that molded to his body quite nicely. "It was all my pleasure."

I nodded, a little lost at what else I could say. I wasn't shy or uncomfortable around men. But this one was a little too close for my liking, and since I had zero interest in him, even though he could definitely be my type, given the fact that *someone else* had all my attention, I didn't want to continue this conversation.

"Lucien Mikael." He presented me with his hand. I remembered he told us his name last night, but I didn't tell him mine.

I took his palm in mine, shaking it. "You can call me, Lila. It's nice to make your acquaintance."

Instead of shaking my hand, he turned it over and brought my hand to his lips. He kissed the back of it, his lips lingering there for a second too long. His eyes met mine over our entwined hands. "My pleasure, *ma belle*."

Oh dear. Yup. Mr. Frenchman was flirting.

I glanced around Lucien and saw that Maddox was lounging

back in his stool, his long legs stretched out in front of him, a drink in his hand, and he was staring directly at me. His face was expressionless.

Lucien turned to the bartender and said something to him in French. I didn't understand the words, but I quickly figured out what he said when he turned back to me.

"It's on me. A treat for a lovely lady."

I was already shaking my head. "Oh. You didn't have to –"

His hand tightened around mine. "Please, allow me."

"Thank you."

Lucien opened his mouth to say something else, but he was interrupted by the ringing of his phone. "Excuse me, *chérie*."

As he moved away, I caught sight of Maddox again. Our eyes met, and I stopped breathing. His gaze was dark, and his jaw was clenched so tightly that I wondered if it'd crack under the pressure. I could see the ticks in his sharp jaw as he gritted his teeth. His face – I didn't know how to describe it. Anger made his eyes appear darker, almost deadly. A shadow loomed over his face, his expression almost threatening. There was a predatory feel in his glare as he watched me closely.

He constantly pushed me away, putting more and more distance between us. Why was he so angry now? I couldn't tell. I. Couldn't. Fucking. Think. Especially when he stared at me like *this*.

Maddox was maddening. He pulled and pushed; he loved and hated. I always thought I understood him better than anyone else. But right now, he confused the hell out of me.

"Lila." My eyes snapped away from Maddox, and I looked at Lucien. He was apparently done with his phone call, and his attention was back on me. Before I could pull away, he gripped my hand in his once more. "If you need anything while you are in Paris, please call me. I could take you sightseeing. I know many beautiful places."

He let go of my hand, and I turned my palm over to see his business card. Smooth trick, Mr. Frenchman. "Umm, thank you."

Lucien leaned down and quickly placed a chaste kiss on both my cheeks before pulling away. "Au revoir, *chérie.*"

I didn't watch him leave. All my attention was on the man sitting beside me. He took a large gulp of his drink.

"He likes you," he said, once Lucien was out of hearing range.

"Jealous?" I shot back immediately.

A smirk crawled onto his face, and he chuckled, his wide chest rumbling with it. "He wants to fuck you, Lila."

My stomach clenched, goosebumps breaking out over my skin. My breath left me in a whoosh. His words were spoken dangerously low, although the harshness in his voice could not be mistaken.

"How would you know?" I retorted, angry and confused. He played with my feelings, turning my emotions into a little game of his. Maddox had me in knots, twisting me around like a little plaything.

He grunted, shaking his head, and then he let out a laugh. As if he was sharing an inside joke with himself. "I'm a man, like him. I know what he was thinking about when he looked at you like that."

"Maybe he wasn't thinking about sex. Maybe he's a gentleman. Unlike you." I was playing with fire, I knew that. I was testing him, testing *us.*

"*I dare you,*" he whispered so softly, I almost missed it. Maddox looked down at his glass, his fingers clenched around it. Even in the dim lights, I could see the way his knuckles were starting to turn white.

He was giving me a dare *now*?

He didn't finish his sentence, and I wondered if he was contemplating his dare. Maddox's jaw flexed from obvious frustration. For a brief moment, I thought maybe he wasn't angry at *me*. Maybe, he was angry at *himself*. He was fighting *himself*. Could it be that the problem wasn't me?

He drank the rest of his drip in one gulp and then slammed his glass on the counter, before swiveling around in his stool to face me. Maddox stood up and walked a step closer to me, until my knees were touching his strong thighs. He leaned forward, caging me in between the counter and his body. Our gaze locked, and he licked his lips. He had me captivated for a moment until he mercilessly broke the spell.

"I dare you to sleep with him."

I reared back in shock. *Wh-at?* No, I must have misheard him. That couldn't be…

"What?" I whispered, my throat dry and my tongue suddenly heavy in my mouth.

Maddox's eyes bore into mine, staring into my soul. When he spoke again, his deep accented voice danced over my skin dangerously. "I dare you to fuck him, Lila."

A tremble started in my core and then moved through my body like a storm. Not just a quiet storm. A tsunami of emotions hit me all at once, reckless in its assault. I submerged under the dark waves, suffocating, and then I was being split open so viciously, it sent tiny cracks of my heart and fissures of my soul in all directions. I clamped my teeth together to stop myself from saying something —anything that would make it worse.

We had done too many dares to simply count on our fingers. Countless silly dares over the years, but we had never dared each other to sleep with other people. Granted, I had asked him to kiss a girl once; they made out, but it was years ago. But our dares had never crossed that line.

Sex... that was never on the table. We never explicitly talked about it, but it was almost an unspoken rule.

Why would he even ask me to do such a thing?!

"What's with that look, Lila?" he taunted.

My eyes closed. I refused to look at him, to look into his beautiful eyes and see nothing but pitch-black darkness. He wasn't looking at me like he used to. The light in his eyes was gone.

It scared me.

It hurt me.

It was destroying the rest of what was left of me.

"Look. At. Me."

I didn't want to. I didn't want him to see the hurt in my eyes.

"Open your eyes, Lila," he said in his rich baritone voice.

I did as I was commanded. He crowded into my personal space, forcing me to inhale his scent and feel the warmth of his body. "Are you serious? Or are you already drunk?" I asked quietly. It was hard to breathe with him this close.

"I never take back a dare."

And I never lose. He knew that. We were both very competitive, and to this day, neither of us had backed down from a dare.

Maddox's hand came up, and he cupped my jaw. His fingers kissed my skin softly. He smiled, but it didn't match the look in his eyes. "What's wrong? You don't want to do it?"

"I don't play to lose." *Asshole.*

Maddox leaned closer, his face barely an inch away from mine. Our noses were almost touching. My heart fluttered when he tipped my head back. *Take back your dare. Take back your dare, Maddox. Don't make me do this.*

He curled his index finger around the lock of hair that had fallen out from my bun. His minty breath, mixed with the smell of alcohol, feathered over my lips. I wanted to beg him with my eyes. Maddox tugged on my hair slightly before tucking it behind my ear. He moved, and my eyes fluttered close once again...*waiting*... a desperate breath locked in my throat as my chest caved and my stomach clenched.

He pressed his cheek against mine, and his lips lingered over my ear. "Don't disappoint me, *chérie*."

My body shuddered, and I breathed out a shaky breath. He tore my heart open and left me bleeding. He pulled away and stared down at me.

Maddox was mocking me. Taunting me.

He never stopped being a jerk. He just hid it behind a sexy smile and a nonchalant expression.

I thought he had left his asshole ways behind. But no, I was wrong. So fucking wrong about him. About *us*.

Friends. We were friends.

I thought maybe... he wanted *more*. More of me. More of us, of what we were or could be. I was so goddamn wrong.

Maddox Coulter was still an asshole behind a pretty mask.

And I was the stupid girl who fell in love with her best friend.

CHAPTER THIRTY-NINE

Lila

I waited, my heart thudding in my chest. His warmth behind me had my stomach twisting in anxiety. His shirt brushed against my bare shoulders. Maddox crowded behind me, and my gaze moved to Lucien.

He looked miffed as Maddox came between us. Lucien and I had spent the whole day together. He took me sightseeing while Maddox stalked us from a distance. Lucien didn't know, but I saw him, following us everywhere we went.

Lucien planned to take me out for dinner later at the Eiffel tower. He said it was romantic and beautiful up there. I knew from the look in his eyes that he was expecting something tonight.

Lucien expected us to fuck.

And Maddox dared me... so it was happening. Tonight.

I tried to pull away from my best friend, but then the fireworks went off in the dark Paris sky, and it stole my attention. People cheered on the rooftop of the hotel where we were standing.

Someone had just gotten married; they were celebrating. The City of Love, indeed.

Because of the noise of the fireworks as well as the music and laughter that surrounded us, Maddox thought his secret was safe; he thought it was loud enough that I couldn't hear the words he whispered in my ear. But I *did*.

"If there's a God, He doesn't want me to be happy. Maybe it's my fault because I pushed you into the arms of another man. But He won't let me have you even though I begged him to let me love you freely. I can't remember the last time I asked Him for something. I guess... I'm not meant to have what I want. My parents. A family. You. You. You," Maddox whispered in my ear, his voice a low rasp.

Another set of fireworks went off, loud and booming into the sky.

His lips caressed my neck, warm and soft against my skin. "All of *you*."

He sounded so broken, so tortured.

If only...

Maddox and I...

We were more than friends but less than lovers. That was our relationship; there was no real definition. We were somewhere in the middle, tangling over the edge of something that could forever break us.

I turned around and his face held an expression of a wounded beast: a bleeding warrior, a broken boy.

"Lila," he started, his voice a gruff baritone, but Lucien came forward. He wrapped an arm around my waist, pulling me into him.

Maddox's eyes clouded, and he stepped back, without finishing the sentence and whatever else he was about to say. Lucien's lips caressed my temple, and Maddox stalked away, disappearing into the crowd.

Maybe that was all we were or could ever be: an incomplete sentence and a story without an ending.

But his secret confession changed everything.

Maddox *wanted* me.

God, how stupid could we be?

"So, we shall meet in an hour?" Lucian said, breaking through my thoughts. "Is that enough time for you to dress?"

I nodded, mutely, and sent him a tentative smile before striding away.

I walked inside my room, grabbed a few things, and then stalked over to the adjacent room. His door wasn't locked, and I walked inside to find Maddox sitting in a sofa chair, staring out the window—into the dark night.

He was still in his black slacks, his tie hanging loosely around his neck, his rumpled white shirt unbuttoned and his sleeves rolled up to his elbows. His legs were stretched out in front of him. He had a cigarette between his lips and a drink in his hand.

Maddox looked... rugged. Angry. Intense.

He owned the room, his mere presence sending out a dominating mood. His gaze fell on me, and Maddox tensed. His whole body tightened at the sight of me. His face hardened, his expression dark and brooding.

I wished the situation was different, but there was no other way. I couldn't unlove Maddox, and I didn't want to. We weren't something, but we weren't nothing either.

I sucked in a breath and hung on to my courage, while sashaying inside. I dropped the two dresses on the bed, and my lips curled.

My legs trembled, but I locked my knees together. "I need your help."

He simply grunted in response, his face flashing with uncontrolled frustration. I wondered if the thought of another man touching, making love to me, fucking me was killing him and the fact that it was him who sent me into the arms of another man.

My stomach cramped, and I inhaled. Exhaled.

The room was growing hotter, and a sheen of sweat slid down between my breasts. I slowly pulled the robe off my shoulders and let it pool at my feet, standing in front of Maddox in my lace panties and bra.

His eyes widened before they narrowed on my bare skin.

I'd been half-naked in front of Maddox plenty of time before. This time, it was... different.

I grabbed the first dress and stepped into it, shaking my hips a bit, so I could pull the tight fabric over the curve of my ass.

Once the dress was in place, I turned to face the mirror, giving Maddox my back.

A single beat passed.

One breath.

Thud.

I caught his eyes through the reflection. "Is this sexy enough to tempt him into fucking me before we can even get to his bed?" I crooned.

I was playing with fire.

And I was about to get burned.

His gaze traveled down the length of my body. It was a red fitted, sleeveless dress, and the bodice cupped my breasts like a second skin with my tits practically spilling out. The dress was indecently short, and it was the best way to say–*fuck me.*

Maddox's fingers clenched the glass in his hand so hard, I thought he'd break it.

I smirked. *Am I breaking through your walls, Maddox?*

His eyes grew darker, a vicious glint in his gaze. I smiled sweetly, trying to appear unfazed by his reaction, even though my heart was beating so fast it threatened to burst through my chest, and my knees were so weak, I wondered how I was still standing.

I licked my lips and blinked my eyes innocently. We were still watching each other through the mirror. "Can you zip me up?" I croaked. "I can't reach the zipper."

Another heartbeat.

A low exhale.

Thud.

Maddox stood up, tall and tensed, and the harsh look on his face had me whimpering silently. He stalked forward, eyeing me like a predator.

I was the prey, the willing captive.

Maddox pressed against my back, crowding into my space and pushing me closer into the mirror until the tip of my breasts were brushing against the coldness of it.

A silent gasp spilled from my lips, and his fingers skimmed over my bare back.

He inhaled and exhaled a shuddering breath.

If I died tonight, it'd be a sweet death.

We continued to watch each other through the mirror, our reflection staring back at us.

Not blinking.

Not breathing.

Maddox then slowly zipped me up, before his hands dropped to my hips, and he held me tight. Oh God, my heart catapulted in my chest.

"If he hurts you, I'm going to kill him," he growled low in my ear. His words were thick with threat.

My teeth grazed my lips, and I bit down, waiting for him to stop me from leaving, to take back his foolish dare. His grip tightened on my hips.

Stop me. Take back your dare.

Thud, my heart hammered in my chest. Goddamn it, Maddox!

Beyond frustrated and angered by his lack of words, my control snapped, and I swiveled around. Maddox didn't see it coming, and he stumbled back as I pushed him into the wall next to the mirror. He let out a grunt, and his eyes darkened in warning.

Dizzied by our close proximity, I swallowed past the lump in my throat. I cupped his jaw and pressed my body against his.

He didn't pull away, didn't breathe, didn't say a word. A line had been crossed, and we both knew it.

My mouth was so dry, I could barely speak the words: "It's my turn, isn't it?"

Standing on my toes, I brought our heads closer, my lips lingering over his. "I dare you."

Maddox tilted his head, and his fingers dug into my hips. "I dare you to kiss me," I breathed.

My heart stuttered as I said the words. Point of no return, this was it.

His eyes widened; his breath hitched.

One heartbeat. Thud.

Two heartbeats. Thud. Thud.

Then, Maddox *pounced.*

I cried out as his lips captured mine. Brutal. Harsh. Unforgiving.

Maddox Coulter devoured my lips like it was his last meal, and I fell into his arms, powerless.

I gasped into the kiss, which opened my mouth for him. His

tongue slid inside, tasting me. He licked and kissed and bit on my lips. Savage and cruel.

Anger rolled off him in waves as we became cocooned with our lust and need for each other. He took his frustration out against my lips, and I returned his punishing kiss with a violent one of my own.

He hadn't been the only one struggling with this need… and hunger for each other.

I suffered, too.

My pulse throbbed, and my stomach fluttered. My whole body tingled as he spun us around, slamming my back into the wall. Maddox fisted my hair, his knuckles digging into my scalp. He growled a guttural groan and kissed me harder.

This was everything I ever wanted. Dizzy. Hazy. Full of desire and untamed hunger, I moaned into his kiss.

Maddox shoved my dress up, not so gently, and pushed my panties aside. "Is this what you want?" he grunted.

I moaned.

Yes.

Yes.

Yes.

He growled deeper. "You want to be fucked against the wall like this?"

Yes.

God, Maddox!

I cried out when his thumb brushed against my clit roughly, sending tiny sparks through my body. He tsked darkly. "I didn't know you were such a dirty, filthy girl, *Lila*."

I was already so wet between my legs, his fingers glided easily over my folds. Maddox groaned as he felt my pussy clench against his seeking fingers.

LYLAH JAMES

"Fuck," he swore, pressing his nose against my nose. He bit down, his teeth digging into my sensitive flesh. I clung to his shoulders, writhing in his arms.

Maddox pinched my clit, and I cried out, my body growing tight as a bowstring. He callously dipped a finger inside my pussy, and I clamped down.

"Lila," he said hoarsely.

He pumped his finger, once, twice. "Maddox, *please!*"

"Lila," Maddox whispered wretchedly. He pulled out, and I gasped when he thrust back inside with two fingers. He didn't give me time to adjust to his long, thick digits; he slid in and out in a punishing pace, dragging out desperate moans from me.

I was so close... so... so fucking close.

He pulled his fingers out.

"Maddox!" I gasped.

He shushed me, his lips capturing mine again. Maddox shifted slightly, and then I felt him – his hard length rubbing against my wet folds. He hooked my thigh around his waist, spreading me for him. My panties were still shoved to the side as his tip probed my entrance. His hips jerked forward, and Maddox groaned as he spread my pussy-lips with his cock, his tip seeking out my swollen clit.

He circled his hips, coating his length with my wetness. "How badly do you want me to fuck you?" There was a possessive glint in his dark gaze.

"If you don't fuck me now... I'm going to go crazy." My clit throbbed, and my heart was in my throat.

Every dream... every day I had been left wanting for Maddox...

This was finally happening. After years of refusing to acknowledge this tension between us, I had Maddox in my arms.

Our eyes met. Silent and breathless. Heart pounding.

Maddox shoved inside in one punishing thrust, stealing my breath from my lungs.

I cried out, and my body tightened. He stretched me; my inner walls spasmed around his cock as he seated himself inside my pussy, buried to the hilt.

His mouth brushed against my neck before it found its way to my lips again. I could feel his hardness pulsing inside me. A curse fell from his lips as he pulled out almost all the way, before plunging in again.

I looked down between our entwined bodies, watching his cock disappear inside me. Thrust, after thrust. The sound of us fucking filled the room, echoing around the walls.

His grunts, my moans.

His groans, my whimpers.

My name was a whispered prayer on his lips.

His name spilled from mine as I cried out.

He ground the hilt of his palm against my clit, and my eyes rolled back into my head as my body spasmed. I spiraled down as my orgasm hit. It was the most intense release I've ever had.

One brutal thrust later, Maddox held himself inside me, as deep as he could go. I felt his release, spurt after thick spurt, as he filled me.

My leg fell from his hip as I gasped for breath.

Maddox pressed his forehead against mine, and I saw instant regret in his eyes. Oh no, no. Please no.

"Lila," he rumbled.

"No." I pushed his chest, and he stumbled back. "Don't you dare," I warned.

His face twisted with a brutal look, but I pushed him again, until he was forced to take several steps back.

One final push, and he stumbled onto the bed, his back flat on the mattress. The look of surprise on his face made me smirk. I couldn't let him overthink this, not right now. Not tonight. Maybe tomorrow. But tonight was ours.

The only way to keep Maddox from pulling away was to... use my body against him.

I quickly got rid of my panties before leaning over his wide frame. "My turn," I croaked.

Maddox tensed as I pushed his black slacks to his knees. His hard cock jutted proudly toward his stomach. Long and thick, glistening with his cum and my wetness. My heart drummed wildly as I brought my head closer to his length.

My lips closed around him without warning, and his hips jerked up as he shouted, "Lila!"

I took as much of him as I could down my throat, and I hummed, loving the feel and the musky taste of him in my mouth. "Fuuucck, Lila."

He fisted my hair, and I peered up at him. His head was thrown back in pleasure, and need pulsed between my legs. He thrusted into my mouth, silently demanding for more. His breathing was shallow as I sucked him and it was the biggest turn on to see him this affected by my touch. I licked the tip, following the thick veins coursing the length of him, before I deep-throated him again.

Maddox hissed and groaned. His thighs clenched, his stomach tensing as I repeated the process. Sucking and licking.

"Lila... stop... fuck!"

Maddox was close, and I pulled away. I straddled his hips, both of us still fully clothed. His hardness rested against my wet slit.

His blue eyes locked on mine. "Don't fall for me," he rasped darkly.

Too late, baby.

My lips curled with a smirk, hiding my true feelings. "I just sucked your dick. Who said anything about falling in love? I just want you to fuck me. Do you dare?"

Maddox glowered dangerously, and I moved my hips, slowly gliding down his length as I took him inside my body once again. His hands came to my waist, and he gripped me tightly.

His hips bucked against mine, impatiently. There was a warning in his gaze, so I started moving, bouncing up and down his cock.

He felt so good, inside me... against me.

I never wanted it to end.

Maddox sat up, and his hand wrapped around my neck. My eyes widened, and his fingers curled around my throat. His grip tightened, not bruising, but the pressure was there, and I gasped. Even though *I* was fucking *him*, he still stayed in control.

I moved up and down his length, finding my stride.

Until Maddox grew impatient.

He growled and flipped us over. Hands fumbling, teeth grazing each other, lips fighting for dominance, we tore at each other's clothes until we were skin to skin, bared and vulnerable to each other's desperate touch and hungry eyes.

Maddox flipped me over on my knees, and he spread my thighs apart. Without warning, he plunged inside—one smooth, merciless thrust inside my body as he forced his cock through my tight channel.

His lips grazed the back of my neck, one sweet gentle kiss, even though he fucked me raw and deep, ruthlessly and filled with so much passion. My eyes blurred with unshed tears.

Maddox Coulter was fucking me.

My best friend was making love to me.

My heart cracked and withered.

I was powerless as he continued to ram himself into me, animalistic grunts spilling from his throat.

"Maddox!" I cried out his name, over and over again.

I didn't know where he ended and I began.

"Lila," he groaned in my ear, his breathing ragged. "*My Lila.*"

Tears spilled down my cheeks, and my eyes closed.

Please don't let this night end.

Breathless, heart pounding, pulse throbbing, we found our release, moaning each other's name. We were utterly intoxicated by each other. I collapsed into the mattress, and Maddox slumped over me like a blanket. I teetered over the edge of consciousness, my body achy and sore, and my lips curled into a sleepy yet satisfied smile.

"Maddox," I breathed his name.

His arm tightened around mine. "Lila."

My eyes closed, and I slipped away... far, far away.

CHAPTER FORTY

Lila

I woke up, my body deliciously sore. It was a good ache, and my lips twitched.

And then I remembered, the night before flashing in front of my eyes like black and white polaroid photos. Snap, snap, snap. Click, click, click.

My head turned, and my eyes landed on a sleeping Maddox next to me, both of us completely naked. We fucked multiple times during the night, unable to quench our desire for one another. We passed out, woke up, and then fumbled for each other in the dark, over and over again.

I sat up, my heart hammering in my chest.

Last night had been filthy... beautiful... and everything I ever wanted and didn't know I *needed*.

But we crossed a line, and there was no going back. My stomach churned with nausea, and I suddenly felt sick.

Last night, even though I had been tipsy and Maddox had been drinking, both of us were fully aware of what we were doing. Now that it was the morning after and my mind was clear from the frustration and *need* that had been coursing through my body, I didn't know what to do with myself.

What happens now?

What if Maddox...?

What if he didn't want this to last, what if this was a one-time thing for him?

I didn't even know what I wanted as my mind filled with confusion. My heart was heavy with mixed emotions. My body ached from last night, but my heart *hurt*.

Tears burned the back of my eyes, and I cupped my face, feeling stupid. For a moment last night, Maddox was mine, and I was his.

But that was it.

Just one night.

Maddox wasn't the type to commit, and I needed more from him than just a one-time fuck session. There was no point in risking our hearts when the thin thread between us had already snapped.

We couldn't undo what was done.

I had to walk away; I had to leave, though I would cherish last night for the rest of my life.

I eased off the bed and quickly wrapped my robe around me, before walking toward the door. I turned the handle but never got a chance to walk out. The door was suddenly slammed shut, and I was torn away from it. The world spun, and my back slammed against the wall.

Maddox loomed over me, his eyes dark, his dirty blond hair disheveled, and he was still... naked. I peered up at him through my lashes, my heart racing. His lips curled, and he looked enraged.

At me?

Because I was leaving?

Because of last night?

"Where do you think you're going?" he asked, his voice dripping
with something akin to... possessiveness? His jaw tightened, and
my stomach flipped. "Back to Lucien, so you can fuck him, too?
Was last night not enough?" Maddox snarled.

What. The. Fuck?

I slammed my hands into his chest, pushing him back. But he
was much stronger than me, and he crowded into my space with
a low growl. Maddox kicked my legs apart and pushed his knee
between my thighs, holding me captive.

His palm slid up my throat, and I felt the strength in his touch.
I swallowed, my throat bobbing in his palm, and his hold tightened
on my neck. The slightest pressure and my clit pulsed. His hand
moved up, cupping my jaw.

His eyes were two dark pools, unhinged. "Is your sweet cunt that
greedy, *Lila*?"

Holy Shit. Again. What. The. Fuck?

"Let go of me! What is wrong with you?!" I spat, raising my
hand to slap him. He clasped my wrist and jerked my hand down,
pressing my palm over his chest.

My breath caught in my throat. His heart was pounding
intensely. Thud, thud, thud.

There was a moment, between our heated glance and our volatile
kiss, where time stopped and then...

His lips slammed over mine, and he took my breath away. He
didn't just kiss me. Maddox possessed me, shoving his tongue in my
mouth and licking every inch of me.

Punishing. Hard. Unforgiving.

My nails dug into the skin over his heart. He hissed against my lips, and to my utter surprise, his kiss gentled. Maddox pulled away, only slightly. His breath lingered over my lips, before Maddox pressed his mouth against mine again.

Sweet. Tender. Soft.

"I dare you to kiss me." We were already kissing, but I knew what he meant. He wanted me to kiss him like he kissed me; he wanted me to kiss him like we kissed last night... and he wanted me to repeat the words I threw at him.

"I dare you to stay." His lips touched mine again. *Kiss.*

My heart stuttered.

"I dare you to give us a chance." *Kiss.*

I forgot how to breathe.

"I dare you, Lila."

Then his lips found mine again, and he sealed his dare with a long searing kiss, kissing all the pain and doubt away.

EPILOGUE

Lila

Four months later

Maddox sat on the bed, his head in his hands, a choked
sound coming from him.

"You're the best unplanned thing that has ever happened
to me, Maddox. And I can't lose you. But you're doing everything
to push... me away from you," I whispered, my voice breaking at
the end. "You've been telling lies. Since when have you started lying
to me, Maddox?"

After all we had been through... he tainted everything that we
were with his lies.

His head snapped up, and his eyes flared with torment. He was
decadently handsome, a little bit broken and a mistake from the
beginning.

"I'm sorry," he choked out.

"Is that all you have to say?"

There were tears in his eyes. "I'm sorry."

If it hurts you so much, what kind of love is this?

I knew Maddox would break my heart, but a part of me hoped he wouldn't.

My heart wept, and a lone tear slid down my cheek. "They said you were trouble. I didn't listen. I took a chance on you. And now I regret it."

"Don't leave me." His hoarse voice cracked. "*Please.*"

I took a step back. Maddox looked wounded, and my soul bled to see *him* hurt.

"Lila," he breathed my name. "Please."

I slowly shook my head. "Maddox." It pained me to say his name. "You broke your promises."

My feet took me another step back.

"No," he pleaded. "Lila, *no.*"

I turned and walked away, leaving my broken heart at his feet.

THE CONCLUSION OF LILA'S AND MADDOX'S STORY WILL BE HERE SOON...

ACKNOWLEDGEMENTS

I think first and foremost, I want to thank Oliver. Thank you for believing in me even when I didn't believe myself. If it weren't for you, I'm not sure this book would have existed. From helping me come up with the title – to characters' names – and listening to my endless rants about the plot and helping me figure out this story, you helped me bring this story to life. Thank you for always making me smile every day.

Vivvi, how do I ever thank you? You're my rock and a piece of my heart. Thank you for loving my characters, my babies, just as much as I do, if not more. You're the moon of my life.

My wonderful editor Rebecca – your patience is admirable. Thank you for not hating me. You worked with me on such a tight schedule. It's insane but you legit made this book possible. I thought you kicked me to the curb, but you didn't. For that – I am forever grateful. Thank you for holding my hand.

My parents, thank you for your never-ending support and love.

To my girl, Cat…seriously, what would I do without you? Suse, you've been there, supporting my craziness and I love you even more. You made my book pretty – thank YOU!

Sarah Grim Sentz – I'm so glad I trusted you with these promo graphics.

Special thanks to my STREET TEAM! I'm so amazed by how dedicated you guys are.

Huge thanks to CANDI KANE PR – you're a gem and I'm so glad I trusted you with my book baby because you did magic!

Maria at Steamy Designs: You killed this cover! So gorgeous and everything I wanted!

To the bloggers and everyone who took their time to promote this book, you are awesome! My big thanks to you. To my beautiful readers, a huge thank you to every single one of you. My lovelies. Your never ending support and love has taken us on this path. Thank you for standing with me through all my craziness.

ABOUT THE AUTHOR

Lylah James uses all her spare time to write. If she is not studying, sleeping, writing or working—she can be found with her nose buried in a good romance book, preferably with a hot alpha male.

Writing is her passion. The voices in her head won't stop, and she believes they deserve to be heard and read. Lylah James writes about drool worthy and total alpha males and strong and sweet heroines. She makes her readers cry—sob their eyes out, swoon, curse, rage, and fall in love. Mostly known as the Queen of Cliffhangers and the #evilauthorwithablacksoul, she likes to break her readers' hearts and then mend them.

CONNECT WITH ME!

Did you enjoy *DO YOU DARE?*
Come and join my reader's group:
Lylah's Lovelies Therapy Group
or Like my author page to make sure you stay in the loop!
Instagram: @authorlylahjames
Or you can sign up to my Newsletter!

BOOKS BY LYLAH JAMES

Tainted Hearts Series

The Mafia and His Angel: Part One
The Mafia and His Angel: Part Two
The Mafia and His Angel: Part Three
Blood and Roses
The Mafia and His Obsession: Part One
The Mafia and His Obsession: Part Two

Truth and Dare Duet

DO YOU DARE? (Book one)
I DARE YOU (Book two, the conclusion)